Digging Deep

The Baycliff Valley Series : Book One

H K Brown

First paperback edition October 2024

Cover design by H K Brown

ISBN 979-8-9902545-0-3

-Mom-

Thank you for encouraging me to follow my dreams and teaching me that anything is possible. Limitations only exist if you allow them to. I can't thank you enough for always motivating me in my creative endeavors.

To my mom, who believed in me until her last breath. Thank you for showing me what limitless love looks like. This is for you.

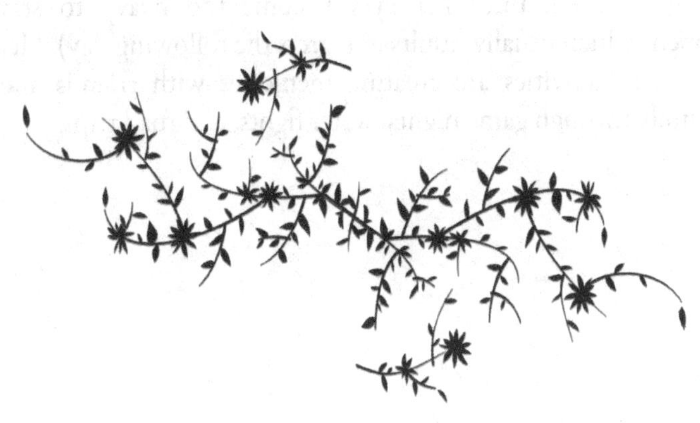

About the Author

H K Brown is an up-and-coming author committed to making her mark in the literary world. Characters come to life in H K Brown's romantic novels pulling you in and making you feel as if you're part of the family. She loves pushing boundaries while ensuring the heavy stuff remains private. As you turn the pages, you can't help but connect with the characters and see them come alive in your mind.

Raised in Southern California, she now calls Oklahoma home.

She's a member of the Alliance of Independent Authors and takes every chance she gets to hone her craft, listening to podcasts, taking classes, and watching videos.

With H K Brown around, boredom isn't normally a problem—she's always working on something, be it with her human family or furry one. She loves snuggling up with a good book until her eyes become too heavy to stay open (which usually results in regrets the following day). Her favorite activities are creating memories with friends and family through game nights, water fights, and road trips.

Content warning

Digging Deep is a closed-door, suspenseful, second-chance romance. It will push boundaries while fading to black when it threatens to get spicy. It is perfect for those who want the emotional roller coaster while limiting the steam.

Please note that Digging Deep also contains content that may be sensitive to some readers. Some scenes include grief, anxiety, panic attacks, (adult) abduction, abuse from a stalker, and the mention of the death of parents.

Happy reading

Prologue

Stepping out of the walk-in, I look to the clock and see that it's 10:45 p.m. "*Shoot*. I didn't mean to stay so late," I say to myself. "No wonder my stomach has been fussing at me for the last hour or so." We're short-staffed right now which means I need to stay past closing to get this count done on time—we always close early for inventory week.

Being the boss—and future owner, when my uncle finally decides to retire—is so much fun sometimes. Sarcastically speaking, of course. I love my job, but so often, I have time for nothing else after working long hours. I could have asked someone to stay and help, but most are nearing overtime for the week already. Until we can get more staff, I have to pick up the slack. The pressure to get things done is unbearable at times.

I walk into my office, grab my phone, and dial my sister, Kayla. I lock up as the phone begins to ring, shoulder my bag, and make my way through the kitchen. I can crash upstairs in Uncle Joe's apartment—he keeps my old room as is, for nights like this—but instead, I decide to go home. Now that he's dating again, I don't want to interrupt.

"Hello?" Kayla answers.

"Hey, will you hang out on the phone with me while I walk home?"

"Sure, why are you leaving so late?"

"Inventory week," I reply. No need to say anything else. She's helped me with it many times.

I don't realize how dark it's gotten until I make my way to the dining room, the only light shining in from the moon outside. With the seasons changing, dark comes earlier nowadays—it's my least favorite part of fall.

"Are you sure you don't want to call a cab, Leah? You shouldn't have to walk alone in the dark."

I detest walking home so late, but calling a cab would have me here for another hour or so—tourist season always slows them down. During the day, Oklahoma City is a family-friendly location visited by many, most of them enjoying long walks along the canal from sunup to sundown. However, once the sun sets, the safety of single women walking alone is questionable. Like in many fast-growing cities, the crime rate has increased significantly. So, my uncle implemented a system, when any of us at the restaurant work past dark, we try to have a walking buddy when leaving.

Like all good things—it works until it doesn't. "It's only four blocks down the canal route. I can walk fast."

Living so close to everything, I don't own a car, there isn't really a need for one. I walk everywhere, and then when I need to leave town, I take Uncle Joe's car, or if he's using it, I rent one. It's one of the perks of living in the busy district.

Taking the steps down to Bricktown Canal, I hug my bag close. I can't stand feeling like I'm in the opening credits of a scary movie the kind where a woman hurries down a dark alley looking over her shoulder, running from every little thing on the way.

Hell, even with my sister on the phone, I'm still creeped out.

"Talk to me, Kay. Give me something to take my mind off the walk home. How's Mike doing?" I look over my shoulder, tighten the hold on my bag, and keep pushing forward.

"For a man who just had surgery on his knee, he sure is getting around well. Damon made it sound like he couldn't do anything for himself when he asked me to stay a few nights."

"You know D. He overexaggerates a lot—it's one of his many charming qualities," I say, sarcasm lacing my words. "I'm glad you're there though. He shouldn't be alone. How long is Damon supposed to be gone this time?"

"He said he'd be back in a few days. He has some sort of tech meeting in Vegas. He mentioned something about obtaining new equipment for his team."

A few days without Kayla is going to be a challenge. I'm so used to her being around all the time. Since our parents passed away, it's been just her and I. The rest of our family stepped back when Uncle Joe stepped up. He's not our uncle by blood, but it's how we've always known him—he grew up with our mom. Best of friends since they were in diapers. When Mom and Dad passed away in the car accident, he didn't even bat an eye. He took us right in and made a home above the restaurant so he could manage home and work life a little easier.

Though I understand now, I hated having to leave our home and friends back then. "A few days like last time?" I ask. "He said he had a tech thing then too."

Damon owns his own company. I don't really know what they do, but from the outside looking in, it just looks like four big guys sitting in a room behind computers. "Remember when he said three days and it turned into six?"

Mike and Damon grew up together in a group home not far from where they live now. Mike is one of my and Kayla's best friends. He and I met one night while speed dating—which I never do by the way . . . I went with my friend Kim. She met her now live-in boyfriend, while Mike and I connected right away and decided to give it a shot. After the second date, neither of us felt any kind of spark and decided being friends was the way to go. It's been five years ago now, and he's like the brother I always wished I had. Damon, on the other hand . . . he's a good guy but he sure does get on my nerves at times. Gotta love him though. He's a good friend and Mike's current roommate. He's always kind to Kayla and me when we're around.

"Better not be. I already told Mike if D's not back in four days, I'm packing him up and bringing him to our place. Their apartment, while nice, smells like a locker room."

"I know, right? This is going to be weird. I'm not used to you being gone for so long. Since you moved in, I think we've spent what . . . three or four nights apart?" Just thinking about being alone makes me miss her already.

"Something like that," she replies. "Don't worry.

Mike and I will be back to annoying you before long."

"I'm sure you will." I laugh.

My sister being on the phone has provided me the distraction, I needed to get home, and the canal hasn't bothered me like normal. I'm just approaching the main street when I catch sight of a man on a bike up ahead. I hug my bag tighter to me and run up the stairs.

I hate being so jumpy, but after being assaulted four years ago by a date—I was lucky I was able to get away—I avoid being alone in the dark as much as I can. In my rush, I nearly miss what Kayla's saying.

"Don't give me flack," she huffs. I can picture Kayla standing with her hand on her hip, rolling her eyes. "Are you close yet?"

"I'm just about to cross the street now. I'll be there in a minute."

Normally, I make it home in sixteen to eighteen minutes. Tonight, from Uncle Joe's Restaurant—that's the name of the place; inventive right?—to my apartment, it took me thirteen.

"Okay, I'm here," I announce. I enter our building, closing the door firmly behind me. "I made it faster than I thought I would." I try to turn on the stairway light only to realize it's burned out. Again. Walking into a darkened hallway is not what I need right now. Just breathe. You can do this, I chant to myself while I head up the three flights of stairs to my landing.

"No more scary movies," I say to her. "This is creepy." I take the steps two at a time, trying like hell to cut my time in half. "Stairwells in the dark make me think of *The Grudge.*"

Kayla laughs. "You got this, you big ol' baby. Move that pretty little butt and get upstairs. Let me know when you're there."

I huff, knowing she's right. I do have this. Being assaulted has left me fearful to the point that I'm always looking over my shoulder, ready for the next hit. I've worked hard to get out of that mindset, but walking home alone in the dark doesn't help make me feel safe.

I lunge up the stairs before my own wariness makes me too scared to sleep tonight. Even when the lights are working, this stairwell creeps me out. Though the owner took the time to restore most of this building, he left the stairs as they were when he bought it—minus a fresh coat of paint. So, those of us living here have been stuck with a narrow staircase that squeaks and moans at every step. Not to mention the lights that don't work half the time and the creepy tree right outside the window that's scary in the dark.

"Remind me to buy lightbulbs when we go shopping this weekend." Having invested in this building with the owner of the complex, I'm part owner in a way. I used my inheritance to make the purchase. I own my apartment, the storage unit next door, and just over half of the roof that I had sectioned off. The owner installed a stairwell for the other portion, so my area is private. That's where my ownership stops. I don't have anything to do with the rented units or building maintenance, but in this case, I don't mind buying a box of bulbs to make sure I can see when coming home.

"Will do," Kayla chuckles. "Now move it, sis. I've got to give Mike his meds in a minute."

Finally, after what feels like an eternity, I make it to my landing, my head down as I dig for my keys.

The hair on the back of my neck rises. I look up and take in my surroundings. To the far left of me is the only other apartment on my level. Mr. Donaldson never leaves his light on—no matter how much I ask him to. His side is always so dark.

I hate to think about what could be hiding over there. I would have left my light on this morning if I'd known I'd be home after dark.

Just to the right of the stairs on the landing is my front door. As I gaze that way, I spot a shadow that I hadn't noticed before. Forgetting the keys, I frantically search for my mace. If that's someone, they're about to get a face full of pepper spray . . . if only I can find it.

The shadow grows closer as someone steps out of the dark corner by the window less than twenty feet from where I stand. I can't make out who it is, but I sense trouble. If I were to open my door now, I'd be inviting it in.

He looks right at me, his hoodie pulled down over his face. In a rough, grief-stricken voice, he says, "Kayla, you can't leave me . . ."

Surprise has me floundering to readjust my grip on my bag before I drop it.

He approaches, and I catch a glimpse of the man's face. I'm puzzled. I've seen him before, but I can't place where. If only I could see a little more.

With his comment about Kayla in my head, I try to get my voice to work, but the words won't come.

He stretches out his hand, but I remain unable to speak, frozen midstep.

"Hello Leah, are you there?" I hear Kayla shout through the phone.

Finally, my fight-or-flight instincts kick in and I make a move, backing up just before he's able to grab me. I'm one step closer to the edge and have to do something.

"Help," I scream, dropping my handbag, ready to fight with all I have.

Stepping back one last time as he approaches, my heel slips off the landing, making me wobble. Trying to right myself as I begin to tumble, I grab hold of the lurker. I reach for anything I can get my hands on. If I go down, he will too.

He yanks his hoodie from me, sending me plummeting to the landing below.

My body arrives at the bottom of the stairs with a thud as my head hits the ground, hard. Spots flood my vision.

"Hold on, Leah. Help is on the way!" I hear Kayla yell from somewhere in the distance.

Through the fog, I can barely make out the man descending from the third-floor landing, then leaving my building.

With no fight left in me, I succumb to the darkness.

I come to when I hear a commotion next to me, causing me to grunt in discomfort.

"You're going to be okay, sweetheart. Hang in there," a

baritone voice says. I don't know who that is, but the sound of his voice is soothing.

I attempt to open my eyes, but the lights shining my way cause me to shut them up tight. "Ugh, my head," I groan.

"Do you hurt anywhere else?" a lady's voice from my opposite side asks.

"I'm not really sure. My head is pounding so bad right now."

"Let's try and sit her up. I don't see any visible broken bones or lacerations," she states.

They each put a hand behind my back and neck on either side and begin to help me up. The dizziness gets so bad that I have to lean forward as I dry heave, causing me to shudder in pain. I feel like I've jumped in the ring with Mike—him being an ex-MMA heavyweight champ, versus me, plain Jane, average female in her late twenties. I'd be a walking bruise for sure. The first time he attempted to teach me self-defense a few years back, I nearly had to crawl home. This feels like that again, but worse.

"Officer Cameron," the lady says. "Can you please holler down at my partner and tell him to bring up the stretcher?"

"No," I say. I look up at her through the corner of my eyes. "I can walk. No sense in blocking the landing when I can do it."

"Are you sure, ma'am? It won't take us long to get you situated."

"Leah," I state. "My name is Leah, and I'm sure. I'd rather walk."

"It's no prob—" she starts.

I reach out and touch her arm. "I'll be fine. Besides it's

not like I'm walking down alone. You'll be right next to me if I get dizzy."

"I don't want you falling again," she states. "Officer Cameron, would you mind hollering down at Brooks asking him to come up and help me get her downstairs?"

"Why don't I just help her down the stairs? I'm already here."

I cock my head to the other side to get a look at him. Seeing as his arms stretch his shirt in the way they do, I bet he wouldn't need any help getting me down the stairs.

"Okay, then. Let's try and get you up," the woman says. "Let me know when you're ready."

I take a deep breath and remind myself that I've got this. "Ready," I reply. They try to help me stand, but the dizziness threatens to take me down again.

I don't got this, I nearly cry out.

"If you're okay with it, I can carry you," Officer Cameron announces. "You look like you're ready to fall over."

"Okay," I say weakly. I feel so defeated, but I also know when to admit that I need help.

I'm swept off my feet into a pair of tree trunks called arms just as quickly as I speak. I tuck my head into the crook of his neck when it feels too heavy to hold up. I could fall asleep right here in his arms.

When we get downstairs, he puts me on the waiting gurney and takes a step back. I look up to thank the officer but can't find words as I look into the deepest, most beautiful, ocean-blue eyes I've ever seen.

The guy waiting does something to the bed, then begins to wheel me in the direction of the ambulance.

Officer Cameron walks alongside us until I'm put in

the back. Just as the door is being shut, he smiles, making my stomach flutter. Through the little wind-ow on the door, after it closes, I see him lift the corner of his shirt to his nose, the same spot where my head was just lying.

When the guy next to me starts asking questions, taking my attention off the window—and what's just on the other side—my hope is that one day, I can meet Officer Cameron again. Maybe next time in street clothes.

Chapter One

Ten months later

I'm filling in for Susan—our lead hostess—while she's on break. Being up front is something I dread nowadays, but it comes along with the job. All customers are seated, so I make rounds checking to ensure drinks are full. I fill water and coffee cups along the outer section of the dining room, then grab a fresh carafe and turn back to focus on the remaining tables.

That's when I see her, his girlfriend, Tillie, sitting here in my dining room at work, causing my heart to race. It's nearing a year since the incident in the hallway of my apartment building. John—the guy who attacked me—had his girlfriend testify in court that she was with him all night. It was then that my lawyer brought up that he'd been stalking Kayla for months prior. She'd broken up with him and he hadn't handled it too well. My lawyer made sure that the judge knew of his character. He might not have been after me, but he still meant to be there that night. That bit of information sealed our case—he got eighteen months for his crime. Most thought he got off easy, and maybe he did, but I was just glad he got taken off the streets.

Mike and Uncle Joe started upping my self-defense lessons after that, and Kayla even joined us sometimes. Mike and his buddies took the brunt of the teaching me to ensure that I was taught right, I had such bad anxiety after the attack that I couldn't go anywhere alone, and when I tried, I panicked.

Out on a walk one day to get a coffee, I had the biggest panic attack that I've had to date. I knew I shouldn't have tried to go alone, but I was so tired of feeling like a burden. Officer Cameron and his partner happened to be along the canal when it began. Cam—his name is Butch Cameron Jr., but everyone calls him Cam—came to my rescue yet again. He talked me through it and gave me the name of a therapist that had helped a friend of his with a similar situation. The panic attacks came on strong back then, but they have become more manageable over time.

After that day, he came to my place every morning before work and walked with me down the canal. He helped me work through a lot of my paranoia as far as going out alone. A few months ago, he quit coming around altogether, and I haven't seen him since. I'd hoped that something might build between us, but I guess that was wishful thinking. I miss him being a part of my life.

I'm steps from Tillie's table when she looks up and notices me. I've seen her here several times since the incident, but it's been months. I've never come face-to-face with her. I take a deep, steadying breath and push forward while looking out toward the other tables.

"Leah Covington," she sneers. "Fancy seeing you here. You'd think after getting my boyfriend thrown behind bars, you'd tuck tail and run."

"Tillie," I reply. I leave it at that and try to walk past to avoid confortation.

"John didn't deserve what he got because of you." She reaches out, grabbing my arm. "He said it was an accident. I don't know how you can go on living out here in the free world like nothing happened while he's locked up with all those criminals."

"This is not the place to discuss it," I grit out through clenched teeth. Yanking my arm from her bruising grip, I put on a plastic smile. "It's over. He's already doing his time. No sense in dwelling on it. Now, if you'll excuse me, I have a restaurant to run." I move past her table—two minutes until Susan comes back—and finish my rounds filling drinks. A couple of tables in, I see Susan coming down the hall on her way back from break, and I politely excuse myself from the dining room.

I send Mike on his break, then it's my turn. My stomach rumbles so I make myself a club sandwich on whole wheat. I dang near burn myself trying to grab the bacon from the grill pulling back midjump. "*Ouch*, son of a—" I look up, peeking around to make sure nobody heard me. "Thank God, nobody's in here." The dish crew is clanking around loud enough that they can't hear. Mike is on break still, and Alex—the other cook—is in the walk-in, which means no one caught the boss nearly swearing. Starving, I continue to pile my plate.

Alex walks in moments later with full trays to fill the prep station. "Hey, boss," he says. "Mike's back. He went to get his side work started. He said he'll be here in a minute."

Side work in a kitchen is the simple things that keep it running that most don't think about. When you're at home, it would be the prep done for a meal, like slicing an onion, cutting a tomato, and cleaning up messes. In a restaurant it's the same, except on a larger scale.

Nobody—management included—leaves their shift's mess for the next.

"Thanks, Alex. I'm taking my lunch break now. If you need me, I'll be in the office." I grab my plate and take off for some much-needed R&R, kicking off my heels as I enter. I close the door behind me so I'm not disturbed and plop down in my chair, grab my sandwich and take a big bite. This is heaven on whole wheat.

I flex my poor feet. I wish I could get away with wearing tennis shoes to work, but Uncle Joe likes his management to dress for the job—that means a pencil skirt, blouse, and heels. Even though they're short heels, they still aren't ment for kitchen work.

I work through my lunch break, completing the schedule and readying the bank deposit. I didn't think I'd get this all done today, as it usually waits until Monday. I don't even notice that a couple of hours have passed without incident until my office door creaks open. I glance up from my paperwork to see a smiling Kayla holding two wardrobe bags and a chocolate bar. She's wheeling in her ready bag behind her.

She stands just over six feet tall and has sandy-blonde hair, Tiffany-blue eyes, and legs for days. I can anticipate Kayla's thoughts without her opening her mouth: *I don't have curves like you. Having to be a size two for work sucks.* I'd hate being critiqued for my weight too.

Kayla gets her beauty from Mom, while I get my looks from our dad. I'm five feet, four-and-a-half inches tall. I never forget that half because every inch—or half—inch counts. My curves make me a steady size twelve, and I have dark-brown eyes—that many mistake as black—that match my hair. We couldn't be anymore opposite in looks than we already are. Seeing as I'm four years older—I'm twenty-eight, and Kayla is twenty-four—I've taken on the motherly role in our relationship.

"Boss lady's done for the day. Let's show this town what the Covington sisters are made of." She tosses the garment bags on the chair across from me and I'm shocked by what she's wearing.

"Are you crazy, Kayla? You could ruin that back here. A dress like that belongs on the runway, not in my kitchen."

Leave it to my sister to come in through the kitchen wearing a designer bridesmade dress, rolling her bag behind her. We've gotten changed back here many times. Still, I've never seen her or anyone else come back here in something from the Vera Wang White collection. Until now. It's beautiful, short, and blush pink, but it doesn't belong in the kitchen of a restaurant.

At least the smell has improved. With Kayla comes the scent of Coco Chanel. It's almost like walking through a garden, enjoying a fragrant orange.

"I know, I know. I'm changing." Kayla sticks her tongue out at me, turning to show off her dress. She puts her bag in the corner, takes off her heels, then turns to look me over. "Bennett dropped me off here." Bennett is a photographer that Kayla has worked with many times now. They have developed a little friendship through time. "I didn't want to carry all this upstairs. This was the next best place.

Don't worry. I made Mike back up before walking into the kitchen. He even took his coat off the hook to cover me as I walked through."

"I swear, he's going to make a good husband one day. Let me text Uncle Joe, make my rounds, and grab the till. I'll be ready in ten."

As I walk through the kitchen, checking in on the dish crew and Mike, I see that he's just about done. "When Uncle Joe comes down, you can clock out. Kayla wants us ready soon," I say. Knowing Kayla, I'm in for it. I hate getting all dolled up. I'd rather throw on jeans and a nice shirt than a pound of makeup and a dress that leaves nothing to the imagination. If she weren't moving to New York for work soon, I probably wouldn't even be going tonight. "I'm sure she's going to torture me while I count the till."

Mike chuckles, knowing I'm right. He's seen Kayla put me in those torture devices she calls curlers before.

After making my rounds and grabbing the till, I head back to my office and shut the door behind me.

"Sit your gorgeous butt down and let out the teacher bun you have going on today," Kayla says. "It's time to show these guys what you're working with under this mess of clothes. I wish you wouldn't hide behind this manager look. You have a beautiful body, babe. Why cover it up like this? You can be subtle and sexy rather than look like you're hiding from the world. You draw the wrong kind of attention that way."

She constantly fusses at me for how I dress; I know it's not her style, but hers isn't mine either. I get that she wants me to show off, but it hurts sometimes that she wants me to show off, but it hurts sometimes that she can't see me as I am. I don't mind showing off if I'm around people I'm comfortable with, but when I'm not, I'd rather blend in.

"Kayla, I know you want me to show it off, but I don't want to. Plus, I'm not hiding behind this manager get up. I *am* the manager, and this *is* my uniform. I don't try to change you, so quit trying to change me."

"All I'm saying is that you should give it a feminine touch rather than looking like Nanny McPhee before she becomes a knockout."

"Jeez, thanks for the confidence boost," I say. I didn't think my clothes were *that* bad, but now she has me second-guessing myself.

"You know what I mean," she replies.

"I'll think about it. Maybe I can add a bit of something, but I'm not flashing someone to appease you." I can add a pair of earrings and gloss or something, but I'm not one to want to stand out.

"That's all I ask."

After cleaning my face and letting my hair down, I take two Advil, knowing what's coming next.

Kayla primes my face before putting hot curlers in my hair. "You're going to score some numbers tonight," she says.

"Not interested, Kayla. What about you? You haven't dated in a year. That's gotta be a record."

She spins me around in my chair fast enough to make me dizzy. "What the heck, Leah? Are you calling me a floozy?" she asks, with a hand on her hip.

Unable to conceal my shock, a gasp escapes my lips.

"No! Why would you think that? I know you're not that

way. There's a difference between dating a lot and sleeping around. You like to date; there's nothing wrong with that. You're making sure that you find the one instead of settling." Seriously, how could she think I'd say that? Let alone think it. "Gah Kay, I didn't mean to come off like that. I'm sorry," I state frantically.

I see a hint of naughtiness flash behind her eyes before a slight smirk appears on her face. "Gotcha," she says, her voice playful.

"That's *so* not cool. You brat." She really had me going there for a minute. She can be so annoying sometimes.

She's laughing so hard that she holds her stomach and crosses her legs. "You're so easy, Leah. I know you'd never call me a floozy. But you should've seen your face. You were tripping over your own tongue to cover your butt."

Lifting a brow, I nod at her. "Love the model pose, killer," I tease. I swear, I love her, but there's never a dull moment when Kayla's around.

She straightens quickly before smacking me on the shoulder. "Not funny. I dang near peed myself."

"Good. Maybe next time you won't mess with me like that." I smirk and break off a square of her Hershey's bar, tossing it in my mouth.

Kayla's look turns serious a moment before she puts on that practiced smile she uses for work.

"Are you going to tell me what you've got going on in that head of yours?" She begins tugging at my hair again, not even acknowledging my question. Kayla's not one to keep things from me, normally. I look up at her and see a glimmer of a tear in her eyes and yet she won't budge. That makes me pull out the big guns, figuratively speaking of course. She needs to get this off her chest. I put my hand up to stop her from pulling another curler out of my hair. "Fine, if you don't want to talk, then don't, but I'm going to the bar as I am. I don't want all that stuff on my face anyway."

"Really, Leah?" she huffs. "You're going to go there?"

"Yeah, I am. Kay, you need to talk about something. I can see that you're on the verge of tears, I bet you haven't even told Megan. If you don't let it out now, it'll keep eating at you." Meg is one of her closest friends outside of Mike and me. They spend a lot of time together, considering they're both models.

"Fine." Kayla throws her hands up, plopping down in the armchair across from me, hugging the throw pillow to her chest. "I know we normally tell each other everything, but I didn't want to stress you out anymore. You're already dealing with so much."

"I'm here for you no matter what. That's what sisters are for. I don't want you to ever feel like you can't tell me something. I don't care what's going on in my life—there is always room for you." I get up and lock the door before returning to my chair.

Kayla takes a deep breath before looking me in the eyes. "I quit dating because I'm scared." She squares her shoulders then shrugs. "If it weren't for me dating and breaking up with that creep, you wouldn't have gone through half the stuff you have. John hurt you, Leah. He wouldn't have been there if it weren't for me." With a pout, she bites her lip and hugs the pillow closer to her chest. She lets out a big huff, hanging her head in a defeated motion.

I hate that Kayla's beating herself up over this. "Why didn't you ever tell me this? We could've talked it out." I sit back in my chair, looking over to her so she has my full focus now. She shouldn't feel bad for the choices another made. She couldn't have stopped him from hurting me. If not me, it could have been her.

"Because you would have forgiven me, and at that time, I didn't want to be." She wipes the fallen tear from her face. "I knew John had issues. He was the sweetest guy on the planet one minute, but the moment he was told he couldn't have something, he got a little scary. I didn't think in a million years that he would wait for me on the stairs. I volunteered to help Mike when D asked because I had broken up with John a couple weeks before that and his girlfriend started harassing me. I didn't even know that they were dating. I thought she was just a friend." She looks up from her hands and straight at me. "He can be violent, but I never thought he'd hurt you. *I promise, I didn't.* I'm sorry. I felt so guilty but didn't know how to approach you. You were already having those panic attacks, and I didn't want to be any more of a headache than I already was."

"You're right, I would have forgiven you right away. It wasn't your fault, Kayla. None of it is. You picked a creep, but even I can say that he hid his true colors well. I thought for sure he was a good one. It was hard to take him out of that box in court when I realized who he really was. Now, I'm glad he got thrown behind bars. You should have told me all this back then." I grab a tissue and move to Kayla, kneeling to dry her eyes. "You. Are *not*. A burden. Sure, a lot has happened to us over the years, but we're still here and we're stronger now because of it. We never gave up, Kay. Don't take this on your shoulders. It's not your fault."

"It might not be my fault, but I still brought him into your life. I need to learn to make better choices in men.

Quality over quantity."

Grabbing her chin in my hand, I turn her face to look at me. "Listen, we're the Covington sisters. We're here for each other no matter what happens. Right? When we had nothing else, we had each other. No matter how much life throws our way, I got you."

That is one statement I can make without falter. There is not a thing I wouldn't do to protect my sister.

Chapter Two

Being in my old room brings back all kinds of memories, some good, some not so. It's like a time capsule of my childhood, my basketball trophies and rock band posters right where I left them all those years ago. I really should talk to Uncle Joe about updating it. I think the last time I changed anything was on my fifteenth birthday when I begged him to let me ditch the princess-pink walls and paint them black. I begged for a month, until finally, we came to a compromise on one sage-green and three gunmetal-gray walls.

Standing in here now, looking back, I can say that the road I was headed down in high school was not a good one. I'm grateful now—not so much back then—that Uncle Joe gave me a job in the restaurant as soon as my work permit came through. Keeping busy helped me keep my nose clean and led me to where I am now.

"Leah!" Kayla yells from the other side of my door.

"We need to go soon. Are you almost done?"

"Be out in a minute!" I yell back.

I take the dress bag off the back of my door and unzip it, looking it over.

The dress is a mixture of my style and Kayla's. She got me a shimmering, rose-gold dress with a Queen Anne neckline.

It's a bit short for my liking, but it'll be manageable so long as I remember to bend at the knees. I step into it and notice that it's also a bit tighter than I'd like, as it hugs every curve in my body. Overall, I'm pleased. She kept my comfort level in mind, only pushing a little. This is something I might have picked for myself a few years ago.

I look good tonight.

Taking in a deep breath, I grab my strappy, tan heels and clutch purse from the corner, paste on a smile, and step out of my bedroom.

Kayla looks like she's ready to go. She's in a short, scarlet-red number that sits just under her rump with an off-the-shoulder neckline to keep a hint of modesty about the look. She has on her black six-inch pumps with matching clutch and hoop earrings that settle on her shoulders. Her hair is up in a tight pony, providing a killer look that ends with bright red lips and a clean face.

"Put your shoes on. We've got to get out of here," Kayla mutters, shoving her lipstick in her clutch.

"I'm going to need your help with this one. The strap is messed up." I walk over and sit on the couch as Mike walks in.

He's a large man whom many find intimidating. Mike is six foot three and built like a tank. He's a good-looking man, not one gray hair on his head. I like to tease him about being older than us. At thirty-two, he's older than most of his friends, except Damon, who's a couple years older, I believe. Kayla swears that Mike "breaks the Richter scale of male hotness." He has jet-black hair shaved on both sides and left a little longer on top. He wears it slicked back and has the brightest bottle-green eyes. I've never seen anyone with more tattoos than him; he's a walking piece of art.

But to us, Mike is a big old teddy bear—few see that side of him. He's had a lot of pain in his life, but no matter what is thrown his way, he overcomes it and is one of the best guys I know. Having him with us tonight is a good idea, considering how rowdy things can get at the bar. It's Saturday night in the busy district, after all.

We head downstairs to meet Uncle Joe on our way out. He's a six-foot-tall biker with sleeve tattoos. Even though he has me dress up for work, his dress code is more lax. He's always in biker gear, and he wears his boots everywhere he goes—I've even seen him wear them to the lake while in swim trunks. He is always presentable, though, with salt and pepper hair slicked back for work, a neatly trimmed beard, and amber eyes. His black Uncle Joe's T-shirt is clean and form-fitted, and the black pair of Wranglers and chain hooked to his wallet complete the uniform.

"Hey, Uncle Joe," I say upon approach. "I'm going to grab the deposit then we're heading out."

He sets down the pan that he's holding and looks over at me, whistling. "Beautiful. Both of you. Stay there, baby doll. I'll grab it for you. I'd hate for you to get dirty."

Uncle Joe is always good for a confidence boost. For most of our lives, he's told us not only how beautiful we are but how smart and strong we are. I swear I don't know how he never married.

He brings the deposit bag to me, handing it over with a kiss on the side of my head. "I nearly forgot, Leah. Susan brought this note to me before she left. She said someone left it for you." He hands it over and I read.

Leah,
Sorry, I had to go so soon. I'll be seeing you again.

That's odd. There's no name or anything. This can be from anyone—I serve so many people in a day.

"Thanks, Uncle Joe. She didn't say who left it, did she?"

"No. Why? Is it something I need to ask about?"

"It's fine. I'm sure they'll surface before long."

I toss the note aside—I have enough going on right now to worry about it.

"We better get moving soon," Kayla interrupts.

"You got my girls covered tonight?" Uncle Joe asks Mike.

"Of course," he replies.

"Thank you, son."

Mike isn't technically a relation, but he might as well be. He's always with us and is as close to Uncle Joe as we are. We're Mike's family—aside from his gym buddies and Damon, he doesn't really have one. Here in the South many people argue that Oklahoma is Midwestern, but the Census Bureau disagrees, when we consider someone family, we make it known. Hence Uncle Joe calling Mike "son."

"Is Janet coming over tonight?" I ask. Janet is Uncle Joe's girlfriend. They met at the hospital while I got checked out after the incident. She was the charge nurse, and sparks flew between the two. It took a bit for her to accept him since she's been widowed for only four years now, but Uncle Joe finally wore her down and now they're inseparable. They are so cute together. She's soft where he's hard, but she has no problem telling him how it is, and he has no issues accepting that she's probably right.

"Yeah, she'll be here after her shift at the hospital."

"Give her a hug for me, will you?" I ask. I like Janet. She's so much better than some of the others he's dated.

"Sure," he replies. "I better let you all go now. I have a

restaurant to run."

"Bye, Uncle Joe," Kayla replies. "See you tomorrow. Tell Janet I said hey."

He gives Kayla and I both a quick kiss on the cheek before Mike escorts us out and along the canal route.

The bank is only a few doors down from us, so we stop there first and make the drop. Since they're already closed, I use the overnight slot after making sure the bag is securely locked—the bank manager has the other key. Since the bar isn't too far from here, we decide just to walk. Along the way, Mike drapes his leather jacket over my shoulders. His coat is so big, it swallows me, but I have no complaints since it brings warmth. I'm always cold for some reason.

We are nearing the Devon Tower and see that someone is impeding traffic—*I wonder if the cops will get called to get him off the street*. Several people stand around him, looking up.

Mike and I walk over to the crowd to see what's going on, while Kayla walks off on her own to try to figure out what's going on.

"Look," a guy says next to me, pointing up.

"Looks like someone's BASE jumping," Mike says.

"Isn't that illegal?"

"Who knows," Mike replies. "I'm sure you can probably get some kind of permit or something. Nowadays, there's a permit for just about everything."

"Right." I look around, not spotting my sister. "Where's Kay?" I ask.

"There." Mike points toward the person in the street. It's a little hard to see that far out, but I can make her out. Let's grab her and get out of here."

"Sounds good. I'd rather get to the club and get off my feet for a few anyway."

Mike and I start heading that way when she saunters over, throwing an arm over my shoulder and turning me back in the direction of the sidewalk. "Let's get out of here, shall we? I'm ready to get my dance on."

Without argument, I turn back and head in the direction we were walking. With the club being just down the road, we're there in under five minutes. There's no line yet, so thankfully, we get right in. Smirking Tree Saloon is a new, two-story country and Western establishment. At the door, they check our ID and stamp our hands to show we're clear to drink. As soon as we walk in, we're hit by loud music, laughter, and the pungent smell of alcohol, sweat, and a mixture of everyone's cologne. There's a stage to the back for live music, a riding bull in the middle, and a large dance floor taking up much of the space. Tonight, the band is doing a Gretchen Wilson cover. *They aren't bad*, I think to myself. Overall, the saloon is modern and feels more like a sports bar with a Western twist. Posters are splattered about from the bands that have played here. The servers wear jeans, form-fitted red T-shirts with the bar logo, and black aprons. Pretty classy for a Western bar.

As soon as we clear the bouncer, Megan approaches Kayla and hauls her onto the dance floor. Meg catches my eye and sends me a finger wave hello. I wave in return before Mike and I find a large booth in the back. He goes to the bar and comes back a few minutes later with a couple beers.

"I ordered some nachos and asked them to bring some change for darts."

I love to get nachos and beer when we come here—they're the best things on the menu, as far as I'm concerned.

"How've you been doing? The real answer, not the response you give us to get us off your back," Mike says. He scoots to the back of the booth and settles in.

"I'm fine . . . well, I will be. I've had a few rough nights, but I'm keeping it together." I take a swig of my beer and kick my feet up on the booth across from me.

The server brings our nachos and two rolls of quarters, setting them on the table alongside two more beers. I grab a loaded chip, popping it into my mouth. When I look in Kayla's direction, she's having the time of her life on the dance floor. "I think it's more the thought that John will be up for parole soon that's got me on edge more than anything else right now."

"Do you think you'll be going to the hearing?"

"Probably not. The letter said that if I didn't want to go, I could write a letter in response. I'm not really sure what I'm going to do yet."

Mike puts his hand on my arm, drawing my attention from the nachos. "No matter what you decide, I'm here for you. I'll be by your side every step of the way."

"I appreciate that," I reply. I really do. Without Mike, Kayla, and Uncle Joe, I don't know if I'd be where I am today. They're an amazing support system.

I look over and spot an open dartboard. Then I change the subject to try and lighten the mood. "Come on, let's play. How about you try to beat me for once?"

"You're on. I'm not gonna go easy on you. Hope you're up for the challenge."

"You know I am."

When we get there, I'm up first and completely miss the board. "I meant to do that," I tease. "Let's see if you can beat me after I helped you out like that."

"Oh, *please*," Mike says. "Just because you won last time doesn't mean you always do. You can quit rubbing it in now."

"Never," I mock. I love playing games with Mike. I'm not a fan of going to the bar, but anything competitive with him is always fun.

An hour later, were settling a tie, on the best of three. Were down to the last round when a hand lands on my shoulder, startling me. I throw the dart and miss the board so bad, I end up hitting the one next to us, a few feet away. "Sorry . . . I'm so sorry," I say to the man playing on the dart board next to me. He looks pissed and I can't really blame him. I would be too if someone interrupted my game like that.

I turn back around, and my eyes go wide.

"Damn, it sure is nice to see you again," Cam states.

"What are you doing here?" I ask.

I thought for sure when he up and disappeared that I'd never see him again. I mean, here we are, months later, and I haven't gotten so much as call or text. *Who does that?* I wonder. I'm peeved that he could string me along for so many months and then drop me like hotcakes. We might not have been an item, but I thought we at least had a friendship after spending so much time together.

Mike turns around, assessing the situation.

I momentarily panic, not wanting Mike to butt in. He was upset with the way that Cam all of a sudden dropped off the face of the earth. Cam had won my family over when he kept showing up to help me through a tough time, but when he disappeared, it upset them. We all gave him a long while, knowing his job could have taken him away, before we even attempted to reach out.

"Would you mind checking on Kayla for me?" I ask Mike.

He turns toward the dance floor, but before taking off in Kayla's direction, he looks between the two of us, his eyes finally landing on me. "I'll be keeping an eye on you. Holler if you need me."

"Thanks," I reply. I turn toward Cam and look him in the eyes as best as I can, considering he's a foot taller than I am. "Why are you here?" I growl. In a challenge, I put my hand on my hip and raise a brow. "You know, friends tell each other when they plan on leaving for months at a time."

I see the confusion flash in his eyes, but I need to know. "I'm not here to cause trouble. I didn't know you and Mike were together, or else I wouldn't have bothered. I just wanted to see you."

"We're not. Mike and I are just friends, but that's not important. Why, Cam? You made me think you died or something. That's not cool."

I'm so confused on how I should feel right now. I want to hug him—I've missed him so much—but I'm still mad enough that I could punch him.

I signal the server for another beer and point toward the table, then look back at Cam.

He looks good in street clothes; I've seen him like this a handful of times since I've known him. Cam is a few inches taller than Mike, six and a half feet tall at least. He has chocolate-brown hair that's a little shorter on the sides than on top, and deep ocean-blue eyes. His chest is broad, rounding out his build with huge arms and a slim waist. He looks good in Western wear—a flannel shirt unbuttoned over a white T-shirt, dark-blue Wranglers, and a pair of cowboy boots.

He steps toward me to let someone pass behind him. I catch his smell—leather and pine with a hint of spice.

I'm not strong enough for this yet. I'm livid, yet all I want to do is hug him—I could get lost in his scent. When someone calls and leaves messages, people should call back. It's not fair to be there for them one day and gone the next.

Life isn't fair, Leah, I remind myself—a hard lesson I learned a long time ago. Still, it's just not right. That's playing with someone's heart.

"I know you're mad at me, but I wanted to see you. I'm back in town now, and I plan on making it all up to you if it's the last thing I do."

"Back in town?" I question. Where the hell has he been?

"If you want, we can get a table and I can tell you everything."

I start to turn toward my table, but he stops me, pulling me into him for a tight hug. "I'm sorry, I just really missed you."

The struggle between heart and head can be a real pain sometimes. I want to melt into his arms, but instead, I force myself to pull away, slugging him on the arm as I do.

I'm frustrated, and even though he feels like home, I can't lose myself until I know what's going on.

"I guess I deserve that," he says with a chuckle. "Want another? Or are you good?"

"Yeah, you do." I smirk. "But I'm good . . . for now."

"How about I buy you a drink, instead?"

Getting a drink with Cam is going to change things.

Either I'm going to get the closure I need, or we'll move forward from here. How, only time will tell.

Chapter Three

I take another drink of my beer as I process the information I was just given. "So you left state to take care of your grandma, who'd been injured," I start. Then I nod at the server as she sets down a basket of fries and two fresh beers. "I can't blame you for that—family should come first—but what I don't get is why you didn't at least shoot me a text at some point to let me know you'd be gone for a while. I would have understood." I could imagine how hard that would have been to pack up decades of memories in a few months' time. Moving her into a full-time care facility wouldn't have been easy on anyone. I sit back in my seat, but when he doesn't respond, I move on. "I waited for you every day for two weeks. I thought for sure that you'd show up for our daily walk to the coffee shop. I even called and left a couple messages for you at the station. Why didn't you call me or at least send me a text to let me know that you were okay? I didn't take you as the kind of man who would just up and disappear without a word."

Cam looks at the bottle in his hand for a moment, picking at the label. When he looks up, I can see the sorrow in his features—his lips are downturned, and he has nearly folded in on himself. "I'm sorry," he groans. "I'm not gonna give any excuses. The day before I got the call from

Mom asking for help, I got asked to provide backup on a case at work that took me down. Some things that we see as cops, we can't ever unsee. That night, I had my best friend, Mark, meet me at my house after work. I wanted to drink myself to sleep. I'm not an alcoholic by any means but . . ." Cam shakes his head as if he's trying to rid himself of the image. "The call was over a husband beating his wife and daughter within an inch of their lives. I was not in a good place; I couldn't bring that to you. So when Mom called, I took care of the paperwork I needed to at work and left."

Some guy walks to our table, sitting down next to Cam, interrupting us. "Hey, bro. We're gonna take off. You good?"

"Yeah, I'm good. See you tomorrow," Cam responds. The guy gives me a chin lift before getting up and heading toward his crew waiting by the door.

I feel bad for him, but I'm still upset. Frustrated at the interruption, I cross my arms over my chest and look back at Cam, waiting for him to finish.

"Sorry about that." He takes another pull from his bottle. "As I was saying, I hopped in my truck that next morning, put in for a temporary transfer of positions at work, and headed out. Cap said under the circumstances, he'd push my vacation days until the transfer went through, allowing me to work from her place through conference calls until things got settled."

"I get that, Cam, and I can't say I wouldn't have done the same, but why didn't you call me back? That's the one thing I still don't get. When you walked away, I began to believe that you meant more to me than I did to you. Now that you're here, I'm not sure what to think."

He breathes in deeply, his eyes closed, clearly struggling with the memory. "I'm not proud to admit this, but the night I assisted in that case, I got so mad that I threw my phone, destroying it. It was that or lose my cool on Mark. I never get that worked up, but there was something about that man and the way he smiled when his wife coded . . . it hit harder than any case I've ever been on before." He throws back the rest of his beer and begins to white-knuckle the bottle.

I reach out and take his hand. I'd have been pissed enough to hurt someone if I'd stumbled upon a scene like he's describing. "Cam. You're a good man. I can't imagine being in your shoes, and seeing how it's still affecting you, I can only assume it's still raw." I can't help but feel for him. Seeing the pain written all over him in this moment makes my heart reach out to him.

He takes in a steadying breath and looks back to me with a shy smile. "I'm sorry. I shouldn't still be so worked up over it."

I would be. I can't really fault him for that.

"Can I get you two another drink?" a server says, startling me.

"I'd like a black coffee and water please," I say.

"Same," Cam states.

When she walks away, he turns his hand in mine so that his palm is now facing up. "When I broke my phone, I didn't have time to get another before I left. I didn't get one until I was with Grammy. For whatever reason, the store couldn't back up my contacts, so I didn't have your number. I did get the messages you left me with the station, but you never left a phone number and I never thought of calling the restaurant. I should have, with as many times as

I walked you to work. It just never crossed my mind. I'm sorry. I should have tried harder."

"You're right, you should have, but . . . I forgive you."

What good would it do to hold on to these feelings when I can understand what caused his actions? I'm still upset that he didn't try to reach out, but it won't do any good to dwell on it.

"I can only imagine what you faced in that time."

We're briefly interrupted when our coffee and water is set in front of us. After thanking the server, I take a sip of the hot liquid and let it warm me from the inside out.

"So, is Grammy okay now? I hate hearing that she fell." Cam laces his fingers with mine and smiles. "She's as ornery as ever, already making friends and enemies." He chuckles. "How have you been? How are the panic attacks?"

"I've been good, working a lot right now. You know how it is. The panic attacks are a lot more manageable than they were. I still get them, but nothing like I used to."

I lean back in the booth and carry on a conversation with Cam that has us catching up as if he's been gone a week rather than months. It is so nice having him back. I've missed spending time with him. Since the moment I met Cam, there has been this draw that I just can't shake. I'm not sure that I want to.

During a lull in our conversation, I look out to see if I can find Kayla and make sure all is well. I look down to see our hands linked, his big fingers dwarfing my little ones in a way that makes me feel protected—safe.

"Leah," he says, gaining my attention. "I'd like to ask you something. Would you—"

Frustratingly, Kayla plops down in the booth, interrupting us. "Hot Cop's back, huh? We good here?"

"Yeah, he's back," I huff.

Of course, now would be the time she'd show up. I'd like to know what he wants to ask, but I guess I'll have to wait.

I scoot back toward the middle of the booth, creating room for Kayla. When Mike approaches the table, Kayla scoots closer to me, causing me to move even more, invading Cam's space. She pats the booth for Mike to sit next to her.

"Move your sweet little tush over. Can't you see I need to rest my feet? Heels aren't exactly forgiving, you know." She has me move until my entire right side is pressed up against Cam. Then she lies back, snuggling up to Mike.

Cam looks at me with a smile on his face before putting his arm on the back of the booth behind me.

Mike smiles down at Kayla, kissing her head, then looks at me with a smirk before glaring at Cam with a raised brow. "Are you back to stay this time, *Officer Cameron*, or do you plan to up and leave again while ignoring all attempts of communication?"

"*Michael*. Be nice," Kayla says. "I wouldn't have told him to meet us here if I'd thought you'd make things weird."

"Wait, what? You invited him?" I ask, not bothered by Mike.

"Did you not see your man standing in the middle of the street stopping traffic?" She flashes her eyes at him, taking him in. "Of course I asked him to come. You two needed to talk."

Well, that's news to me.

"Anyway," Mike says, getting our attention, "I'm not trying to make things weird. It's not like I asked him to meet me out back. I can't be considered a good friend if

I'm not watching out for her." He nudges her chin to look him straight on. "I can't believe you didn't tell me you invited him."

Kayla folds her hands over in her lap, but before she can start, Cam cuts in.

"I didn't mean to hurt her," he says. "Leah and I will figure out where we go from here. I don't expect you to like me, but I hope you respect that I'm here to make things right if she'll have me."

Mike nods his head. "Just don't hurt her. If you do, I might just have to take you out back after all."

"*Michael*," Kayla says, fussing.

Not bothered by her, he pulls her in to him and kisses her head, silencing her once again. I know he means nothing by his comments, and apparently so does Cam, who gives him no reaction at all.

When the bartender yells, "Last call!," we decide we're done and start heading out.

"I have my truck here if you guys would like a ride," Cam says.

"That sounds great," I say. "I'm running on fumes."

Mike takes his jacket off and drapes it over Kayla. "You two go ahead. I'll walk with Kayla."

I look over to Cam. "Are you sure you don't mind giving me a ride?"

"Not at all," he replies.

After Mike and Kayla turn and head down toward the canal, Cam leads me toward his truck. It's an F-350 on steroids. It looks like he took an already-big truck and had it lifted. Unless I want to flash everyone, I can't climb into it wearing this dress without help.

"I normally wouldn't have any issues, but I'm not dressed to climb into your truck."

He chuckles, opening the door before taking off his shirt, leaving him in his T-shirt. He puts his button-up over me, which reaches my knees—at least I won't flash anyone. Being surrounded by warmth and his scent has my eyes wanting to close in absolute delight.

He opens the passenger door and lifts me in as if I weigh next to nothing. "There, nobody can be flashed. And I never expected you to crawl in. I always planned on helping you."

He rounds the hood of his truck before climbing in and getting seated behind the wheel. He has a slight smile on his face as he shuts his door, turns the key, and allows the engine to roar to life. "Are you still in the same building?"

"Yup," I reply.

He nods and pulls his truck out of the parking spot. Once we get to my building a few minutes later, he parks and comes around, helping me out of his truck. His face is so close that I can feel the wind of his shallow exhale on my cheek. He's trouble for sure.

I step away and put my key in to let us in the building. After reaching my landing, I shrug off his shirt, attempting to hand it back.

Cam leans in, close enough that we're cheek to cheek, and whispers in my ear, "Keep it, sweetheart. I saw how much you enjoyed it." His breath on my ear causes a shiver to go up my spine.

I close my eyes and take a deep breath to ensure my voice doesn't break. "Come on in," I croak. Clearing my throat, I move to unlock the door.

Cam being in my home is not something I thought I'd ever see again. I stand back, taking in the way he walks around, looking everything over. When he walks into the living room, I catch the curtain move. The window is ajar, and I wonder if Kayla opened it. I didn't have a chance to double-check it before leaving for work earlier. I'll have to ask her when she gets home. We normally lock it, knowing people can access it from the fire escape.

In the living room, he points to the open window. "Do you leave this open?"

"No. It must have been overlooked when we left this morning."

I'm glad he came up with me. I'd have been creeped out if I were alone and found it like that.

Cam closes it before turning back to face me, catching me midyawn. "You must be tired."

"Yeah, I am. I'm exhausted."

He sits on the loveseat, leaning back, getting comfortable.

"I'm going to go change," I say as I walk toward my bedroom.

I shrug my dress off as soon as the door shuts behind me. I grab my usual boy shorts and tank and throw them on. The warmth of Cam's shirt has me wrapping it back around me as I catch a chill. Unable to stand the makeup any longer, I run into my bathroom and wash it off before putting my hair up in a messy bun. Then I rejoin him in the living room.

He looks up from the magazine he grabbed from my coffee table and clears his throat. "Damn, you look good in that."

I look down and realize how inappropriate I look in the moment. If it were Mike, I wouldn't even bat an eye—there's no attraction there. But with Cam, I should have thought this through more. Being up for . . . going on twenty hours now messes with your thought process.

I grab the blanket from the back of my couch and sit down next to him and cover up. "Thanks."

Cam puts his arm across the back, and in a matter of moments, I feel the faint tug on my hair from him touching the ends.

"Now that we have a minute, why don't you tell me what you planned on asking me?"

Cam puts the magazine he picked up back on the table, then turns his body so that he's looking at me directly, eating up a large chunk of the cushion that was left between us.

"I'd like it if you'd give me another chance," he states.

"Give you a chance for what, exactly?" I sit up a little taller and take a breath. "To be friends again? Sure, I can do that, but you need to communicate with me." I raise a brow in challenge and wait for him to reply.

"I'd like a chance to be more than friends if you'll have me," he replies. He looks me in the eyes, and when I don't respond right away, the lamp on the side table behind my head becomes very interesting. "I should've called you and I'm sorry that I didn't. Leah, I've only ever been in one relationship before. She didn't want me to bring my problems to her. I know that sounds like an excuse and Mark chewed me out for not talking to you, but I promise, if you're willing to give me a chance, I'll do better."

Wow. I didn't expect him to lay it all out for me like that.

I reach out my hand and put it on his knee, drawing his attention back to me. "Can you give me a little time? I'm still trying to adjust to the thought of you being back. I don't trust easily, and I did trust you once, but it's not easy to trust you again."

Cam takes my hand in his, bringing my knuckles to his mouth and kisses them, sending tingles though my entire hand and down my arm. Feeling the heat in my ears, I'm sure I'm blushing. *Great.*

"Okay. I can work with that. I just want the chance to prove to you that I am so very sorry. Leah, I promise I'll do better."

"I have no doubt." I look into his ocean blues and get sucked in for a moment.

If not for Mike and Kayla choosing this moment to walk in and join us, I might have done something stupid, like hugging him again—or worse, kissing him. When I'm ready, I can only imagine how right it will feel, but for now . . .

Cam stands and extends his hand out to help me so I can follow. When we get to the door, he opens it, looking back at me.

"Do you have my number?" I grip the doorframe, trying to keep myself from reaching out to touch him.

"I do now. Kayla gave it to me earlier."

"Well, I hope to hear from you sometime then."

He smiles. "I bet you'll be sick of me in no time."

I shake my head with a slight smile on my face. "I still walk to the coffee shop at the same time nearly every morning. You're welcome to join."

He smiles brightly. "I'd love to. See you in the morning?"

"See you then." I give him the door code and bite my lip. I hope I really do see him in the morning.

He leans in and gives me a kiss on the cheek before righting himself. "Lock up, sweetheart." He turns toward the stairs and heads down as I'm left wondering what tomorrow will bring.

Chapter Four

The next morning, I wake at my normal four-fifteen a.m. and take a quick shower. This is one thing about being an opener for the restuarant that sucks. On occasion, I fill in and close, but my normal schedule has me opening five to six days a week. Thankfully, my favorite coffee shop opens at five, allowing me to get my fix along the way. We don't open until six, but by the time I make it there and get things ready, I'm lucky to unlock the door in time for the first set of customers to stroll in.

I dress in my normal knee-length black pencil skirt, three-inch black heels, and this morning's choice of a wine-red button-up shirt. I take Kayla's suggestion and throw on a pair of hoop earrings and a bit of mascara, then pull my hair up into a high pony so it stays out of my face. I grab my vitamins and overnight oats along the way. Once I make sure things are locked up tight, I pull the door open.

I'm startled to see someone on my landing but calm quickly when I notice it's Cam. His smile grows bright. "Good morning."

"Morning, Cam," I reply.

"Did you sleep well?"

"I did, thank you." I turn and close the door behind me, locking it before heading down the stairs. "How about you?"

"I slept like a baby." He looks over at me as we make it to the second-floor landing. We round the landing and head down to the first. "Are you ready for a pumpkin latte?"

"Cam," I chuckle. "It's not even August yet. Pumpkin doesn't come out for a while still."

Cam smiles. "If you could, would you get one?"

"Uh, yeah. What kind of question is that? You know they're my favorite." What is he up to? I wonder.

We step out of my building, making sure the door latches behind us, and head in the direction of the coffee shop.

Ten minutes later, I'm holding my first pumpkin spice latte of the season in my hands, sipping that heavenly flavor. I now know why Cam asked.

"How did you get them to make me one? I didn't think they got the ingredients in this early."

"I'm the cop that saved the owner's daughter from a bad situation. She told me that if I were ever in the area, I could stop by and get whatever I wanted." He winks. "I asked her if she could make pumpkin spice lattes off menu for this special girl I know."

It's too early in the morning to blush, but my body doesn't get that note. "That's so sweet of you. Thank you, Cam." I lean into him a bit in an awkward, no-hands hug.

He chuckles, putting his arm around me in a brief embrace. "It's no problem, really. You deserve it." He smiles at me as we continue our trek to work.

In no time, we stop at the front door of the restaurant. I almost wish that this morning's walk could last a little longer.

"Well, here we are," Cam says. "Thanks for letting me walk with you again. See you in the morning?"he asks.

"Same time, same place."

"I'll be there." Cam leans in to kiss my cheek before turning to leave.

As I watch him walk away, my stomach flutters. I quickly grit my teeth and shove the feelings away. I'm still not sure if I'm ready for what he wants. I don't know if I can deal with the heartbreak if he leaves again.

Two weeks—it takes two weeks of Cam walking with me in the morning for my walls to start to come down. Once bitten, twice shy, and all that jazz. The more I understand about him leaving, the more I open up to him. No matter how much I've wanted to dive in headfirst, I've held back. Tomorrow, though, I'm going to his best friend Mark's weekend-long birthday adventure—as a friend. I can't help but feel a little disappointed that he didn't ask me to be his date.

Kayla, Mike, and I are getting ready for our weekly game night. I garb a chocolate- covered pretzel from the bowl at my side and toss it in my mouth, enjoying its salty-sweet deliciousness. Mike is finishing up the dishes while Kayla shuffles the cards in preparation for the game. On nights like this, we normally choose what new meal we want to make, turn up the music, and give it a shot. It's something we've enjoyed doing together for the last few years now. Tonight was Mike's choice—carbonara Florentine, something none of us have ever tried. It was delicious.

"Are you ready for this, sis?" Kayla asks.

"Yeah. Are you ready for me to hand you your butt again?" I take a sip of my water and put my phone face down on the table so I'm not distracted by it.

"No, not this. I'm talking about going out with Cam. You're going to be with him and his friends and family for the whole weekend. That's a big step."

"I guess. If it were a date, it would be, but he specifically said, 'as friends.' You heard him."

"His mouth might have said 'as friends'," Mike says, nosing in, "but his eyes said he's about to make things more than friends, if you know what I mean." He pulls my attention his way. Mike hands us each a longneck beer before taking his seat at the table across from me.

"Eww, Mike," Kayla adds, swatting his arm. "You know Leah's not like that."

Of course she'd bring that up. Yes, I'm still a virgin. It's something she doesn't like to let me forget. It's not like I'm trying to save myself for marriage or anything, but I'm not willing to sleep around either. I want to know that I'm with my life partner before I give myself fully to anyone.

"I didn't mean it that way, Kayla. I just meant that he doesn't plan on staying friends for long. I think he's just playing it safe."

I stand and move to the kitchen, grabbing a chilled mug from the freezer. "Want one?" I ask. The beer Mike brought over isn't quite as cold as I'd like. When they nod, I grab two more and head back to the table, handing them theirs before taking my seat. "Him playing it safe is starting to drive me crazy. Part of me is glad, but then again, it's time to move forward. I'm a little scared, but he's shown me that he means what he says."

"Tell him," Mike says. "Why do the guys always have to do the guesswork?"

Kayla raises a well-manicured brow, then starts passing out the cards. "Not all have to guess," she says under her breath.

"I don't want to push his hand," I add. "What if I say something and he isn't ready?"

"Not happening," Kayla says. "Tell him. I bet you money he'll be over the moon."

Maybe . . . but what if he's not? "I'll think about it," I reply. We're ten minutes into our game when Kayla stands and does a victory dance. "Woohoo!" She turns her card facing her and does a round in front of our faces with it, showing us that she's down to her last card. Mike has three and I have five.

He reaches to grab her card when it's in his face once more.

"You're just jealous," she says. "I'm gonna win, and you know it."

"Do I?" Mike asks. "Last I heard, you never win."

"Hey," she retorts. "Just because I normally do something doesn't mean it can't change."

"You two need to quit distracting me from the game," I say. "You're just worried that I'll win."

"In order for anyone to win, it means you need to take your turn," Mike jokes. He takes a drink of his beer and waves a hand to the table as if he's Vanna White from Wheel of Fortune.

"If you two would quit acting like children, maybe I would," I return.

I lay down my set and discard, leaving me with one card. Kayla takes her turn, then it comes to Mike. He grabs a few cards from the draw pile and lays them down, discarding the final card in his hand.

"Rummy!" Mike states with a big grin.

"Of course you won," I say playfully. "You distracted me." I yawn big and stretch my arms over my head. "I hate to say it, y'all, but if I'm going to hang with Cam tomorrow, I better get some sleep."

Kayla grumbles a bit but caves, standing to help clear the table. "Go on, sis. Mike and I can clean up. Go get your beauty sleep."

I say my good nights, then climb into bed, my mind still swirling around what Kayla and Mike said at the table.

Should I make the first move, or should I wait for Cam to? What if I'm waiting forever?

The next morning, I lean over and check my phone to see if I have any messages. While scrolling, I hear my door creak open, then feel Kayla crawl onto my bed. I get a smack on the butt just before she starts bouncing. I pull back quickly, dropping my phone and flinging my blanket aside in my haste.

"Morning, sleepyhead. It's time to get up and get ready for your date."

"Give me time to wake up before you start in." Before I can pull the covers back up, she rips them off the bed in a flick of her wrist.

I sit up to stop her, failing in my sleepy state.

"Oh no, you don't. We can't have you being a grouch today. This is your first date in years. You need to make this count."

I flop back on my bed, launching a pillow at her head. "It's not a date, Kayla. Remember he said, 'as friends.' His words, not mine. Why do you always have to annoy me? I swear, you do it on purpose."

"That's what sisters are for. It's my job to be a pain in your rear, and it's yours to be a thorn in my side. Now get up before I start singing."

Oh, Lord help us all. I love her to death, but she couldn't sing if her life depended on it.

My phone beeps. I reach across the bed, grabbing it from the floor. Kayla tries to smack my butt again—something she has always done to get me moving at her speed—but fails to connect as I turn over just in time to stop her. Looking at the screen, I see a message from Cam. "What if he's canceling?" I ask, worrying my lip.

Kayla puts a hand on her hip. "You have no clue, Leah. That man worships the ground you walk on. Answer him already."

Cam: *Morning. I hope you're ready for this weekend. Make sure you wear something you don't mind getting muddy.*

Me: *Morning, Cam. I'll be ready after my shower and a strong cup of coffee. Are you sure there's room for me and they don't mind me coming?*

Cam: *Of course there's room. Becca would have my hide if you backed out now. She rented a huge cabin for Mark's 30th birthday. I hope you don't mind sharing a room with me, though. We'll have a set of twin beds.*

Sharing a room is something I've never done with a man before. Hearing that is a little scary—the thought of drooling in front of him is terrifying. Hearing that we'll have separate beds and that he thought of it without me having to ask warms my heart. Then again, what if he doesn't see me that way? Rather than getting caught up in the unknown, I opt for humor.

Me: *Will you even fit on a twin?*

Cam: *LOL I'll make it work.*

Me: *Ok then, I guess I'll see you soon.*

Cam: *See ya.*

Kayla grabs my phone, taking a quick picture of me lounging in bed, wearing Cam's shirt, bedhead and all, then sends it before I can get a grip.

"What the hell, Kay? That's wrong on so many levels."

When my phone pings, I check it to see his reaction.

Cam: *Thanks for the picture, sweetheart. You don't make it easy on a guy, that's for sure. I'm gonna make it my background.*

Not really knowing what to say, I attempt to keep calm. He doesn't need to know Kayla sent that picture.

Me: *You're welcome. Gonna go get some coffee. See you in a few hours.*

Cam: *See you then.*

Kayla's excitement is loud enough to wake Mike. He comes running into my room, hair a wreck, bed splotches on his face and drool still on his chin, ready for a fight. Seeing there's no danger, he wipes off the drool before sitting on the bed next to Kayla. Often on game nights, he'll pull out the hide-a-bed in the couch rather than walk back across the canal toward his apartment. He lives about the same distance we do from the restaurant on the opposite side.

"You know, one of these days, I'm going to learn not to jump every time you squeal like that. I thought something was wrong." He wraps Kayla in his arms and looks at me. "You two throw on some clothes. Coffee's on me this morning."

Kayla leans her head back onto his shoulder. I wish they'd throw caution to the wind already and decide to date one another. I don't know why they keep fighting it.

Kayla smirks. "I'm all for free coffee, but it would make it so much more interesting if you didn't throw on any clothes. You know, I never thought I'd find a man with morning breath, bedhead, and Looney Tunes boxers hot, but dang, Mike, it's really working for me right now."

"Oh my God! Out," I say. "I so don't need to hear that. Now all I can imagine is . . . You know what? Never mind, go get dressed. I'll be out in ten."

I'm all for them getting together but I don't want to hear it. Yuck.

On their way out the door, I catch them bickering.

"Seriously, Kay, You had to go there, didn't you?"

"What?" she says, shooting me a wink. "I didn't mean any—"

Finaly, I'm left in peace to get dressed as the door clicks shut behind them.

We dress quickly and head to our normal coffee shop just a few minutes' walk from the house down the canal. Kayla goes to the counter to place our order with Mike's money, and once we have our coffees in hand, we head back down the canal toward my place so I can take a shower and start getting ready.

Mike, Kayla, and I jab at one another along the walk. It's when I mention Kayla's dating life that she hip-checks me, causing me to trip and stumble into a man walking down the canal. Mike catches my arm and steadies me as I turn to apologize.

"Hey, watch it! I should push you into the canal for a stunt like that," the man says, and I feel a prickle down my spine.

I can't see his face as he has his hat pulled low on his head, but the way he has his hands in his pockets and is folded in on himself tells me that he's in a hurry to get away from something.

"I'm sorry, it was an accident," I say. "I tripped."

The guy steps closer. When he takes one hand from his pocket, Mike grabs me by the elbow, putting me behind him so that he's now facing him. "Of course she would hide like a coward," the man says, laughing threateningly.

Mike nudges me toward Kayla. "Stay together," he growls, his voice deep with anger. He turns toward the man and pulls himself to his full height. "You need to leave, man. I've had enough of you talking to her like that. I suggest you move on."

The guy laughs in Mike's face but smartens up and turns to walk away.

"Wait," Kayla says quietly. She crouches a bit, looking toward the man as he turns. She moves along the partition wall, keeping her distance, following him as if she's trying to figure something out.

What is she doing? I wonder.

Kayla stops suddenly, standing to full height with her mouth wide open, then runs back. "Oh. My. God, Leah. I think that was Ryan."

"Ryan?" I question.

"Ryan." She nods furiously, widening her eyes as if it'll help me understand.

Then it hits me. My ex, the one who assaulted me years ago. The one who made me fear so many things.

"No, it couldn't be. I thought he left the state after—" I move to the bench nearby and take a seat, trying to steady my breathing. He and I dated not long after Mike and I did. Ryan and I went out all of four times before he tried to assault me. That's when self-defense became a priority for me. I dread going to the gym, but I will so long as I know I can protect myself if the need ever arises. Again.

"Are you sure?"

"Pretty much."

My nerves are rattled, but I can breathe knowing that Mike and Kayla are here with me. The tension that came over us a moment ago starts to settle now that Ryan's gone. Hopefully, we can put this behind us now. I don't notice an officer approaching until I stand and turn.

"Ladies. Mike. Everything good over here?" he asks. "I got a call to walk this area." Officer Shane and his wife, Marge, have been coming around the restaurant regularly since I was a little kid. Sometimes it pays to have officers that eat there frequently. He's like family to us after all these years.

"All's good now, thanks," Mike says.

"Well then, y'all have a nice day. I heard the weather is supposed to be beautiful today. Better enjoy it while you can."

"Thanks, Shane," I add. I take a sip of my now luke-warm coffee. "Tell Marge hey for me."

"Will do, hun," he says as he slips into the coffee shop. "You know, it's hot when you go all beast mode to protect us," Kayla says.

"There's nothing hot about that Kay. I was just looking out for my friends."

Still a bit uneasy, I try to shake it off, knowing these two have my back no matter what. I interrupt them before this gets out of hand. "Thank you, Mike. I'm grateful for what you did."

"That's what friends are for. Now, how about we get you home so you can get ready to see your man?"

We walk in peace, drinking our coffee along the way.

Is Cam my man? I think. I'd like to hope so.

Chapter Five

Mike, Kayla, and I are sitting in the living room chatting when a knock at the door puts a pause on our conversation.

Mike gets up and opens it, and I'm taken aback the moment Cam appears. I know I'm staring but hell . . . He's looking mighty fine today. Cam's wearing tight, Wrangler blue jeans and a fitted V-neck, giving me a better look at his tattoos. It looks like one is an eagle and I can make out the words "service," "honor," and "sacrifice." Cam once told me that he joined the Marines the week he turned eighteen. He served four years in active duty and four in ready reserve. That's when he went to the academy and became an officer.

"Better wipe your mouth, sis. You're drooling," Kayla says, stepping up beside me. "Hey, Cam. Take good care of her this weekend, will you?"

"Of course," he replies. He chuckles when he notices I haven't said a word. I'm still too busy staring.

When I snap out of it, I move toward Cam, but all I can think is, *Good Lord, he smells so good*. "Ready?"

"As ready as I'll ever be." He grabs my bag from beside the door, shouldering it, then takes my hand and leads me down to his truck. "You look amazing. Are you sure you're okay getting muddy in those clothes? It may ruin them."

Today, I'm in my high-waisted, dark-blue skinny jeans, a vintage Skillet band crop top with my bikini underneath —it tastefully covers all my juicy bits—and my Ariat boots. While Converse might work better, my boots are much more functional for the mud pits. I kept my face clean, and since I let my hair air-dry, it's down, resting midback.

"I'm fine. If these get ruined, I have others."

As we step outside of the building, I catch sight of his truck, his Jeep on a trailer behind it. This thing is insane—mud tires, a snorkel, a soft top, and a light bar. I can't wait to see what it can do!

"Do you need help climbing in?" he asks as he opens the door of the truck for me.

"I'm good, thanks though," I reply and step into the truck.

Cam shuts the door and walks around the front, climbing into the driver's seat before starting the truck. "Ready?"

"Sure am," I reply. "I'm excited. I haven't gone muddin' in a long time. I work so much that it's hard for me to get out nowadays. Plus, Kayla isn't big on getting dirty."

"I'd love the company but don't feel like you have to get out there today. You can always hang back with the others if you want."

"I'd love to join you," I say a little too excitedly.

"I'm glad, because there's no place I'd rather you be than beside me."

I feel a blush rising to my cheeks. I fan my face, trying to cool the heat before I embarrass myself any further.

"Are you hot? I can turn on the air."

"No, I'm good. Just excited to get this day started."

Cam shoots me a wink before turning his focus to the road ahead. The ride to meet the others will take nearly half an hour. I use this time to get to know him better.

"So, Cam. How old are you exactly? It seems silly to just now ask. I feel like I know you so well but not at all."

"I'm thirty. I get what you mean. I feel like I could write a book on you but couldn't fill out a form at the doctor's office if I ever had to."

"How about we get to know each other better?"

"Sounds good."

"So you already know that I'm twenty-eight. When's your birthday?"

"September eighteenth. When's yours?"

"Are you serious? Mine's August eighteenth. That's crazy how close they are."

"It is. Would you rather be outdoors doing something or inside?"

"I love being outside as much as I can be, but I also love to be in the kitchen creating something new. I guess it just depends on what kind of mood I'm in. You?"

"I love the outdoors," he says. "I like to hang with the guys and play Xbox from time to time, but I much prefer being outside."

"What kind of movies do you like to watch?"

"Don't laugh," he says, a slight blush on his face.

"What do you mean? I'm not going to laugh at you, but now you have me more curious than before."

Cam takes a quick glance at me. "It might seem weird, but my mom used to do these mother-son date nights. She wanted to make sure we knew how to treat a woman. I hated them when I was young, but the older I got, the more

I enjoyed them. We used to watch rom-coms. Now I have a soft spot for them."

"I think it's cute. Your mom raised you right. You can tell her that for the most part, you're the perfect gentleman."

He smirks but moves on. "Are you an animal person?"

"I love dogs, but I've never had one. Hopefully someday. Maybe after I have kids, but for now, I just don't have the time. What about you?"

"There's a barn cat on the property. I like him and even sneak him some treats from time to time. Otherwise, I've never had one other than farm animals. My sister, Janelle, has a dog. I like him too. But like you, I just don't have the time right now." There's a pause in the conversation. "What kind of hobbies do you have?" Cam asks.

"I haven't had much time lately, but I love to go fishing and camping. It's been well over a year now since I've been, though. Life kind of got in the way. Other than that, I love to host game nights at the house. Kayla, Mike, and I have this thing where we take turns picking something we've never eaten and attempt to make it before we bring out the cards. It's a blast." I smile. "What about you?"

"I love fishing myself. There's a pond on my property, so I go as often as I can. Lately, it hasn't been as much as I'd like." Cam takes my hand in his, putting our joined hands in the bench between us. "How are you feeling about this weekend? You're not still nervous about coming, are you?"

"A bit. I mean you told me a little about your family." He has a sister, Janelle, two brothers, Pat and Tom, his mom, dad, and Grammy. "But you said only Tom is coming, right? Who else? You mentioned Mark and Becca, his wife, and that she's rented a big cabin. I'll be meeting a bunch of strangers. It's a little unnerving."

I can't help but think about how different our families are. He's from a large, close-knit family, while I barely have one person, and most of my family is adopted.

Most of his works in service positions—they've served our country or our great state in some way. He has uncles in the Navy and Army, and there's even an airman in the mix, Cam's service in the Marines rounding it out. He has a paramedic, fireman, and several police officers for siblings and parents. Cam says that they live by a motto: "Live life while you're still breathing." Considering their career choices, that makes sense.

He hands me his phone and rattles off his passcode. "Pull up the photo album and have a look. I want you to be comfortable around them if possible."

"I don't want to snoop, Cam," I say, trying to hand it back.

"It might help you. In a way, it'll be like you know them—or at least *of* them—if you look and ask questions."

He's right—it might help a lot. I open his phone and start looking.

He doesn't have much to look at, but with what he does have—you can feel the love. At least now I can put a face to the names and avoid the weird *Uh, what was your name again?* questions. Thank God I'm good with names and faces. Maybe I'll survive the day after all.

As I give him back his phone, we exit the interstate. From the number of trailered Jeeps in the parking lot of the charming little café with a gas station next door, I assume this is where we are meeting his friends. Cam stops at the gas station to fill up his Jeep.

"Last time we came out here, Tom ran out of gas midtrail. I'd hate to do that with you here. We'll head over there in a minute, then you can meet those knuckleheads."

Cam steps out of the truck, setting the nozzle, and then comes around to my open window, leaning on the side of the door.

"Who all will be here?" I ask. I'm unsure if everyone is meeting at the café or at the cabin later.

"Mark, Becca, and their daughter—my niece, Aubrey. My baby brother, Tom, and some of Mark and Becca's friends. The others come around from time to time, but Tom, Mark, Becca, and Aubrey are around all the time. They're my Mike and Kayla in a way."

"I'm excited to meet them. You said that Aubrey's your niece? Is Mark your brother too?" I ask in confusion.

"No, but he might as well be. As long as we've known each other, he's hung around the farm. Mom and Dad consider him one of us. The whole Cameron family has taken them in."

"Gotcha."

Cam excuses himself to finish up. After paying, he gets back into the truck and we drive to the restaurant, parking next to the other trucks pulling Jeeps. The first to approach us is a large man who looks like Cam. As he opens my door, I recognize him as Cam's brother Tom. Height-wise, there's only about a half-inch difference—Cam is a tad shorter but broader in the chest. They both have ocean-blue eyes. Tom has blond hair, unlike Cam's dark brown. The way his brother carries himself makes him look like a tough guy, but the smile on his face and his eyes says he's kind. Tom offers me a hand in getting out of the truck, then looks over to wink at Cam.

As Cam opens his door to get out on the other side, he's bombarded by a bunch of kids and a few other adults.

I put my hand in Tom's and jump down out of the truck, releasing it midjump.

"A pretty lady that doesn't need my help. I like you already," Tom says.

Cam looks over. "Tom, don't you even think about it. I didn't bring Leah here for you to fall all over her and embarrass me. Sorry, sweetheart, this is my pain-in-the-butt little brother. Pay him no attention. He's harmless."

I start to respond but am distracted when the kids on the other side of the truck start teasing Cam about bringing a girl. The kids are circling him now and singing. "Uncle Cam has a girlfriend! Cam and Leah sitting in a tree, K-I-S-S-I-N-G!"

I can't help but smile.

"Oh, *yeah*?" Cam says with a laugh. "If I catch you, I'll be kissing *you*."

I hear a chorus of "Yuck!," "No way!," and "Gross!" as they all scatter.

I feel eyes on me and turn to see a nice-looking couple approaching. Shutting my door to the truck, I recognize Mark and Becca. They're adorable together. She's shorter than I am but not by much. She has dirty-blonde hair up in a half pony, dark-brown eyes, and an average build. She seems friendly with a bit of a firecracker fuse. The way she looks at the others, pointing to the restaurant and seeing how they start to fall in line, makes me think she's the ringleader. The way she carries herself says it all—stiff posture, head held high. There is a confidence coming from her that I'd love to have. When she looks at me with a smile, and a wink, I can tell right away that she's friendly and approachable despite her appearance screa-ming otherwise. I guess you need thick skin to hold your own in a group full of cops.

Mark can't be much over six feet. He's short compared to the other guys here. He's built solid but is lean, with short, auburn hair, and some of the rarest, most hypnotiz-ing eyes I've ever seen. One is emerald green, and the other sapphire blue.

"Shoot, sorry. I didn't mean to stare," I say. "It's just that you have amazing eyes."

He sticks his hand out for a handshake and introduc-tion. "Don't worry about it. I'm used to people staring." He puts his arm around his wife, pulling her to his side. "It's nice to meet you, Leah. We've heard a lot about you. I've been telling this guy," he says, pointing his thu-mb over his shoulder in Cam's direction, "to bring you around for a while now. It's about time he listened to me." He glances in Cam's direction, then continues. "I'm glad you could make it."

"Thanks, me too," I reply.

Meeting Cam's family and friends has me a bit nerv-ous. It's not like I'm meeting his mom though. *That* would stress me out. Being friends takes some pressure off, but when I think about us both having feelings for one another and wanting to see where this can go in the future, the pressure of making a good impression comes back. Full force.

I'm pulled in for a hug, startling me. "Hey, hon, I'm Becca. It's so nice to meet you in person."

Cam walks over, bouncing a cute little girl on his hip. "This here is my niece, Aubrey. She's Mark and Becca's daughter. And the one with the awesome knock-knock jokes."

"I'm four," she says. She holds up her hand and puts up four little fingers.

"Well, you're a big girl then, and your jokes are fantastic," I say. "They had me laughing so hard I started crying."

Aubrey is the spitting image of her mom, except for her curly, strawberry-blonde hair and the freckles on her cheeks. "Aubrey, has anyone ever told you that you look a lot like Princess Ariel?"

She squeals, looking at Cam. "Unkie Cam, is she your gillfiend?"

"Maybe one day, baby," he says as his eyes trail over to me, shooting me a wink.

"We better get inside," Becca says. "They have our table ready."

We all shuffle inside, and when we reach our table, Cam pulls out my chair for me. I thank him and take a seat. After placing our order, Aubrey asks to sit in my lap. While we color together, I try to pay attention, but as the others start in on Cam, my attention pulls that way.

"Have y'all had the talk yet?" Tom asks. "You know, like when you want to marry, have kids, settle down, and what-not?"

I glance in Cam's direction. He looks a bit confused, with a slight blush growing on his cheeks. I can't help but chuckle.

He looks in my direction and smirks. "Care to answer that, sweetheart?"

Not wanting to fold, I decide playful is the way to go. "We've talked about getting hitched someday, but nothing's set in stone. I'm sure when it is, you guys will be among the first to know." I look at Cam and wink. "Your brother wants a family right away, while I want to wait a few years. You can't really settle without being on the same page. We still have a few things to work out befor we move forward."

I look over at Cam and see his mouth hanging open. I graze his chin with the tip of my finger, shutting it. "Don't go catching flies, babe. That's what fly tape is for."

"Damn, Leah, that was freaking awesome," Tom says. "I didn't expect you to throw it back at me like that."

Mark and Becca nod in agreement.

"I couldn't let you have all the fun. Really, though, I'm just here as a friend," I say. I turn to face Cam. "You good?"

"I'm great," he replies.

Brunch is a blast. As we're finishing up, Cam leans over to me. "Thank you. You have no idea how much you being here means to me. I love seeing you all get along so well." He looks at me as if we're the only people in the room, sending shivers down my back.

Becca interrupts. "Ladies and children, bathroom break. Men, pay the tab, and we'll meet you at the trucks."

I try to give Cam money for mine, but he refuses. Becca comes over, linking her arm in mine, leading me to the restroom. It can be hard for me to connect with others at times, so feeling comfortable with this group is amazing. After washing up, we load up and head down the road, following behind the others.

Cam squeezes my hand, gaining my attention. "You

good over there" I said your name a few times and got no response."

"I'm fine. I get caught up in my thoughts sometimes. Sorry, what is it that you wanted?"

He takes his hand from mine, putting both on the steering wheel as we turn down a dirt road full of potholes. "Hang on to something. I don't want you hitting your head on the door. You can scoot in closer if you want," he says as he slows to a near crawl, allowing me to scoot in.

I unbuckle and move closer to Cam before bracing the best I can, planting my feet firmly on the floorboard and buckling back up.

"This can be rough, especially since it rained a couple days ago. It's a private road, so until we pitch in to have it graded, it's going to be a bumpy ride. We don't mind, but you might hear Becca fussing about it."

Just then, he hits a bump that I'm not expecting. It shoves me into him, hard.

"Are you okay?"

"Fine," I say, midlaugh. He wasn't kidding, this is rough.

Chapter Six

This place is amazing and I can't help but take it all in. There's a big, open field for us to park and play in. Some are already setting up an event tent across the field. The kids are out, running around in the middle. To the left is a hose setup with clumps of dried-up mud. Just behind that is a trail with big rocks on one side and trees on the other. This looks like the perfect spot. I'm kind of jealous I never knew this was here.

Tom has been giving Cam grief about "slowing down so much a snail could pass" and Cam's been trying to blow it off, but I don't see that happening much longer.

Cam's voice pulls me back to the situation at hand. "Dude, chill out. I didn't want Leah to get hurt. You should've seen her bounce. She nearly hit the roof."

Tom starts to laugh, but I swat his shoulder. "Be nice. You know you'll do the same thing one day."

Cam looks like the Cheshire Cat with a big grin on his face.

"You just defended my brother," Tom says. "Are you okay?"

They remind me of Kayla and me, in a way. "Yes, I did, and I'm great."

Tom looks pleased. Glancing over to Cam, he gives a chin lift. "I'm sold. It's gotta be love."

I shrug my shoulders and look back at Cam. "I don't know, maybe," I say and hop out of the truck.

Tom laughs. "Dang, girl. You're cruel."

I leave the guys to their bickering and walk with Becca to the tent to help the ladies set up and get the kids settled. Just as I'm about to set up the second to last table, Cam walks in.

"We came to see if you ladies still want to ride."

"Of course I do. Unless you'd rather me go with someone else," I say, a little unsure.

Tom's head snaps in my direction.

"Don't you think about asking her," Cam says, then turns back to me. "I want you with me."

Tom looks our way tauntingly. "Don't worry, I can give her a ride."

Becca shrugs off their behavior. "I'm glad I'm not going to be the only lady out there with these knuckleheads. They're always like this. It can get annoying sometimes."

Mark interrupts. "You're going? What about Aubrey?"

"Aubrey's taken care of. I'm going on a ride with my man for his birthday. Is there a problem with that?" she replies.

He smiles big, shaking his head. "Nope."

"Good. Let's go, stud." She smacks Mark on the butt before running off toward their Jeep in a fit of giggles.

"I love when she's like this," Mark says as he takes off running after her.

I can't help but chuckle and admire what they have together.

"Seeing them gives me hope. They're made for each other," Cam says.

I nod, watching Mark catch up to Becca. He picks her up bridal style and kisses her midspin. "They're cute. I can see why they give you hope. They seem to have something solid."

"They've overcome a lot to get where they are today." Cam puts his arm around my shoulder as we approach his Jeep. "I'd like to make sure that your harness is secure if you don't mind. We've had one fail in the past, so now most of us inspect them before letting anyone ride."

"Works for me. Safety first," I reply.

After climbing in, he secures the harness, then checks it for safety before going to his side and doing the same. After he's pleased that we're secure, he leads the way, lining us up with the others. "Okay, guys, make sure you set your hand-held to hands-free and secure them. I don't want anyone getting stranded or left behind this time." Cam secures his walkie-talkie on the dash in a special sleeve before turning it on and testing it.

While they're setting up, I check the trail ahead of us. This is unlike anything I've been on before. It looks like an old dirt road that's been washed out by the rain. There are some big puddles of murky water, but most of it is mud.

We take off, and in a matter of minutes, it looks like Cam drove over a mud volcano centered under me. Kayla's paid for a mud bath and facial before, but mine's free. I'm going to shine for a week at this rate.

He looks over to gauge my reaction.

I laugh loudly from deep within my belly. "Why'd you slow down? I was having fun."

He raises his brow. "Are you ready for more, then?"

"Yeah, I am. Aren't you? It's been years since I've been out in the mud. Show me what this trail has to offer."

Tom's voice breaks through on the radio. "If you let her go again, I might call her myself. I know how a phone works."

Cam clenches his jaw, white-knuckling the steering wheel. He takes a deep breath and releases it before looking over at me. "Leah may be single at the moment," he delivers with a wink, "but you're the wrong Cameron to change that."

I look away, both to avoid their brotherly rivalry and the flutters that wink created. "Are you ready to show me more?"

"As you wish, sweetheart," Cam says.

An hour later, as we're nearing the end, we pull over when Mark and Becca get stuck. Cam gets out of the Jeep so we can help push if needed, then undoes my harness and extends his hand to me. "Come on. Just be careful."

Becca's on the side where Cam asks me to stand. "How are you doing?" she asks.

"I'm having a blast." I glance over at Cam, then back at Becca. "Though it bothers me a bit that Cam's treating me as if he's worried that I'll break or something."

"He'll get there, hun. Show him what you're made of." She looks back at Mark. "Think of it like this. The guys see all kinds of stuff at work that nobody should ever have to see. They're used to helping others, taking care of them in one way or another. When they find someone they care for, the worry amplifies. It's our job to tell them when they're being too much."

"Thanks, Becca. That makes a lot of sense."

Thinking about the case from the night he walked away hits home. I can imagine.

I watch as the guys actively try to pull Mark and Becca's Jeep out of the mud, but notice that Tom's winch has seized up. "Hey, Cam, why don't you hook up to that tree and back in? Then you can hook their Jeep to yours," I suggest.

Cam nods his head toward his Jeep. "Might as well give it a shot. Go get the Jeep and I'll meet you by the tree."

I head to his jeep and climb in before reversing it back to the tree. It's been a long while since I've driven, but it's nice to be behind the wheel of a vehicle again. Once I get there, Cam walks my way. He goes to the front, hitching his winch around the tree.

Becca walks over, grabs my hand, and pulls me out toward her Jeep. "Don't worry, Cam. You pull it, and we'll push," she says as Mark walks over to meet us at the mud pit's edge.

"You ladies know that once the wheels turn, you're going to get mud flung on you, right?" he says, offering both of us an arm that we gratefully take.

"I know, babe," Becca replies. "We'll be fine. Hey, it gives you a reason to shower with me later."

"I'm muddy already," I respond. "I'll be fine."

"Cam will kill me if something happens to you, Leah." Mark looks down at Becca. "And I know I couldn't handle it if you got hurt."

"Mark, why don't you let Becca guide your Jeep out, then I can help you and Tom push?"

After some debate, Becca hops in the driver seat of their Jeep as Tom, Mark, and I step behind it and get into position. Becca gets it rocking in a snap. When we see it moving, we jump into action.

After we get the Jeep out of the rut, my boot gets stuck, causing me to fall on my butt in the mud. I let out a wail of laughter in response.

"Leah, are you hurt?" Cam asks. He heads my way, marching through the mud and stopping right next to me. "Are you okay? Did you get hurt?"

I look up at him, shielding my eyes from the afternoon sun. "No. I'm good." I take his offered hand but pull him down in the mud with me instead of getting up.

Cam lands with an *oomph*, then turns to me after gathering himself and smiles. "Better?"

"Much." I take some muck and rub it onto his clean cheek. "You look good covered in crud."

"I look good, huh?" he asks in a teasing tone.

"I haven't hidden the fact that I think you're good-looking. How many times have you caught me staring?"

"Well, the feeling's mutual. Even lying here in the dirt." He extends his hand to wipe some mud off my cheek but stops when he realizes his hand is covered in muck also. "You're the most beautiful woman I know."

Thankfully, I'm covered in crud or else he would see just how red my cheeks can get.

"Come on, Cam!" Becca yells out. "Quit trying to put the moves on her. We aren't here for a show."

"Speak for yourself," Tom adds. "I'm taking notes."

"Come on, Hot Cop," I say, putting a hand on his chest trying to conceal a chuckle. "Help me up would you? We have an audience."

Mark laughs from afar. "I forgot she called you that."

"Shut up, man. You guys sure know how to ruin a moment," Cam says, standing before offering me a hand up.

We all get back into our respective vehicles and head toward the well to get washed off, where Becca has us pose for pictures. Once we're done, I move over to the faucet and strip down to my bikini so I can rinse off my clothes. Immediately, I feel eyes on me. The smoldering look Cam's giving me is enough to send chills down my spine.

A whistle breaks through the gawking. I look over to see Tom staring. He glances away quickly, but there was no mistaking it. I shake it off and turn back to Cam. He looks . . . worried? No, that's not right. Irritated, maybe? But why?

Mark approaches, patting Cam on the back. "Sorry to interrupt, but I need to borrow this guy for a minute."

I nod, walking to the hose with Becca to rinse off the worst of the mud before we have a chance to go take an actual shower.

"Don't mind them. Let's get this mud out of our hair," she says.

After rinsing off, we meet up with the guys at the back of the trucks where they already have the Jeeps trailered and are waiting on us to shower. The showers are in a tent the size of a large porta potty and consist of a warm water bag hooked up at the top with a nozzle. The bags are solar powered to heat the water. Cam has three in his. He tells me he borrowed them from his mom and sister so I'd have enough water for a decent shower. I'm lucky that he's so thoughtful. My stomach is in knots after the day we've had. If he doesn't make a move soon, I will. I'm tired of waiting. The man doesn't always have to make the first move, right?

Becca leaves my side, running into Mark's welcoming arms before heading into their shower. Cam walks over as

I hang my wet clothes on the back of his truck.

I grab my shower bag and towel as I turn to face him. "Will you help me get the rest of the mud out of my hair?"

Without argument, he steps inside with me before lowering the door. Cam turns around and looks at my body, still covered by my bikini. "My God, Leah," he whispers under his breath. "You're perfect."

I don't think he means for me to hear him, but I do. I turn to look over my shoulder. "I got a lot of the mud out, but it's still in there pretty good."

He clears his throat and forces his eyes to meet mine. "I see that."

Cam grabs my shampoo, putting a generous helping in his hand. He reaches around me, tilting my head up with a finger touch under my jaw. His chiseled chest brushes my back, and I close my eyes and try to even out my breathing. He wets my hair and begins to massage the soap into my scalp with his long fingers, sending shivers down my spine.

When I release a soft moan, he leans in so that his lips are nearly touching my ear. "Feel good?"

"I'm in heaven right now." I hum.

"I'd be more than happy to wash your hair anytime you ask."

"I might just have to take you up on that." I turn around and wrap my arms around his waist. "Cam, I'm sorry about what happened out there with Tom. I should've thought before stripping like that. Since I came here with you, I didn't think it would be a bother." I honestly wasn't thinking at all. I was just reacting. It goes to show how comfortable I am around this group. I scoot .

back a tad as the soap nears my eyes.

He rinses it away from my face. "Don't do that. You have nothing to be sorry about. I'm the one who should be apologizing." He takes a moment, then speaks up. "You need to know why I'm so wary." Cam closes off the water nozzle so he can focus on me. "When I brought my ex around, she didn't get along with the others. I let her come in and act a fool and did nothing to try and stop it. I should have tried to talk to her about it, but she had this way that made me feel guilty if I brought up any issues I had."

He shouldn't have felt bad for trying to work on an issue in a relationship. That's not how it's supposed to work.

"She nitpicked everything I did. Flirted with Tom—even if he declined her advances, she still tried—and she'd compare us to one another often. I know it wasn't his fault, but it still did damage. When they met, he treated her the same as he did you." The hurt in his eyes is hard to witness. "Well, not the same, but he still did the same annoying brother stuff. In the end, she tried using me to get to him. She wanted to be with Tom, not me. People either love him or hate him," he says. "The thought of losing you . . . it's too much. But the thought of losing you to *Tom*? No matter how much I love him, that would destroy me."

"Oh, Cam," I say. "I understand, but I'm not here for Tom. He's great, but he's not who I'm interested in. I can promise you that you're it for me." Standing on my tiptoes, I lean in and wrap my arms behind his neck. With our bodies pressed together, I join my lips to his in a long-awaited kiss. After what started in the mud earlier, I have to know what it's like.

I feel Cam's hand inch up my back and land on the crook of my neck. The rapid beat of our hearts between us and the deep sigh in his chest puts me at ease—a little. Pulling back for air when my lungs begin to burn, I bite my chapped, swollen lips and look down to hide the blush on my cheeks.

Looking up through my eyelashes, I try to gauge his reaction.

Cam is still breathing heavily. "I hope we can do that again." My smile begins to grow. Cam nudges my chin up with his finger. "I want you know that I don't see us as just friends. There's too much chemistry here. If that kiss didn't prove it, I don't know what will."

"Cam, I—"

"Move your butts, lovebirds," Tom interrupts. "The grill won't run itself."

Can huffs and starts the shower back up. "Can we talk about us when we get to the cabin tonight?"

"I'd love that," I say, leaning in to give him a sweet kiss. Frustrated we can't continue this but happy we put a pin in it, we finish our shower.

After getting changed and looking in on the others, Becca and I grab the meat for the grill and a beer for each of us before heading back. Cam spots us first and runs our way to help, Tom and Mark following closely behind.

"The guys and I were going to throw around the football while the meat's cooking," Cam says. "Would you like to play?"

If I can't have another private moment with him, this will do. *Let's play.*

Chapter Seven

Placing my hand on my hip, I watch the back-and-forth between Cam and Becca. I don't remember the last time I threw a football around—maybe in college but I'm not sure. Today has been a *long*, fun-filled day. It's now nearing dinner. Tom started the grill and has decided to sit out of this little football game that Becca tries to turn into a guys-against-girls game. The icing on the cake is that she also placed a bet—whoever wins has to pay for a night out on the town for the others, essentially a double date.

"I know you ladies can handle yourselves, but it's not a fair game. We're twice y'all's size," Cam says. "How about we mix the teams into boy-girl so it's fair?"

"I said it was guys versus girls," Becca cries. "Don't go changing it up now."

Cam looks in my direction as if he's debating it.

"I'm game. Guys against girls sounds fun to me." I wink at Cam, and out of the corner of my eye, I catch Becca throw a fist into the air in triumph.

I smile at him and turn to walk to where Mark is waiting.

Cam grabs the ball out of the back of the truck and runs to catch up to me. He throws an arm around my shoulder and walks with me to the open field. "We'll be nice and give you ladies the ball first."

"Thanks?" I say in question, not knowing whether he's being nice or placating me. I almost can't stand the thought, but I'm going to take a page out of Kayla's playbook. With our size and lack of experience, there's no other way we'll win this. Here goes nothing.

I look over to Cam. "You ready, handsome?"

He winks, tossing me the ball. "Show me what you've got, sweetheart."

This is about to get dirty—metaphorically speaking, of course. I'm not proud of what I'm about to do, but he asked for it.

I get on my tiptoes, giving him a quick kiss on the cheek. "No hard feelings?" I ask. As he's about to answer me, I spin around, taking off toward Becca.

Cam shakes it off and starts running my way.

Knowing that I can't outrun him, I slow down and shake my backside with every step. I must say, those hula lessons I took with Kayla sure did pay off. Cam is so distracted that I'm able to toss the ball to Becca, who is unguarded by a stunned Mark, scoring us a point. If I hadn't distracted him, I know he'd have grabbed me, and I wouldn't have been able to go anywhere.

"Dude, get your head in the game and your eyes off Leah's backside!" Mark hollers at Cam. "I can't believe you just stood there and drooled over the show she put on rather than grabbing the ball. Come on. Don't make us look bad."

Tom laughs from the sidelines. "You can't tell me you'd have your head in the game if Becca was shaking her bum like the Chiquita banana lady. At least he isn't drooling like a teething toddler. There's only a little bit of spittle on his chin."

I can't help but laugh, swatting Cam on the chest. "Sorry, big guy."

He shakes his head. "No complaints here. I got one hell of a show."

Based on the heat in my cheeks, I must be beet red.

Since we scored, the ball is ours. I throw it Becca's way. She catches it with ease and starts running to make the point. Mark catches up as she stops and turns to look at him with one hand on her hip and an eyebrow raised. Instead of grabbing her or the ball, he looks at her as if he isn't sure whether or not he can take the ball.

That leaves me open. I run and grab the ball as she holds it at her side. I hear her saying something about tonight but choose to ignore what I don't want to hear. Cam doesn't even attempt to catch me; he's still standing there watching Becca and Mark.

After scoring another point, I ask, "Y'all know we're playing a game, right? Are you going to start trying, or are you handing it to us?"

As they laugh it off, I decide it's time to make this interesting.

"Since it's two-zero in favor of us ladies and you didn't even try the last time, how about you fund a girls' night out rather than a double date if we score again before you do?"

"Not a chance. You asked for this, sweetheart. I hope you're ready." Cam walks over to Mark with a big smile on his face. "What's all this about not making us look bad? At least I got a show out of it."

Becca comes back toward me while watching the guys. "You know he's got to do the whole 'I'm a man, hear me roar' thing now. Right?"

"I know, but I don't want to hear them say they handed it to us either. This way, the score will speak for itself. We may play dirty, but we still played."

"Smart thinking. Let's do this then."

I have the ball in hand when Cam grabs me by the waist, stopping me. He takes it from me, swinging me up on his shoulder like I'm a sack of potatoes. He takes off in a light jog on the way to score a point. Becca's no help. I look over, seeing that Mark is holding her also. I can't help but laugh. I knew the men would make a point about their strength.

Cam makes the goal, then sets me down while smiling.

"Now that you've scored, know that that won't happen again. We're going to kick your butts," I say. I pat his chest, turn, and wink over my shoulder before skipping away toward Becca, who is standing a few feet away.

Cam chuckles as he heads toward Mark.

"What did you say to him? He looks like the cat ate the canary," she says with a laugh.

"I told him that they won't be scoring another point, so to speak."

"Seriously?"

Sharing a laugh, we walk out to the field.

Becca walks to Mark, going in for a kiss. When she does, I grab the ball out of his hand and take off running. As I'm heading in to make the point, I feel Cam closing in on me. I take a knee, knowing he's much taller. With his speed, he should go right over the top of me. Cam stumbles, trying to stop in time, but it works; he sails on over. I'm back on my feet before he fully regains his footing, and I score our point just as he stabilizes himself. That leaves us one point away from the win.

Once the men pick their jaws up, Mark says, "Good play."

Cam gives me a side hug. "I didn't expect that—nice play."

I chuckle. "One more point and you'll have to take us out for some fun." Before he can respond, I walk back toward Becca, pulling her in for a huddle. "We need one more point. I've got an idea. Mark shouldn't be covering you too hard. We can use that. I'll start with the ball. Cam will cover me . . ." I trail off, looking over at the guys, who are looking at us like they already know our game.

This should be interesting.

Becca covers Mark in her flirty way, and I take off running with the ball. The setup is all part of the plan. We've got to psych them out for this to work. I look to my left, giving Becca the signal. *Hurry up,* I say to myself, knowing that any minute Cam will be on me.

She turns, running in the same direction I am. We both head toward the goal. Feeling Cam close in, I throw the ball to Becca as he narrows the gap. Mark, running in her direction, is mere steps too late. She reaches the goal line and spikes the ball, winning us the game. The look on the fellas' faces is priceless.

"Oh my God, I can't believe that worked. We won!" Becca exclaims as she hugs me tight.

Mark and Cam walk over to us in congratulations, as Tom yells out to get our attention.

"Dinner's ready! Meet y'all at the tent!"

After a quick bite to eat, the guys put the trailer locks on and unhook their Jeeps. Apparently, one of them owns this piece of property so they can leave their trailers here if they need to. I was worried that someone might hook up to them and take off with their stuff, but Cam assures me that they have cell cams all over the place.

"Ready to head out?" he asks.

"Yep, so ready."

Cam walks me to his truck, opening the door for me. "We have about an hour until we get there." He shuts it, rounds the hood, and hops in before starting his truck and pulling out. "Care to talk about us now?"

"Are you sure you want to do that while you're driving?"

"If you're game, I am," he adds, as we follow the others down the road. The ride back to the interstate is much quicker without pulling a trailer. It's also a lot less of a jumble.

"Alright. Let's hear it," I say.

Cam is quiet as we pull onto the interstate, then he settles in. Waiting on him to talk has me feeling nervous suddenly. My palms are slick, my knee starts bouncing, and my heart feels like it's ready to beat out of my chest.

Cam reaches over and rubs my leg, and I turn to give him my full attention.

"Sweetheart, I told you that I'd do anything to prove to you that I'm here, that I won't be going anywhere. You said that you needed to learn to trust me again. I hope that I've shown you that you can." Putting on his blinker, he changes lanes to pass a slow driver. Once passed, he starts back up. "I know it's only been a few weeks since I've been back, but if that kiss was any indication of where we're headed, I'm happy to see it. There's something between us, and I don't wan to keep fighting it."

"I agree, there *is* something between us, and you *have* shown me that you're here for me. So . . . what are you saying?"

"Well, I didn't plan to ask you this while driving, but I can't wait anymore. Leah, will you be my girlfriend?"

The nerves are real now that I know I have to tell Cam the one thing I dread telling guys I'm interested in. "Before I answer you, there's something you should know about me. It wasn't important until now, but if you want to be with me, you need to know." Squaring my shoulders, I take a deep breath. "Cam, I'm a virgin."

Without skipping a beat, he states, "That's something to be proud of, sweetheart. Not many can say that at our age."

"You're not mad that I didn't tell you sooner?"

"No, why would I be? It's not like we've been dating or anything. Besides, that's your business to tell when you're ready."

"So you're good with this, and the fact that I don't move at the same speed as many others?"

"I'm perfectly fine with it. I'm in this for the long haul, Leah. I have no problem waiting until you take my last name. It'll be kind of fun making out like a couple of teenagers."

"You sound so sure of yourself over there," I tease. "I'm not waiting on marriage; I'm waiting until I can see myself heading that way."

"Why shouldn't I be sure of myself? You've had me since I found you—my fallen angel—at the bottom of the stairs."

Cam glances over and winks. "I can respect that you're not waiting, but I think it might be fun to try."

So no sex until marriage—if we head that way. I've never met a guy that wanted to wait before. It's kind of nice.

"I guess if you're sure then, I'd love to be your girlfriend." I so badly want to unbuckle and crawl closer to kiss all over him right now. I'm falling for him, faster than I'd thought I'd ever fall for anyone.

"I'm sure," he says, turning his hand over and interlocking our fingers before lifting my hand to his mouth to give it a kiss. "You have no idea how happy I am right now. If I weren't following Mark, I'd pull this truck over and kiss my *girlfriend*."

Not knowing how to respond without putting my foot in my mouth, I stay quiet and try to calm the heat rising on my cheeks. When I don't respond, he chuckles, kissing my hand once more before falling into a comfortable silence for the remainder of the ride.

Once we pull into the driveway, I feel my mouth drop. "This is a cabin?" I ask. This is the biggest one I've ever seen. "It looks like one of those you'd see on *House Hunters*. You know, the ones that no normal person could afford but they make you think you can?"

Cam laughs. "Now you sound like my mom. I know what you mean though. When she showed me the reservation, I had the same reaction. She saved for months to pay for today." He turns off the truck. "Stay put. I'll come around and open your door."

"Cam, I can get out on my own."

"I know, but you're my girlfriend now. You shouldn't have to."

"Such a gentleman," I concede with a chuckle.

Cam makes good on kissing his girlfriend as he helps me out of his truck. The moment my feet hit the ground, he frames my face with his hands, touching his lips to mine. Until we're interrupted anyway—unfortunately.

"Hey, you two," Tom says, patting Cam's shoulder on his way past the truck. "You're drawing an audience. How about we get inside and find our rooms?"

"Can't a man kiss his *girlfriend?*" Cam asks.

"*Girlfriend?*" I hear Becca squeal from across the way. "Are you serious?"

Cam grabs our bags from his backseat, tossing them over his shoulder. "Yep, she finally took pity on me and agreed to be my girl."

"Oh. My. Gosh," Becca cries. "I'm so happy right now."

Cam puts his arm around my shoulder, pulling me in. "Come on, beautiful, let's go find our room."

Stepping into the cabin, I'm in awe. The wall of windows at the back of the house overlooks the rolling hills on the other side of an impressive pool. The décor is modern, not so much that it doesn't feel homey, but enough that it doesn't feel like a hunter's lodge. Cam tugs on my hand, pulling me toward the stairs behind him. I can hardly get over the view. This doesn't look like a cabin at all. It's big enough to be a small hotel. *This is crazy!*

Walking into our shared room, I take it all in. "This is cute," I say.

"Sure, if we want to have a tea party, we're all set," Cam adds. He points to the little kid setup in the corner with a grin on his face.

"At least there's two beds and a bathroom."

Setting our bags down, Cam starts to reply when he's cut off by my phone ringing.

It's Kayla. I hit accept and put her on speaker. "Hello?"

"Hey, sis. How's it going?"

I sit on the edge of one of the beds and nearly sink into it, it's so soft. "Good, how about you?"

"I'm fine. I'm calling to let you know that you had a delivery of flowers today. I put them in your room for you."

"What do you mean flowers?" I look at Cam, but he shakes his head no. "Is there a card?" Who else can they be from? Uncle Joe maybe?

Cam sits on the bed across from me, brow raised.

"Hold on, let me look." There's a pause, then, "Yeah, there is. It says, 'Sorry.'"

"There's nothing else?" Cam questions.

"Nothing but the card, the name of the flower shop is House of Blooms. Maybe you can call them and ask who they're from."

I've never known anyone to buy me flowers except for special occasions. I'll have to figure it out when I get back home.

"Can you text me the shop's phone number? I'd like to call and find out," Cam states.

"Sure," Kayla replies. "I don't see the big deal in getting flowers. I'd love for someone to send me a bouquet."

"There isn't," Cam says. "I just want to check in. Leah wasn't expecting them, and I didn't send any flowers, so it raises concern for me. Are you sure there's no name on the card?"

"Nope, and all it says is 'Sorry.' They were sitting by the door when I got home."

"Thanks," Cam says. "I'll check into it."

"No problem."

"Thanks, Kay. I'm going to get back to my boyfriend now," I say with a big grin on my face.

"Wait, *what*?" she screams. "Boyfriend? When did this happen?"

I giggle, looking up at Cam. "About an hour ago."

"Well, I'm happy for you two. I'll let you go, but I expect details when you get home."

"Done. Love you."

"Love you, too, sis."

She's not the only one who's happy. I can't quit smiling. For once, I found a good one.

Chapter Eight

I attempt to crawl out from under Cam's arm without waking him. I look back to make sure I didn't once I'm standing. He snuggles into my pillow and lightly snores, letting me know that all is good. I slept like a baby, wrapped in his arms. After showering last night, we snuggled in to watch a movie while sharing some cocoa and popcorn. We both fell asleep somewhere in the middle. I'm not ready to be sharing a bed in a sexual way, but after last night, being held while I sleep is my new favorite pastime. I hope he slept well. A twin bed for me is pushing it, but for the both of us . . . that must have been uncomfortable for him.

I walk into the attached bathroom and do my business. Then I grab some clothes and throw them on before slipping out of the bedroom and head downstairs. The house is quiet this early. I slept in a bit according to the clock on the far wall, but I guess six a.m. is still early when on a mini-vacation. I enter the kitchen and locate the coffee pot; I get it started, then find a pitcher to make some cold brew—I know that Becca and Tom drank it cold yesterday, so I'm going to cover all bases. I grab myself a cup of hot coffee and begin scouring the fridge to see what I can whip up for twelve people. Last night, Mark and Becca had some groceries delivered for this weekend. I locate sausage, eggs, and the ingredients for biscuit bombs—there is something amazing about biting into a biscuit and having gravy burst into your mouth. Then I spot the fresh fruit and set it all out on the counter before tying up my hair and getting started.

Hearing a thud on the stairs, I look across the way and see Becca walking down carrying a sleeping Aubrey and a little pink suitcase. I wipe my hands and jog over to her to grab the bag.

"Thank you," she whispers.

"No problem."

One of the other moms comes down the hall with her kid wrapped in her arms. "Is Pam here yet?" she asks.

"No," Becca replies. "But she should be pulling up any minute. Are the others ready?"

"Yeah. They should be out soon."

I feel like I'm playing that old game Pong, watching the back-and-forth between these two. "Are y'all leaving already?" I interrupt.

"No," Becca answers. "Some of the women have a baby shower for another friend to get to. Pam from church agreed to watch the kids while they go, and Lily is taking Aubrey so that Mark and I can have a kid-free weekend."

"Oh, okay."

"Thanks for getting someone to come pick us up," the woman I now know as Lily says.

"I'm glad to do it. Thank you for keeping Aubrey for me. We'll be by Sunday evening to pick her up."

When there's a soft knock at the door, I move to open

it, and three others with kids draped over them walk down the hall. I help carry bags and walk them out to the waiting passenger van. They all load into it with their children.Becca helps Aubrey inside last, setting her on her booster seat before giving her kisses and shutting the door.

"Alright, let's get these men fed, shall we?" she states.

"Let's do it."

Becca and I walk up the driveway arm in arm and back into the cabin. We head to the kitchen and wash up before warming the oven.

Becca is standing at the sink washing her hands while I dry mine. "What is it that you do at the restaurant?" she asks.

"I'm the manager. What do you do for work?"

"I stay at home. I'm on disability." She chuckles when I look confused. "Not everyone's disability is visible, Leah."

"Oh, I didn't mean—"

"Don't worry about it. I don't take offense to it anymore. So what are we making? It looks like you have something planned already." Becca looks over the ingredients on the island. You'd think in such a big kitchen that there'd be some decent small appliances, but aside from a coffee pot, can opener, and a toaster, there are none. Looks like I'll be mixing the biscuits by hand.

"I planned on biscuit bombs, sausage, eggs, and fruit."

"Biscuit bombs?" Becca questions. "What's that?"

I outline what exactly they are as I whip up the gravy and get it set in the freezer. With there being no ice trays in this house, I put a layer on a cookie sheet. It won't be the same burst, but I can double up if I need to.

"Those sound delicious. I'll make some skillet potatoes

and bacon to go with it. These guys can eat." Becca pulls out her phone and clicks a few things. "How about some music?"

"Yes, please."

After turning on K-Love—a local station—she pulls out a bag of potatoes and begins washing them as I grab a bowl and mix up a good amount of biscuit batter. Once I'm done, I begin cutting them with a cup since there are no cutters in the drawers. When the gravy center is added, I put them in the nice, warm double oven.

"How are things going with Cam?" Becca asks.

"Things are great," Cam says, startling both of us. He walks into the kitchen in swim trunks and a white tee, his hair still wet from his shower. Seeing as it's a pool day, he must have wanted to get a head start. He steps in behind me, snaking his arm around my waist and pulling me in to kiss the side of my head. "Morning, beautiful."

"Morning," I echo. "Sleep good?"

"The best night's sleep I've had in some time." He kisses me once more, then scoots across the way to pour himself a cup of coffee. After taking a drink, he moves my way once again. "Need help?"

"Oh God, no!" Becca exclaims.

"Why not?" Cam asks, looking puzzled.

"Seriously? You can burn water, man. Sure, you can grill with the best of them, but it's best that you stay out of the kitchen."

"I resent that. I can cook," he fusses. Turning to me, he smirks. "I can."

"How about you help me make a fruit salad, then?" I'm Switzerland—neutral territory. It seems to be the safest.

Cam sets his cup down and moves to wash his hands before coming back to help me. I grab a pineapple and set it, a knife, and a cutting board in front of him. He grabs the knife and stares like he has no clue what to do.

"Never cut a pineapple?" I ask.

"No, but it can't be that hard, right?"

I snatch it up out of harm's way and set a container of strawberries in front of him instead. "You can take the tops off and quarter them."

Cam takes the paring knife and starts sawing at one. I drop the pineapple and wipe my hands on a hand towel, turn his way, and wrap myself around the side of him, grabbing his hand to help. Cam lifts his arm, pulling me in front of him, leaning down so that his head sits in the crook of my neck. "What am I doing wrong?" When his warm breath hits my skin, it causes me to shiver.

"You don't need to saw the knife." I wrap my hand on the outside of his and attempt to show him the proper way to slice a strawberry. "Try it like this."

"Whoa," Tom says as he enters the room. "If I got cooking lessons like that, I might actually pay attention."

Cam jerks the knife, nicking my finger. "Ouch!" I move to the sink and run it under water until the bleeding stops.

"I'm so sorry," Cam says, coming up behind me. He steps up to the sink and grabs my hand, looking at the cut. "Let me find a Band-Aid. I can't believe I did that." He pulls away, but I stop him.

"It's fine, it was an accident. This kind of stuff happens in the kitchen every day. It's not like this is a first for me."

"I still hate that you got hurt."

"I'm fine, Cam. I promise."

"How about you take her up to the room? There's a first aid kit in all the bathrooms. You can doctor her up and get ready for the pool I can help Becca finish up," Tom says.

I start to argue, but Cam is not having it. He lifts me, tossing me over his shoulder, and heads toward the stairs.

"Cam put me down. I can walk."

"I know you can, but if I put you down, you'll head back to the kitchen instead of where I need you to be."

"Don't worry, I got this!" Becca yells out, followed by her laughter.

I place my hand on Cam's back, trying to brace myself as we head up the stairs. Once he has me in our room, he sets me down, taking my hand and tugging me into the bathroom. He opens and closes a few cabinets until he finds what he's looking for, then sets it down on the counter and comes back for me. He walks me over and lifts me so that my bottom is on the cool counter. Never in my life have I been treated like this before. It's . . . I don't really know what to think. It's not bad, by any means, but it makes me feel things I've never felt. I don't know how to handle it, so I just let him take care of me while I peek up at him through my lashes.

He takes my finger, holding it over the sink, then pours peroxide on it, causing me to wince. He looks up at me, then lifts my finger to his face, blowing on it, sending shivers down my spine once again. He grabs a fresh hand towel and dries it up, then applies a bandage. My heart pounds as he kisses it all better. I am so far out of my comfort zone right now. My stomach is in a frenzy of flutters.

I'm scared it will take flight at any moment.

There's a knock at the door before Mark sticks his head inside. "Hey, sorry to interrupt. Becca sent me to tell y'all that breakfast is ready. She said get your suits on and head on down. We'll meet you out back by the pool."

"Thanks, Mark. Be down soon." Cam steps out into our room and comes back with a swimsuit that I haven't seen before. "Get changed. I'll wait for you in the room."

"Where did you get this? It's not mine."

"What do you mean it's not yours? It was in your bag."

I hold it up and notice that I've seen this before. I think this might be the one Kayla was trying to get me to buy when we went shopping Thursday. *That little sneak.* "Never mind. This has Kayla written all over it." I toss it on the counter and look back at Cam. "Can you close the door behind you? I'll be out in a minute."

This suit is smaller than the normal full-coverage bikini that I would wear. It's cute though. I put it on and tie the strings. It's a deep purple with little stars all over it. Once it's on, it's not as intimidating as I thought it would be. Nothing is hanging out, even if I'm showing more than I normally would. I'm covered in all the areas that matter.

I open the door and walk out toward my bag. I look over as I hear something fall and see Cam's eyes darken as he looks me over, his hand held out in front of him as if he is holding something, his phone at his feet. I guess he was. "I can't get over how good you look in a bathing suit, and this one . . . I'm going to have to keep you close."

I walk his way as if there's an invisible string pulling me in his direction. I can't help but stare. He has his shirt off and I can see just how built he really is. He isn't as defined as I thought, but he is pure muscle. When he catches me gawking, I hear a throaty chuckle and witness his pecs jump. His Marines tattoo that I caught a glimpse of previously is beautiful and takes up most of his upper-left side, but on his right ribs is a colored flag that looks weathered, full of holes and jagged edges.

He lifts his arm when I reach out to trace the edges of it. There's a pair of combat boots at the far bottom with a large gun of some sort tucked in and a helmet hanging from the top, centered with the flag. Off the top-left side, it says, *"For our freedom"* and the bottom right, *"I will serve."* I trace a ragged, raised scar hidden beneath, causing Cam's muscles to tense.

He reaches out, grabbing my hand. "Another time. Right now, let's get your sunscreen and head downstairs before they beat down the door."

I flinch at the sudden change but head toward my bag and grab my sunscreen, then hurry downstairs for breakfast. I would love to hear his story but the way he pulled back has me wanting to pump the brakes. When he's ready, he'll share.

Cam and I are sitting around the firepit, cuddled up in a chair, enjoying a quiet moment together. After breakfast, we played courtside volleyball for a while before it got too hot, then we took it to the water. Some time later, Tom hollered out, "Weenie roast!" and so the fire was built. It's been an eventful day. The guys wanted pizza for dinner, so Cam ordered a dozen, claiming that it was on him as a gift for Mark.

Cam fiddles with his beer next to me. I grab it and take a drink, not wanting to get up from his warm embrace to get my own. I turn so that my legs hang over the arm of the chair. Cam leans his head on my shoulder, so I lie mine on his.

I could stay in this moment forever. I look out at the others, some playing horseshoes and some back in the pool.

"It was my fault," Cam says, drawing my attention. "The wound you saw. It was my fault. I was on watch while the others in my squad cleared a building. A kid came walking down the road . . . he couldn't have been much older than Aubrey." His fingers dig into me a little, biting my skin but not enough to hurt. "When his ball came close to me, I stepped out just enough to kick it back. I shouldn't have, but I got distracted." He shakes his head. "Bad things happen when I get distracted."

I place my hand on his cheek, rubbing my thumb back and forth for support. If he doesn't want me to see how haunted he looks right now, the least I can do is provide him with some comfort.

He takes my hand, kisses it, then places it back on his cheek. "They came out of nowhere," he groans. "It was my job and I screwed it up. Three of us got hurt that day, all because I was stupid. I knew better."

I sit up, get him to look at me, and cup his cheeks. "You did what anybody would do, Cam. How were you to know they'd use a kid as a diversion?"

He doesn't say anything to my comment. I start to worry, but then Becca plops down into a nearby chair. He seems to shake his mood.

"S'mores time," she announces.

He kisses my shoulder as the makings are being passed around. Now that we've had our moment, he seems to be back to his normal self, all jokes and laughter. I know he still blames himself, and I hate that.

An hour later, I begin to grow tired. These have been a couple fun-packed days. Because Cam just opened a fresh beer, I settle in for the long haul. In front of all his friends, I fall asleep in his arms. I don't even wake up until Cam's tucking me into bed. Startled, I try and get up.

"Sleep, sweetheart. Everyone's going to bed now."

"I'm sorry. I didn't mean to put a damper on things."

"You didn't. You gave me the perfect ending to a wonderful day." He leans down and kisses my head before climbing into his own across the way.

I already miss his arms being wrapped around me. As the chill runs down my spine, I contemplate crawling into his bed with him. Before I fall asleep again, I run through the day's events in my head once more. Cam's not the lucky one. I am.

After having breakfast with the group, Cam and I head home. I got a call early this morning asking me to come in to work this evening. After stopping to pick up his

Jeep, we get back on the road. Three exits before the one I'd take to get home, Cam gets off and heads south a few miles. Baycliff Valley is a small farming community with so many old, abandoned buildings that would be nice picture opportunities. There is a Dollar General and an adorable micro gas station with a shop attached for things like milk or bait. We pass a church the size of a small house and a volunteer-run fire department. If I were coming down this road without Cam, I wouldn't even think of this as a town. It looks like a straight shot from Interstate 40 to Highway 9.

Cam slows past the church, readying us to turn left down a dirt road. Less than a block down, he takes another left, heading down a long driveway lined with white rock and trees. A sign overhead announces that this is Cameron Farms.

Nerves creep in as it hits me that I'm about to see where Cam lives.

Chapter Nine

I fiddle with my hands as Cam turns onto what I assume is his property. He has to make a stop after dropping me off, and pulling his Jeep would make parking that much harder to find. It just made sense for him to drop it off on his way to take me home.

"This is my family's land. Each of us kids have five acres. Mom and Dad have a total of around 120 more." He looks off to the left toward a house. "I've never brought a girl out here. Hopefully, they won't come running. They can be a nosy bunch."

I chuckle. "Nosy? You've met Mike and Kayla. I'm used to family sticking their noses where they shouldn't. Why wouldn't you want them to come over and say hi though?"

"My family doesn't believe in privacy. I love them to death, but I'd like to keep you to myself for now. Let's figure us out before Mom has us walking down the aisle."

If he doesn't want me to meet them yet, I'm not going to argue. I turn my attention back to the view in front of me. Behind a fence to the left are several cows. On the right is an obstacle course. I'm sure a family full of emergency personnel often uses something like that for both training and fun. I can only imagine how tough it is. At the end of the driveway, the trees part at a fork.

"To the left are my parents, Butch and Marie. To the right, my sister Janelle and her three kiddos. Straight ahead and down the way is my house. Tom is to the right, and Pat, our oldest brother, is to the left."

This place is fantastic. I wish I had a family like this. Mine is great, but this is next level.

"If Pat is the oldest and you're the second, is Tom or Janelle the baby?" Tom give me those vibes, but I haven't met Janelle yet.

"Tom is." He laughs. "Could you not tell?"

"Yeah. I kind of thought so. Like Kayla, he seems to love attention." I chuckle. I look over and see three kids playing behind his sister's house. They start running toward the fence, waving as Cam and I pass. "This is an amazing setup you guys have out here."

Cam waves back and continues. "I bet you can tell who's single and who isn't by our homes. Mine and Tom's look sad compared to the others."

"It's not that bad. Maybe a bit plain, but that's normal for bachelors." *This is a dream.*

Continuing down the drive, he takes my hand and gives it a firm squeeze. He nods in the direction of his home as we start to pull up. It's a white, two-story, farmhouse with a covered front porch overlooking a pond. I can picture myself sitting there with Cam, watching the sunset.

He clears his throat, and I notice my mouth gaping open.

I snap it shut, and try to hide my embarrassment by looking away. "Your home is stunning. Its just like what I have always imagined buying when I decide to move on." He puts the truck in park, and i hop out. "I love your porch."

I would normally help unload, but this view has me under its spell. I wander over and sit on the stairs, looking out at the view across the pond. Leaning my head against the railing, I'm in a daze, lost in the beauty in front of me. I could stay here forever. When I hear footsteps approaching me from the side, I look up to see Cam staring at me.

"It's the most beautiful sunset I've ever seen," I tell him.

"It's breathtaking," he says, still looking at me.

Cue the flutters and the heated cheeks. He has a way of making me feel more girly than normal. Cam offers me a hand up from his stoop before placing it on the small of my back, guiding me inside. He opens the front door, then steps behind me, allowing me to take it in.

The house's layout is impressive. His kitchen is a dream, but everything screams bachelor pad. The walls are empty except for the big-screen TV in the living area. It feels more like a stopping place than a home.

To the left is an office through a set of French doors, and to the right is a living area. The home has an open floor plan, making it feel bigger than it is, not to mention that all the windows open to a beautiful view of nature surrounding the home. Along the back wall of the living area is a staircase, with a half bath tucked in underneath. Across from the living area is a dining room with a massive, custom-made dining table that could easily seat a dozen or more people. It looks as if the table and benches were carved from the trunk of a tree, not something easily picked up at a local furniture store.

Through the dining room and to the right is the biggest and the best kitchen I've ever seen outside of a commercial one. There are top-of-the-line Hestan appliances and an island that rivals the dining table for size. The light over the island looks custom made to match the table. Just outside the roll-up window over the sink is an outdoor kitchen, making it convient for handing off food and cleanup.

"This kitchen is amazing!"

Cam smiles, following me around while I take in everything that makes up his house.

"You have a great home, Cam. I can tell you put a lot of thought into the build."

He hands me a cold water that he just pulled out of the fridge. "Thanks. I designed this house with the thought of my future family enjoying it for years to come. The kitchen especially—it's typically the heart of the home. I'd love to be able to cook a meal for my wife in here one day." Chuckling, he adds, "I guess I'd have to learn to cook for that to happen."

"Maybe I can teach you how to make a few dishes."

"I'd like that, but no knives for me next time." He looks around the empty kitchen. "I guess I'd need to buy some kitchenware first. Why don't you go upstairs and freshen up? My room is straight across from the stairs, or if you turn left at the top, about halfway down the hall on the right is the main bathroom. There are towels in the closet just outside the door."

"You're sure you don't mind me using your en suite?"

"Not at all."

I set my water down on the counter, walk to Cam, and pull him down for a quick kiss, then head toward the stairs. If he were anyone else, I might not enter his room so willingly, but I know that I'm safe here, so I do.

"Huh." This is not what I expected. The downstairs is

empty, but I thought for sure that I'd find his touch on things in his bedroom. I step into the room and straight in front of me is a big king-size bed on rails, neatly made, but there is no headboard or anything. For a night table, there are a few stacked milk crates on the side of the bed. There's a recliner beside the big, beautiful picture window to my far right that looks like an optimal place for stargazing.

I can picture us curled up there for hours upon end. Not a knickknack in sight. I open the first door on my left and find a huge walk-in closet that's nearly the size of my room. This suite is huge. I walk into his closet, running my fingers along Cam's neatly hung clothes, imagining how my things would look hung next to his. There's enough room in here for mine, plus some. This would be Kayla's dream closet.

Stepping back into the room, I go to the door next to the closet and I'm taken aback when I step inside. The big picture window on the far right is mirrored in here, straight back from the door. The windows are a little darker than normal, meaning they're most likely tinted, thank God. I would not be using this bathroom otherwise. Directly in front of the window is a claw-foot tub. I'm in love already. To the left is a double sink with a makeup counter that is a little lower, with a stool tucked underneath. Opposite the counter is a huge walk-in shower, big enough to fit four easily.

I hear ringing coming from somewhere in the distance, snapping me out of my daydreaming and back to reality. I clean up quickly and head back downstairs. "You have the perfect setup out here."

He walks over and takes my hand. "I'm glad you like it,

but you coming down these stairs smelling like the soap from my bathroom is a thing for the memory bank." He hands me my water. "Are you ready to go? We've gotta get you home for work."

"If I must." I smirk and follow him out. What I'd really like to do is curl up on the couch with Cam and forget that I told Uncle Joe that I'd come in and help.

Twenty-five minutes later, he's walking me into my building.

"Don't forget I'll be picking you up at four tomorrow for the game."

"I'll be waiting," I reply as we make it to my landing. "I had fun this weekend. Thanks for taking me."

"I did too. Thanks for coming. I don't want to leave, but I know you need to get to work." He hooks a finger in the belt loop of my shorts, pulling me into him. "But I want to kiss my girl before I have to leave."

I brace a hand on his chest, looking up into his eyes, inching my hand up until I'm wrapping it behind his neck, pulling him in for a memorable good night kiss. Our lips meet, causing my eyes to flutter shut, allowing him to take over. Too brief of a heart-swelling moment passes before the front door to my apartment is being whipped open, putting a damper on the moment. Cam leans his forehead against mine as we both turn our heads to take in Mike backing out the door.

"Tell Leah I'll meet her . . ." he says, stopping in his tracks as he turns and notices us. He looks a tad shy, the tips of his ears reddening when he notices that he's interrupted something between us.

"No need to leave a message," I reply. I pat Cam on his chest and push back to standing on my own. "Give me a minute to change and we can head out." I turn to give Cam my attention. "I better get moving. I'll call you after work."

He leans in, kissing my forehead, then waves in at Kayla and Megan, who are sitting in the living room. "I'll make sure to have my phone on me. Talk then." He hands Mike my bag, then turns toward the stairs and heads down.

Mike takes my bag to my room, dropping it just inside, then heads back to the kitchen.

"Hey, Meg. Sorry I don't have time for a visit."

"It's fine, maybe next time."

I walk into my room and immediately spot the vase of wildflowers sitting on my bedside table. I take a quick picture and send it to Cam. He mentioned to us the other night that he was going to talk to the flower shop about them. I hope this helps. I then grab the flowers and toss them into the trashcan by my door. If another man is sending me stuff, he can keep it. I grab my work clothes from the closet and quickly put them on, put my hair up, and refresh my deodorant, then head back out.

Coming home early so that I can fill in when someone calls off work sucks. I'm just glad that Cam is picking me up tomorrow so I can go to the basketball game with them. I don't want to miss that.

Let's get this night over with already.

Unable to get away for an early dinner like we had planned, Cam picks me up from the curb near my apartment so we can head to the game. After closing the restaurant last night and opening this morning, I barely made it out of there in time to shower and grab a bag of Goldfish on the way down. I hop in and scoot to the center, leaning in to give Cam a quick kiss before I buckle up. He hands me a sandwich covered in a napkin. I look at him in question.

"Mom was nearby when you called saying you had to work a little late and had to cancel dinner plans. She figured you wouldn't have time to eat, so she made you this."

"Oh my goodness, that is so sweet. Thank her for me, will you?"

"Will do." He leans in, kissing the top of my head, then puts a hand on my knee and signals to pull back into traffic.

Ten minutes later, we're pulling up to the stadium. Cam parks next to Tom's truck and we hop out. I make my way around to Cam, where he links his hand in mine and leads me to the others. A couple of their other friends that were at the cabin with us have shown up but are off to the side on their own. They seem to be their own group inside a larger clique of people.

"Leah!" Becca yells. "I'm glad you came back."

"Of course. I told you I would," I chuckle.

"I was sure you'd be fed up with all of us by now." She pulls me in for a hug.

I pat her back as we pull away. "Not even close."

"Why don't you ladies go on in and find the seats? We'll grab a few beers and meet you there," Mark says, handing me my ticket.

"Fine, but grab me a souvenir cup this time," Becca huffs. She links her arm in mine and leads the way.

Once we get to our seats, she notices that the tickets Mark gave us put the men next to each other with us on either side of them. "No way," she says to me. "Here, sit with me. They can take ours." After we're all settled in, Becca checks in with the other ladies who are a little further down before turning back to me. "I'll be in the city most of the day on Wednesday. Wanna meet for lunch?"

"I've got to work, but you can come by the restaurant if you want. I can take my lunch when you get there and introduce you to some of my family and friends."

"It's a date," she says. Then she hands me her phone to put my number in. "Don't let them make you move. They're bigger than us we'd—never be able to see around them."

"What are you ladies up to?" Cam asks upon approach. He holds out my beer for me, and I gladly accept. Then they shuffle in, finding seats.

"Were setting up a lunch date," I reply. I pass Becca back her phone, then take a drink, enjoying it as it cools me from the inside.

Mark looks over at Cam with a raised brow. "Before you know it, Becca will have her looking at wedding dresses."

Cam slaps Marks arm lightly. "Don't go scaring her off. Leave the wedding talk for later, not right after y'all meet her."

"You know . . ." I start. I decide to carry on with the conversation from brunch the other day about us getting hitched. "Dress shopping's not a bad idea. We might not have a date yet, but looking won't hurt. Right?"

"Right," Becca adds. "Plus, if it needs to be altered, you're going to need to order early."

Cam shrugs his shoulders. "Fine, have fun with it."

I can't help but laugh. "Oh, come on. I'm just playing."

"I know but I'm not wearing a tux," he says smirking.

"Really? Why not?" I ask in all seriousness. "When you get married, you only plan on doing it once. You should do it right."

"I guess I haven't thought about what I'd wear. Just that I'd hate wearing a tux."

"That's a shame. I bet you'd look good in one," I say. "Everyone should look their best on their wedding day."

"What do you plan to wear when you marry?" Cam asks seriously.

"I never thought of what I'd wear. I just know that when we marry, I want to look my best. As I think everyone should."

Becca sniggers under her breath. All three of the guys appear to be shocked.

What did I say? Now, I'm confused.

"You look like I said something wrong."

"No, sweetheart. You did nothing wrong," he says, wrapping his arm around my back.

I try to laugh it off since the game's starting.

The first part is slow, and the score goes back and forth. After a while, Becca heads out for a bathroom break with some of the other ladies from the group. I stay back with the guys and watch the game. It starts to get good. All it takes for me to yell is one crap call from the ref. The game is close. The score is 107 to 104 in favor of Oklahoma City Thunder—our NBA team. As a result, there's a lot of shouting.

The others shuffle in a good twenty minutes later. I'm just about to ask Becca where she got her foam finger from when my phone vibrates. I take it out to make sure it's not the restaurant or Kayla needing me. It's neither, nor do I recognize the number.

Unknown: *Sorry, I didn't stick around the other day.*

Me: *Who is this? I don't have your number programmed in my phone.*

Unknown: *I'm a little hurt that you don't know. Think about it. It'll hit you.*

Me: *You must have the wrong number because I have all my friends' numbers programmed.*

Unknown: *No, Leah, I know who you are.*

Whoever it is, it's not funny. I hate creepy games like this.

Me: *Who are you then?*

I look at the others to see if one of them could possibly be messing with me. Nothing. Nobody is on their phone except Becca, but her number's in my phone. I wait for the reply.

I debate on telling Cam now or later. Relationships are something I'm not used to, but I know I'd want to know if someone was messing with him. I put my hand on his and hand him my phone, open to the text for him to see. I hope it doesn't get him all worked up, but I also want to show him that we're a team and I trust him.

Chapter Ten

I stand here with Cam wrapped around the back of me breathing into my hair, just outside the stadium. OKC Thunder won 114 to 104 only minutes after the texts came through. When Cam saw them, he helped me to my feet and shot through the crowd, telling the others to meet us out front. Minutes later, Tom flung the doors open, looking for us, followed closely by Mark and Becca.

Cam held out my phone. "Check this out and tell me if I'm just being jealous or if I have right to be concerned."

Standing here now, I'm waiting for a reply as they look over my phone and the pictures Kayla and I sent Cam with the flowers. They've had our phones for a good five minutes; it's eating me up inside.

"You're not being jealous at all," Tom says. "I'm sending this over to Jazz. She's who you gave the information about the flowers to, right?"

"I agree," Mark says. "I'd be livid if this were to happen to Becca."

What? If all three—they're all cops—are suspicious, maybe I have reason to worry.

"Yeah," Cam replies. "Thanks, bro."

"Who's Jazz and why are you sending her information

about me?" I ask. "Aren't you guys overreacting a bit? It's just some flowers and a few texts." I'm sure it's just someone I know messing with me.

"We see this kind of stuff all the time. I don't think we're reacting enough," Cam replies. "I'll explain Jazz when we get somewhere quieter."

The stadium is still clearing out, and rowdy people are everywhere. It is quite loud. I guess I'll let him take the lead here. He is the cop, after all.

I nod. Tom finally hands us back our phones. We pocket them as Cam starts tugging me down the sidewalk.

"Hey!" Becca fusses. "Don't leave. We're supposed to go get cocoa. It's tradition."

"We'll meet you there," Cam hollers back.

I look over my shoulder to see her pouting. I'm about to say something, but Cam beats me to it.

"I missed you last night," he says. "Walk with me. I'd like a moment alone with my girl."

Who am I to say no to that?

He steps behind me again, wrapping me in his arms, kissing my neck.

"*Cam.*" I giggle when his whiskers tickle me.

"Fine," he huffs. He steps to my side, taking my hand in his. He looks over at me and winks before bringing my hand to his lips for a kiss, before tucking my arm into his and sending tingles through my body.

Along the walk from the stadium, which is less than half a block, he has been more affectionate than any one of my exes ever has been with me. I'm completely enamored.

"What are you thinking about over there? You're awfully quiet." He grins.

I raise my brow. "You're driving me crazy."

"How is that?" He chuckles before kissing the back of my hand again.

"You're gonna make me say it, aren't you?"

"I have no idea what you're talking about, gorgeous," he says innocently.

I smile, then look out in front of us. "You haven't given me a real kiss since you picked me up. Since we left the stadium, you've been so affectionate, it's driving me nuts. Just kiss me already." I can't help but blush. I can hardly believe I just said that out loud, I'm not normally so forward with a man.

"I knew we should have taken my truck." He laughs softly. "If I were a teen, I wouldn't care if we made out right here in the street."

Seeing the restaurant grow closer, I pull him to a stop, stretch up on my toes, and lean in to give him a sweet kiss. It has me melting into him when he draws me closer, my heart rate picking up.

He pulls away long enough to breathe out, "I guess I still don't mind."

Sealing our lips once more, I'm completely lost in all things Cam.

"Get a room!" someone yells from across the way.

I break our kiss with a chuckle, lean my forehead against his chest, and breathe him in for a moment to calm my racing heart. I can't seem to get enough of this man.

Cam rubs the back of my neck soothingly. "Come on, sweetheart. I promised you some cocoa." He steps in front of me and gets the door like the gentleman he is.

A hostess greets us as we enter. Biff's is a cute fifties diner with classic black-and-white floor tiles, a jukebox in the corner, red-and-chrome seating, and neon lights. The cherry on the sundae is the fifties attire worn by the staff. The men are in white button-up shirts, black slacks, and red-and-white-striped aprons with soda-jerk hats, while the ladies are in black poodle skirts, white button-up shirts with red-and-white-striped half aprons, and saddle shoes.

Cam tells the hostess we're expecting three more to show before she seats us in the back corner in a round booth. She hands us our menus before taking our drink order and walking away. We scoot in so that we're next to one another at the back of the booth, leaving room for the others on either side.

The cute, older server appears, carrying our hot cocoas with extra whipped cream. "Well, aren't you two lovely. I'll be back to take your order when the rest of your party joins you. If you need anything, just give me a holler."

I nod, and she walks off. I snuggle into Cam's side as he drapes his arm around the back of the booth.

My phone beeps with a text—Becca telling us they're on their way. I show Cam the message and cuddle back in, leaning on his shoulder for a bit.

"Cam, who is Jazz? You said you'd tell me."

He sits me up for a minute so he can look me in the eyes. "Do I sense jealousy?" He smirks. When I don't answer, he kisses my nose, then nudges my chin, so I look back at him. "Don't worry, sweetheart. Jazz is like a little sister to me. I was in the service with her brother. I mentioned to him that I was going into the academy around the same time she was. He asked me to watch out for her."

"So do you work with her now? Is that why you sent her my information?"

"Yeah, she's at the same station as me. She's a darn good officer and I trust that she'd be willing to help on this."

Looking into his eyes, I don't see even a hint of malice. I can trust him. I doubt they would have brought her up if it was anything more.

"And what is *this*, exactly?"

"Right now, it's just a friend helping another out. I don't know who's messing with you, but I don't think it's friendly. At the moment, I don't have enough to state otherwise, but my gut is telling me to keep an eye on it."

"You're scaring me a little," I say, fiddling with my fingers. If he's really this paranoid, maybe I should be too.

Cam nudges my chin so I'm looking at him. "There's no need for you to worry, yet. I've got you. As long as you keep telling me if anything happens and always have someone with you, everything will be fine."

"But you think that something can happ—"

"You two doing okay over here?" the waitress interrupts.

"We're fine, ma'am, thank you. The others will be here in a minute," Cam states.

"Please, call me Bella. None of that ma'am stuff with me. I'll give y'all a moment's peace and come back when the others arrive." She shuffles off again.

This is the perfect opener to move on from that heavy conversation. I'll just be more cautious than normal. I'm sure Cam's right—everything will all be good in the end.

I elbow him playfully in the ribs. "Yeah, sir. Make the lady feel old and we'll have to watch our food for sure."

He goes to tickle me, but thankfully the door opens, and we hear the others arrive.

"There they are. Look how cute. The lovebirds are all cuddled up," Tom announces to the whole restaurant as he walks in.

My phone pings with another text. It's from Becca again but, this time, with a photo.

I open the photo and see Cam and me cuddling in the booth. It's so cute—he has his arm around me as we lock eyes. She snapped it when I was messing with him about our server, but it makes us look like we're ready to kiss. I show Cam and send it to him before putting my phone away.

Bella comes back over to take our order. Cam and I order a shareable plate of loaded cheese fries, a club sandwich, and some cheesecake, then Tom rattles off his request with a considerable amount of charm.

Bella giggles. "Sure thing, sugar. You're one handsome guy, you know that? We might've had something if I wasn't a happily married woman."

I can't help but laugh.

"Oh, honey. You got to keep these young ones on their toes," she says to me.

We hear the cook holler out the swinging door.

"Bella!" She looks over her shoulder, then back at us.

"Coming! Gotta go, kids. The hubby needs me."

"You guys would've been such a cute couple," I say to Tom. "Too bad she's taken. I'm sure I could've set you up."

Tom snaps his head my way. "Ha ha, funny." The others can't stop laughing, though. "I didn't expect *you* to roast me. Becca or Cam, sure, but not you. I thought we were friends," he says.

I chuckle. "Sure, we are, but I'll still pick on you. It's when I don't like you that I'm quiet."

Not long later, Bella brings our food out before excusing herself again.

We dig in while chatting.

After a few bites of the cheese fries drenched in ranch, I look up to see Becca staring at us with a smile. "You know, you guys are way too adorable. Mark, what happened to us? We used to be a cute couple. Now we're the old married one," she pouts.

Mark kisses her head, pulling her in to him. "Baby, we *are* a cute couple. The new just wore off a long time ago. That doesn't mean I don't still worship the ground you walk on. You know I'd do anything for you. You're my queen."

"I think you two are a cute couple, and after hearing what Mark said, you guys still hold that title. I wouldn't worry about anything," I say. Those two are relationship goals.

He nods in thanks. "See, baby? We're still cute."

I lean back in the booth just as my phone vibrates with a text.

Kayla: *Hey, sis. Where are you? I thought you said you'd be home by now.*

I startle when I notice the time. It's way later than expected. After showing Cam Kayla's message, we decide to get moving. Kayla will worry if I'm not home soon.

Me: *Be home soon, lost track of time.*

We head back to the truck as a group. Once there, Becca pulls me in for a hug.

After she releases me, Mark pats me on the shoulder. "Thanks for coming. It's been a blast. I hope to see you around a lot now."

I pass my phone around so they can put their numbers in as I put mine in theirs. When I get mine back from Tom, I pull up the contact list and see that he entered his as "Your Favorite Studly Brother."

I look at him. "Really, Tom?" I ask.

He sure did miss his calling; he should be doing standup.

"What? You know I look good, and I *am* your favorite. You don't have to admit it; I already know." Tom brushes the invisible dust off his shoulder while grinning, then pulls himself together. "I'm sure you'll be sick of us soon enough, but call if you need anything. Even if that help is carrying groceries. We're here for you."

"You know she lives in a three-story walkup," Cam interjects, "and you just offered to help carry her groceries in? You barely help Mom, and that's just a few bags from the car to the kitchen. No stairs involved."

"That's different. I've *got* to give Mom hell—it's what I do," Tom says.

"I'm sure I can make a grocery haul sometime soon. It's been so long since I've had a chance to stock up. Thanks for the help, Tom. I hate carrying my groceries up all those stairs." Opening the door of Cam's truck, I climb in, leaving Tom to wonder whether I'm playing or not.

Cam hops in behind the wheel, laughing. "I'll see you later, man." He closes the door, then turns to look at me. "I love how you mess with him."

The drive to my place is full of comfortable silence. Once parked, Cam comes around the hood of the truck and opens my door for me. After hopping out, Cam doesn't move but, instead, takes full advantage of our proximity by pulling me in to him. Not wasting a moment, he places his lips on mine. After a spell, he pulls back and leans his forehead against mine. "I've had the best time with you."

"Me too. Thank you for taking me with you."

"No thanks needed. I'm the one who should be thanking you," he says. Cam reaches up and tucks a stray piece of hair behind my ear. "Let's get you upstairs, sweetheart."

Walking upstairs hand in hand, I can't help the flutters in my stomach. I should've known being with him like this would have me wanting to jump in headfirst.

Cam, being the gentleman that he is, walks me to my door, kisses me softly, and waits until the door is locked behind me to leave. Leaning my head against the door as I turn the last lock, I sigh.

I turn around just in time to see Kayla step in from the fire escape. "How was it?" she asks.

"How was what?" I ask. "The game? I met—"

"Not the game—the kiss. It's not like you guys were trying to hide it or anything. I didn't think you had it in you, sis." She fans herself. "Please tell me that kiss will happen on repeat."

"If I have a say in it, it will," I say. Thinking of the way Cam looked at me downstairs after pulling back from our kiss has my cheeks burning. I'm almost certain that was the look of a man in love. "Wait, how do you know he kissed me?"

"I heard his truck while I was out on the fire escape. Don't blame me for seeing y'all smooch when you guys practically made out for the whole apartment complex to see."

Feeling the heat rise on my cheeks, I start to defend

myself but realize there's nothing to say. If I want to kiss Cam, I can. Unfortunately, the lack of sleep is catching up with me. Through a yawn, I say, "I need to lie down. Do you mind if we catch up tomorrow?"

"Fine, but I want to hear it all."

"How about you text Mike and set up a game night for tomorrow after work?"

I'm ready to crawl in bed. I walk into my room, kick off my shoes, and strip down before throwing Cam's shirt back on. It has become my new favorite thing to wear. No sooner than my head hits the pillow, I'm out.

Game night doesn't work out since Kayla got called away on assignment and Mike and I had to close the restaurant. Again. But a week later, we have one set up, and now that Uncle Joe has a new hire that's fully trained on night shift, it might just happen. It's been a week since becoming Cam's girlfriend, and nothing has changed other than he calls me "sweetheart," "beautiful," and "babe" more often. He and I walk to the coffee shop and the restaurant nearly every day. Our time is full of hanging out with each other or friends when we aren't at work. Becca has come to the restaurant and had lunch with me a few times. She even met Kayla after she came home, then the three of us and Aubrey had a slumber party while Mark was working late on a case around midweek. It's been nice blending his friends and family with mine.

Tomorrow morning is our first day off since we started dating. I glance at the clock on my way to the kitchen. Cam should be here soon. As if my thoughts conjure him, I hear a knock at the door, followed by it cracking open. "Morning, beautiful," he says, walking in.

"Morning, handsome." I get on my toes and wrap my hands behind his neck to give my man a warm kiss.

"Do y'all have to be doing that every time I see you?" Kayla asks as she walks in behind me. "You guys are too sweet—you give me a toothache."

Chuckling, I pull back. "Morning, sis. I'm about to head out. See you tonight?"

"I'm staying at Megan's, remember?"

"Oh, yeah. I guess I'll see you tomorrow then."

In no time, we're out the door. The walk to the restaurant is filled with laughter and stolen kisses. Cam finds a little dark nook under the canal's bridge and pulls me in to him for a moment alone to get his lips on mine before heading back down the canal. He was right when he said it'd be fun making out like teenagers.

I pull him down the street, eager for my morning coffee and to get to work on time. Cam walks me the whole way, never once releasing my hand from his. When we get to the restaurant, I dread letting go.

"I'll see you this evening, sweetheart," he says. "I'll pick you up here after work." Leaning down, he gives me one last kiss before turning to leave.

Seeing him leave makes me miss him already. Forget falling—I'm already head over heels in love with this man.

Chapter Eleven

I flip the pancake on the griddle. It has been a crazy day at the restaurant so far. I'm used to Mike being on staff with me—he can hold his own—but he's filling in on night shift tonight. After these next two days Drew, our new cook, will be on his own. He and Uncle Joe will have opposite days off here on out. Let's just hope he stays on with us. He's good from what I hear. I haven't met him just yet.

Alex and Trayvon need a lot of help in the kitchen. So much for my office work getting done today. We have been so short-staffed on my shift that the paperwork I left three days ago is still sitting on the desk, untouched. Normally, Uncle Joe's the one to take care of it, but right now, whoever gets to it can do it. Ever since that big chain restaurant came in offering nearly double our pay per hour plus benefits, we've had a high turnover. It's getting ridiculous. Even after giving a two-dollar bump, it hasn't helped much. All the mom-and-pop stores around here have been hurting.

I walk back into my office after all the orders are plated and in the window. I get a drink and am ready to go relieve Ronny in the dish pit while he takes a break. Before I can head back there, though, Susan pages me.

I call the front to see what she needs. "Hey, Susan,

what's up?"

"I need you out front, please. I have a customer here who's been waiting for around ten minutes. He knows we have no tables right now, but he swears if you don't make one for him, he'll start trashing the place."

Great, just what I need.

I rub my temple as my head begins to throb. "I'll be right there." I know I'm about to have an issue on my hands. It's just before noon and the front of the house is already full. I have two cooks and three servers right now. We've been handling it just fine, but this guy is about to throw a wrench in the mix.

I get out my phone and call Mike.

He answers on the first ring. "What's up?"

I hate making these calls, but here goes nothing. "Hey, I have a guy up front acting out, with a packed house and I'm short-staffed. I'm about to deal with him, but if you know anyone in the area right now, please ask them to stop in and make sure this place doesn't get flipped. I can deal, but I need to make sure everyone is safe."

"Where's Uncle Joe?" he asks.

"He's in Tulsa. I don't know when he'll be back."

I hear Kayla talking in the background.

"Done. Kayla is calling Cam." The line goes quiet for a minute before he says, "Yeah, okay. He and a few coworkers are in the area. They should be walking in soon. Good luck. I'll be there a little early, but I can't leave just yet."

"Thanks, Mike. See you in a bit."

I didn't want to disturb Cam, but I'm glad he's coming.

Ending the call, I straighten myself out, then walk to the front of the house where I see the customer standing near the podium. *Great!* This guy has been in here several times, harassing my waitstaff each time. Mike has warned him once before to chill or he won't be welcomed back. He's from the road construction crew that's working on the interstate not far from here. He's a shorter man, I'd say five ten maybe, unkept brown hair, a stubbly jaw, and heavily overweight. He's still in his bright-yellow safety vest, so he stands out in here.

I square my shoulders and step up. "Hello, I'm the manager. How can I help you?" I ask, smiling tightly.

He steps even closer still. I can see flecks of dirt on his skin, but when his rancid breath hits my nose, I nearly gag.

I try to keep space between us by moving back. "Sir, please step back."

The door opens. I quickly divert my eyes, looking in its direction. "Welcome to Uncle Joe's. We'll be with you in a moment."

A few customers trail in, followed by Cam and some other officers. He winks as one puts their name down on the wait list and they all step toward the back wall to wait.

"I asked to see the manager," the angry customer says, spewing hate in my direction.

"I *am* the manager, sir," I say. "What can I help you with?"

"*You're* the manager of this place?" he spits. "No wonder this place is so crappy. Nobody I know would respect such a tiny woman. How can you command someone to do something when you're the size of a child?"

Customer service is a gamble. It's Russian roulette. I have a loaded chamber, and it's ready to blow.

Cam steps forward. "Sir. If you'd step outside with

me, I'll see what I can do to help."

"I'm not stepping outside. I'm sure the moment I do, they'll seat someone else. I need to get lunch and get back to work."

"I'd be more than happy to seat you at the bar in the sundae shop—a separate dining room off the side of our main one, which is kept for birthday parties or used as overflow when we have the staff to run it—or I can take your to-go order if you'd prefer. I just don't have a spot in my dining room just yet." I hope I never have one open for him either. I'd rather never see him again. He's always so hateful.

"That sounds reasonable," Cam says. "Will that work for you?"

"No!" The customer starts to escalate again. He looks angrier now than he did before. "My issue is this *woman*. Is there not a *man* here to get things done? I've been waiting ten minutes for a table, and I'm running out of time." The disgust in his voice makes me wonder what caused him to be so full of hatred.

I smile warmly through clenched teeth.

Another officer steps up to Cam's side, providing a united front. "Sir, she said that she'd be more than happy to seat you at the sundae bar. Is that not what you want? To be seated?"

"I work hard out in the sun all day. Do you think I want to sit at the bar? I want to be able to kick back and enjoy my break. Sitting at the bar won't cut it."

Some people act like we can move mountains or, in this instance, already seated customers. It's frustrating. Sometimes, I'd rather a customer not stay and take up a table for hours upon end, but a paying customer has every right to their table so long as they aren't harassing the other customers or staff. Besides, this is the lunch rush—these customers are eating lunch and heading right back to work . . . for the most part.

"Again, I'm going to have to ask you to step outside with us," Cam says. He looks up to see that they're drawing an audience and urges the man toward the door.

The customer starts to argue, but when the officer who joined Cam flanks him, he steps outside, despite his continued protest.

Once the door closes behind them, I breathe out a sigh of relief.

A couple of customers make their way to the cashier on their way out. Ronny steps into the dining room to help clear the two now-vacated tables that I quickly clean and seat with the next names on the wait list. If he'd only been a little more patient with us, he'd have a table now. I look outside just in time to see the angry customer throwing over one of our specials signs as he turns and storms down the stairs to the canal.

Cam picks it up before walking back in. I hate to imagine how things could have gone if not for him and the other officers coming in when they did. I hope I can get a moment to thank them properly while they're here. At the very least I'll comp their meal for the help.

I take a deep breath, then turn toward everyone seated in the restaurant. "I'm sorry you all had to witness such behavior. Dessert is on me today." I feel a sting in my eyes. It has been one of those days for sure.

I step into the dining room and get everything moving again. Once everyone is served and lunch is ending, I give Ronny his break. Thirty minutes later, I take to my office to have my lunch—a BLT and fries. I wish I had the time to sit with Cam while he was here, but that just wasn't in the cards for us. By the time I finished my tasks, he was gone. That's okay, though, I know I'll be seeing him soon. I take my phone out of my desk and shoot him a quick text while shoving another fry into my mouth.

Me: *Thank you for coming to my rescue again. I don't know what I'd do without you.*

Cam: *No need to thank me, beautiful. I'm just sorry he spoke to you like that. Everyone says thank you for the meal. It was nice of you to cover it. How's your anxiety?*

Me: *It's the least I could do. It's not good, but I'm in my office about to do paperwork so I should be ok.*

Cam: *Good. We had to head out on another call. See you after work. xoxox*

Me: *Xoxoxo see you later.*

Even though he is off to God-only-knows-what, he's still worried about me and my anxiety level. I'm in so deep.

Dinner with Cam is the highlight of my day. He picks me up, carrying in a bouquet of wildflowers and a Hershey's bar, then takes me to a bar and grill around the corner, making good on his mention of grabbing a beer with dinner. We decide to call it an early night for once. Cam wants to make sure that I get plenty of rest after the day I had, plus he needs to check in with his parents.

Kayla's out of town with Megan, Uncle Joe's having dinner with Janet and her out-of-town son, and Mike is working, so there's really nothing for me to do other than call it a night. I shower before bed, then wrap my hair in a towel and one around my body. As I walk to my bedroom, I grab my phone and check to see if I missed any calls. There's a text.

Unknown: *Have you figured out who I am yet?*

Me: *No, but you need to stop. Since you won't tell me, leave me alone!*

Unknown: *I'll see you soon.*

Me: *I guess I won't know if I don't know who you are.*

Unknown: *Until a week ago, I hadn't seen you in some time. I'll see you again soon though.*

Who the heck did I see last week that I hadn't seen in a long time? Why wont they just tell me who they are? This is so frustrating! I close out the text and open my social media instead. That'll distract me.

Scrolling through my notifications, I come across a post that I'm tagged in. I click it, and my heart nearly beats out of my chest. *Breathe*, I chant to myself. The post is a news article about John Knorr—Stalker John—being released from prison. I guess my letter to the parole board was for nothing.

The pressure in my chest escalates until I think I'm having a panic attack.

Somehow, I manage to pull up Cam's name in my contacts. I hit call, and he answers on the first ring.

Before he can say anything, I say, "C-Ca-Cam." I struggle to take a breath.

"Sweetheart, I need you to breathe for me. Can you do that?" he asks, jumping into action. "In on three . . . and hold it. Out on three . . . now, repeat. Let's do it a few more times."

It feels like I'm in the deep end of a swimming pool, unable to reach the top. My hearing is muffled and pulling in air is a chore. If not for Cam's reassurance, I might not be able to pull through on my own.

We do this over and over until I start to cough, finally able to breathe . . . kind of.

"Good girl, you can do this. You're so much stronger than this attack."

I feel myself slowly relaxing. Hearing Cam helps calm me. We do this for a few more minutes until I feel better.

"Thank you," is all I manage before I start yawning. Thankfully, I caught this early. It could have been so much worse.

"What brought this on?" he asks.

Even though I'm tired, I manage to explain the social

media post. "Do you think he's the one texting me? I thought it was just someone playing with me."

"Hey, don't think like that, sweetheart," Cam says. I hear a car door and his truck start. "I'm coming over. I don't want you to be alone right now."

"I'm fine," I say. I want no more than to be wrapped in his arms, to feel safe, but I don't want to be a burden. It's not like he lives right around the corner.

"Please don't argue it—I'm coming. I don't care if I have to sleep on the floor next to the bed. I'll be there in twenty. This is as much for me as it is for you. I need to see that you're good."

"Okay, I'll see you then." Feeling relief that he saw through my protest, tears begin to fall. These attacks are scary.

I get up and throw on some sleep shorts and a tank top before going to the bathroom to finish getting ready for bed.

Cam's twenty minutes turns into fifteen. The moment I open the door for him, I find him in sleep pants and a white T-shirt with a bag on his shoulder. He pulls me into a tight hug, dropping his bag. Not wanting to let go, I jump up, wrapping my legs around him in an embrace. He adjusts his hold on me, closes my door, locks it, and walks to my room. Burying my nose in the crook of his neck and breathing in his scent is calming, like coming home after a long week. Once we get to bed, he pulls back, causing me to whimper in protest.

He chuckles. "Are you okay?"

"I'm better now that you're here. Thank you for coming."

"Babe, there isn't a thing that I wouldn't do for you," he

says, nudging my chin to look him in his eyes. "I love you."

Hearing those words from his mouth is next level. I throw my arms around his neck, pulling him back into me. "I love you too."

Cam lies down on my bed, motioning with his hands for me to crawl in with him. I start that way. As I'm not moving fast enough apparently, he pulls me in to him so that my chest meets his. I chuckle, then lay my head on him and snuggle in.

He kisses the top of my head, then runs his hand through my hair. It feels so good, I could fall asleep. "These texts," he says. "I'd like to see them."

Nodding, I roll over, grab my phone, and hand it to him, then take his hand that settles on my hip and move it back to my head.

He chuckles but continues his loving strokes.

"Mike's bunch of friends are full of pranksters. I thought it was one of them playing with me at first. I wouldn't put it past them, but things just don't make sense. Then the flowers. I'm starting to wonder. Maybe it *is* John."

"The date of John's release and the start of the texts don't add up. The article could have the date wrong, but that's unlikely. If you don't mind, I'd like to ask Jazz to investigate this officially."

I tuck myself into Cam further. "It's your call. I trust you." He wraps his arm around me and puts his phone down. "I'll see if she can meet us at the coffee house when she gets back in town."

Alright." I kiss his chin, seeing how I can't reach his lips. "Did you bring your hygiene stuff? I have an extra toothbrush, but if you use my shampoo, you'll smell awful girly. You're welcome to it though."

"I just got ready for bed before you called, but yeah, I brought my stuff. You're not saying I stink, are you?" he teases.

"No." I bury my head in his chest in embarrassment.

"Good. Let's get some sleep, shall we? I've got to look good for the hot date I have with my girlfriend tomorrow."

"As if a lack of sleep would hinder that? You always look good to me." I smile.

"Quit trying to butter me up, beautiful," he teases with a tickle to my side. "Where do you want me?"

"Here, in bed with me. Being in your arms feels good."

"Are you sure? I don't mind the floor."

I snuggle in a little further. "I'm sure," I sigh.

Turning us so that we're spooning, Cam pulls me in to him snugly. He whispers in my ear, "Good night, beautiful. I love you."

"I love you too."

Despite Cam's arrival under less-than-great conditions, I feel so incredibly grateful that I can feel his heart- beat beside mine.

Waking in Cam's arms is better than I remembered. After the day I had yesterday, I would've normally had the worst night's sleep, but last night was restful. I almost don't want to get out of bed, but I know I need to. Rolling out from under his heavy arm without waking his is difficult, but when his lip twitches and the slight snore starts again, I step into my en suite to freshen up.

After a quick shower, I head into the kitchen and start the coffee pot. By the time I have it going, I feel Cam snaking his arm around my waist, pulling me in to him.

"Happy birthday, beautiful."

"Thank you, babe. I'd completely forgotten that it was today."

As Cam is about to reply, there's a knock. He removes himself from my grasp and walks to the door. As soon as he opens it, Becca, Mark, Aubrey, Tom, Kayla, and Mike walk in. In their full arms are the makings of a birthday party.

"Surprise!" they say in unison.

My hands cover my mouth as tears fill my eyes.

I look at Cam, but he just smiles. "Surprise."

I walk his way and cuddle in to his side.

"Thank you, all," I say. "I can't believe you did this."

"This was all Cam. I was planning our yearly rummy match with Uncle Joe and Janet. That's apparently not good enough for your man though," Kayla says jokingly. "It's still happening, just not today."

"Joe's bringing some food," Cam says. "I hope you don't mind, but I invited my parents and other siblings. I wanted them to meet you."

"Um." What? Is he serious right now? Wow. I guess, I'm about to meet his parents. This is huge. *Breathe*, I have to remind myself as my heart tries to run off. "How long have you been planning this?" I look around the house, then down at myself, cringing. "I wasn't expecting company. Cam, I'm not dressed to meet your parents."

"I gave everyone a heads-up last month so most could make it. Or at least try to." He looks me over and grins. "You look good to me. I'm sure they'll love you, just like I do."

I'm sure I'd look good to him if I were wearing a potato sack. I planned to have a morning in—I'm in sweats and a plain white tee. Not something that screams, *I love your son.*

There's more commotion at the front door, and I turn to see Uncle Joe carrying trays of food, followed by an older couple, a few kids, and two other adults. Then Kim—an old friend, the one I went speed dating with when I met Mike—walks in behind them.

"Kim?" I say in confusion.

"Leah?" she says, not seeing me yet. Pushing past the others, she looks around, finally spotting me. "Oh my God! It *is* you. It is *so* good to see you, girl." She pulls me into a rocking hug. We can't help but laugh when we feel Kayla engulf us both from behind before taking off to help with the decorations.

Nearby, Cam is talking to the guy I vaguely remember her posting as her man on her socials. They both look like they have questions, but that can wait a few minutes. They'll understand soon enough.

Kim, Kayla, and I go way back. She is one of the few friends that I have from school that came around and actually liked it when Kayla would tag along. Since we met in the third grade, she was by my side when our parents died. We haven't spoken in at least four months now. I used to follow her on social media, but after her boyfriend was hurt in action, she took a hiatus and has dedicated all her time to helping him. I sure have missed her.

"What are you doing here? Last I heard, you packed up and moved in with that man of yours. It's like you forgot all about us little people."

"First, I never forgot about you, never could. Second, I *did* move in with my man. Who just happens to be Cam's brother Pat."

My eyes go wide. "No way!"

She nods her head enthusiastically. "I lucked out when Cam invited us all. As soon as we pulled up out front, I knew it was you. I just *knew*. God, Lele, I'm just so happy to see you." She turns to look behind her, bringing Pat back around front with her.

He's a little shorter than Cam, maybe six four. He wears a scowl and has longer hair than I'm used to seeing on men. It's covering the whole left side of his face. His eyes match his brothers', and his coloring is like Tom's, but his appearance is much harder than both of them.

Cam steps away to greet a few more people.

"Lele, this is Pat, my *fiancé* Pat, this is Leah." The way she drags out what he is to her has my eyes widening yet again. I'm so happy for her—if anyone deserves happiness, it's her.

I stick out my hand to shake his.

"Nice to meet you," he grunts.

"You too," I reply, before looking back to Kim. "OMG I'm so stinking happy for you. When did this happen? You should've called me."

Kim looks up at him, and smiles. "I should have but . . . well, well catch up later and I'll tell you everything." Pat put his hand on her shoulder, causing her to look his away again, then nods. "We'll be over in the corner. Happy birthday."

"Thanks." They walk off and I'm left standing here taking it all in.

When I look up, I see Cam approaching with whom I can only imagine are his parents.

Oh Lord, help me now. I'm a nervous wreck. I can only hope I don't hurl.

Chapter Twelve

Cam introduces me to his parents—Butch and Marie—who share stories about the Cameron clan. I share a few in return about Kayla and me growing up. They have me in stitches, laughing so hard that I can hardly breathe. Cam is a carbon copy of his dad with his mom's coloring. His mom, however, has brown hair and eyes and is just about an inch taller than me. Some might say that he and his dad have similar taste in women.

"Check this out," Marie says. She pulls out an envelope and starts sharing pictures. The first is a little Cam in nothing but his dad's boots and hat.

The laughter fades as I'm left in awe. "How cute," I gush.

"He's not nearly as cute now that he's all grown," Butch adds, ribbing Cam a bit.

"Really, Dad?" Cam says. He puts his arm around my shoulders, pulling me in to him. "You're supposed to talk me up, not try and make me look bad."

"You've already got me," I say, poking his side. "I don't need to hear a sales pitch."

"Oh, you'll do just fine," Marie adds. "These Cameron men are charmers. It takes a strong woman to win their hearts." She pats my arm just as a woman a little younger than me walks over with a young child on her hip. She looks like Marie's younger sister rather than daughter.

She smiles at me and hands the kid over to Cam. "Hiya. I'm Janelle, Cam's sister. These little ones," she says, patting the heads of two young children, "are my kids—Sage, Peter, and the one Cam's holding is Eric."

"Nice to meet you all," I reply.

"I'm fwee," Eric says.

"Wow, you're such a big boy. Three years old, and super strong, I bet."

He nods his head vigorously, then turns to face Sage. "See, 'age? I a big boy. I stwong."

"Whatever," she says with an eye roll. "Mom, I'm going to go talk to Kim." Without waiting for a reply, she turns and walks off.

"Can I go now?" Peter asks.

"Sure." Janelle looks back at us. "Sorry. Those two have attitudes lately. Eight and ten going on fifteen, I guess."

"Sage is going to be one heck of a challenge in a few years," Marie adds. "Ten years old and already worse than her mom as a teenager. I don't envy you, honey."

I can only imagine.

"Alright, everyone," Uncle Joe says. "The food is ready."

I excuse myself and head toward the kitchen—I'm ravenous. I get a plate and join the others who are sitting around the foldable tables that someone brought with them.

When we're done with breakfast, Uncle Joe calls me to sit in the living room in my favorite chair by the fireplace. Apparently, it's time for gifts. I haven't had a party and gifts since . . . I don't remember. Maybe my eighteenth birthday?

Each person takes a turn bringing me a gift. Tom got me an apron that has Cam's face over the words, "Cam's cupcake." I also get enough gift cards to have a full day out and not be out of pocket for anything. I love it.

When it comes time for Kayla's, she looks nervous as she hands me a large gift bag. "I didn't even know I had these until recently. I hope you like them."

"I'm sure I'll love it, Kay." As I take out the tissue paper, my breath catches at the sight of deep-red yarn. I look up at Kayla, and she nods her head. When I was five, Mom commissioned our neighbor to make me life-size—for a five-year-old—Raggedy Ann and Andy dolls. After Mom and Dad passed away, they were lost in the mix. I thought that I'd lost them forever.

Tears fall, no matter how hard I try to hold them back. "How did you . . ."

She kneels next to me. "I've never gone through the boxes that Uncle Joe saved for me. I had a rough spell where I missed Mom. I wanted to find a blanket or something of hers. When I opened the boxes, these were staring at me."

Pulling one out, I hug it to me as I stand and pull Kayla in for a wet hug. "Thank you, Kay. I thought these were gone forever."

We take a moment to hug it out, then I dry my eyes and sit back down.

After I settle back in, Uncle Joe hands me a CHEF'STORE gift certificate and a ticket to the monster truck show this year.

"Thank you, Uncle Joe," I say. "You still plan on going with me, don't you?" He and I have gone every birthday since I moved in with him. What started as something I loved as a kid has become a gift I enjoy as an adult born from tradition.

"Every year. Baby doll. If you'll have me."

"Always, Uncle Joe, always."

Cam steps up next, holding out a manila envelope.

I open it to find papers and a brochure. "What's this?"

"I thought we could take a trip—a sort of combined birthday adventure. What do you say?"

The brochure is for Grand Lake in Disney, Oklahoma. I look up and wait for him to explain.

"You had such a fun time when we took the Jeeps out. I figured why not do it again but in a nicer location? I rented a few cabins, so there's plenty of room if you want to invite anyone."

Standing up, I throw my arms around his neck and lay one on him right there in front of everyone. "Thank you, Cam. I love it!" I really do. Part of me wishes that he'd have taken us on our own private weekend getaway, but seeing as how it's a birthday adventure, I'm more than happy in a group of friends.

I see Kayla grab the papers and scrunch up her brow.

"What's up, sis?"

"I can't go," she pouts. "That's the same time Mike and I are supposed to be in New York."

As much as I hate the thought of her leaving, I'm glad that Mike will be going with her this time.

"Let's do cake," Janet says from the kitchen. She snuck in sometime during breakfast, and I haven't had a chance to greet her yet. Either she's busy hosting or I'm busy with the guests.

I sneak away from the others for a moment to give her a

hug. At fifty-four years young, Janet is four years younger than Uncle Joe. She has the fullest head of thick, blonde curls I've ever seen, and her gray eyes make her stand out. I always thought Uncle Joe would end up with a woman in leathers of her own, but Janet is soft and wears sundresses and lip gloss—no leather in sight, unless she's in Uncle Joe's. It's sweet, really. Just as she's ready to cut into the cake, I move in and wrap my arms around her.

"Happy birthday, honey." She puts down the knife and turns into my embrace. "That man of yours did good."

"He did. Thank you for coming."

"There's no place I'd rather be. Now, you better run off and grab your guy before your uncle ropes him into helping him clean out the walk-in later."

I make my way back out to the others just in time for the cake to make its rounds.

After a bit more time together, Cam stands. "Alright, everyone. It's time to start wrapping it up. Mark and I owe these two beauties a day out."

Marie and Butch take Aubrey home with them, and Janelle follows closely behind to let the kids run wild after all the cake they had during the party.

I can hardly believe Cam pulled this off. This man of mine is something else.

For our double date—the one we won playing football—Becca and I choose to go to Frontier City, our local theme park. We've been here a few hours already. It's been a blast! By the time we get to the front of the line for the log ride, I'm bouncing from toe-to-toe.

"Dang, girl," Becca says, chuckling. "You haven't stood still since we got in line. You're wearing me out."

I've enjoyed today so much that I can hardly contain it. I haven't been on so many rides in *years*. I loved coming here as a kid but then life happened, and I just quit going at all. Now that I'm here, it's just too much to control.

"Tell me about it," Cam says. He wraps his arm completely around my chest, leaning his head into the crook of my neck. "Someone's excited. It's really cute."

"Four," Mark says to the ride attendant.

The guy steadies our log, letting us on. I'm in the front, followed by Cam, then Becca, and finally Mark.

"Ready for this, sweetheart?" Cam asks.

"Yep!" I say, bouncing in my seat.

Going through the dark tunnel, I can't see a thing. I feel puffs of air on my face from the ride and a mist coming in from somewhere. Cam pulls me back to him and I snuggle in.

As we inch toward the top of the drop, the jitters get real. "Good Lord, this is high. Maybe I should have—"

The log plummets. The pit of my stomach falls out, and I scream. I scream and scream some more until we hit the water and I get a face full of it. Even though I'm drenched, it's a blast. My favorite ride today.

"Want to go again?" I ask.

Cam chuckles near my ear. He stands and extends his hand to help me out as we dock. "With that line, we wouldn't have time to get dinner before Mark and Becca have to leave," he says.

The line twists and turns around the barriers and is down the walk a good fifty feet or more. Cam's right, we would be in line forever

"Come on. Let me win you a stuffed animal before we head out."

Since I was in the front of the log, I'm drenched. Water is not just dripping off me as I stand—it is pouring off. It's puddling in my shoes and starting to chafe as I walk. Thank God Cam thought to have me bring an extra set of clothes and shoes today.

We get to the carnival game area, where Cam and Mark start off by climbing a rope ladder that extends over an inflatable and end with a round of balloons being popped with a dart. By the time we finish, Becca and I both have a few large stuffed animals each. I even win a gigantic pair of neon pink sunglasses and a tie-dye cape for Cam. He puts them on proudly, wearing them everywhere. He looks all kinds of silly, but that won't stop him from beaming in pride as the onlookers gawk.

Cam wraps his arm around my shoulder, kissing my head while humming. "I love my glasses. Too bad Cap won't let me wear them to work."

Mark laughs, holding up his phone to take a picture. "Nope, but I'm sure everyone will love to see this. How about we put this one right in front of the mudding one with her on your desk?"

"You have a picture of me on your desk at work?" I ask in wonder. I know he has some on his phone, but his desk? Wow.

"Sure do," he replies. "A few in my locker too."

This is the kind of love I have always wanted—a man who is proud to be with me, no matter how silly we might look or the occasion.

"It's a place of honor, hun," Becca says, linking her arm in mine. "When they're busting their tails on a case and putting in all that overtime, they have a piece of us with them to help pull them through." Becca moves back to Mark. "I'm hungry. Let's get changed and go get dinner."

Since the bathroom is empty, Becca and I set our bags down in front of the sinks. The stalls are tiny, but I make it work.

Someone walks into the bathroom, just as I get my shoes and jeans off. She pushes on the stall door.

"Occupied," I say, "I'll be just a minute."
Moments later, I hear the faucet followed by the door. I guess she couldn't wait.

When I step out, I put my wet clothes in my bag and grab my brush. I accidentally knock my tote over, causing its contents to go everywhere.

"Oh no, here, let me help you," Becca says. She rushes over from the stall she just left and crouches down to help me gather my stuff.

Once we have everything that we find on the floor, I notice that my keys are missing. "Becca, do you see my keys?"

"No, are they not there?"

I open the bag and dig once more to make sure I didn't miss them. "No." Frustration begins to set in. "I know they were just here. I had to have them when I locked up earlier."
Where are they?

"Let's look again."

After five minutes, there's a knock at the door. It cracks open. "You ladies good in there?" Cam asks.

"Yeah, but I can't find my keys," I reply.

We spend some time looking but come up empty-handed. I'm beyond upset. How in the heck could I lose them at a theme park? They were in my bag the whole time. I never even unzipped it until I got my dry clothes out.

We head to customer service and report them missing in case they're handed in. I can't believe I lost my keys.

"You good, babe?" Cam asks as we get to his truck.

"Yeah. Just upset that I can't find my keys."

"I'm sure they'll show up."

"Yeah maybe."

We head to a little hole-in-the-wall Italian eatery about a block from the theme park. It's not much to look at, but the food is so good, I nearly lick my plate clean—well, not really, but I do soak up every drop with a piece of bread. When the server sets the check down, Mark grabs it and pays for us all, despite Cam's argument.

"It's our treat. Consider it a gift for Leah's birthday."

"Thank you," Cam and I state in unison.

"Sorry to eat and run, but Mark has to work tomorrow, and Aubrey has dance in the morning," Becca says.

"We're done here anyway," I say. "How about we walk you out?"

When we make it to their truck, Becca and I hug while the guys shake hands. With the promise to meet up again soon, Cam helps me into his truck.

"Would you come home with me tonight?" Cam asks

after hopping in. "I'm not planning to start anything. I just want to hold you in my arms." This will be the first time staying at his place. "Can you have me back for game night tomorrow?"

"Sure," he replies.

"Then let's go pack me a bag." I smile. No matter how nervous I am for this, it feels right.

When we make it to my place, I let us in using my hide-a-key. Cam agrees to check the windows to make sure everything is locked up before we leave again. Grabbing my weekender from the top of my closet, I throw everything I need for tomorrow, then dive into my dresser, looking for something to wear tonight. I grab a pair of sleep shorts, and a tank top and call it good.

"Hey, Cam?" I holler. "Do you have a coffee pot or a pan or anything in your kitchen?"

"I have a coffee pot and disposable dishes. Why?" How does he not have anything in his kitchen? That would drive me crazy. "Do you mind if I bring a pan or two so I can make us breakfast?"

"Bring whatever you want, sweetheart. I planned on taking you to eat in the morning, but if you'd rather cook for us, I'm fine with that too."

I grab my bag and walk out to the kitchen, grabbing all that's needed for my stay. I open the fridge. "How does French toast with fresh fruit, sausage, and eggs sound?" I planned that before everyone showed up this morning and am still craving it.

"It sounds like I'm never going to want to let you leave," he replies. He comes up behind me and wraps me in his arms. "You're spoiling me again."

"Not spoiling," I say, turning around in his arms to face him. "Just taking care of my man."

"I like it when you call me that." He leans in, kissing my nose.

I smile. "Well. Get used to it." I lift onto my toes and lean in for a kiss.. "I love saying it."

"No! No, no, no," Kayla says from the doorway.

"Coming through. I don't want to see all that. Give me a minute to get to my room." She shields her eyes and walks through the kitchen. I swear, she's so dramatic.

"Hey, Kay," Cam says.

"Hey. Hold on a second and I'll be out of your way."

"Kayla, can you stop a minute? We need to talk," I say. Leaving Cam behind in the kitchen, I pull her back to my room for privacy.

"What's up?" she asks, dropping her schtick and lowering her hands.

"I was about to leave you a note, but since you're home now, I can tell you. I won't be home tonight. I'm going to stay the night at Cam's."

"Hold on. You're *what*?" Kayla says, plopping down on my bed.

"I'm staying at Cam's," I say, joining her. I turn to look at her, and she at me.

"No offense, but are you sure you're ready for that?"

No offense? Really?

Feeling annoyed, I huff. "Kayla, I stayed with him in the cabin, and he stayed here last night. I don't see a difference."

"There *is* a difference, a *huge* one. Once the sleepovers start, the moving-in talk is closer than ever before. The first night was for a party—last night, an emergency. This would be by choice. Leah, sis . . . this is different. If you're ready for that, then I'm happy for you, but you need to make sure that's where you see this headed first."

"Kay, I love him. If I didn't see a future with Cam, do you think I'd ever let him talk me into any of it? Give me some credit. You know me better than that." I stand and start pacing.

"Leah," she says as she stands. She puts her hands on my shoulders, bending to look me head-on. "Then you two lovebirds get a move on. I didn't mean to make you angry. I just don't want you moving faster than you're comfortable with. I love you, sis. I just want to see you happy."

"I *am* happy," I sigh. "*So* happy." More so than I have been in a long time. "Kayla, I think that he's the *one*."

"I've known for some time, I just wanted to make sure you knew too." She pulls me in for a sisterly embrace. "I'm happy for you." She smiles shyly. "Forgive me?"

"Always." We hug it out for a minute before drying our eyes. "Love you," I say.

"Love you too. Don't forget, game night tomorrow. Uncle Joe, Janet, Mike, you, and I. Cam can come if he wants. I think Becca might be coming too. She said she'd let me know for sure by morning. Mark has to work and she doesn't want to be home alone."

"Won't she have Aubrey?" Mark must be on a case if he'll be gone all day.

"I guess she has a sleepover or something. Not sure, though."

"Okay, then. See you tomorrow."

Even though I'm hurt over her assessment of me staying with Cam, I know she's only watching out for me. I've never stayed with a boyfriend before Cam. She's right—this is a big step. One I'm ready to take.

Chapter Thirteen

I snuggle further into Cam's side, enjoying the warmth of his body. Staying the night has been amazing! I've rather been enjoying our morning make-out session too. I don't want to leave but I don't have a choice with game night being tonight. Last night, we sat out on the front porch and stargazed for hours until my eyes became too heavy to stay out any longer. Cam lifted me, carrying me up to bed, when I didn't want to move. Managing two days off together is rare, and I don't want to leave this nice, warm bed or the arms of my man. I imagine folding my arms and stomping my foot to get my way. I chuckle at the thought. It didn't work when I was little—I doubt it would now.

"What's so funny?" Cam asks.

"Nothing really. I was just thinking."

"Care to share?" He nudges me, so I look up at him.

"I was just wondering if I pout—you know, a foot-stomping, arm-crossing pout—if I can stay in bed longer."

"I wish, but you know at some point we're going to have to get up and get sustenance," Cam chuckles.

"You might, but I'm fine right where I am."

He rolls me over on my back, hovering over me, then looks into my eyes. Right when I think he's going to make a move, he gets up from the bed, causing me to growl and cover my face. "That's just mean!" I screech.

"If I kiss you now, we'll never get out of bed. You know it as well as I do. It's almost noon. We need to get up and get you fed."

I love how he takes care of me, but right now, I'd rather lie here and make out a little longer. Who needs food?

"You better take all the time you can get now. You know as soon as our feet hit the bottom of the steps, it'll be like alerting everyone to join us."

Cam laughs. "I'm sure we'll be fine until tonight. I told Mom that I was asking you to come back with me and for her to tell the others to give us some space. How about you teach me how to make brunch, then we can cuddle up for a couple more hours before we have to go?"

"Fine," I grumble. I crawl out of bed and grab one of his shirts, slipping it on over my tank and shorts. "But I bet you money once we're down there, we don't get to cuddle up like you said. Our lazy morning will be a thing of the past."

"How about we make it more interesting than money?" Cam mutters. He snatches me up by the shirt, pulling me into him. Then he buries his nose in my neck, kissing just below my ear in an open-mouth kiss. He is driving me crazy, and he knows it. I feel the smile stretch across his lips when my body vibrates from delight. "How about if you're right?" Kiss. "I can be your errand boy for a day in the clothes—or lack thereof—that you choose." Kiss. "If I'm right, I get the same." Kiss. He lifts his head to look at me. "I'm thinking that little purple string number Kayla snuck in your bag would look real good right now," he delivers with a wink.

"What do you mean, 'errand boy'?" I pull back from his embrace. He keeps his hands on my hips but loosens his hold.

"I mean, I guess it'd be more or less a cabana boy. I'd be more than happy to give you a massage, feed you grapes, wash your hair. I'd say cook you a meal, but that might be a bad idea. I can bring you drinks or fetch your phone or whatnot."

"I'd do the same if you win?"

"Yes. If anyone interrupts us—in person—between now and the time we leave, then you win. We can collect at any time, so long as we are in private."

"You're on!" As much as I don't want to be interrupted, I so want to win this. *Come on, guys, don't let me down.* He told me that his family doesn't know boundaries and is always at each other's houses. I hope that's the same for today.

Cam grabs his shirt from the end of the bed, putting it on before he takes my hand and leads me out of his room and down the stairs. When we get to the bottom, he turns off the porch light, then joins me in the kitchen. I wash my hands, start the coffee brewing, then get out the makings for brunch. I pop a strawberry slice into my mouth before taking everything back to the island.

Cam walks back in, and instead of joining me, he sits at the island and watches my every move. "Damn, this is nice. Seeing you enjoying the kitchen like this makes the hassle of picking it all out worth it."

"What do you mean?"

"I know nothing about kitchens, so I had to do a whole heck of a lot of research to make sure I was getting the best of the best in here. Watching you dance around, humming, I'd do it all over again."

I should be used to the way he talks to me by now, but the flutters are still very real. I set down the egg carton and walk around the counter to where Cam is sitting. I wrap my arms around his neck and lean in for a kiss. He takes that moment to put his hands on my bottom, lifting me as he stands. He then turns, sets me down on the island, and begins to devour me as if I'm the only brunch he wants. Caging me in with a hand alongside either hip, he leans in further, moaning at the sweet strawberry flavor left behind from the berry I just ate.

"Hey, Cam?" someone says from the door. "Would you mind—"

I hear something fall, followed by a screech.

"Oh my God, I'm so sorry. I didn't know Leah stayed over."

I look over Cam's head as he lays it on my shoulder and see Janelle and her kids. Her hand covers Eric's eyes while the other two turn away.

"Mom was supposed to tell everyone to stay away," Cam grumbles under his breath.

I push him a little to get him to step back, hop off the counter, and walk toward Janelle.

"Sorry. Cam didn't think anyone would be stopping by today. I can go get changed so you can talk to your brother. Just give me a minute."

"Oh, no. That's my bad. I didn't know you were here. He never brings girls home. I'm the one who should be sorry. I'll start knocking."

Cam grumbles from the kitchen as I start to walk away. He steps to my side, stopping me from leaving. "What's up, Janie?"

"Sage, can you take your brothers around back to play for a minute? I'll be out soon," she states.

"I'm going to go get changed." It sounds private, and I don't want her to be uncomfortable.

"It's fine," Janelle says. "I don't mind you staying."

"Out with it then," Cam says. "What did he do this time?"

"How did you know he did anything?" She looks at me, then at Cam.

I feel out of place here, like I'm in a conversation that I shouldn't be in, but she asked me to stay. I don't want to be rude and leave.

"Because you come to me or Tom when Bryant does anything. You know Pat is a loose cannon. What did he do, Janelle?"

"I was just going to ask you to watch the kids, but that was before I knew Leah was here. I'll go ask Kim. She can watch them at my place."

"What did he *do*?" Cam growls.

What kind of man is this Bryant guy? I've never seen Cam so mad before. This is a little nerve-wracking.

She bites her lip to hold back the tears building in the corners of her eyes as Cam clenches his fists at his side.

I step into him, wrap my arm around his waist, and cuddle in a tad. I know he's mad, and from the sounds of it, he might have that right, but she's stressed enough as it is. She doesn't need him stressing her out even more.

"I need to go see my lawyer, is all."

With Cam not getting anywhere, I step in. Maybe a softer touch will help. "I don't know anything about what's going on, but I hate to see you two at odds." Cam is livid and she's on the verge of tears. "Janelle, if someone hurt you or one of the kids, you need to tell someone. Even if . . . even if it's not one of your brothers." I look over at Cam, who flinches when I say that. I hate to, but she needs to know that she can tell someone without facing her brother's wrath. "Nobody should ever have to live in fear."

"He hasn't touched me since he was thrown off the property," she breathes. "He's just messing with the kids' minds. I need to talk to my lawyer and see if we can do anything else to get his rights stripped."

"What's he doing to the kids?" Cam growls.

"Come on, man." She throws her hands up in the air and begins pacing. "Sometimes having all brothers sucks. Cam, you can't come off halfcocked, you know that. You're a cop—use your training. If you go at him again, you can cost me my kids. I have to do this legally. He can't come on the property or go to the school. His visits are limited, but he's getting in their heads. They'll be fine, but I have to go to see my lawyer and see what I can do."

I can only imagine her frustration. I'm frustrated *for* her.

Cam calms down a bit, though I can tell he's still mad. I can also tell that he knows she's right. "Fine, but I swear if he hurts any of you . . . Cop or not," he says.

"I know, Cam. I know." She smiles over at me, then up at him. "I've got to go. I'll have Kim watch the kids. Thank you, Leah. You guys really are good together, you know." She pulls us both in for a hug, then goes to gather her kids.

I sure hope they're all going to be okay.

I step back into the kitchen a little less hungry than before. I want to say something about the way he stressed her out, but I don't really know the story there. I can't fault him for wanting to protect them—they are family, after all. So I decide to keep my mouth shut.

I put up the bread and decide eggs, sausage, and fruit will be good enough. I get the sausage started in the pan and feel Cam sneak in behind me.

"Thank you."

"For what? I didn't do anything."

"You just being here helps." He leans in and kisses my neck. "I just get so frustrated. Bryant is a degenerate and he's been messing with her and those kids for way too long." I can understand that. "I know, I need to calm down when I talk to her, but after finding her in the pasture the way I did? I just get so worked up."

I flip the sausage it doesn't burn. "What do you mean finding her in the pasture?"

"That's not my story to tell. Maybe one day she'll explain. Can we just get back to breakfast please?"

"Sure, if that's what you want." I'd love to know the story, but he's right that it's Janelle's story, not his.

"It is. You were right, you know?"

"Right about what?"

"You win." He looks over my shoulder at me. "You won the bet. What do you want me to wear?" He chuckles.

I take the sausage out of the pan and set the pan on the back burner so I can fry the eggs soon.

"I didn't want to win like that, Cam. You don't have to pay up. It's fine." I hate that I won at the expense of his sister's happiness.

"I'm glad you won. That means I get to spoil you. Now what do you want me to wear?"

I'm not going to argue that. "I guess since you wanted me in a tiny bikini, you can be in boxers and an apron."

He smirks, grabs something from a drawer by the sink, then heads up stairs. "I'll be back. FYI, I still want French toast."

As Cam goes upstairs to change, I grab the bread back down and mix the batter on a Styrofoam plate. It is so hard to cook in here without any dishes. He walks back down a moment later in nothing but his boxers, socks pulled up to his knees, and an apron with my face plastered across the entire front.

I burst out laughing, I can't help it. "Oh my God, does that say, 'Property of Leah'?"

"It does," Cam laughs. "Tom got it for me when he ordered yours. He said if I'm going to learn to cook, I should do it in style."

"You wear it well," I tease.
Cam walks into the kitchen and I can't help but stare. He is a good-looking man, even in this silly getup.

"Care to show me how to make French toast? I can make eggs already. Just don't tell anyone."

"You can? This, I have to see."

"Take a seat. Your cabana boy's got this." He leans in and kisses my head before turning me and giving me a swat on the backside on my way out.

I round the island and sit at the bar to watch him. "The pan should be warm now. You can add a dollop of butter. Then dip both sides of the bread in the batter, and put it in the pan."

"Like this?" he asks. He puts a hunk of butter in the pan. It's a little much, but it'll work. He drops a piece of Texas toast on the plate, sloshing the mixture over the edge. Then he turns it and tosses it into the pan.

"Yes, like that, but be softer."

I watch as he attempts a second, doing much better.

"Take the spatula and flip the first one before it burns."

He does so, squishing it in the process.

I pick up the powdered sugar and let a little fly his way, chuckling. "Be softer. You can cook, but you need to learn to be gentle."

"Are you starting a food fight?" Cam tosses some my way, forgetting the food.

I get up when I can tell it's burning and turn off the flame as Cam dumps—I mean *dumps*—more sugar on me.

He smiles down at me. "Oops, looks like you need help washing your hair now."

"Cam," I laugh. "You didn't have to waste so much powder sugar."

He nods and looks around the kitchen. "Breakfast is a wreck." He lifts me bridal style, carrying me toward the stairs.

"I thought you said that I needed to eat," I tease.

"I changed my mind. I'll buy you food on the way to your place."

I chuckle and can't help but needle him once more. "We should at least clean up the mess."

"Leave it," he says. Cam looks at me and winks. "If you're done teasing me now, I'd like to shower."

Thankfully, I have my swimsuit in my bag—the one

Cam's been chomping at the bit to see again. After a nice, long shower, we lie in bed while he gives me the most amazing back rub of my life. Sure, it leads to a make-out session, but I'd be a liar if I said I don't enjoy it.

Being out here on the farm is a dream—maybe one day it can be my home too.

"Becca, you made it!" I say. Tonight is game night. Uncle Joe, Janet, Mike, Kayla, Megan, Damon, Cam, and now Becca all sit around the table. This is my annual birthday rummy game. I said we could play something else, but Uncle Joe wanted us to stick with tradition.

"I did. Mark said he'll stop by when he gets off work."

"Awesome. I'm glad you're here."

I fussed about coming tonight. I didn't want to leave Cam's place, but now that we did, I'm glad we're here. Though when he begged—he literally got down on his knees and begged—me to come back tonight, I thought he was messing with me like he had been all day, but when I noticed that he was being serious, I put him out of his misery and agreed.

"Sweetheart," Cam says. He leans in so that I can hear him without raising his voice. "I'm going to go use the bathroom in your room if you don't mind. I don't want to have to wait on Mike to get out of the other."

"Go ahead. Can you grab me a sweater out of my dresser on the way back? I'm sitting right under the AC vent."

"Sure thing." He stands and heads into my room as Uncle Joe starts to deal out the cards.

"You two look awful good together," Janet says across from me. She's sitting snuggled up to Uncle Joe's side. She kisses his shoulder before smiling back at me. "Don't you agree, Joey baby?"

"'Joey baby'?" Kayla chokes out. "Oh, please tell me that nickname has stuck." She laughs hard.

"Kayla," Uncle Joe fusses. "Control yourself, kiddo."

"What? It's cute. I didn't think I'd ever see the softer side of Mean Ole Joe come out for anyone other than his girls. I'm eating this up."

"Mean Ole Joe?" Janet questions.

"All my friends thought he was a grouch because of his permanent scowl," Kayla replies. "Back in middle school, my friends started calling him Mean Ole Joe because he was only ever nice to me and Leah. Not that he was mean—he just wasn't open to others."

I trail off from their conversation when Cam walks back out carrying one of my favorite baggy sweaters—I stole this one from Uncle Joe when I was in college and missed home.

"There's my sweater," he says.

I turn back to look at Uncle Joe. "Let's face facts—you're never getting it back." I stick out my tongue and smile.

"Some things never change." He laughs.

I reach up and take it from Cam when he makes it to me. "Thanks, babe."

He leans down, giving me a quick kiss. "When did you get your keys back? I didn't even know they found them."

"I didn't," I say. "Frontier City never called."

"Really? I just saw them sitting on your dresser."

I look over at Kayla, then back at Cam. What's going on?

Could I have just misplaced them, or is someone messing with me? My nerves are on edge, and I feel my chest start to tighten. What if the same person that's been texting me took my keys"

"Leah, baby, breathe," Cam says. He turns me to face him, putting my legs between his. He runs his hands up and down my arms, bringing me out of my near freak-out. "What are you thinking, sweetheart?"

"Cam, I had to have taken my keys with us when we went to the theme park. Everyone had cleared out already. I couldn't have locked up without them."

He nods, following the steps that I'm retracing.

"How could I have picked them up? I've been with you the whole time," I start, "and no, they didn't call me to have them picked up either."

I look into his eyes and see recognition of what I'm saying.

His hands on my arms begin gripping a little harder than I'd like, but he soon drops them. He runs his hands through his hair and stands. "Stay here. I've got to make a call." He leans down to give me a quick kiss before walking out the front door.

"I bet he's calling Jazz," Becca says. "Mark said she was coming back soon."

"Who's Jazz?" Janet asks.

"A good friend and fellow officer," I reply.

If this person who's been messing with me was in my home, I won't be staying here again any time soon, that's for sure. At least tonight, I'll be at Cam's where I feel safe.

Chapter
Fourteen

Two nights turns into two weeks of staying at Cam's house. After the night Cam found my missing keys in my room, neither of us felt good about me going home alone, even though I had all of the locks changed the next day. Kayla hasn't been staying there either. She's been alternating between Mike's and Megan's houses. Cam has made me feel at home here—he even gave me a drawer of my own. Meanwhile, Jazz told us that she'd investigate and be in touch with her findings.

Cam has been enjoying his cooking lessons since I've been here and finally admitted that he needed to get some kitchen stuff. So yesterday, he and I went shopping after work. But tonight, I'm back home. I miss Kayla, and Cam said the same about the guys. He's going to try to get them all together for a few beers while I hang out with Kay.

That flies out the window when I find out she has plans. Mike is at work, and Uncle Joe is out of town with Janet. So here I am, all alone, bingeing on some cookies-and-cream ice cream while I look for something to watch. When my phone vibrates, I forget all about the remote.

Kayla: *I might not be home tonight. Are you good with being alone until Mike can come over?*

Me: *Yeah, I'm fine. Have fun, but please be safe.*

Kayla: *Don't worry about me, sis. I'm staying with Meg, I'm safe. She's having a crisis. See you tomorrow?*

Me: *See you then.*

Even though I want to be nosey, I drop it. For now. Instead, I decide to check in with Cam.

Me: *Hey, babe, Kayla backed out. She's going to Megan's. I'm looking for a show to watch. Any ideas?*

When Cam doesn't respond, I put my phone back down and start looking for a movie. I settle for a romantic comedy—*Life as We Know It*. I swear, I'm a sucker for a happy ending.

I hear a clanking noise come from my room . . . My heart stops. I listen again, but nothing. I try to go back to my movie, but I hear it again. I grab the bat from beside my front door and investigate, but I see nothing. It's hot as heck in here, though. I know the air is on, so I check the window, finding it cracked open. I don't remember opening it. It's not something I would have done in a heatwave—104 with an index of 112—either. I close it before walking back out to the living room and grabbing my phone. Still no response from Cam.

I shoot Becca a quick text.

Me: *Hey, girl. I texted Cam a couple hours ago. He hasn't responded yet. Do you know if he got called in?*

Becca: *Yeah, he did. Mark said that he got a call shortly after he got there and had to run. Is everything okay?*

When I hear a noise coming from my room again, I nearly jump out of my skin.

Me: *Yeah, just on edge, I guess. I keep hearing noises and being all alone has me freaking out a bit. I found my window cracked open again and I don't think I'd do that in this heat, but I'm not certain I didn't do it either. Things have been crazy lately.*

Becca: *Aw, what kind of noises? Are you okay?*

Me: *I'm fine. I went to look and didn't find anything. Maybe the window being open knocked something over. I don't know, I've heard it a few times.*

I start pacing back and forth. Since all of this has started, I can hardly stand the thought of being alone in my own home. All my life, I've had to fight. I just want to be happy and not have to always look over my shoulder.

Becca: *One of the guys can come check it out if you want.*

Me: *I don't want to be a bother. I'm sure I'm just overreacting again.*

Becca: *If you're safe, I'll let it go. You can always come to hang out with us if you want. We have a spare room. It sounds like Cam's working on some big case, so it might be a while before he gets in touch.*

Me: *That sounds fun, but I don't have a car. I'd hate for y'all to come pick me up just to go right back. Besides, I've got to work in the morning. I think I'll just shower and turn in early.*

Becca and Mark live just on the other side of the Cameron farm, so I don't want to bother them for a ride. They'd have to go twenty minutes either way just to get me. I can do this. I'm sure I'm just overreacting.

Becca: *Tom's in town. I can have him pick you up on his way back. Plus, Mark works in the morning, so he can take you back. Pack a bag and come stay. Aubrey would love to see you. She's been mad at Cam for taking all your time anyway.*

Me: *Are you sure? I don't want you to make a fuss.*

Becca: *I'm sure, now move your butt. Tom will be there in five. Hope you're hungry. He just picked up pizza and beer.*

Me: *Sounds good. See you soon.*

Becca: *<3*

As I head to my room, I shoot Kayla a quick text.

Me: *Staying the night with Becca. See you tomorrow. Love you.*

Kayla: *Have fun. Give Little Miss hugs for me. Love you too. I'll let Mike know.*

Me: *Will do. Thanks sis.*

In a matter of minutes, I get a call from Tom, who's right out front.

"Hey, I'll be down in a minute," I tell him. "Locking up now."

I hang up and shove my phone into my back pocket as I turn around and lock the door behind me. When I look up, I notice a small note stuck to it.

I'll see you soon.

I stall in my steps. The window could have been accidental, but a note is not.

I grab my phone out of my pocket and hit dial on Tom. "Hello?"

"Can you come up?" I hang up, knowing he'll try to carry on, but I need him here now.

Moments later, I turn to see Tom taking the stairs two at a time. "What's up? You sounded frightened."

"There's a note." I point at the door, then explain about the window.

Tom takes his phone out of his pocket and hits call before stepping away. "Call Becca and let her know that we'll be late." He holds a finger up, then focuses on his call. "Hey, I'm at Cam's girl's house. Can you come over? Yeah, there's a note and an open window this time. Yeah . . . right, my thoughts too. No, we'll wait out here for you. Sure, see you then." He looks back at me, appearing a bit saddened. "Jazz is on her way. I think it's time you and Cam accept that you have a stalker."

My legs suddenly grow weak. I rest my shoulder against the wall and slide down to sit on my landing. I knew this was a possibility, but hearing it come out of his mouth so matter-of-factly is a shock to the system. I know living in denial is not a healthy place to be, but it is an easier place to accept.

"Are you alright?"

"I will be. It's just a bit much to take in."

"I bet. I know I'm not Cam, but I'm here for you if you need anything."

Tom is an amazing guy. He's always joking around, but he does have a softer side to him too. One that we don't get to see too often. I'm glad that he was so close. Had I seen this note and nobody was around, it could have been bad.

Tom's phone rings. "Hello?" A pause. "Yeah." He rattles off our door code. "Third floor. We're sitting outside the door." He hangs up and helps me to stand. "Jazz is on her way up."

No matter that he's here now and that he's handling this in a way that I know that Cam would be proud of, I can't help but wish that Cam were here instead.

Jazz steps up onto the landing. She reminds me of an Irish princess—thick, curly, red hair; green eyes; cheeks full of freckles; and powder-light skin. She's beautiful with a powerhouse attitude. She walks over, shakes my hand, and starts in. "Tom told me about the note and the window. Did you by chance look to see if anything else was out of place while you were inside?"

"I didn't. I thought I might have opened the win-dow and forgotten I did it. Things have been crazy lately; I'm not exactly thinking straight." My nerves are wrecked.

"That's fine. I know last we spoke, we weren't sure of what exactly was going on yet. I'm with Tom on this, though. With the flowers, the odd texts, the keys, and now this? I think we've got a stalker case."

I feel like falling apart. Instead, I take a deep breath and try to maintain my composure, even if I feel like falling apart right now. Nothing will come of this if I do.

Tom puts a hand on my shoulder. "I'm right here with you every step of the way."

"Thank you," I reply. "Come on in."

Jazz steps up and takes a picture of the note on my door before grabbing it with a gloved hand and putting it into a baggy. When she nods, I open the door. We walk around the whole apartment, but I don't notice anything out of place. When I open my bedroom closet, hanging right there in the middle is a wraparound yellow dress that I know is not mine. I tried it on while Kayla, Becca, and I were in the mall recently, but I put it back. I decided not to buy it. I didn't think I'd wear it enough to spend that kind of money on something.

I take a step back, holding my hand to my mouth. "Um," I cry, "that's not mine." I point to the dress.

Jazz walks over and takes a picture of it, then walks back toward the bathroom still looking. We meet in the living room minutes later.

"I'm going to make a report off the information I've gotten from you already. I should be able to fill out a victim's survey for you. I'll reach out if I need anything else. I'll bag that dress on my way out." She looks to Tom, then back to me. "I wouldn't stay here alone if I were you. I'd also always have someone with you while you're out and about. We don't know who's behind this yet or their motive. Better safe than sorry." She takes out a card and hands it to me. "If you have any questions or you remember something that you haven't yet told me, give me a call." She walks into my closet and returns with the bagged-up dress. "I'll be in touch in a few days."

What in the hell am I supposed to do now? Life as I know it has just been turned upside down.

I take out my phone and text Kayla everything that happened while Tom drives us out to Becca's.

Me: *No more staying at the house alone.*

Kayla: *I was talking to Mike earlier today about that. He and D can't stay at their place for a while due to the remodel. Mike said he can stay with us. That would make me feel better. What do you say?*

Me: *Sounds good, plus I think we need to call the security company and have them come out too.*

Kayla: *Sounds good. TTYL sis. Heading into the theater.*

I put my phone up and sit back for the remainder of the ride.

When Tom pulls up, the front door is flung open, and Aubrey starts running in our direction. "*Leah!*" she yells.

Opening my door, I hop out, chuckling. I crouch and open my arms, waiting for her amazing hug. I'm not disappointed—this girl can hug! She's just what I need right now.

"I missed you, kiddo."

"I missed you too," she says. "Come on, I wanna show you my woom."

"Lead the way, Little Miss."

Tugging on my hand, she leads me in, past a smiling Mark and Becca, right to her room. She directs me to take a seat at her table, then puts a tiara on my head. "You get to be Pwincess Leah now."

"Oh, I do, huh? What about you?"

"We can both be pwincesses. I have another tiawa." She walks over to her dresser, grabbing a second, and puts it on herself.

"What about your mom?"

"She's the queen, silly."

I giggle a little at her seriousness. "Oh, gotcha. I guess that makes your dad the king. What about Uncle Tom?"

"He's the ges . . . gew."

"Gesgew? Do you mean jester?"

"Yeah. He's the clown," she says, matter-of-factly.

God, I love this little girl. The whole ride over, I couldn't get out of my head. If nothing else, these few moments with her give me an escape.

"I heard that, princess," Tom says from the doorway. "Dinner's ready. Come eat."

Seeing that the pizza is piping hot, I'm sure they had to

throw it in the oven for a quick reheat. Sitting around the table with them is a load of fun, even if I keep catching looks of pity. I hate that everyone is looking at me like I'm about to break.

Toward the end of dinner, I get a text.

Cam: *Hey, sweetheart. Sorry I didn't message sooner. I've been working. I don't know when I'll be off. Are you ok staying at your place tonight?*

Me: *You're fine. When you didn't text back, I kind of figured. I'm staying the night at Becca and Mark's. Just finishing up dinner now.*

Cam: *Good, I'm glad they invited you. How'd you get out there?*

Me: *Tom was picking up dinner nearby and grabbed me.*

Cam: *Have fun. I have to get back in there. I'll call when I can. Love you.*

Me: *Love you too. See you soon.*

"From the grin on your face, I take it that was Cam?" Tom says.

"It was," I respond. "He was just checking in." I set my phone down on the table and take a drink of my water, opting out of drinking alcohol tonight.

"Feel better now?" Becca asks.

"Yeah. I do."

"You didn't tell him what happened, did you?" Tom asks.

"No. Not in a text or while he's working. I can take care of this, and when I see him next, I'll let him know then. I don't want him to worry about me when he needs to be focused right now."

"Good decision," Becca says. "He might get upset, but you're right. It needs to wait."

"Okay, enough of that," Mark says. "Who's up for Pictionary?"

"I'm game," I say. We stand and clear the table. Since everything used was disposable, we fill the trash can that Mark takes out, then head to the living room.

Tom, Aubrey, and I are on one team, and Becca and Mark are on the other. Aubrey is my helper.

"Uncle Tom," Aubrey says. "That's not how you dwaw a cop. You made it look like a clown." She has her hands on her hip, foot cocked out in front of her, looking up at Tom.

He mirrors her and looks down in debate. "Isn't that what you call me? I'm an officer, silly."

"Yeah, but a clown isn't a cop. They have guns and handcuffs and stuff."

"So do I," Tom says.

"*Ugh*," Aubrey huffs out in frustration, throwing her hands up in defeat. "Mommy, can I have a bubble bath now? Uncle Tom is annoy me."

"Annoy*ing*, honey," Becca corrects. "Yes, you can. I'll go run you some water. Go get your pajamas."

Aubrey tugs on my arm, so I lean down. "I have to go to bed after my bath. You can sleep in my woom if you want to. Mommy does when Daddy woks late. She says it makes hew not lonely."

I catch a glimpse of Mark looking at Becca with sad eyes. She shrugs it off before walking down the hall toward the bathroom.

"Thank you, Little Miss. Maybe another time."

"You can sneak in latew if you miss Uncle Cam. Just don't hog the bed ow take my teddy. If you do that, I'll be mad."

I smile and bop her nose. "Don't worry, princess. I won't touch teddy."

"Aubrey, get a move on before the water gets cold!" Becca yells from the hallway.

"I bettew go so Mommy won't blow a gasket," she says, shocking me.

"*Aubrey Leanna,* what have I told you about that? Move now!" Mark says.

Aubrey turns and hightails it to her room, grabs something, then runs down the hall toward the bathroom.

"Tom, you've really got to watch what you say around her."

"My bad, that was one time. I didn't think she'd pick up on it," he defends. "I'm out. Y'all have a good night." Tom heads toward the door, looking back over to me. " Call if you need anything."

"Will do. Thanks, Tom."

"I'm going to head on up. I'll be leaving at four," Mark says as soon as the door shuts. "I can take you then or you can ask Becca to take you later."

"Four's fine. Thanks. Mark."

"No problem. Good night." He turns and heads to lock up before going to his room.

I walk down the hall to the guest room. Then I shut the

door, I strip down and pull on one of Cam's shirts. It's a close second to being in his arms. It'd be better if it smelled like him. I plop down on the bed and pull out my phone to look at the few pictures we've taken since being together.

It looks like we've lived a lifetime together already.

I have pictures from our outing with the gang, our double date, and my time teaching Cam how to cook in his kitchen—I think that's one of my favorites. Cam is in nothing but his boxers and an apron. It would look good on the wall in the kitchen if I weren't worried about so many other eyes seeing what's mine.

Exhaustion taking over, I let my eyes close while thinking of all the moments yet to come.

Chapter Fifteen

Something shakes me, waking me from my sound sleep. I was worried that I wouldn't get any rest, but I slept hard. I move to turn onto my back and bump into a wall of muscle. Turning over quickly, I smack right into a sleepy-looking Cam.

"Oh my God!" I shriek, sitting up fast, the sleep wearing off quickly at the sight of him. "You scared the heck out of me. How'd you get here?"

"I drove," he says, a smirk on his handsome face.

"That's not what I meant, and you know it," I say, swatting his chest. "How'd you get in?"

"I had Mark leave a key out for me. I told him I was going to sneak in once I got off. I have to go back pretty early, but with all the ugly I've seen, I needed to see you for a little bit." He snuggles his nose into the hollow of my neck.

I lean in and kiss his bare shoulder. "What time do you have to go in?"

"I have to be back at ten."

"Where's my phone?"

"I put it on the charger behind you. Why?"

"I'm going to call Mike and make sure he can handle things this morning. I want to be here with you." I turn the best I can in his grip and pick my phone up, then make the call.

"Hello?" Mike answers in his sleep-worn voice.

"Morning. Sorry to wake you so early," I say. "Cam just got in, and he doesn't have to be back until ten. Can you cover me until then?" I never ask for favors, so surely, he'll know if I'm asking, it's important to me.

"What time is it?" he grunts.

"It's one. Sorry it's so early. I figured I better ask right away."

"It's fine. Is he okay?"

I look over my shoulder at Cam. "Physically, yes."

"Good. Yeah, go take care of your man. I've got you. I'm going back to bed now."

"Thanks, Mike." Hanging up, I turn back and snuggle further into Cam's chest, burrowing in as close as I can get. "I'm all yours."

"I'm lucky to have you. All night, all I could think about was getting to you and washing off the stuff I've had to see."

Looking into his eyes, I see how haunted he is. I hate to add more, but I know if I don't tell him, he'll be pissed that I withheld it. The least I can do is let him get some sleep first. "I know you can't talk about it, but if you want to, just know I'm always here."

"Knowing that you're here and safe in my arms is enough. You have no idea how much it means to me that you'd call in for me."

"Cam," I say, pulling back while holding his face between my hands. "I love you. There isn't anything in this world I wouldn't do for you."

"I love you, too, sweetheart," he says with a handsome smile on his face.

I pull him in for a quick kiss. Cam snuggles his head to my chest as I rub my hand through his hair, just how he likes it. "I'm not going anywhere. Sleep. I've got you."

He came to me instead of going home after a long, hard day. He sought me out, of all things. I love this man so much that my heart feels like it's overrun with joy. I've never been so happy in my life.

Cam is not happy hearing that my place was broken into, but he is happy that Tom was there to help me through it. With him being on a case, the others step up to make sure that either someone is home with me or I'm with them while he's at work. Over the next two weeks, he's run ragged at work. He's away more than normal, but knowing that I'm going to wake up in his arms helps get me through each night. I give him a key to my apartment so he doesn't have to drive home every night to an empty bed. I want him with me as much as he wants to be here. Cam hasn't missed a night yet. He doesn't have more than ten hours off a day in all that time. It makes spending time together hard.

The text I get from him before I turn in for the night has me smiling.

Cam: *Case closed, sweetheart. I'll be home soon. Love you.*

Me: *I'm so happy to hear that. Good night, love you too.*

The next morning I'm in my office at work, and Cam is sitting across from me on his phone. He followed me to work today, claiming that he missed spending time with me. I love that he wants to hang with me, but I need to be working right now. He's distracting—one of the main reasons he never hangs out here other than for a quick bite to eat. Knowing that he hasn't had a guys' night in some time, I suggest that he go out with them. "There's no sense in you hanging here today. I know you miss being around me, but I have to work. It's fixing to be lunch rush anyway; it's going to be crazy. Go have some bro time. You can see me later."

"You know *bro time* involves alcohol, right? If I leave now, I might not see you tonight. Would you be happy sleeping without me?"

"I'd hate to sleep without you. But if you drink, I'd rather you safe than sorry. I want you to have a good birthday, and since I can't get out of work, you should at least go have fun. Just don't forget I have a little birthday thing for you tomorrow." I have a private party planned—just him and I. I went and bought all the stuff to make his favorite dinner—meatloaf and mashed potatoes—and then I'm taking him to iFLY to go indoor skydiving. It's going to be a blast. I hope. I figure since he's been working so much, a private party is something he'd like much more than being with everyone. Especially since we're about to be with them for nearly a week straight.

"Will you have someone with you tonight if I don't make it back?"

He is so protective of me—I love it. I just don't want him to skip out on things because he feels responsible for me.

"Kayla and Mike will be home tonight."

"Good." He tugs my chair over to him so that I'm now sitting between his outstretched legs.

"Then it's settled. You go out and have fun tonight. Tomorrow, you're mine, and then we head off to Disney the next morning. You'll be tired of me before you know it."

"I'll never grow tired of you, beautiful." He leans in, kissing me on the nose. "Never." He then moves to my mouth, putting his hand behind my head to deepen the kiss, but grunts in frustration as a knock sounds at my door.

"Boss, you're needed on the line. Alex is falling behind," Ronny announces.

"I'll be out in a minute."

"Come on," Cam says. He pushes my chair back and stands, extending his hand for me. "Walk me out."

Times like this, I wish I could take an extended vacation from my job, but then again, I'd be bored if I couldn't be here. This is all I've ever known, but seeing how Cam looks right now makes me wish I could ditch my responsibility and spend every waking moment in his arms.

Heading back to my apartment after work knowing that Cam is out with the guys and might not make it to see me has me bummed. I know I suggested it, and I meant it. I don't want to be the cause of him not having any time with his guy friends. I refuse to be one of those girlfriends, but I sure do miss him. At least starting tomorrow, I'll have him all to myself, followed by four more days in a row, since we'll be heading on our weekend trip to Disney. I can hardly wait.

I text Cam a quick message before unlocking my door.

Me: *Hey, babe, hope you're having fun. I just wanted to let you know I made it home safe. Love you. See you tomorrow.*

Cam: *Good. I switched to coffee already. You might find me in bed before long if things die down here anytime soon.*

Me: *I'm fine, Cam. Stay, have fun with the guys. I'll see you tomorrow. I'm going to shower and head to bed now. I'm exhausted.*

Cam: *Okay, sweetheart. Good night, I love you. See you in the morning.*

Putting my phone away, I see Mike and Kayla at the table playing UNO when I walk in. "Hey, guys," I say on my way to my room.

"Hey, wanna play?" Mike asks.

"Rain check? I'm worn out. I just want to hit the shower and crawl into bed."

"Yeah, that's fine," Kayla says. "Hey, wait! How'd you get home?"

"I called an Uber. I was too tired to walk tonight, besides I didn't bring my umbrella." It's been raining off and on for the last couple of days. I'm so over it already.

"Well I'm glad you're home. Night, sis."

"Night," I say just before I shut my door.

After my shower, I crawl into bed, and in a matter of minutes, I'm out.

At some point in the middle of the night, I'm awakened by a crash next to me. I shoot up in bed fast, reaching for the light. When I can't find it, I search for my phone. I'm spooked when I see light coming in from the window. I know it was closed when I went to bed.

Finally finding my phone, I pull up Cam's name and press call, shouldering my phone as I reach for my bat.

Though muffled, I hear, "Hey, sweetheart. You alright?"

When I see the curtain move, I shift my focus to grabbing the bat, dropping my phone mid reach. Once I untangle my feet from my bedding, I stand.

"Leah, are you there?" Cam asks somewhere in the distance, though it doesn't fully register.

Stepping around the foot of my bed, I'm taken aback when I see a shadowed figure step out of the corner of my room and move toward me.

"Oh my god! Who are you?" I ask loudly. "Mike, get in here! Someone broke in!"

The figure moves frantically, turning and pushing through the window, breaking a pane before stepping out.

When Mike comes in, it's almost like watching a mad grizzly on a hunt. He's all growl and rippling muscle. He climbs through the window before I can stop him.

Remembering that I called Cam, I search for my phone. "Babe?" I say, putting it to my ear.

"Leah, sweetheart. Go to the living room with Kayla. Call Jazz and Uncle Joe. Tom and I are on our way," he says.

"Cam, I'm . . . I'm scared. Someone was in my room," I say as the seriousness of the situation begins to sink in.

"I know, beautiful. I'm on my way now. We're already in the truck. I'll be there in a minute. You're okay, sweetheart. You're safe. I'm right here."

"But you're not. Cam, you're not here and I'm scared," I say with a shaky voice. I fall to the floor, barely able to catch my breath.

I can hear someone in the background, but I can't make out a thing they're saying. Time is at a standstill as I drift. It feels like I'm drowning, and no matter how much I fight, I can't get air. Rocking back and forth, I feel like I'm about to lose the fight.

I feel two big, strong arms lift me and pull me in to them. Cam.

He sits down with me on his lap and tucks my head against his chest. His hand rubs up and down my back. I feel numb, nothingness taking over as my vision begins to darken.

"Come on, sweetheart, I need you to breathe. You're safe now," Cam says.

He pulls me in to his chest as the tears roll down my cheeks and darkness takes over.

I wake in Cam's room, the sun shining in through the window, warming my skin. He must have brought me here last night after all that mess. I hope Mike and Kayla are okay.

Sitting on the bed next to me is Little Miss Aubrey. When I fully open my eyes and smile at her, she returns it. "Mommy, Leah's awake!"

"Cam isn't here. He and Tom went to the station for a bit," Becca says, walking in. "He tasked Mark and me with staying here with you while he's out." She sits down on the bed, patting my knee. "How about you hop in the shower? By the time you get downstairs, breakfast will be waiting on you."

Aubrey runs out of the room; Becca begins to stand.

"Hey, Becca." I stop her just before she gets up. "How's Cam after last night?"

"As good as expected, I guess. Finding you the way he did brought back a flood of memories for him from when he found Janelle in the pasture. He'll be fine, but I do have to warn you that his protectiveness will be ramped up, I'm sure."

I nod. "What happened to Janelle? This is the second time I've heard of it."

"That's her story to tell, but I can say that her ex is not a good man. He used to hit her, and she went through hell getting him out of her house." She pats my knee and starts to stand.

"Do you know how Mike's doing? He ran out after the guy last night." I feel horrible that he took off so quickly to protect me and I don't even know if he's hurt. A tear falls. If not for him and Cam, I don't know how last night would have turned out.

Becca pulls me in for a quick hug, then takes my hand as she pulls back. "You're safe now, hun. Mike is safe. His feet got cut up from the broken glass, but he was bandaged up and is right as rain now."

I hate that he was hurt at all, but I'm glad that he's safe. "Shower up. We'll take you to town to grab your things when you're ready. Cam and Tom are going to meet us there."

"Thank you, Becca . . . for everything." I really don't want to go back to my place after last night, but considering that I need a few things, I guess I kind of need to.

"You don't have to thank me for anything, hun. Family takes care of each other. We love you. We'll see you downstairs when you're ready."

I go to my drawer and grab some shorts and a tank top and head toward the bathroom. After a nice, long, hot shower, I walk back into the room and look for my phone. When I find it on the side table—still milk crates—I sit and check my texts.

Kayla: *When you get this, text me to let me know that you're ok. You scared the hell out of me last night with that episode. The EMT said all was well and that you just needed rest, so I agreed to let Cam take you home with him. I'm staying with Mike.*

Me: *Morning, sis. I'm doing fine. A bit of a headache like normal after a big attack like that, but I'm ok. Honestly, sending me home with Cam was probably the best thing you could have done. I love it here. I don't know if I ever want to go home again. I was so scared. I'm glad Mike let you stay. I would have hated for you to be there alone after that.*

Kayla: *Thank God you're ok. I've been so worried. After your trip, we need to have a talk about what we want to do. I'm with you on not wanting to be there anymore.*

Me: *Sounds good to me. You and Mike, be safe on your travels. I can't believe you're going to New York this weekend.*

Kayla: *I know, me either. I'm just glad that Mike's coming with me. I want to check it out before I move out there.*

Me: *I don't blame you. Love you, sis.*

Kayla: *Love you too.*

Closing my text with Kayla, I open the one from Uncle Joe.

Uncle Joe: *Please tell me that you're ok, baby doll. Kayla nearly gave me a heart attack when she told me what happened.*

Me: *I'm ok. Sorry I didn't call. The panic attack I had last night was the worst I've had in, well, maybe ever, but I'm good now.*

Uncle Joe: *I heard. I'm just glad to hear that you're ok now. Is Cam taking good care of you?*

Me: *Yes, he is.*

Uncle Joe: *Good. Love you, Leah.*

Me: *Love you too Uncle Joe.*

I close Uncle Joe's chat and I see that I have one more text.

Cam: *Morning, beautiful. Tom and I came to the station. I wanted to talk to Jazz about what happened last night and to my Cap about taking some time off. Becca and Mark should be there before you wake up. I asked them to bring you to town to grab a few things. Let me know when you're on your way, and we'll meet you there.*

Me: *Morning, babe. Does she need to talk to me? What do you need to take time off for? Love you too.*

Cam: *We can talk about it when I get home. I'll explain everything. See you soon.*

I tuck my phone into my pocket and head downstairs to the kitchen. Walking in, I find Becca and Mark with a dozen donuts and three to-go cups of coffee.

"Morning," Mark says. "You ready to go to town?"

"I suppose," I say in response. Moving to the counter, I reach for a glazed donut and accept the piping-hot coffee that Becca pushes my way.

"Eat up, then we'll head out," she adds. "Come on, Aubrey, let's get you cleaned up. Grandma Marie's coming to get you in a minute."

I don't really want to be going back to my place, but considering that I'll have so many people there supporting me, I'll make it work.

Chapter Sixteen

I lie on the couch at Cam's house with my head in his lap, him running his hand through my hair aimlessly. With full bellies from the pizza we grabbed after loading his truck full of my belongings from my room—Cam packed it all—we sit here watching TV, neither of us fully paying attention. So much for his birthday surprise that I had planned. With the happenings of last night, he said he'd rather hang out on the farm today than go out. Cam loved the certificate I bought and says we can use it later for a date night, but he's too tired to do much more today.

"How'd it go with Jazz and Cap?" I ask.

"I gave Jazz all the information I could give her. She said she'd call you, Kayla, and Mike in a bit to follow up. As far as Cap goes, I put in for a sabbatical. I asked if I could take a few weeks with the possibility of extending it."

"What did he say?" Surely, he's not taking time off because of me. I already feel like a burden. I don't want him to have to rearrange more for me than he already has.

"He had me finish up the cases I was working on. Cap didn't want them left open while I was gone." He glances up at the TV, then back to me. "I'm supposed to hear back from him as soon as he knows. He doesn't see any problem with it though."

"That's good. Is a sabbatical like a vacation or what?" I ask, a bit confused. "I've heard of them but have no idea what they really are."

"It's a benefit we get after being active duty for five years. We can take up to a year off with full job security."

"That's a nice benefit, but you didn't need to use it on me. I'm fine," I lie. "I don't want you uprooting your life any more than you already have because of me."

He pulls me up and into his lap so that I'm now straddling him and nudges my chin so that I'm looking him straight on. "After you broke down last night, you can't tell me that you're fine. Be honest with me. The break-in took you to your knees. What kind of boyfriend would I be if I wasn't there for you? Of course I'm taking some time off." He kisses my nose. "I'm not uprooting anything; I'm protecting what's mine."

I blush when I can't stop the tingle that goes down my spine at him calling me his in that gravelly tone. Cam pulls me in for a hug, kissing the top of my head. The break-in did take me down, and then today, having to go back and see my apartment afterwards nearly took me out again. One look at my room and Cam had me sitting on my couch instead of going in. I don't know if it was more for him or me, but either way, I'm glad. But him going in instead of me means he packed nearly everything I had in there. Now it all sits upstairs in his room, mostly still in bags.

"You're an amazing boyfriend. I hope you know that," I say, tucking in further.

Cam's phone rings. He maneuvers so he can grab it while keeping me on his lap. Seeing that it's Jazz, he answers on speaker. "Hey Jazz, what's up?"

"Hey Cam, is Leah still out there at your place?"

"Yeah, why?"

"I'm on my way home, not far now. Do you mind if I stop by?"

"Babe?" he asks me.

I nod.

"Sure, come on out."

"Alright, be there in ten." The line goes dead.

He sets it on the cushion next to us.

"I need a beer for this," I say, standing. "You want one while I'm up?" Since Kayla and I both decided we aren't going home until at least after we get back from our trips—if at all—we divided the food and drinks in the house between Cam's and Mike's houses so that we have something to eat.

"I'd love one, thanks."

I walk into the kitchen and grab two cold beers from the fridge, then turn back to head to the living room when there's a knock at the door. Cam gets up and goes to answer it while I make my way back to the couch.

Jazz walks into the living room as I pull the blanket I brought over from the back of the couch and cover up. I open my beer and take a long pull.

Jazz lingers on the other side of the room, not quite sure what to do with herself. "Hey, Leah. Is this a bad time?"

"No. Have a seat. Would you like a drink?" Anything to pause the anxiety creeping in.

"No, thanks." She does as I say and pulls up a chair opposite me. "We need to talk about who this could be. Let's talk it through, even if it may not be useful. I want to know everything."

Cam lifts his beer to his mouth, taking a swig. If this is uncomfortable for me, I'm sure it is for him, too, seeing how protective he is of me. I really don't want to be talkingabout all this right now, but I know it needs to be done. I take a portion of the blanket in my hand and start twisting it as I think about who all could be out to get me.

"This is harder than I thought it would be," I say. Who really wants to bring up their past drama?

Cam puts his hand on mine, and I look up and smile softly.

"Maybe if we start slow, it'll jog your thoughts. Has anyone made threats to you in recent history?" Jazz asks.

"Yeah," I say. "I had an angry customer not long ago. Cam and a few others came in and got him to leave. It happens a lot in food service though." I look over at Cam, then back to Jazz. Cam's hand covers mine. I turn it over and start tracing his lifeline with my finger. My hands are so tiny in his huge ones.

"What else? Has anyone come back into your life lately that hasn't been there in some time?"

"Oh." My eyes go big, and I sit up straight, letting go of Cam's hand. "I almost forgot. The morning Cam picked me up for Mark's birthday weekend, Mike, Kayla, and I went to go get coffee. Kayla hip-checked me, and I stumbled into a guy along the canal. He became hateful, going so far as to threaten to push me in the canal."

Cam growls, taking me from the story. He tightens his hand into a fist on my lap. I take it in mine again and begin playing with it. Not only does it help me, but I guess him too.

"What happened?" Jazz inquires.

"Mike stepped in. He put Kayla and me behind him, and in time, the guy backed down and took off down the canal. But . . ." I look up at Cam through my lashes.

"But what?" Jazz asks.

"Not long after I met Mike, I met this guy named Ryan. We started dating. We only went out a few times. I thought he was a nice guy at first. One night, he was dropping me off after we had a dinner date. I leaned over the console to give him a quick goodnight kiss, but he wanted more." I hate telling these stories—they make me feel so weak. "Anyway," I say, linking my fingers through Cam's, "I was able to get away. He didn't hurt me too bad, and Uncle Joe and Mike demanded I learn to protect myself afterwards. Kayla thinks he was the guy on the canal. I'm not so sure. I never got a look at his face."

"Did you fill out a police report after the incident?" Jazz asks.

"When Ryan assaulted me, yes. After the coffee shop, no." I'm so over filling out reports. It seems like every couple of years, I'm filling out a new one. It's frustrating.

"It's a stretch, but I'll see if I can get any footage of the incident on the canal and look for the file involving you and Ryan. Do you know that date?"

"No, just that it was the day we left for Mark's party."

"I mean for the previous incident."

Oh, that. "I have the paperwork at home in my file cabinet if you need it. It was nearly five years ago."

"Good, anything else?"

"Well, there's John Knorr. He got out of jail. He's the one who caused my spill in the hall of my apartment." The one that brought me Cam. Though I hate that it happened, I also wouldn't change it. I know that sounds funny, but if I wasn't there, I might never have met him.

"Yeah, but," Cam interjects, "he was still in jail when all of this started."

"He might have been, but I'd still like to rule him out as a person of interest," Jazz states.

"There's one more person I can think of."

"Who's that?" Cam asks.

"Tillie." I look to him to see if he recognizes the name. "John's girlfriend, the one who testified in court, saying that he'd been with her the whole time rather than causing me to fall down the stairs."

He looks over as if he must be remembering. "You saw *her* again?"

Oh, I knew he didn't like her, but his reaction confirms it. "Yeah. She's come into the restaurant a few times since court." Though I can't stand the thought of her coming in, I can't refuse her service either. Other than her messing with me a little, she's never really threatened anyone. If I were to give her the boot, she'd make a big fuss in front of my customers. If she did something to earn it like that one guy did, that's one thing, but for just sitting there and enjoying her meal is another. "She never really starts any drama or anything. She says a few choice words to me when she spots me, then leaves it be."

"She shouldn't be in there at all," Cam says.

"I wish I could refuse her service, but it'd be more trouble than it's worth," I say.

"Well, that gave me a lot to look into. If you can think of anything else, day or night, feel free to give me a call."

"Thanks, Jazz. I'm sorry you had to drive all the way out here."

"No problem at all. I live just down the street in Wagon Springs. We're practically neighbors out here."

"Oh, nice. Isn't that where Becca said she's from?"

"I believe so," Cam says.

He walks Jazz to the door, letting her out.

After the door shuts behind her, I stand and clap my hands. It's time to get my stuff unpacked and get ready for our early-morning road trip.

Standing at the fridge the next morning, I pack the ice chest with plenty of drinks and snacks for the road, then grab the brown bag of breakfast burritos I made for the trip.

Cam walks over and grabs the ice chest to take out to the truck. "Hey, babe, can you lock up on your way out? I've got the truck loaded up and am ready to hit the road as soon as they get here."

"Sure." I walk to the door, grab my phone from the entry shelf, and look around to make sure we didn't forget anything. I grab his keys off the key hook near the door, set the alarm, and head out, locking up behind me. I get to the truck and load the food up in the middle, then walk around so I can grab a water from the chest. Cam's standing next to the truck, so I toss him his keys.

He turns, placing them in the truck, then grabs something from the door. I grab a water from the back and turn to find Cam standing nearby. He reaches out taking my empty hand in his. I feel something cool drop in my hand before he removes his.

"What is this?" I ask, looking down. A key. Hanging from it is a tiny pair of handcuffs, a whisk, and a navy-blue ribbon tied to it.

"I was going to give these to you yesterday, but things happened. Leah . . . sweetheart, will you move in with me? I don't want you to think that I'm asking because of what's going on now. I want this—I want you."

I cover my mouth in shock and start to respond, but Cam interjects.

"I'll understand if this is too soon for you." He runs his thumb across my cheek to wipe away the tear that has fallen. "I hope these are happy tears."

I nod my head frantically. "They are," I squeak. "Yes, Cam. I'd love to move in!" I throw myself at him, wrapping my arms around his neck and my legs around his midsection. "My God. I love you so much." Pulling back, I lock eyes with him and see the fire in mine reflecting in his. I take his face in my hands and mold our lips together in a passionate kiss. His hand finds its way to the base of my neck, fisting the loose hair there.

Someone clears their throat behind us as the heat ramps up. I pull back and bury my face in Cam's neck, frustrated at the interruption. I knew they were coming, but their timing sucks.

He chuckles and looks over at the intruder. "What's up, Tom?" he asks in a raspy voice. Thankfully, he doesn't let me go. He trails his hand up and down my back in comforting circles, allowing me to calm myself.

"Um, this is . . . nice and all, but umm . . ." Tom clears his throat again. "We need to get moving."

Cam puts me on my feet and then rounds the truck and

opens my door for me. I look over at Tom, whose cheeks are probably as red as mine are right now. I smile, then glance at Cam, who looks like he won the lottery.

I swat his stomach. "You're having fun with this, aren't you, sir?"

"What can I say? It's a rare moment when Tom gets tongue-tied. Plus, you're cute when you act all shy. So yes, I'm enjoying it. I can't help it," he says.

"Does this mean you . . ." Tom asks.

Cam cuts him off. "Yeah, I asked her to move in. Looks like you got a new neighbor."

I look over at Tom to gauge his reaction. He looks genuinely happy for us. *I'm* happy for us.

"Congrats, you two," Tom says. "I'm happy for you. I could have gone without seeing all that, but I'm glad you guys are doing this." He opens the door to his truck and starts to get in, but stops, looking back at me. "If you decide to sell the apartment, let me know. I know a good realtor. We went to school together."

"Thanks. I need to talk to Kayla before I decide, but I'll keep that in mind."

We finish loading up, then head out to meet Mark and Becca. I text Kayla while we're waiting on the others.

Me: *Cam asked me to move in with him and I said yes.*

Ripping the Band-Aid off, I jump in right away, then think twice about my approach. Too late now.

Kayla: *I figured that was coming. I'm happy for you, sis. Looks like the Covington sisters are starting a new chapter in life.*

Me: *That we are. I'm going to miss you like crazy.*

Kayla: *Same, but you're kind of stuck with me, you know. We share this thing called DNA. You're not getting rid of me anytime soon.*

Me: *I wouldn't want to if I could. I love you, sis.*

Kayla: *I love you too.*

Me: *What should we do about the apartment?*

Kayla: *It's up to you. It's your place.*

Me: *It's ours.*

Kayla: *Not anymore. Sell it if you want. Be happy and make a life with your man. Do something you've always wanted to do.*

Me: *Are you sure?*

Kayla: *Why wouldn't I be? We're both moving on. Be happy. Hey, got to go. I'm being called. Love you, have fun. See you next weekend.*

Me: *Love you too. Let me know when you land.*

I put my phone in my pocket and lean my head back against the headrest for a moment to take it all in. I've never been to this point in a relationship before. It's a little nerve-wracking now that it's sinking in, but it's also amazing. I feel more at home on the farm than I ever did in my apartment. Should I sell my place or keep it as a backup? What if I move in here and, down the road, Cam decides it was a mistake? I'd have to find a new place then. It's not like he'd be leaving his family's land. I guess I have some thinking to do.

Cam hops in the truck and grabs my hand. "Ready to head out?"

"Ready," I say.

No matter the outcome, I'm in this. I love him and am ready to give this relationship my all.

Chapter Seventeen

Cam and I play the ABC game—the one where you start at A and end at Z, naming things you see along the trip—and slug bug. That one is so fun, especially when you see a truck full of Volkswagen Beetles. I quickly find that road trips with Cam aren't boring by any means.

An hour from our destination, I get a text.

Becca: *Tell that man of yours that I need a bathroom and food break.*

Me: *Gotcha.*

I turn in my seat and look to Cam. "Becca says to stop at the next exit for a food, fuel, and potty break."

"If you don't mind, I'd kind of like to take our food to go."

"No problem. We'll make it quick."

The stop in Broken Arrow, Oklahoma, takes maybe twenty minutes. Once we get back on the road, we've barely finished our lunch when we're pulling off and parking again.

It's a battle of the seasons right now, for sure. We had a week of rain and now it's 103 outside. *Ugh, I'm ready for fall.*

Stepping inside, we're greeted by the attendant. "Welcome to Cozy Cabins; are you here to check in?"

"We are," Cam says.

"Name?"

"Butch Cameron Jr."

Sometimes I forget that his name is not actually Cam.

"Here we are. We have three cabins reserved for you. Are you the ones trailering those Jeeps?"

"We are." Cam looks a little questioning when he says that.

"We've had a lot of rain as of late. There have been warnings of some areas washing out and others being a little sketchy at best. So far, they haven't closed anything down and are just asking everyone to use caution while on the trails."

"Thank you for letting us know. We'll make sure we're careful."

I put my hand on Cam's arm to get his attention. "I'm going to slip away and get a cold drink and use the restroom. Be right back."

By the time I get back, Cam has secured the keys and is waiting for me by the exit. After handing out the keys, we all go our separate ways for the rest of the night. Tom leaves to check out the local bar, while Mark and Becca are in an argument, leaving Cam and I to have a quiet night.

The cabin is nice. It's a one-bedroom, one-bath with a kitchenette and a small living area. On the back porch is a Jacuzzi tub and some loungers. When dark hits, I tire of watching movies and go into our room, put on a bikini, and walk out to the living room.

Cam looks up at me from his reclined position on the couch, looking like a deer in headlights—open-mouthed and bug-eyed. "What's this for?" he asks, motioning to my bathing suit.

"You don't like it?" I tease. "I thought we could stargaze from the Jacuzzi tub out back. Want to join me?"

"Hell yeah, I do," he says, standing in a hurry. Off goes the shoes, then the shirt. When he starts hurriedly walking my way, I turn toward the door, but he catches me, tossing me over his shoulder.

"Cam, stop! Put me down, babe. You're going to make something fall out that shouldn't."

"I guess that's a good way to see if it fits properly, right?" he asks, swatting my backside. "Maybe you should have thought of that before you appeared in front of me nearly naked."

"You've seen me in a bikini before. What's wrong with it?"

"Not a dang thing. You're gorgeous. But if you remember last time, I could barely keep my hands off you. What makes you think now would be any different?" he asks. Cam sets me down on the bed instead of taking me outside. "Stay here. Give me five minutes and I'll come and get you. Can you do that for me?"

"Um, sure," I say in confusion. Sure enough, Cam is back in under five, wearing nothing but boxer briefs. He takes my hand. "Come with me, sweetheart." He leads me to the back of the cabin. Just as we get to the door, he has me cover my eyes, then guides me outside and stands with me on the porch. "Open your eyes now."

"Oh, Cam," I say in awe. Not only has this man started the hot tub, but he set out candles everywhere, along with red fabric rose petals on the ground. There is a radio in the back, playing soft rock. Next to the Jacuzzi is two flutes with what appears to be champagne and . . .

"Are those chocolate-covered strawberries?"

"Yes, they are."

Turning in his arms, I kiss him softly. "How did you pull this off? I know you didn't have the time or the stuff to do all of this."

"When you stepped away during check-in, I asked if they had a way of romancing our cabin. When he offered all of this, I took it. All I had to do was keep you busy long enough for them to set it up."

"Thank you, babe. I love it, and I love you."

He gives me a long kiss. "Now let's hop into that hot tub. It's calling my name."

Toeing into the tub is heavenly. It's almost too hot at first, but the scalding water hitting my sore muscles feels amazing.

Cam slips in behind me, pulling me to his chest. I lean back against him in awe. This is so romantic. I've never had this before, but now that I do, I never want to lose it.

When I see a shooting star, I point it out. "Make a wish."

"I don't need a star to make my wish come true. It already has."

I turn my head to look back at him. "What do you mean? There has to be something you want."

"I have you in my arms, in our home, and in my heart. What more could I want? I know my dreams are coming true. The day you take my name and we start growing our family, I'll have everything I have ever wanted."

Cam has a way of turning me into a blubbering mess. I can't help it as tears begin to fall.

He lifts me, turning me to straddle his lap before wiping my cheeks with his thumbs. "I hope these are happy tears, and not those of realization."

"Of course they're happy, Cam. You're my everything. Now that we're together, I can't picture life without you."

"That's good because I don't plan on ever leaving you. You're stuck with me, beautiful."

Cam and I barely gaze at any stars before we decide to turn in for the night. Having shared a moment like that, the stars are no longer as important as being wrapped in his arms.

The next morning, the others come over for breakfast, which Cam has delivered. Becca, needing to prove something to Mark, talks me into putting on my bikini—after a lot of begging on her part—just as she does. I want to talk about things, but she says sun therapy is in order first. As we step out of mine and Cam's room, Tom notices first, before the others turn to take us in.

As we walk by the guys, I run my fingers across Cam's chest. "Will you come lotion my back?"

"Damn straight, I will," he growls. "You know I can't keep my hands off you when you wear that." Cam turns to grab a towel and my sunscreen while Becca and I head toward the beach.

Tom runs behind to catch up. "Hey, ladies, I know you need a moment, but I don't feel like I should let y'all wander off alone. I'll stand back, but I need to stay close just in case."

"Thanks, Tom," I reply.

Becca grabs my arm, pulling me off with her until we find a spot she approves of on the sandiest part. "Did you see the way Mark was looking at me? It's like he wants to hide me away. We used to go out and *do* stuff all the time." She shakes her head. "It's almost as if he's scared that I'm going to fly off the handle at any moment. I'm surprised he let me around you. Leah, how am I going to get him to listen to me? I love that big dummy more than anything and want to make our family grow, but he's so worried that I can't handle it," she says before she turns, crying on my shoulder.

"I can't really help you if I don't know the situation. If you want to clue me in to what's going on, I'll do my best."

Becca dries her eyes just in time for Cam to step up and lay out our towels for us. We get comfortable on them, keeping quiet for the moment. As Cam begins applying my sunscreen, I take her hand in mine after I see her wipe at a stray tear.

Mark's shadow looms over us. I look up to see him looking like a scolded child. "Becca, can I put sunscreen on you so you don't burn? You know how red you can get near the water if you don't."

"Sure, but leave me alone after, please. I need some time without you breathing down my neck." She looks over at me and shyly smiles at Cam. "I'm sorry to steal your girl from you, but I promise no mischief. Just relaxation and maybe a swim."

"I don't mind. It sounds like you need her right now. I'll be with the guys enjoying my view."

I swat his chest playfully. "*Cam*."

"What? There's a lot to look at around here." He winks at me. "You ladies enjoy your time."

Cam and Mark stand and walk away, Mark's head hung low. These two have been couple goals since the moment I met them. I don't understand what's going on, but I need to get to the bottom of it because if they can't fix it, how can I have hope that we'll stand a chance at the long haul?

Becca and I have this whole side of the beach to ourselves. That's a rare thing but seeing that school's back in session and it's still kind of early for many, it happens. The guys are across the way, throwing the football back and forth. I'm sure they're checking in with Mark. It's my chance to get Becca talking.

"Care to tell me what's going on?" I ask.

She nods. "It's over me wanting to have a baby and him not wanting to chance it. Instead of him talking to me, he's been shutting me out."

"I didn't know you even wanted another. Mark doesn't?"

"I guess for you to understand, I should tell you everything." She sits up and looks out at the water. "Did I ever tell you that I'm a twin?"

"I don't think so," I admit.

"Well, I am. My sister, Rachel—Chelle—and I were best friends. Growing up, we were the spark in our parents' eyes. Walking into their place was like walking into a shrine. They put us on a pedestal nobody could compete with. Now that I'm a mom, I can understand, but still, they took it too far. They had to do IVF to get pregnant, so when they had us, the camera was a permanent fixture in our faces. Looking good was a must; acting anything less than perfect was frowned upon."

She takes a quick drink of the water Cam gave us and takes a deep breath. "The older Chelle and I got, the more we rebelled. When I met Mark, I calmed down a bit. I was fifteen and he barely saw me. I wanted to be someone he noticed. Anyway, Chelle didn't want to calm down. She wanted Mom and Dad to notice her, not as the perfect kid she had to portray but as her true self. She started acting out more than normal." Becca shakes her head and wipes her eyes. "When she got with Johnny, she was out of hand. She got black-out drunk at a party and let him touch her. She didn't even remember it the next day. Only that she knew she felt different."

Unable to take it any longer, she stands and begins pacing. I sit up and give her all my attention.

"Chelle wound up pregnant. When Mom found out, she saw us, alright. She was so mad." Becca shakes her head at the thought. "She didn't hit us, but it might have hurt less if she had. That night, we decided it was enough. We packed our bags, and after our parents were asleep, we snuck out."

I start to reach out my hand to offer her some comfort,

but she shakes her head no.

"We went to a school party with Johnny. Chelle hung out with him while I went to find Mark. I should have known better. I should have been by her side." She stops pacing and hugs her arms around her midsection. "She told him that night that she was pregnant and that the baby was his. What I didn't expect was for him, in front of so many people, to become so violent. He beat her, Leah. He hit her until someone pulled him off her. When she fell to the ground, she hit her head on the curb."

I wipe away the tears streaming down my cheek as I try to focus on what she's saying.

"I tried to get to her, but there were so many people in the way. Finally, Mark helped me reach her." Releasing a sob, she sits, putting her face in her hands.

I move in, cradling her to me, giving her as much comfort as I can.

"It was too late. She was alone and scared when she took her last breath." She shudders. "I should have been there. I should have been at her side."

"It's not your fault, honey." My heart breaks for her right now. I couldn't even imagine losing Kayla in that way.

"I know that now, but I didn't then. Mom and Dad made sure that I felt guilty. After a few years of therapy and pushing Mark away, I can honestly say that I know that I'm not the cause. But you know, trauma like that plays a factor in your mental health. It also increases your risk for postpartum. Mine was so bad with Aubrey that I almost took my own life."

"Oh, Becca," I cry.

"I've been seeing a counselor ever since. She said that she'd work with my OB during my pregnancy if we decide to

try again. Mark knows this and he still won't even consider it. I love him, I really do, but I don't know if I can
keep doing this. He won't even talk to me like a
normal human being. He'd rather shut me out every time
I try and talk about it. If he would just hear me out and
then conclude that it's not for us, as much as I hate it, I
could deal. But he won't even do that, and I can't handle
it anymore."

"I can see why you're upset. Do you think he'll go to
therapy with you so you can speak in a place where you can
be heard? Is that even something that you're willing to do?"

"Yeah, I am. I don't know if he'll go for it, but I can ask."
I look over at the guys and see them all standing there,
looking over at us. I can only imagine how much Mark
wants to be here for Becca right now, but his actions
are what hurt her. I feel for these two. I just hope that
they can talk this out and move forward in a way that's
best for them both.

The day flies by with us working on our tans, girl talk, and
even swimming. The water won't be warm much longer.
Now that we're nearing the end of September, we better
enjoy it while we can.

That evening, we go our separate ways for dinner so Mark
and Becca can work on their issues. Tom goes back to the
bar to shoot some pool and have a beer with a local officer
he met there the night before.

A couple hours later, I get a text.

Becca: *Things are better. Thank you for talking to me. It helped a lot. Mark heard me out and said we'll talk to my therapist together.*

Me: *I'm happy for you guys. See you in the morning.*

Becca: *How about we hit the trail tomorrow? I can have the front desk bring us some food for a picnic. It's supposed to be nice out.*

Me: *Sure! I know Cam wants to take me on a date the night before we leave, so tomorrow sounds good to me. I'll let him know.*

Becca: *Sounds good. See you guys in the morning.*

I walk into the bathroom where Cam is showering. "Hey, babe? Becca and Mark are back on track. She's going to arrange a trail ride and picnic in the morning. Hope that's cool."

"Yeah, that's good. I'm glad they worked it out. Thank you for being there for Becca."

"Of course I'm going to help if I can. I like her. She's like an adopted sister."

Cam's phone goes off. "Can you get that, sweetheart?"

"Sure." I reach down into his discarded jeans pocket and get his phone. I put it on speaker. "Hello?"

"Is this Butch Cameron?"

Who on earth would be calling and asking for Butch Cameron rather than Cam?

"No, this is Leah, but he's right here. Do you need him?"

"No, you're the other one he said to call if his brother didn't answer."

"Who said to call us?"

"Tom Cameron. He said to call you and ask you guys to come and get him."

Cam turns off the shower, pulling back the thick curtain and putting a towel around his waist, then steps out.

"Why? Is he okay?" I ask.

"He's a little banged up is all. He stepped in when the whole thing went to hell. There was a bar fight, and my daughter—the bar's waitress—got caught in the middle. He got her out without so much as a scratch. Tom took a few blows to the head and a kick to the ribs. I brought him to the emergency room to have him checked out. The doc said he'll be sore for a bit but is clear to go home."

"Okay, thank you. We're on our way. Can you text me the address?" I ask.

"Sure," he says as he hangs up.

"Always the hero," Cam says.

"Let's go get him. I'm just glad he's safe."

Getting to the local hospital doesn't take us much time at all. When we see Tom, I'm irked.

Cam leans down to my ear. "He's fine, sweetheart. You good?"

"I'm fine. I just don't like seeing people I care for hurt. Look at him, Cam. He has blood and bruises all over him."

"I like knowing you care for my family, but he's seen worse. I promise he'll be fine."

"I know, and if he were at work, I would have been fine. Being on vacation, I didn't expect this. Let's get him back so he can rest. I'm just glad it wasn't you. I don't know how I would've reacted."

"I love you too," Cam says, winking at me.

"Hey, guys," Tom says, sounding as if he's on something. Pain pills, if I had to guess. "I'm so glad you could come." He puts his arm around my shoulder, leaning on me a little more than normal, causing me to stumble.

"I assume you're Cam and Leah?" A man walks up, shaking our hands. "I'm the one that called. He's a little out of it. The doc gave him some painkillers and said he'll need to be watched tonight, but otherwise, he's in good shape considering."

"The girls like a shiner," Tom slurs, poking me in the cheek. "Don't they, sis?"

Cam looks over at Tom, notices me struggling under his weight, and takes him off my hands. "They do. Just not my girl. She was worried about you, man." Cam looks back at the gentleman who's now standing with a lady a little younger than me. "Thanks for calling. Do you by chance have his keys?"

The man tosses them over. "No problem. Make sure to thank him for me when he's a little more with it, will ya? He really saved my girl. I'll forever be grateful."

"Alright then," I say. "Let's get you back to the cabin. You're sleeping on the couch so I can keep an eye on you."

"Awe," Tom says. "I knew you loved me."

Cam looks over at me, chuckling as he attempts to walk Tom out of the hospital. I'm glad that he's going to be fine. I hope I can get used to the guys getting banged up. Cam acted like this is a normal occurrence, and considering their jobs, I guess it might be.

Chapter Eighteen

The next day, we're loading up the basket of food that was sent down from the main cabin when Becca and Mark join us. After one look at Tom, Becca is all questions and concern. Mark drapes an arm around her shoulder, pulling her back from her perusal.

"What happened to you?" he asks.

"I got caught in the middle of a bar fight," Tom states.

"Bro! What did you say?"

"Seriously?" Tom questions. "I didn't do anything other than save the waitress that almost got taken out."

I nudge Cam in the ribs. He walks that way, putting a hand on Mark's shoulders. "Let's hit the trail, shall we? It's supposed to be nice out today. I want to take advantage while we can." Cam turns to look at Tom. "You good on your own, or do you want to ride with us?"

"Nah, man. I'm good. Thanks, though."

Every so often along the trail, we stop and take photos. This is more of a joyride than a thrill ride for us. With everything going on lately, we'd much rather take some time and enjoy the calm. After taking some pictures at our third stop, we all head back toward our Jeeps.

"You guys about ready for lunch? Becca said she's starved and wants to stop soon," Mark says before getting back in his Jeep.

"Sure, let's find an overlook and stop there. Maybe some tables or restrooms for the girls. What do you say, sweetheart?" Cam asks.

"Let's do it."

"Alright, let's go then. I'll pull over as soon as I spot somewhere that looks decent."

We travel another ten minutes before we come across a rock overhang that looks over the lake. Back off the trail is some parking, a few tables, and a cabin with showers and restrooms. I guess this place is as good as any.

"This look good to you, babe?" Cam asks.

"Sure, it's beautiful. I bet we can get a good picture of us looking over the water for the living room."

Cam parks and helps me out of my harness. Climbing out, Becca finds me, grabs my hand, and pulls me off to the restroom with her. When we come back out, the guys have the picnic ready. We share some decent food and many laughs. After lunch is over, Cam grabs my hand, walking me to the rock overhang.

"This is one of the nicest places I've been in a long time," he says. Cam steps behind me, wrapping himself around me. We turn so our back is to the water and take a picture that I just know will be my favorite so far.

"I love it here; I can't believe how peaceful it is." I came once as a child, but seeing it now, with Cam at my side, it's much better.

"I don't think I've ever seen you so happy. I'm thrilled I get to share this with you."

"You get to share life with me. I hope you're ready for forever," I say. I turn in his arms, lock my fingers around the back of his neck, and lean in for a kiss.

Beneath our feet, the earth begins to shift.

Cam twists me around and tosses me hard. I hit the ground with a thump and a roll. As I look in his direction, I see the ground beneath him crumble, taking him down with it.

"Oh my God, *no! Help!*"

I crawl closer to the edge, desperate to find out if Cam is okay, if he's alive. Desperate for someone to help, I look over my shoulder and see the others running my way.

"*Help!* Cam is down there. I can't lose him. Please help!" I yell.

I crawl closer to the drop-off, but Tom yells for me to get back. "You can't fall too!"

I can't, though. He needs me.

"I need to help him, Tom." I cry. "*Cam!* You have to be okay. *Please* be alright."

I'm about to turn and free-climb my way down when Tom stops me with a hand on my shoulder. "No way in hell, Leah. Cam would kill me. I have gear in my Jeep." He turns to yell out to Mark. "Grab my emergency tote!" Then back to me. "Mark and I are trained in emergency situations. Go get in the glove box of your Jeep. Cam has a sat phone in there—call this in. The sooner you do it, the quicker help will get here."

Even though I don't want to, I push back from the edge and stand, wobbling a little. "He has to be good, Tom. I can't lose him!"

Breathing is getting harder by the moment.

Grabbing my shoulders, Tom shakes me enough to get my attention. "Leah, you need to be strong. Pull yourself together and help me save him. Mark is getting our gear—now get over there and call it in. That's my brother down there. Do you think I'm going to let anything happen if I can help it?"

Taking in the deepest breath I can manage, I try to find my strength. Even though I'm terrified, I have to do this.

I nod and run off to Cam's Jeep. I call in the accident on his satellite phone. The dispatcher assures me that help is on the way. I run back to the cliffside just as Tom is being lowered.

"Leah!" Mark says with enough force to let me know that he's called my name more than once. "Tom needs help securing Cam. Becca is a wreck. I need to work the pully. Are you good to go down there?"

I was ready to go down there for him without so much as a harness on me. Of course I'll go. I'm scared senseless, but I need to know that he's good.

Nodding, I can't seem to say the words.

"I need to hear you, Leah. I need to know that you can pull it together and not freak out when you see him. You could make it so much worse if you can't."

"I can do this. Cam needs me."

"That's what I thought. Good girl. Let's get you harnessed up." He looks down over the side to where Tom must be with Cam. "I'm going to send Leah over," he yells. "I'm bringing the rope back up."

"Have her take a few deep breaths! Cam's hurt bad," I hear Tom holler up.

The tears come with such force that I can't stop them.

"You good?" Mark asks.

"I'm fine," I say, sucking in a breath. "I can do this."

No matter how much I want to crumble, I can't . . . I won't.

Mark connects a harness to me before hooking me up to the rope. He goes over how I need to hold it and even how to slow myself from going too fast if I need to. When I take my first step over the side, I take in my surroundings. Cam is lucky he landed where he did. There are two landings that he could have hit. Directly attached to the side of the ravine is a small one—maybe big enough for him to sit on—and the other about ten feet or so from the side of the wall. This one is where he lies, with Tom on one side and enough room for me to stand or crouch on the other. Other than these, there is a direct fall to the water and or rocks below. This could have been a search of a different kind if he had fallen just three feet in either direction.

By the time my feet touch down on the ledge Cam and Tom are on, I notice that there's not as much room as I initially thought. One wrong move and we'll all tumble over.

"His arm is in horrible shape. He's going to be in surgery for a long time with this," Tom says. He pulls out a tarp with handles on all sides and a rope with a connecting harness on one end, branching out in many directions like a spider's legs, to connect to the grips. He joins them as needed on one side before laying it down next to Cam on the side with his good arm.

He shakes his head, almost as if switching from brother mode into cop mode. "I'll have to roll him to get it out from under him to sling it. I'm glad he's out of it for this, but if he comes to, he needs to see you. I need you to talk calmly to him and give him soft touches while I work."

I nod, and we both get into position.

"On three."

When Cam is rolled my way, I place my hand on his cheek. Though he's out of it, his brow is furrowed as if he's in pain. "Cam, baby, you're going to be fine. Tom and I are both here. We got you. We're getting you the help you need." I run a hand through his hair and kiss his forehead. "I love you. You're so strong. Hang in there for me. Keep on fight—"

"Done," Tom says. Looking up above us, he hollers out, "Mark, pull him up. Nice and easy."

As Cam is being hoisted up, we stand watch in silence. After he reaches the top and is pulled over the edge, Tom turns to face me, swatting me on the arm.

"You scared the hell out of me. What were you thinking trying to climb over the edge like that? I could've lost not one, but two siblings today. Do you know what that does to someone? Huh?"

I know Tom's mad and emotions are running rampant, but did he seriously ask me that?

"What was I thinking?" I ask, flabbergasted. "I was thinking that the love of my life was down here, alone and hurt, if not worse. You were hurt already, and Mark has Becca to think of. I have Cam. If these were his last moments, I'd be damned if I wasn't with Cam to tell him that I love him," I say. I wipe frustrated tears from my cheeks in a huff.

Tom pulls me in for a big hug that nearly cracks a rib. "Don't you ever do something like that again. You hear me?"

"I'm sorry I scared you," I sigh.

The rope drops, breaking us from our talk.

Mark looks over the edge. "Cam's secure in my Jeep. The

ambulance still isn't here, so Becca and I are taking him to the closest ER. I'll text you when we get there."

"Is there someone up there to run the pully to get Leah and me up?" Tom asks.

"Yeah. An EMT came along the trail with his friends in his personal vehicle. They helped me get Cam strapped in. They're going to get y'all up."

"Drive easily and make sure he gets there quickly. We'll be right behind you."

Mark disappears from above, then Tom starts strapping me in. "I hope you know that even though you scared the hell out of us, you also showed me how much Cam means to you today. He's lucky to have you."

"I'm the lucky one," I say in return.

He nods. "I hope you're ready for Becca. She's a wreck. She damn near pushed me over when she thought you would climb down."

Thankful that Tom's back to his playful ways, I'm able to step out of the now.

"Awe, poor guy," I tease.

He pouts. "I got knocked down another spot on Becca's list of important people. It hurts, ya know."

"You're just a big ole teddy bear under all that muscle, aren't you?" I ask, motioning up and down with my hand.

"Hush your mouth. My teddy side is a well-kept secret," he teases. Tom tightens the harness so we're both secure. "Tell anyone and I'll have to kill ya. Now, let's move. I've got some nurses to check out. You're slowing me down,. Go on, I'll be right behind you."

Once we're up top, we get in the Jeeps and head back to the cabin as quickly as possible before climbing into

Tom's truck and heading out. The drive to the hospital seems to take forever, and when we pull up outside, I'm a nervous wreck.

"Do you think they'll even let me see him? It's not like I'm family," I say, biting my lip.

"Most have policies about it, but are pretty relaxed in most circumstances. I'm sure they'll understand. You're his live-in girlfriend, after all. There has to be exceptions."

I hope he's right. I walk ahead of him and right up to the welcome station.

The older woman behind the desk turns toward me, smiling. "Can I help you, miss?" she asks.

"Yes, ma'am," I say with a polite smile. "Can you point me in the direction of Butch Cameron Jr., please? He was brought in maybe an hour ago and would've needed to be taken to surgery."

"May I ask who you are to the patient?" she asks while tapping away at her keyboard.

"I'm his girlfriend, Leah Covington."

"I'm sorry, ma'am, but hospital policy prohibits me from letting you go back there without permission from the patient. There is a waiting room around the corner. The couple who brought him in was headed that way. When he's out of surgery, I can let him know that you're here. If he expresses that he wants you back there, I'd be happy to personally walk you back."

"He'll want me there with him when he comes out," I beg.

"I'm sure he will, and I'll be happy to come and get you as soon as I have permission." She smiles sweetly. "I'm sorry, hun, it's policy. I wish I could help you."

"She's my brother Butch's live-in girlfriend. He'll very much want to see her the moment he comes to. Are you sure she can't go back now?" Tom asks.

"I'll page the nurse in charge of him right now and see if she'll allow it. I'm sorry, there's nothing else I can do. Since you're his brother, if you'd like, you can go back until she gets the okay to go."

"Go, Tom," I say. "You should be with him. I don't want him to wake up alone. I'll go sit with Becca. Text me as much as you can with updates."

Tom pulls me into a tight hug when he sees the tears gather in my eyes. All I want to do is tell her to shove her dang rules where the sun doesn't shine, but that won't help get me to Cam any sooner. Besides, I understand that rules are rules. She's just doing her job. I can't fault her for that.

"I'll let you know when I hear from his charge nurse. I really am sorry, Ms. Covington."

"Thank you."

As soon as I walk into the waiting room with Tom, I'm immediately pulled into two sets of arms.

Mark pulls back from the hug. "What are you doing out here?"

"They wouldn't let her back there because of hospital policy," Tom snarls.

"That sucks. How about we stay here with Leah, and you go back and check on him?" Mark replies.

Tom shakes his head. "He's in surgery, so it may be a while. I'll check in soon. Besides, they know where we're at if they need us."

Becca pulls my attention from the guys. "There's a bathroom here in the waiting room. Why don't we go in there and get you cleaned up? You two," she says, pointing to the guys, "go to the gift shop and see if you can find her something to wear."

She's right, I'm a mess. This morning's jean shorts, pink tank, and Ariat boots are caked in dirt.

"Sure," Mark says.

"Be back soon," Tom adds. "Be listening in case they come in looking for us."

"Will do," Becca says as she ushers me into the family bathroom, locking the door behind us. "Strip down. I had my gym bag in the truck, so I have some stuff in here. Just no clothes. You can use the sink to clean up and I'll keep an eye out."

Taking the bag from her, I walk to the sink and dig out some shampoo, body wash, aerosol deodorant, and mouthwash. I find a clean hand towel and lip tint. Getting busy, I take a trucker's shower in the sink. Not the best job of being clean, but it'll do.

When a knock comes on the other side of the door, Becca cracks it open and hands me a bag from the guys. Inside is a yellow sundress, flip-flops, and a light blue scarf. Looking through Becca's bag again, I find a comb and a scrunchie. I throw the clothes on and my hair up, feeling somewhat human again.

I peek out of the door. "Thank you, Becca. I feel a lot better."

She pulls me in for a quick hug. "No problem. You'd do the same for me."

Tom walks into the waiting room holding a white bag with blue writing on it. "This is Cam's stuff. They said that he's still in surgery. He did wake briefly after he got here. The nurse I spoke to said that he was asking for you. She said as soon as she gets a free moment, she'll come and get you or send someone else."

"Oh good." It feels like I can breathe again. "Did they say how he's doing?"

"No. She said that his arm appeared to be the worst part of his injuries, though. They'll go over everything after he's out and his doctor comes for a visit. I'm going to step out and call Mom real quick."

After he leaves the room, I find a seat in the corner and lean back into it, resting my head against the back wall. This is a lot to take in right now.

Tom walks back in and takes a seat next to me.

"How'd it go with your parents?"

"Mom wanted to get in the car right away and race up here. Since they're several hours away and they have the kids right now, Dad talked her into waiting. They plan on calling you or Cam a lot, she said. How are you holding up?"

"Better now that I know that he woke up asking for me. How about you?"

"Now that I know that he'll be okay, I'm good. I wasn't, when it went down. I think it's all the training that kept me going. I'm more worried about you than anything."

"You're a good brother, Tom," I say as I lean on his shoulder, settling in.

He really is. Tom and I might not be related, but he is very much the brother I always wished I had. The way he cares for me, his brother's girlfriend, I can only imagine the kind of man he'll be when the time comes for him to settle down. These Cameron men are a force to be reckoned with.

Chapter Nineteen

I push the green bean around on my plate as I sit in the hospital's cafeteria, thinking of all the changes over the last week since Cam's fall. His initial surgery went well. The doctor wanted to keep him for a few days due to a concussion. In that time, they had to do a second surgery to fix a pin that didn't set properly. There were multiple breaks in his arm as if he'd put it out to break his fall. Dr. Harland said at the rate he was falling, it makes sense that his arm was in such bad shape. She did the best she could, considering. At times, the pain meds haven't been enough to dull the pain, causing Cam to be unbearable—so much so that he yelled at me for the first time ever. It hurt, but Tom stepped in, reminding me that it's the pain talking, not Cam. He sent me down for coffee while he stayed with Cam to give me a break. By the time I got back, things were better than they were before. It's now been ten days since we got to Disney, and I'm crawling out of my skin to go home. I haven't left the hospital since the moment I walked in after the accident.

"Are you Ms. Covington?" an orderly asks. He's

standing at the side of my table, looking down at me.

"I am. Can I help you?"

"Sorry to interrupt you, but I was sent down to get you. I guess you left your phone in the room. Your family is looking for you."

I didn't leave my phone by accident. I needed a me moment and not taking it with me was supposed to ensure that I got it. "Thank you." I stand and take my tray to the dish window before heading out toward the elevator.

Last weekend, Kayla and I decided to sell the apartment. Tom called Ella, his friend, to set things up for me. Kayla let her in to look it over since I couldn't. I spoke with her to confirm that I indeed wanted the sale, then e-signed some paperwork she sent over for it to get started. From what I heard, she might know of a potential buyer—one of her clients has been looking in the area—so I guess we'll see how that goes.

Reaching the elevator, I press the up button and wait for one of the doors to open for me. Once it does, I step into the empty lift and press four, bracing myself on the far wall while it takes me to my level.

Cap relegated Tom to desk duty, allowing him to stay with us while working from his hotel room. The cabin was booked up, so he had to swap locations, finding a hotel just down the block. Mark and Becca headed back the morning after, as scheduled, taking Cam's truck with them.

When the door opens on my level, I exit and walk down to his room right across from the nurse's station. Room 417 has become our home away from home. I wave at Nurse Kelly as I pass, grateful she's the one on Cam duty today. She's been so helpful; not only does she care for him, but she is always offering me warm blankets and drinks.

Cam's supposed to be released tomorrow if all goes well with the doc today. I'm looking forward to getting back home and back to work. Mike's been covering for me the whole time. I owe him so much.

I push the door open and find Cam sitting up in bed talking to Tom with a big smile on his face. They stop whatever they're doing when they see me walk in. "There you are," Cam says. "I was worried when I no-ticed that you didn't take your phone."

"I'm in a hospital full of people. I'm safe here. I just needed some me time." I walk to his side and lean in to give him a kiss. "Did you need something?"

"No. I was just concerned. Your phone has been blowing up."

Frustrated that he'd send someone down to get me just because I didn't have my phone with me, I sidestep his attempt to grab my hand and walk to get my phone.

"Babe," he says.

"It's fine, Cam. I'm just going to see what everyone wants."

Tom starts talking to Cam, giving me a moment to breathe. I love him, I really do, but things have been so strained this last week. I know emotions are running wild with the fall, all the calls, the pain, and such, so instead of talking, I push it down and try to keep myself cool.

I grab my phone and see a scroll of missed texts and calls. "I'm going to the waiting room to return these calls and texts. If you need me, I'll have my phone."

"You want to play UNO when you come back?" Tom asks. "I stopped at the dollar store on the way in. I know we're all bored. We need something to do with our time."

"Sure, I'll be back in a few." I walk to the door and then straight down to the family waiting room near the elevators. I pull out my phone and start sending replies, but it rings before I can. Seeing that it's Marie—Cam's mom—I answer right away.

"Hello?"

"Hey, honey, it's Mom. How are you guys doing?" Since the accident, she and Butch have asked me to call them Mom and Dad. At first, I didn't think I could ever call another woman "Mom." I've never called anyone other than my own mother that. With her being gone, it never felt right to call another by that title, but after talking to Kayla, I realized that our mom would have wanted me to be happy, and if Cam really is my forever, then Marie is another mom to me.

"Hey, Mom. We're good. Cam's restless, but they're letting him leave tomorrow, so he'll be fine. How are things around there?"

"All's good. I'm fixing to go check on your house again. Do you need me to stop and get you guys anything before you come home?"

"Let me ask Cam. I'm not sure what all he asked Mark to do. I'll have to call you back on that."

"Sounds good. Shoot . . . Hey, Leah, let me call you back. The alarm's going off at the house again," she says just before hanging up.

Whose house? I hope not ours, but then again, I hope not theirs either. I guess I'll find out later. I take a minute to check my texts and socials and give her time to call me back.

I pull up Jazz's text thread and shoot her a quick message.

Me: *Hey, I was on the phone with Marie, and she said the alarm was going off again. Would you mind swinging by on your way home just in case?*

Jazz: *Do you know whose house?*

Me: *No. That's all she told me before she hung up.*

Jazz: *I'll swing by after I finish up here.*

Me: *Thanks.*

Jazz: *No problem.*

Since I'm here to check in with everyone, I switch over and check my family group chat.

Uncle Joe: *How's it going?*

Me: *Going well. Cam's in with Tom so I'm bored.*

Uncle Joe: *Glad things are improving.*

Kayla: *Same.*

Me: *So how was New York? Sorry I haven't asked before now.*

Kayla: *You've been busy, that's understandable. It was nice but the people and the overcrowding is going to take some time to get used to. Did you know that Walmart around there is a rare thing?*

Me: *Really! That's crazy. Yeah, I heard that it kind of grows on you though.*

Kayla: *Right. I hope so.*

Mike: *You should have seen her when we finally found a Walmart. It's two stories, she went nuts. I got a few pictures. I'll show you when you get home.*

When the door of the waiting room opens and another family walks in, I'm pulled from our conversation. Looking at the clock on the wall, I try to finish up so I can get back to Cam.

Me: *Awesome. Though a two-story Walmart sounds fun to me too and I don't even like to shop that much. Talk soon. Love you all.*

Uncle Joe: *Love you all.*

Mike: *Love you.*

Kayla: *Love you too.*

I'm just about to get up when I get a text.

Ella: *Ms. Covington, this is Ella with Global Realty. I wanted to make sure that it's ok with you that I show the apartment this week. I have two buyers who have shown interest in your listing, and I'd like to show them it ASAP.*

Me: *Please do. I can have Kayla get you a key if she hasn't already.*

Ella: *No need, she gave me one when we met last. I just wanted to confirm.*

Me: *By all means. Thank you.*

Ella: *I'll be in touch.*

Two people interested in my place so soon after listing? That's awesome. I mean if it's something I want, in this market I had better act fast. This is a little nerve-wracking, but I know I want it. No matter how much Cam has been on my nerves lately, I still want to build a life with him. I pocket my phone and head back to his room.

When I walk in, I find Tom and Cam amid a muted conversation, again.

"What's up with you two?" I ask.

"Just talking about barbeque details. I figured I could text Becca with a list of things to get done. It might be helpful if we all pitch in," Tom says.

"We're having a barbeque?"

"We were supposed to have one for Cam's birthday when we all got back. Since the fall, it's been put off, but now that he's being released, we can plan it again," Tom states.

"Sounds good," I say, getting cut off when my phone rings. As soon as I see that it's Marie, I put her on speaker as I reach the guys. "Hello, you're on speaker. The guys are here with me."

"Hey boys, Dad asked me to call you and let you know that the alarm at Cam and Leah's went off. Dad, Mark, and Jazz are over there now checking things out."

Cam sits up in bed, throwing his legs over the side. I put my hand on his shoulder, standing next to him. "Did you go in and look? Does it look like anything is out of place?"

"I got there before Dad but only made it to the porch by the time he stopped me. It smelled like cigarettes and the door was open, so he didn't want me going in. I tried to look, but he told me to go home and call you right away. They were going in as I was leaving."

Since Marie is the only Cameron that isn't an officer, fireman, or EMT, they tend to protect her more than the others.

"Crap," Cam says. "Thanks, Mom. Tell Dad to call me when he can, please."

"Will do," she replies.

"Thanks, keep us posted," I say as I hang up.

Tom grabs his phone as it chimes, then holds it up to look before turning it to Cam. His flared nostrils and deep intake of air are not good signs.

"What is it?" I ask.

Tom turns his phone to face me.

Mark: *Standing in Cam and Leah's dining room. Not good, man. Leah's stalker has just upped his game.*

The attached image is of a torn notebook piece of paper with writing scrawled across it.

You're mine! You tried to hide but you didn't try hard enough. I'm tired of these games, Leah. The longer we play, the harder this will be on you. Why do you make me

I have a moment of panic before my fight kicks in. "I'm done hiding, I'm done being scared. This is my family too and I'll protect them at all costs," I say through clenched teeth.

"What do you mean you're done hiding?" Cam growls. "I'm not just putting you out there as a sacrifice, Leah. No way in hell. I'm not okay with that."

He might not be good with it, but if the fight comes knocking, I'll sacrifice myself before I let him.

"I'm not about to put myself out there, but I do think that I need to be ready for a fight in case he ever gets to me. I know how to defend myself, but I want to know more. I'm going to ask Mike to train me hard, and I'd like it if you guys would teach me how to shoot."

Cam looks like he's taking in what I said. I look to Tom, who is also gauging Cam for a reaction.

"I agree that you need to train just in case, but I don't want you taking risky moves. If we do this, I want you to continue only leaving the property when someone is with you. Can you do that?" Cam states.

"Yes, but I still have to work, Cam. I don't want to have to fight, but this guy is bound to either catch me or be caught. I want to be ready to fight if I must."

After some back-and-forth, Cam says that we'll talk to Mike when we see him next. He thinks it'll go over easier if Mike can see with his own eyes that I'm determined to protect myself.

"Now, can we talk about upgrading the security and putting up cameras on the property? I'm ready to catch this guy," I state.

"I can talk to everyone about updating the system. I think cameras are a good idea though. I don't see that being an issue," Cam adds.

"I'd like to pay for the update to ours," I say. "Before you argue, you need to see my side. The house has been yours for so long and now you want to share that with me. I have nothing invested in it. I want to feel like I've helped in some way, like it's my home too. Let me contribute. And I'd appreciate it if you all would let me buy the cameras for the property too. I know that's a stretch, but I want to feel like I belong and am not just an afterthought."

"I think that's reasonable," Tom says. "I'll upgrade my security, but I understand if you want to buy the cams. I'm sure everyone will."

Thank God at least one Cameron is in. That means I stand a chance.

"I'd normally say no," Cam interrupts, "but you're right. I'm fine with it. Since Mark and Jazz are helping, you should text Mark and ask him to pick them up."

"Thanks, babe, I will."

I pull out my phone before I forget and shoot him a text.

Me: *Hey Mark. Cam, Tom, and I are talking about updating the security around the property. If I buy some cameras, can you pick them up and get them installed throughout?*

Mark: *Sure thing, that's actually a good idea. Now that we know he can get in here, installing cameras might help us catch him.*

Me: *Right, that's what we were thinking. Thanks, I'll send you the details as soon as I get them.*

Mark: *Tell the guys I say hey.*

Me: *Will do.*

I pocket my phone, look at the guys, then grab the UNO cards. "Mark's on it. Now, let's play." Knowing that I have people in my corner no matter the cost helps me move forward. I'm not in this alone, and that means the world to me.

Chapter Twenty

Pulling onto the Cameron's farm is almost surreal. I've missed it something fierce. It sure is nice to be home.

Home.

That's going to take some time getting used to.

Once parked, we head inside, where we're met by Butch and Marie, followed by Mark and Becca as they enter from the side door off the kitchen. There is hugs all around, and some back-and-forth about the break-in.

Cam starts yawning.

"We won't stay—we just had to see y'all with our own eyes," Butch says as he tries to usher everyone out. "We'll visit after you have a nice rest."

I hate that everyone plans to run off so fast, but Cam should get some sleep, so I don't argue. That trip was a long one. I'd kind of like a nap myself.

Marie stops next to me, putting her hand on my shoulder. "There's several heat-and-eat casseroles in the freezer. Some quick lunches and pan ready breakfast scrambles in the fridge. His meds are on the counter. If you guys need anything, Leah—I mean *anything*—call me."

"Will do. Thank you for everything," I reply. I love how they all pull together in a time of need. I feel so loved.

"No need to thank me. That's what families are for. See you both this weekend," Marie says. She pulls me in for a hug before she walks over to Cam.

"I got the cameras," Mark states from beside me. "Jazz and I will put them up this evening after her shift. I'll get with you after. You two rest up. We have a busy weekend ahead of us, so we won't bug you between now and then unless it's needed. Glad y'all are home."

After a few more goodbyes, everyone clears out.

"Would you like to head upstairs and nap, or I can set you up down here if you'd rather?" I'm so tired but I also wouldn't mind just lounging.

"Honestly, babe, I'm tired of lying around. Can we just cuddle up on the couch and watch a movie or something?"

"Sure, sounds good to me. Let me get something set out for dinner and then I'll join you." I help Cam get situated on the couch, then head to the kitchen.

When I walk in, I see a bouquet of white roses and sunflowers sitting on the counter. They're gorgeous. Whether these are for Cam or me, I don't care—I love them. I grab the little card at the bottom, my hand going to my mouth and tears beginning to fall as I read.

To my sweetheart, my angel. You make me want to be a better man. I want to be the one to walk through life beside you, holding your hand. Thank you for being there for me during one of the hardest times in my life. I'm sorry I've been so cranky, I'll do better. You have shown me what true love is. This is my promise. I will love you today, tomorrow, and always.

— Forever yours, Cam.

Wiping the tears from my eyes, I move to smell the flowers. Cam has no clue how much they mean to me.

"I'm glad they came on time," Cam says, walking up behind me. "I doubted they'd make it before we did."

"How did you know? Did you talk to Kayla or Uncle Joe?" I ask through tears.

"Know what? I haven't spoken to either of them in a while."

If he hasn't heard from my family, this is one heck of a coincidence.

"Cam, these flowers . . ." I point to them. "They meant a lot to my parents. The first flower my dad ever gave mom was a white rose—not red, like so many guys give. I remember she had it dried and pressed in their wedding album. My mom used to keep white roses on our dining room table when I was little because they made her happy. One time, she put a sunflower in the mix. When I asked her why, she told me, 'Because baby doll, your daddy grew up across the way from a sunflower field. He used to run and play in them with his friends. It reminds him of the good times, just like white roses do for me.' For their wedding, Mom carried a bouquet of white roses and sunflowers." I try to dry my eyes, but since I'm fighting a losing battle, I give up. "These mean more to me than you can imagine. Thank you." I reach out and touch the flowers as if they'll anchor me to the memories of my parents in some way.

I've been thinking a lot about Mom and Dad lately. *I miss them so much.* Cam choosing these for me has got to be some sort of sign. *Right?* Maybe it's their way of showing me they approve. Kayla tells me I'm crazy when I talk like this, but things like this just hit home. It feels like they're with me in that moment. It's special.

"I didn't mean to make you cry," Cam says.

"You didn't. I've just been missing them lately. I just wish they were here to meet you, ya know?" I wipe my eyes and take a steadying breath. "I'm sorry I'm such a blubbering mess. They're beautiful, babe. I love them. Thank you."

"I'm here for you, Leah. If you ever want to talk about them or need a shoulder to cry on, I'm your guy." He smiles.

I know he is, and I love him for it.

<hr>

"Seriously, Cam! Just take the dang pills already," I fuss. We've been fighting about this for the past three days. It's been a week since we got home now. We had to postpone the barbeque due to a bad storm that blew through. Today, Cam is supposed to go to the doctor about his arm, and yet he's still not willing to take a pain pill.

"I'm not taking them. I already told you that, Leah."

I'm over this already. Last night, I couldn't take it anymore and slept in the guest room. I came into our room about ten minutes ago to get dressed for the day to find Cam doubled over in pain with sweat rolling down his forehead. Rather than letting me care for him, he snapped at me.

"Why won't you take them? I know you don't like the way they make you feel, but at least they dull the pain. Take one now before you leave and then talk to the doctor about changing them. You know the ride and casting is going to hurt like hell if you don't."

"Would you quit trying to mother me already? I've got this. I think I know my own body," Cam hisses.

Gah, he's so frustrating. I throw my hands up in the air and let them flop at my side. "Cam, you made me a promise that you'd do better. You said that you'd stop all this and yet you've gotten worse. Hell, you ran me out of our room last night with this attitude. Are you trying to run me out of the house too? If that's what you want, I can go back home. The house hasn't sold just yet."

Ella did text me this morning to tell me that she has a client that is talking about putting in an offer. They have one more house to look at, and if it doesn't click, they've said mine is it. I'd hate to sell if Cam doesn't want me here anymore.

"If that's what you want, then you know where the door is."

Rip my heart out, why don't you?

My mouth hits the floor. Cam is sitting there, emotionless, staring as the sting behind my eyelids warns me of the tears I'm fighting to hold back. I can hardly believe he said that to me. *Does he really want me to leave?* I wonder. He must. Cam's not one to just say stuff.

"You know what? Fine, I know when I'm not wanted." I turn and yank the closet door open in a frenzy and wipe frustratedly at the tears that I fail to hold back. I grab a duffel bag and start throwing stuff inside. Once I'm sure I have a few outfits, I move and grab my hygiene products and undergarments. Then I walk to the door, grabbing my tennis shoes along the way.

Cam, still on the edge of the bed, hasn't moved an inch since saying those words. I put my hand on the bedroom door and pause, hoping I'm just overreacting.

"Are you going or staying?" Cam asks. "Make up your mind."

"You're a real jerk, you know that?" I swing open the door, throw the strap across my chest, and run down the stairs and right into the rock-hard chest of Tom. I look up and then around him and then down to my feet in embarrassment. In the living room is none other than Tom, Mark, Becca, and Marie.

I sit down on the bottom step and slip on my shoes. "I'm sorry you all walked in on that mess, but I can't stick around. Not when he's like this. I'm going home. Please watch out for him. He's really hurting right now, but that's no excuse for the way he's been talking to me." I stand, pulling my bag with me.

Tom nods. "Mom, can you give Leah a ride to town please? I have to get Cam to his doctor."

He's not going to argue. Of all people, I thought he'd be one of the ones to try to stop me.

Marie steps forward and puts a hand on my arm. "Come on, honey. I have to stop by the house on the way."

Mark says something to Becca, then walks my way. "How about Tom and I go get Cam, and Becca takes you to town? She has to go anyway."

"I don't want to be a bother. I can call Mike or Uncle Joe. It's not a problem, really."

It's not. I'll just walk into town and meet them at the dollar store.

"No," Tom interrupts. "If either of them come out here, they'll want to defend you—and they have that right, but it'll make things worse for you and Cam. Give him a chance to get his head straight. Please. You have the right to leave, and after the way I heard him talking to you, I'd take you myself, but he really does need to get to his appointment and I'm not going to let him take his pain out on Mom too. I hope you understand."

I do. I'd be pissed if Marie got caught in the crossfire. She doesn't deserve that. Nobody does, really.

"Come on," Becca says. "How about we have a girls' night or two? Aubrey's at dance camp for the next three days, so I can sneak away."

I hear Cam open the bedroom door upstairs and start moving.

That's my cue to leave. I inch my way away from the stairs. "That sounds good. I could use a break from everything," I say.

"A break?" Cam asks defensively. "I thought you'd be gone by now. You sure ran out like you had a fire under your a—"

Tom looks up at Cam. "You're being a jerk, man. Give her room to breathe."

"*I'm* being a jerk? How would you even know? You haven't been around in days," Cam says.

I stop and turn back, around ready to . . . what? I don't really know.

"I might not have been around, but that doesn't mean that I haven't checked in with Leah to see how you're doing."

"You've been calling my girl?" Cam asks. He looks at me as if I've hurt him. "You know my ex went behind my back. Why would you do that, Leah?"

Seriously? I did nothing wrong. I only kept everyone updated.

"That's enough!" Marie cuts in. "Why would you even compare her to someone like that? Son, you need to calm down."

Feeling the tears well up in my eyes, I move to step away. "No, that's not *enough,* Mom. Why wouldn't I if she's going behind my back to talk to Tom too?" He looks at me with disgust in his eyes before turning to Tom. "How could you? Why would you—"

"*Cam,*" Mark interjects. "Marie's right—you need to stop. I've never seen you like this. Take a pill and chill."

The hot tears begin to fall. I hate this. Everyone is defending me, so I know he must feel like everyone's ganging up on him. No matter how much of a jerk he's being, I don't want that for him right now.

"Stop it!" I cry. "I don't want y'all fighting over me. Cam made it clear that he doesn't want me here, so I'm leaving. Please don't argue with him over his decisions. It is what it is. I'm sorry I made such a mess of things." I take my keys out of my pocket and move to the coffee table, setting them down. I look back at worry-filled eyes. "I'm so sorry." I head toward the door—and out of Cam's life.

Becca catches up to me a moment later, linking her arm in mine as we walk to Mark's truck. She hits the button on her keychain, unlocking the door. I hear a commotion behind me but ignore it and hop in. I toss my bag over my shoulder into the back seat and put on my seat belt. As I look up, I see Cam walking down the drive after us as we back out and turn to leave. Becca pauses. I want no more than to stop her and run into his arms, but I know better. If I do that, nothing will change.

I can't do this. "Drive," I say.

She nods and gets us moving. Becca reaches over the console, taking my hand. "Are you okay?"

Cam. I hit ignore and toss it on the console. "I will be in time. Thanks for getting me out of there." Just past the fork, my phone rings. I adjust and pull it out of my pocket. Cam. I hit ignore and toss it on the bonsole.

"Any time." She stops at the entrance of the farm and looks over to me. "Are you sure this is what you want? I can turn around if you'd rather work on this."

My phone rings again, and this time, I silence it. "I'm sure. I can't handle him talking to me like that. You can drop me off at my place or . . . better yet, Uncle Joe's."

"Mark said that he was reserving a suite for us. We have today through Sunday. If you still want me to take you there, then I will. Let us do this for you, please. You're our friend too. I need to know that you're good."

I hate that they're doing this, but I'd probably do the same if the shoe was on the other foot. "Fine, but let me pay. I'm the reason we're going anyway."

"I'm sure by now he's already taken care of it. Mark knows someone at the Regent and will get us a penthouse at a steal, so he knows we're safe. Nobody can get to us without private access."

A penthouse? "Becca, that's too much. I mean, that sounds wonderful, but I can't ask you guys to spend your money on me like that."

Can they even afford that? It's not really my business, but I'd feel bad if it hurt them financially.

"When Mark makes up his mind, I can't change it."

Once we get to the high rise in downtown OKC, Becca checks us in. She ensures that Cam can't get a card in case he finds us, then orders an in-room spa night.

I pull out my phone to see twelve missed calls, all but one from Cam, the other Tom. I hit call on Tom.

We turn and walk toward the wall of elevators just below the staircase.

"Hello. Where are you?" Tom asks.

"We're fine. Mark reserved us a room for the weekend. We're safe."

Safe but broken.

"Are you okay?" Tom asks soberly.

"No, I'm not," I say, entering the now-vacated elevator.

Becca swipes her card and the doors close, taking us up.

"What he said . . . it's not alright."

"I know, and believe me, he's beating himself up for it now. Are you sure you two are safe? You don't have to tell me where you are, but if you want, I can ask Jazz to come to you."

"Thank you, but no. We're fine, I promise. If anything fishy happens, Jazz will be my first call." I look over at Becca and smile weakly. "Can you please make sure Cam is good? I know he hurt me, but I still don't want him to be hurting in return."

"You're too good to him," Tom huffs. "Are you and he going to be okay?"

Is that a trick question? It sure feels like one right now. "I don't know."

"Please be safe. Both of you."

"We will. And Tom? Thank you."

"You're welcome, sis. See you soon."

I hang up and turn back to Becca to ask her what's next when the elevator opens to a wide-open living area. It's beautiful. Straight ahead is a wall of windows. Along the back wall on either side is a bedroom and bathroom, and at the front right is a kitchenette. Fancy but not so that I'm completely uncomfortable.

"Now what?" I ask.

"We can call Kayla and have a true girls' night, or we can relax. No drama, no responsibility for now. That's up to you." She takes out her chirping phone, smiles, types out a response, and puts it away.

"Can we just chill for tonight? I'd love for Kayla to come over, but she's out of state this weekend. Besides, if she hears about Cam and me, she'll sic Uncle Joe on him."

Becca chuckles. "He kind of deserves it, if you ask me. I've never seen him act like that before. It was crazy."

It was. I've never felt so empty before. It hurt being on the receiving end.

"Are you sure you wouldn't rather be home with Mark? I mean, you have a kid-free weekend. That's got to be special in the Banks house."

"It is, but Mark wants this for us. You were there for me when Mark and I had trouble, so now's my turn. How's *Coyote Ugly* and burgers sound? I'm starving."

"Sounds perfect."

It really does. An afternoon with a movie, fatty food, a good friend, and no drama. What more could a girl want?

Chapter
Twenty-One

I lie in my hotel bed and crack my eyes open. It's finally Sunday morning. I need to decide whether to go back to the Cameron farm or to go back to my place. I feel bad, but I shut out everyone this whole weekend—well, all except Becca, though she avoided all Cam talk unless I wanted to vent. She refused to comment, as she didn't want to sway me either way. This decision is all on me. I needed that, and even though I hated it in the moment, I'm glad for it now.

I made one call to Kayla on Friday around dinner to let her know that I was fine and that I was in a safe place but that I would not be reaching out for a few days. I think she knew something was going on, but I refused to elaborate because I didn't want her opinions at that moment. Besides, she and Mike are out of state with Megan and Damon, and I didn't want to ruin their fun. Now, I feel guilty because I know she only wants the best for me, and if she knew I really didn't want her opinion, all I had to do was say so and she'd just support me however I asked.

After that call, I turned off my phone and have been unreachable since, unless they got me through Becca or the landline, which they didn't. I kind of dread turning it on now, but I know I need to deal with it at some point, and the time is now.

I sit up in bed, stretching my arms above my head, and yawn. I grab my phone from the charger and turn it on, letting the pings begin. I get out of bed and slip on the comfy house shoes provided by the hotel and head to the en suite to take care of business. When I get back, I grab my phone and head out in search of the coffee pot, finding Becca making herself a cup also.

"Morning," she says. "Sleep well?"

"After I quit tossing and turning, yeah. That bed is amazing. I almost want to lift the sheets and find out what kind of mattress it is so I can buy one."

"I know, right?" She takes a sip of her coffee and sobers. "Are you feeling any better about making a decision?"

"Not really. I did turn on my phone, so there's that." I grab a cup and pour me some liquid gold, then add a bit of cream and sugar before taking that first burning-hot sip that puts everything right in the world. Or not. "I dread reading all those messages."

"Then don't. If you really think about it, when it comes to his messages, the only ones you really need to read are the last few." She takes a sip of her coffee and wanders over to the couch to take a seat, grabbing the room service menu. She puts her coffee on the table in front of her and pulls her feet up underneath. I follow and do the same.

"Why only the last few? Shouldn't I read them all?"

"If you want to get mad again, sure. We both know how things were when you left. He was messaging you so much that you turned your phone off and shut everyone out. I can only imagine the kinds of things he said in the moment."

She turns and grabs the room's phone. "I'm going to have a veggie omelet and toast. Want anything?"

"Same, but can you get on with it? I get that the first messages will be bad, but why shouldn't I look at them?"

"Leah." Becca puts down the menu and scoots to the middle, grabbing my hands. "Look at them if you want, but if you do, you're going to feel that hurt all over again. I'm sure you don't want to go through that again. We both know that the pain he was in had him all kinds of messed up. The way he was Friday is *not* the Cam I know, and I've known him most of my life. I've never seen him like that before. That doesn't excuse the way he treated you in any way, though. So if you don't want to face that all over now that you're ready to communicate, move past the pain, and move on to the important stuff." She grabs the menu and scoots back, then proceeds to call down for room service.

Even though I want to know what he wrote, I know that Becca's right. It won't do any good to bring all that pain back up. I know that he was not in his right mind. *But is he now?* I wonder. I guess we'll find out.

I pull out my phone and bypass everyone else's calls and texts and find the one person's I need to open. I click his name and scroll down to the last few.

Saturday, 10:23 p.m.
Cam: *Will you please answer your phone? Baby, I'm so sorry. Please come home. I miss you so much. Please at least let me know that you're okay.*

Saturday, 11:45 p.m.
Cam: *I'm lying in our bed, unable to sleep. I haven't been able to close my eyes without seeing the look on your face when*

It's too much. I set my phone down and cover my face as I cry, letting it all out.

Becca moves in, surrounding me in her warm embrace.

"I don't know how to do this. I read two of his messages and feel his pain. I want to make everything right, but the things he said are still so fresh. I love him *so* much, but he hurt me. How can I know that he won't do it again?"

"You won't know. Nobody ever does."

The elevator opens and a bellhop carts in our breakfast. He unloads the tray on the dining table before turning to leave.

Becca takes my hand, helping me to stand, and leads me to the table. "The thing about love is that it's risky. It's the biggest gamble of your life."

I plop down in the dining chair while Becca grabs the coffee carafe, bringing it to the table.

"Let me ask you this. When you picture your life in ten years, can you imagine it without Cam, or is the pain unbearable at that thought?"

She's got me there. When I look ahead, all I see is Cam and me—I see it all. I see us building a family together. I see us chasing our kids around the yard and teaching them to ride their bikes together.

"I know it's hard," Becca says, "but love *is* hard. It's never easy to merge two lives into one. If you can't imagine life without him in it . . . fight. Go home and demand that he pull his head out of his butt and that he treats you like the queen you are."

I reach across the table and take her hand in mine. "Thank you, Becca."

"No need to thank me, hun. Family's there for each other in time of need." She smiles at me, nodding toward my plate. "Let's eat. You've barely eaten this whole weekend. I can't take you home without feeding you first."

"What makes you think I'm going home?"

"I know you better than you think. I also know that you love that knucklehead. You wouldn't be so torn up if you didn't."

I pick up the fork and start eating. My phone pings with a new text.

Cam: *Hey, beautiful. I'm just checking in to see how you're doing. You don't have to reply if you're still mad. I don't deserve your forgiveness, but I hope you find it in your heart to forgive me anyway. I'm sorry for the things I said. I wish I could take them back. It's like I was watching myself say it but was unable to stop it from happening. Sweetheart, I love you with everything in me. I can't imagine life without you. I know you'd never do anything like what I insinuated. I'm just so sorry. If you were here, I'd be on my hands and knees begging you to forgive me. Until then, all I can say is that I love you. I will do anything to make sure you know I mean that.*

I take a deep breath and set down my fork so I can reply. If I'm going to stop running and fight for what I want, I guess that starts now.

Me: *You want to know how I'm doing? I've been better, Cam, but physically, I'm fine. The way you've acted toward* me for a while now is not okay, but then even the thought of comparing me to your ex . . . that hurt. I love Tom like he's my own BROTHER, Cam, and nothing more than that. I love you, you big dope. In time, I will forgive you, but right now, I'm still hurting. I never thought you of all people would treat me the way you did. I'll be back later, and we'll see where we go from there. If you really want me to be at home out there, you have to prove to me in some way that it's my home too. That you won't just up and have me leave at the first sign of trouble. I'm giving up everything to be there with you. Make this right or I'm walking . . . no matter how much it'll hurt me.*

Cam: *I'm sorry. I'm so so sorry. I'll make this right, I promise. If I can make this right, will you still move out here?*

Me: *I know you're sorry. We'll talk when I get back.*

Cam: *Take all the time you need. I'll be here waiting.*

I feel bad for leaving Cam on read, but I really don't know how to reply right now. Do I still want to move out there? Yes . . . and no. I think that'll be decided in the moment.

Becca drops me off at the house. I bypass Cam, who is sitting on the couch, and take my bag upstairs. I then shut myself in the bathroom and amp myself up before wandering back downstairs.

"Welcome home, sweetheart," Cam says as I walk into the kitchen. He's standing at the counter holding a lemonade, which he hands to me before grabbing his own.

"Thank you." I stand on the opposite side of the counter. I'm still cautious of being here, but I know I'm here to fight for what I love. If I walk away from this relationship, I want to know that I gave it my all.

Cam puts down his cup, steps around the island, and takes my hand. "I spoke with my doctor and I told him how the other medicine was affecting me. He changed it to prescription-strength Tylenol. I've been taking it as he recommended. It's a lot better. I should have never let it get out of hand like that. Babe . . ." Cam lowers himself to his knees, lets go of my hand, and hugs my waist, resting his head on my stomach. "You have no idea how sorry I am. Our home felt emptier than it has in months. It was hell. Do you think you can find it in your heart to forgive me? To come home and give me another chance, a chance for me to do better? First thing Monday morning, we can go into the city and see about adding your name to the title. I want you to know this is your home too."

I'm shocked, but I did tell him to prove it to me, and this will prove it. I run my hand through his hair. "You hurt me, Cam, but . . . We can put this behind us now. I'll work on letting go of the hurt as long as you work on your actions. But Cam, you need to know if you ever talk to me like that again, or if you ever try to compare me to your ex, you can take a hike. No matter how much I love you, how hard it'll be to get over you, I will walk out that door and never look back again."

"I understand," he says, standing up. "You're coming home, right?"

"Yes. I'm home. I'm not going anywhere, and I don't need to be added. I just wanted to know that this is my home too."

"Oh, thank God you're coming back. But we're still adding you," he says, releasing a bit of tension from his shoulders. "Can I kiss you now, please?"

I lift onto my toes and wrap my arms around his neck. "Please do."

After thoroughly welcoming me home, Cam pulls back and looks me in the eyes. "I don't know what I did to deserve a woman like you, but I sure as heck am glad it happened." He leans in to kiss my forehead. "Will you hav e a picnic with me for lunch?"

"Sure, but we have a lot to get ready for. Moving, for one, and then I thought we had to go shopping for the barbeque and get the house ready?"

"We're still moving tomorrow evening, and we have a week to get things ready for the barbeque. I'd like to treat you to a nice moment and show you just how sorry I am. Babe, I thought I'd lost you. Please, let me do this."

While I'm still a little guarded, I can see past the hurt. He really wasn't himself while taking those pills. I just hope that moving forward, we can work things out before they blow up like this did.

"I can do that, but I need to work for a bit this morning. Uncle Joe asked me to get a Halloween special put together ASAP. Can you holler when you're ready for us to picnic?"

"Sure thing. I love you. Thank you for coming home to me and for giving me another chance."

"I love you too."

Once things are settled, I head to the office and open my laptop to get started. Since I haven't been able to go into work, Uncle Joe has me working remotely. I oversee all the paperwork. He sends me the numbers and information I need, and I input it. I make tester recipes and send him my final choices. He then tries them out on the staff. Not a bad setup, really. It's nice to know that this is an option for me. When it comes to me having a family of my own, I've always wanted to stay home. I've known for a long time that the restaurant would be left to Kayla and me one day, and knowing her, she won't want to be a part of it. Well, maybe one day she'll love it, but her work is elsewhere for now. I do love this flexibility though.

Family aside, my dream has always been to be a mom—a hands-on one, one that stays home with the kids while little. I think that comes from losing my parents at such a young age, but I'd for sure put my kids before the restaurant. I hope that Uncle Joe understands that the restaurant was his dream, not mine. I love it, but I have dreams too.

I look up when there's a soft knock on the door. Cam's standing there, holding a basket and a quilt. "Ready for our picnic?" he asks.

I stretch my hands out in front of me and groan, ready for a break. "Let me send this and I'm all yours." Once I hit send, I power down my laptop.

I stand and walk toward Cam, right into his open arm. I take the blanket from him and lean in to kiss him before heading out. I wonder where we're headed but don't have to wait long. On the other side of the pond, in a clearing,

Cam hands me the blanket to unfold while taking the basket from me.

"I hope this spot is good," he says.

"It's perfect. You're here with me. That's all that matters."

Once we sit, he pulls out the lunch he packed for us—chicken salad sandwiches, grapes, and two sodas. Not realizing how hungry I am, I scarf down my sandwich then lean back for a few minutes. Cam only picks at his food.

I lean back on my hands as he lies down, resting his head in my lap. I readjust and run my hands through his hair, making him hum in satisfaction. Moments go by with me looking out at the pond, snacking on grapes as he feeds them to me. It's so peaceful out here.

"You know, this is where Grammy taught me to fish." He points to the spot just in front of us at the pond's edge. "Right there. The first fish I ever caught on my Scooby Doo fishing pole was an eleven-pounder. I'm sure you can imagine the fight it put up. Grammy was in hysterics when I fell in. She could barely stop laughing long enough to pull me out."

I can't help but laugh as I picture it. "Little Cammie must have been so cute, all wet and shocked. I'm surprised you didn't give up the fish to save yourself."

"I *am* adorable," he says, teasingly. "There's no way I would've let that one go. That big of a fish was bragging rights in our house." He looks up into my eyes before get-ting serious. "I took this plot of land when our parents offered because of this pond. I have so many memories here." He looks out into the distance as if he's seeing a memory flash in front of his eyes. "I hope

Grammy can teach our children to fish in this very spot one day."

"Any kid would be lucky to have a woman like Grammy in their life. I see why you cherish that."

"I can't believe I almost screwed it all up." He rolls so that he's on an elbow, then takes my hand in his casted one. "I really am sorry, Leah. I hope you know that. You're my heart. I can never apologize enough."

"Cam . . ." Taking his face in my hands, I lean in and give him a quick kiss. "You've apologized enough. Let's move on." I kiss his nose. "So you want Grammy to teach your kids to fish here too? That'll be cute. Do you still have your Scooby Doo fishing pole?"

"*Our* kids, but not until after we marry, of course. I think Mom saved it. Can you imagine our son or daughter fishing with that very pole one day?"

I can. I can see it all. His blue-haired Grammy teaching a little Cam how to fish while another toddles nearby. Cam scooping him up in his arms and telling our son that he's doing a good job. The future looks like a dream come true in so many ways.

Chapter Twenty-Two

Moving day sneaks up on me fast. Tom walks in bright and early with a dozen donuts and to-go cups of coffee for all of us from the local gas station. When he sees a smile on my face, he pulls me in for a hug and lets the rest go. I'm thankful—I don't really want to bring it up anymore.

"Mark got called in last night," Tom says. "I have no idea if he'll make it today, so I'd just count him out. He left Becca the truck so she can help haul stuff. Mom said that she'll come after Dad gets the trailer hooked up. He has to run into work himself, so he might not make it either."

"Mike and his gym buddies should already be there moving Kayla's stuff, so there's plenty of help loading up," I convey. "It's just when we get back home that I'm worried about." Cam can't be lifting a lot with his one good arm right now, and I have a lot of heavy stuff.

"I wouldn't worry much. We can park the trailers, and when everyone's home, we can unload it all into the garage," Cam states.

"Okay, then," Tom starts, "let's get out of here."

"Do you know how to pull a trailer?" Cam asks me. He's

tasked me with driving today.

"I can. I've just never had to back one up."

"When we get there, just pull up and I can back it when we're ready," Tom says.

Before we head out, I pull out my phone and open my family text.

Me: *Are y'all about ready to meet at the apartment?*

Kayla: *I'm already here packing my stuff. Are you sure that you're ready for this?*

Me: *Yeah, I'm sure. I'm gonna miss the hell out of you, but you're leaving anyway. Plus, you know we have a room here for you.*

Uncle Joe: *Don't remind me. I'm not ready for my babies to move so far away.*

Me: *I'm only going to be twenty minutes away.*

Kayla: *And I'll only be a plane ride away. It's not like it'll be forever. My contract is only seven years.*

Mike: *Seven years too long, if you ask me. The guys and I are hooking up the trailer now. Be there soon.*

Kayla: *Mike, you know I need to do this. Don't give me grief.*

Mike: *Not going there, Kay. You know I gave you another option.*

Another option? I wonder what he's talking about. Before I can ask, I stop myself. I have my own drama to deal with right now. I can't get involved. Kayla respected me when I didn't want her in mine.

Kayla: *Seriously? You're going to go there?*

Mike: *Whatever. I'll see you guys in a bit.*

Me: *Y'all, please. I love you. Let's not make this weird.*

Mike: *Not weird at all. I'm just saying that your sister has options. I'm putting my phone up. I'll see you soon. Pop's hollering.*

Kayla: *I'm done. I hate it when you get all high and mighty like that. There's no talking to you when you think there's only one way. See you soon, sis.*

Uncle Joe: *Well, isn't this lovely? I guess I better get out my ref shirt. See you all in ten.*

Me: *See you there.*

I put my phone down and turn to the guys. "Kayla's already there and Mike's hooking up the trailer now. You ready? I have some packing to do."

"Sure am," Cam says, extending a hand for me.

"Perfect." I take a deep breath, ready more than ever to leave the apartment and move on to the next chapter in my life.

When we pull up in front of my apartment building, I'm shocked at how many people have shown up to help. Mike is chatting with Gunnar and Damon, both friends of his from the gym, and Pop, the owner who's practically adopted Mike.

"Cam, I should warn you. These guys can be loud and a bit rowdy. They kind of adopted me as a little sister while I was learning self-defense at the gym. I don't see them much, but when I do, they make sure to pick right back up where they left off."

Cam looks their way as if he's sizing them up.

My phone rings. Seeing that it's Ella—my realtor—I answer, putting her on speaker. "Hello?"

"Leah, this is Ella with Global Reality. Is now a good time to talk?"

Not really, considering everyone's standing around waiting on me, but I concede. "Sure, what can I do for you?"

"I'm excited to tell you that we got a full offer on your apartment. The buyer would like to throw in a contingency of a quick-cash sale, along with a bonus if you can vacate in two weeks and leave it furnished."

Two weeks is no problem, but that's a lot to take in. I was going to sell a lot of the furniture anyway. Cam and I decided to start new and go shopping together for our place. The sale will go a long way in doing so.

"I can do that, but what do they mean by furnished?

Like, as in the furniture I currently have there, or do I need to buy something new? You'll have to walk me through this."

"They have asked that you leave the furniture in the main rooms and office. You do not need to leave any décor, such as decorations or lamps."

"I can do that."

"Great. Should I let them know you accept the offer? I've emailed a copy of it over to you if you'd like to see it."

I look over at Cam questioningly, who just shrugs. This is huge. Am I really ready for this? I close my eyes and picture my future. Seeing Cam, I know I'm doing the right thing.

"Yes, ma'am, I'll accept."

Cam takes my hand, lifting my fingers to his mouth for a kiss.

I smile in return. The others must have gotten tired of waiting, as they all start heading inside. I can't blame them—it's hot today—ninety-eight degrees and humid as all get-out.

"Perfect. I'll draw up the paperwork and get with you as soon as I can."

"I'm at the apartment right now. We just pulled up to start moving. If you need me for anything today, you can find me here."

"Sounds good. I'll try to make it before you leave. Thanks again, Leah."

I look over to Cam, who still has my hand in his. "This is crazy!"

"In a good way, though. Who knew?"

"Right? I didn't expect it to sell so fast." I unbuckle and lean in, giving him a quick kiss. "We better get in there and help. I'd hate for them to break something."

We step out of the truck and lock it up. When I walk around the truck and look up at my building, I'm hit with an overwhelming number of memories—some good, some not.

Cam wraps an arm around me from behind, placing a kiss on my temple. "You good?"

I turn in his arm and lean up to give him a quick kiss. "I'm fine, babe. I was just thinking of all the memories Kayla and I have here. You know, closing a chapter to start another can be sad sometimes. No matter how much you're ready, you still hate to see a good thing end."

He smiles and kisses me on the forehead. "Don't forget the good thing that's beginning."

What a day! We finally make it home after a long, loud, tiring day. Cam and I cuddle up on the couch while we wait for Tom to bring back pizza from the local Quick Stop. I'm too tired to cook, so we're chancing it on gas-station pizza—not my finest moment, but it'll have to work.

Cam's phone rings. I sit up and grab it—it's Jazz calling, so I put it on speaker.

"Hello?" Cam answers.

"Hey, I'm in the area. Is it okay to stop by for a few minutes? I'd like to talk to you and Leah a bit."

"Of course," he returns.

"See you soon."

With Cam in a bad way last week, Jazz met with me on the phone to see if there had been any new developments. Since my stalker snuck into our home, things have been quiet—no more gifts or texts. It makes me wonder what's going on, why it would suddenly stop.

There's a knock at the door before it's pushed open. "Knock, knock."

"Back here, Jazz," Cam says.

He readjusts his hold on me as Jazz enters the living room. She grabs a chair across the way and sits. "How's it going? Has anything happened since we spoke last?"

"No," I say, "nothing's happened lately. It worries me a little. From all I know about stalkers, they don't just up and disappear."

"They don't," she agrees. "I don't think that he's gone, though. I think he's lying low and watching."

I sit up out of Cam's grip as she gains my interest. I'd love to hear that she figured out who he is. *Oh, please be good news. I can really use some right now.*

"Pizza's here!" Tom announces as he walks in. He stops dead in his tracks when he sees this isn't a social call, then quickly sets the pizza on a chair and joins us on the couch. "Sorry, please continue. What did I miss?"

As Jazz catches him up on our conversation, I lie back and sigh in frustration. I knew Tom was coming back but his timing stinks.

"Spill it," Cam says, interrupting their conversation. "What do you know that we don't?"

Jazz fiddles with her notepad as if she's nervous. Since

she's a cop, I would think she'd be able to tamp down her emotions, but with how close she is to Cam, this must hit close to home.

"Mark and I have been walking the property every couple of days since the breakin. We found a few cigarette butts matching the one found on your porch. They were located nearer to Janelle's house but close enough to see your front porch. But that's not what worries me. I believe that he may have an accomplice. There were two different types of cigarette butts out there, one with a light-colored lipstick on it. I don't know for sure, but we set up several cameras in the area to see if we could catch him. From the looks of the beaten-down path, he frequents that area."

I squeeze Cam's hand when he tenses, trying to pull him back to the present.

"I'm sorry," she continues. "I know this isn't what you wanted to hear, but it's progress. We'll get him. I know we will."

Will they, or will he get to me before they figure out who's after me?

Two days later, I go into work for the first time since the accident. It feels so odd to me, like I don't belong for some reason. I don't know why, but I don't like it. It's not that any of my regulars or staff act in any sort of way other than being happy to see me. I'm just not in it. I wonder if Uncle Joe would let me go remote full-time, maybe ask

Mike to step in as acting GM. I'll have to broach that after the holidays.

After work, I head upstairs to my old room to get changed. Tom is picking me up and taking me to the shooting range, then I'm being carted off to the gym for some ramped-up self-defense lessons courtesy of Uncle Joe, Mike, and Damon. Cam said he wouldn't miss it for the world. He'd be taking me to the range himself, but he has a follow-up appointment this afternoon with his doctor, and they might be removing his cast today.

I walk downstairs to a waiting Tom. "Hey. You ready for this?"

"Hey, sis," he replies. "Ready, but I'm starved. Mike handed me a couple of sandwiches while you were upstairs. Said you hadn't eaten either. We'll eat on the way."

I start to argue but opt out when my stomach rumbles in protest. We walk out front and find his truck parked front and center. He opens my door for me, then heads around the back of the truck and hops in.

Ten minutes later, we're pulling into the parking lot of G&H Gun Range. My nerves begin to ramp up, but I know I'll be okay. Tom is a cop; no matter how nervous I am, I'll be taught right. We step out and walk into the store, right up to a case filled with guns and ammo.

"Can I help you?" a big bull of a man asks.

"We'd like a lane, please," Tom states.

After we fill out some paperwork and go over the rules, we're led to the back of the building toward the indoor shooting range. Tom brought in his own gun and ammo, so there is no need to make a purchase other than the lane, making it much quicker than expected. I put on the safety glasses and earmuffs as we walk, muffling the sounds of the other guns being fired. Once there, the guy goes over a few things with us, then turns to leave.

Tom starts setting everything up. I'm so lost—I don't know what's what. This is so far out of my comfort zone that I'm starting to second-guess myself.

"Let's give this a shot, shall we?" Tom turns to look at me and notices me standing off against the wall in a puddle of nerves. "Come on, Leah. I'm a pro at this. I wouldn't dare let you touch a gun if I didn't think you could handle it. Come over here. I'll go over the rules and let you hold an unloaded gun before I let you fire one."

I nod and walk over to him. He goes over the basic rules, like keeping firearms pointed in a safe direction, keeping your fingers off the trigger unless I'm ready to shoot, and a few others. It's a lot to process.

"If you don't think you're ready for this, we will skip the lessons but Leah . . . you really need to get comfortable around guns. You're living with a cop—there are guns in the house and on the farm. I would feel safer knowing that you know how to properly handle one in case you ever have to use it."

I don't plan on it, but he is right. I do need to know how. I'm the one that asked for this. I do need to know. What if my stalker has one? If I learn how to use one now, I'll stand a better chance. I take a deep breath and square my shoulders before stepping forward.

Tom then hands me the gun, calling it a Glock 22. It's got some weight to it, but it's not as scary as I thought it would be.

After he sees me get comfortable with it, he shows me how to hold it, with both arms fully extended at shoulder level, both hands on the gun. "Remember, index finger of your dominant hand needs to be extended against the frame of the gun, not on the trigger until you fire it. Now close one eye and look at the target. If the red dot doesn't move, that's your dominant eye. If it does, switch."

"Got it."

"Don't lock your elbows," Tom says, knocking my arms.

I loosen up a little, then aim again.

"Better. Now fire."

I look over my shoulder at Tom in question.

"It's called a dry fire. There's no bullets in there yet. I just want you to get the feel of it."

I nod and do as I'm told.

"I think you're ready to give it a try."

Tom and I stay at the range for a good hour or two before he decides that it's time to go. I really feel like I got the hang of it. I shot the center of the target—or around it—nearly every time. It was an adrenaline rush for sure. I'm not ready to carry a gun around, but if the need to use one ever rises, I'll be ready.

When we pull up to Pop's gym—Dead Lift—the nerves hit. It's been a long while since I've hit the mat with any of these guys. I know they won't go easy on me now that they know that my stalker is getting closer than ever. That's what I need, but I know I'm going to have to dig deep if I want to make it through this without feeling like a big bruise.

"Come on, Leah," Tom says. "Everyone's waiting."

I hop out of the truck and walk in, followed closely by Tom. I see Xena—Pop's daughter—behind the counter to the left and nod. Then I find my crew—Mike, Damon, Uncle Joe and Cam—to the far right near the mats. I walk over nervously.

Cam meets me halfway, giving me a kiss on the forehead. "How'd she do at the range?" he asks Tom.

"She's a natural. I'd have her watch my six any day," Tom replies.

"Beginner's luck," I state as we get to the mat. I hand Cam my stuff, slip out of my shoes, and step through the ropes toward Mike, Uncle Joe, and Damon. "Hey guys, you—"

Damon cuts me off by swinging in behind me and putting me in a choke hold. He's taller than the other guys, at six foot six and maybe 225 pounds. He's got a runner's body, but he sure can move. "What do you do when someone takes you from behind?" he asks. "Come on, think. You know how to get out of this."

I look over to see Cam standing at the edge of the mat, like he wants to jump in. I wink in his direction to let him know that I'm good. Then I use the heel of my bare foot to come down on the top of Damon's. I throw my elbow back into his gut, and once he's bent over, I attempt to throw him over the top of me. It's been a while, so it takes me two times to get it, but once I do and he's on his back, I get over the top of him and put a knee to his chest.

"Really? No warm-up or tape?" I ask, winded.

"There's no tape in a street fight," D states, patting my leg. "I'm glad you still got it. You need strength training, though."

"Come on, kiddo," Uncle Joe says. "Get your head in the match. You know this stuff—keep an eye on your surroundings. He would've never taken you if you were."

Mike tosses me head and mouth gear. I put them on, and I'm quickly taken down as he swipes my legs out from under me. *Gah, that hurts.*

"Come on, man. Give her a minute," Cam says from the sideline.

Mike extends a hand. "You have to be on guard at all times. You know this."

I do. I take his hand and use it to pull myself up while knocking the back of Mike's knees, making him kneel, then jump on his back.

"Nice sleeper," Uncle Joe says. "Now follow through."

Mike grabs my neck, flinging me over the top of him, causing me to land on my back again. "If you let everything distract you and lighten your hold, you're in trouble."

"You're always so grouchy in the ring," I retort.

"Watch out," Cam hollers.

I turn just in time to see Damon stomp near my side. I roll out of the way and scramble to get up. When he gets near, I do a quick roundhouse kick that has him stumbling back. Mike comes at me from the other side.

"What is this, a twofer?"

When he lunges at me, I sidestep him and end up running into D, who puts me in another choke hold. This time, my dominant arm is locked behind my back.

"You know what to do, Leah," Uncle Joe hollers. "You're in a hold and have another coming at you. Use what you have to your advantage."

Mike steps up in front of me, giving light jabs to my gut, letting me know they got me. "If there are two of them after you and you can't take us, how can you take them? Come on, you know how to get out of this. Think!"

I look over his shoulder to see Tom walking Cam out of the gym.

I'm so tired, but I know I need to do this. I reach up and put my hand on D's arm, using it as leverage to get out of the hold without breaking my neck. I twist in his arm just enough to get loose, then punch him in the ribs, causing him to bend over with an "Umph!" Mike reaches for me as I push Damon in his direction, causing them to collide as I take off running to the opposite side of the ring, just like they taught me. *You get free and then run. Don't stop until you find help—or in this case, exit the ring.*

Once there, Mike nods. "Nice. Now hit the machines for thirty minutes followed by the treadmill. Give me five miles gradually working up in speed. You did good, Leah, but D's right. We need to work on strength training and your speed."

Five miles? I'm tired already, but I'll do it. I need to be able to take care of myself, so I do as I'm told.

Digging deeper than before, I give it everthing in me.

Chapter Twenty-Three

I roll over in bed and moan loudly. I've been training hard every day this week. Now that the weekend is finally here, I get to take a break. Though it'll be short-lived, considering the barbeque is tonight. Yesterday while I was at work, Cam and a few others around here took care of a lot of the prep work so I wouldn't have to. I'm forever grateful for that, seeing as my whole body aches.

"Morning, beautiful." Cam laughs as he rolls to his back, wiping the sleep from his eyes. A couple of days ago, Cam got his cast removed. His doctor was thrilled at the rate it was healing. He's now in a post-cast brace. Cam says it's itchy but he would much rather that than the cast.

"What are you laughing at, sir?" I ask as I face him.

"You're way too cute."

"Why? I'm sore and would much rather spend the morning in bed with my boyfriend than cooking and cleaning. It's been a rough week."

"When you put it that way," he says, tugging me into him, "I'm sure we can make time."

I giggle—I never used to be one to giggle before him—then pat him on the chest. "Shower first, then we need to get to work. You're the one who made these plans. We can't have a house full of hungry people. Up and at it, mister."

"Sure, we can. Get your cute butt back here. You're supposed to be nursing me back to health. Those kisses are where I find my strength, and right now, I feel *very* weak." He smiles, unable to keep a straight face. "Are you going to deprive me of the strength you know I need?"

I stand up while laughing, then turn back to him with a hand on my hip. "Oh, you poor baby. Maybe you need a sponge bath. Give me just a minute to call and ask. I'm sure Tom can spare a moment to help."

A look of pure shock flashes across his face before something bordering on mischief replaces it. Cam hops up out of bed, rounding the foot of it and looking like a hunter about ready to pounce.

I put out a hand to stop his approach. "Oh no, you don't. The bathroom is the other way."

"I'm too weak. I need help, sweetheart." He lunges as if he's going to grab me. "How about *you* give me a sponge bath?"

I jump back in a fit of giggles. "Not happening. If you get your way, we'll be in bed all day with a house full of people. Shower now, then rest later."

Cam lunges again, getting much closer than I expect. I jump up onto the bed, run across it, and head for the bathroom. "If you want that sponge bath, you know who to call."

"Cheater!" I hear Cam laugh out. "You better put on your swimsuit unless you want me to see you in the buff—I'm joining you this morning."

I run and grab my suit, then go back, shut the door, and step into the shower after I slip it on. I turn on the spray of water and check the temperature once before getting under the water's fall. Cam has respected the fact that I'm a virgin and has made no attempt at changing that. Things have ramped up a lot, but as he's said in the past, it's fun making out like a couple of teens . . . for now.

In no time, I hear the door of the shower open, then feel Cam's arm wrap around my midsection. "Better?" he asks.

"Perfect," I say as I turn around, wrapping my arms around his neck and standing on my toes to give him a kiss. *This* is my happy place.

Not long before the barbecue, the full crew—including Mike and Kayla—show up to help get things ready. Cam and the guys take off outside somewhere, leaving me in the kitchen with Becca and Kayla. Jazz texts me to say that she will be here before long, and Marie is supposed to be on her way back from picking up Grammy. Becca works on the pasta salad while Kayla preps the potatoes for the grill.

Twenty minutes later, Jazz walks in. Cam invited her and her brother tonight, and though he isn't coming, Jazz jumped at the idea of coming to a famed "Cameron function." She walks into the kitchen and washes her hands, then starts peeling some carrots. Becca cuts some fruit for the table while I put together the deviled eggs. We've just turned on some music when Uncle Joe and

Janet walk in with a case of beer. He sets the box down, passing us each one before opening his own. We settle back into our jobs as he sits at the bar, watching what we have going on. Janet washes up and jumps in. I've never seen Uncle Joe take this laid-back approach, but he seems to be enjoying it. I look over at him, smiling.

He winks at me before taking another swig from his beer. "You look happy, baby girl. I haven't seen you like this in a long time. Cam and this place are good for you."

I put down the egg tray and dry my hands as I walk over to him, engulfing him in a hug. "Uncle Joe, you're the best father figure a girl could ask for." When he squeezes me back, I continue. "I love you. Don't ever forget that."

Uncle Joe pulls me in tighter than before, hugging me hard. "I love you, too, baby doll. You know, they never tell you how to deal with your kids moving on. I'd rather deal with the younger years for the rest of my life than feel like you don't need me anymore."

"Uncle Joe, I'll always need you. I promise to work harder in showing you that." I kiss him on the cheek and go to say something but am cut off when a buzz echoes through the kitchen.

Jazz looks at her phone as it also begins buzzing—the cameras have been activated. I grab my phone to pull them up as she opens hers. When I see her head toward the door, I know in my gut that something's not right.

"Stay inside, Leah. Y'all stay with her," she says as she runs out of the house.

I go into the office and open the blinds so I can see what's going on. As I do, I see the guys come over the hill in the Gator and head off into the trees across the way—the same area in which Jazz thinks my stalker has been hanging out.

Moments later, I see Cam and Mike walking back toward the house.

As soon as Cam walks inside, he immediately moves to my side and looks me over. "Are you okay?"

"I'm fine. Jazz and I got the alert, and she took off out the door. Is she good?"

"I'm sure she is. Mark and Tom are out there with her. I should be, too, but since I'm still injured, they wanted me out of the way," he says, looking upset.

I'm sure he hated to step away, but I'm glad he did.

With the blinds open, I see more of the Camerons running toward the door. Mike opens it for them, pointing them in our direction. Pat and Butch go to Cam, who meets them halfway, while Kim finds me, pulling me into a hug.

"Are you okay? When I got the alert, I had to come check right away. Pat couldn't even keep me in the house."

Since the cameras are throughout the property, everyone who lives here has access to the app.

"I'm fine. Someone or something got caught on the camera." Oh shoot, my phone. "Kayla!" I holler. "Can you grab my phone?"

She runs to the kitchen, grabbing it for me. I quickly put in my code and open the camera app. A load of bricks drops into my stomach as I see what flashes across my screen. Standing there, right in front of the camera, is a woman in a black hoodie pulled up tight. Her hand is in front of her face, but she startles and moves just enough for me to see her full face.

I put my hand to my mouth and gasp when I recognize who's out there.

"What it is?" Cam asks, coming to stand next to me. I play it again to be sure. "It's Tillie."

"Who?" Uncle Joe asks.

"John Knorr's girlfriend," I explain.

"*What?*" Kayla screeches. "Stalker John?"

I keep watching the video as I see her turn and run. That's when I see him follow behind her. "John too," I state.

Butch grabs for Pat, hauling him out of the house.

I sit on the nearby desk chair, my head in my hands. Cam walks over, rubbing soothing circles on my back as the others leave the office.

He gives me a moment to gather myself before he speaks. "Do you want me to cancel today? You give me the word and I'll get it done."

"I love you for that, but no. I'm not going to let them take another moment from me. I've lived in fear for far too long. I want to go out there and celebrate your late birthday."

Jazz walks back in, moving straight to my side to check on me first. I quickly tell her who I saw on the camera.

"I'll call this in. I have a few things to tie up out there, but you're clear to stay on this side of the property if you want to go out now. I followed them as they ran off the property and jumped into a car. I'll wrap this up, then come find you."

I take a deep breath, finding my inner strength. I'm not going to let them steal another moment of my life. "Let's get this barbeque moving. Cam, can you start the grill? I'll have someone bring out the potatoes and corn in a minute."

I'm thankful to shut this down, at least for now. I refuse to live in fear any longer. Today is supposed to be a happy day. I don't ant this drama stealing that from us too.

While I play horseshoes with Jazz and Aubrey, I look out at a yard full of family and friends. Some have wandered off, likely on cleanup duty so it's not all left for Cam and me later.

This is what I've always dreamed of: a large family full of love.

Jazz hands me a beer and turns on music, a song I recognize called "Hero" by Skillet. As the game winds down, Marie walks over, Grammy with her, and asks me to take a walk with her.

"Sure," I say before turning to let Jazz know that I'll find her in a few.

She pulls me in for a quick hug, then hands me a single white rose.

"What's this for?" I ask.

"Go," Jazz says, turning me toward Cam's mom. "Trust me. Go for a walk with Marie."

I'm so confused, but I comply.

Grammy is a sweet, little, five-foot-nothing, blue-haired older woman with more style than Kayla and I put together. She nods. "Give me a hug, dear."

As I pull back from her, I'm handed another white rose and given a kiss on my cheek.

"Now, go with Marie. You'll be just fine. We'll see you soon."

Confusing me even more, I turn back to Marie, who interlocks our arms and begins walking toward the fence line.

"What's going on? Where's Cam?"

She smiles but doesn't answer, just continues walking until we get past the gate, where we're met by Butch. He takes a lit lantern off the fence post, then joins us, tucking my other hand into the crook of his elbow.

As we walk further out into the field, my heart is racing so fast that I feel weak in my knees. I don't know what's going on, but seeing as Cam disappeared some time ago, I bet he has something to do with whatever this is.

"What's going on?" I ask them both. "Did Cam put you up to this?"

"We've been sworn to secrecy," Marie says. "I'm sorry, honey, but we can't tell you."

If these two weren't Cam's parents, I would turn around right now, but considering that I know they'll do whatever they can to keep me safe, I follow.

We come upon Mark and Becca next. When we stop in front of them, Butch and Marie each kiss my cheek before handing me another white rose and swapping out the lantern for Mark's flashlight. They head back off in the direction we came from before Becca and Mark each take an arm, walking me forward once more. Knowing they won't tell me anything, I stay quiet and enjoy the walk.

When we get to Janelle, my stomach is in my throat. I know Cam's behind this now, but what's he doing? He couldn't be . . . no. I shake that thought from my head. Surely, he's not proposing already, is he?

Mark and Becca each hand me a single white rose. "We'll see you soon," they say as they walk off.

I link arms with Janelle.

"Enjoy the moment and don't overthink it," she says.

"You know us. Nothing but good is coming."

It's more than the others have said to me.

"Thank you, Janelle," I reply.

Coming upon Pat and Kim next, the process goes the same. I link arms and walk until I see Mike and Kayla come into view. I swallow down my tears as Pat and Kim hand me off. At this point, I'm overwhelmed with feelings of love.

After linking arms with Mike and Kayla, we start walking. I know if anyone will spill, it'll be them.

"What's going on, guys? I know Cam's behind this. Is he—"

Mike looks at Kayla and shakes his head. "Leah, don't ask us, please," he begs. "We love you, but we promised to stay quiet. Enjoy the fact that your family is here for you right now."

Saying nothing else, we continue walking.

Once we get to Uncle Joe and Janet, tears fall that I can't control any longer. Mike and Kayla hand me a single white rose, kiss me on the cheek, and hand me and the lantern off to Uncle Joe.

Janet leans in, kisses me on the cheek, hands me a rose, and walks back with Mike and Kayla, leaving me alone with Uncle Joe.

He and I walk, arms linked with one another for a while until I see the Gator. It's decked out in fairy lights.

I can't help but feel giddy. This screams proposal, but I don't want to get my hopes up, so I stamp down my giddiness the best as I can.

Uncle Joe pulls me to a stop, takes my hand, then gives me a sunflower and two white roses. "These are from the three of us—Mom, Dad, and me. They would be so proud of the amazing woman you've become. I know I am. I love you, baby doll. Now I'm going to hand you off to Tom. I have to put this on you, though," he says, holding up a blindfold. "You can trust Tom. He won't steer you wrong. He'll get you where you're going." Uncle Joe kisses my cheek, wipes my tears, and puts the blindfold on me before helping me into the Gator.

After I'm seated, Tom puts his hand over mine in a supportive gesture.

If he weren't sitting next to me, I might be scared. During the ride, I think back to everyone who took a part in this. Cam involved both of our families and I never even knew a thing.

Tom pats me on the knee, bringing me back to the moment, and I realize that we aren't moving anymore. "Stay here. I'm coming around to help you out."

I nod, and soon enough, I feel one hand on my shoulder and another on my elbow, guiding me to stand. Once I'm on solid ground, he links my arm through his as all the others have and guides me a little further. When we come to a stop, he turns me back around to face the way we came from and takes the blindfold off.

"Stay looking at me, please."

When I agree, he pulls me in for a hug. Then he steps back, his eyes are shiny, but there's a huge smile on his face. "Leah, both you and Cam have been through so much. What happened at Disney shook me, but you stepped up when Cam couldn't and got you guys through it. You've shown me just how much you love him. Your love for my brother has given me hope that someday, I'll be able to find a love like yours. I'd like to be the first to welcome you to the family." He hugs me once more. "Now, turn around and go get your man." He hands me another white rose before he walks off toward the Gator.

I'm a mess. After all that, the tears won't stop. I've never been shown so much love before. I am so full right now, I want to run to Cam. Instead, I take a steadying breath, wipe my eyes, and turn around, then nearly faint at the beauty before me.

The love of my life is standing in the middle of a field, before a backdrop made up of the starlit sky. I'm at the head of a path that leads to him. It's lined with battery-operated tea-light candles and white rose petals. Behind Cam is an altar created from old, teal-colored doors and branches wound around pieces of wood. A vintage white chandelier is hanging in the center. At least three dozen white roses and a bottle of champagne sit on a bistro table and chairs off to the side. But the most important part is my man standing in the center, looking like a nervous wreck. He's holding yet another white rose and a sunflower.

I wipe the tears from my eyes so I can see and take my first step in his direction. When I get to him, I lay down the flowers and lean in for a kiss. He kisses me softly before stepping back and getting down on one knee.

Oh my God.

"Leah, sweetheart, I've loved you from the moment I laid eyes on you. You've held my heart in your hands this whole time. My time away from you was hell. I'll never do that again. I don't want to spend as much as a day without you in my life." He produces a ring box from behind his back. "You once told me that you didn't have much family. I hope tonight that you see that's not the case. *You* make us one.

I love you so much, and I can't wait to wake up next to you every day for the rest of my life. Leah Covington," he says with a big smile on his face, "will you do me the honor of becoming my wife?"

I pull my hands away from my face and nod vigorously. "Yes, Cam, *yes*. I'll be your wife."

He stands and takes my hand, struggling a bit to take the ring out of the box with the other. Once he slides it onto my finger, he leans in and kisses me, taking my breath away.

"I was so nervous. I can't wait to tell everyone that my fiancée said yes!" Cam says excitedly with a fist pump.

I can't help but chuckle at how cute he is. "Babe, I'd have said yes no matter how or when you asked me. It's not what you did that mattered. Though I'm beyond happy with what you did—you're one romantic man. What matters is that I have no doubt that this is right. I can't wait to be your wife."

Cam smiles and takes out his phone, turning on some music before leading me to the open field lined with candles. "I can't wait any longer to have you in my arms. Dance with me?"

"Of course," I say. As we begin to sway, I lean my head on his chest. "You really surprised me tonight. I knew something was up, but I didn't expect this. I knew this was coming at some point, but I figured in a year or so. This . . . is perfect."

I can feel him rest his chin on my head as we get impossibly closer. "I've wanted to do this for a long time. After nearly dying in Disney, I couldn't hold off any longer. I want you in my arms, in our home, stealing my shirts for the rest of my life. I don't want to wait anymore."

With a sigh, I think, *the feeling is mutual.*

Chapter Twenty-Four

Standing in the kitchen, I pour myself a cup of coffee, then sit at the island. Last night was amazing. I can still hardly believe I'm an engaged woman. The proposal—it was perfect. I look at my ring now that I have daylight and a moment to myself to take it all in. It's a beautiful, vintage, rose-gold ring, with a morganite center wrapped in chocolate and white diamonds. I love that Cam kept it small. I don't think I would have worn it around if it was gaudy.

"Good morning, fiancée," Cam says. He steps up to the side of me, kissing me on the head before going to make a cup of coffee for himself.

"Good morning, handsome." I pull my hand back and shift to take a drink of my coffee.

Cam turns around to look at me and smiles blindingly. Last night, after we got back to the house, most everyone was still here. They had the place cleaned up and were waiting to hear the news. Cam and I walked into the house hand in hand. He raised our joined hands and announced, "Everyone out! Not to be rude, but I'd like some time to enjoy my fiancée. Alone!"

Even though he gave them the boot, it still took nearly thirty minutes for everyone to clear out. Through all the wedding talk and goodbye hugs, Cam's hand never left mine. When everyone was gone, he threw me over his shoulder and carried me to our bedroom. I wanted to shower, and Cam—even though we're now getting married—had me put on my swimsuit so he could join me.

"Cam, we're getting married now," I said. "I told you before, I'm not saving myself for my wedding night. I only wanted to make sure that whoever I gave myself to was the one. You're it for me, babe."

"I know you said that, but Leah," Cam huffed, "we've waited this long. What's a few more months? It'll be worth the wait when we can finally give ourselves to each other as husband and wife."

Frustrated, my shoulders slumped. Of course, the one man I wanted to give myself fully to didn't want it. Well, at least not then.

"Fine. I'll grab my swimsuit." Even though I felt a little hurt over his comment, it was still an amazing night.

This morning, I woke before Cam did. My phone had started going off at five in the morning. Instead of getting changed, I washed my face, put my hair up in a messy bun, and came downstairs in nothing more than Cam's T-shirt and boy shorts. He told everyone to give us the weekend, so I'm not worried about anyone barging in.

Kayla, of course, immediately started a wedding group chat with all our friends and family members. The questions started rolling in as soon as it got created and haven't stopped since.

I open my phone and start scrolling through the texts when Cam sits next to me.

Kayla: *Do we have a date yet?*

Tom: *Knowing Cam, it'll be before New Year's.*

Marie: *Do you know how big you want it to be? Indoors, outdoors? How many guests?*

Uncle Joe: *I'll take care of the cake, food, and event tent for the reception. Just let me know what you want and when. We'll make it happen.*

Mike: *I can help wherever you need me.*

Seeing all these texts is overwhelming, but I also love that all everyone's so excited that they're trying to help.

"That's a lot to take in," Cam says, looking over my shoulder. "Do we really need to know all of that now?"

It is a lot, but most weddings are. "It depends on when we're getting married. If we wait a year, then no. But if Tom's right, yes." I look at Cam in question. "When would you like to say 'I do'?"

"We can go to the courthouse today, if you want," he replies. Cam kisses me on my shoulder, then looks back up at me. "But I'd like for you to have a wedding. Do you think we can get married before Christmas?"

"That's awfully quick. I mean, it can be done if we ask everyone for help and have it here on the farm, but it'll be a lot of work." I'd marry him today, but I would love a wedding like he said. Nothing big or flashy, just full of love and those closest to us.

"How about we marry toward the end of November or the beginning of December? I don't care how much work it is. I can guarantee with all of us pulling together, it can get done."

"Are you sure about this?" I question. "If we marry that quick, we really need to get started today with the planning."

"I'm in. I want to walk into next year as Mr. and Mrs. Cameron. What would you rather, November or December?"

I love how determined he is—I just hope we can pull this off.

"How about the first Saturday in December. That gives us a little over a month but is a decent distance between Thanksgiving and Christmas."

It will be perfect. In central Oklahoma, it's rare to have any kind of real cold weather by then. Many Okies are still out barbecuing. As long as we plan for any freak storms, all should work out.

Cam pulls out his phone and opens his calendar app. "December second, it is. Looks like we need to tell the others."

I open my text messages again, but Cam beats me to it.

Cam: *Wedding date: December 2nd, this year. Give us a bit and we'll scroll through the messages and answer all the questions that we can.*

"How many guests do you want, babe?" I ask.

"I think we can keep it kind of small, but I know there's a lot of people who will want to show up. Why don't we say no more than a hundred? If we do it here on the farm, where do you want to have it?"

"I can deal with a hundred, but not many more than that. Since it'll be late fall, we can get away with having an outside wedding so long as we have outdoor heaters in case a cold front moves in. How about near the pond? We both love it there, and we can have the sunset at our backs."

I can picture it already—the yellows and oranges of a fall sunset in Oklahoma as the grass and leaves are changing colors. It'll be beautiful and cool enough to enjoy an evening outside.

"I can ask Kayla if she can get Bennett to do the photography. It'll be a long shot, but he's the best. I'd love to have him."

"And I can ask Becca to get ahold of the florist. Maybe she'll help with the wedding on such short notice since she did the engagement."

Cam and I talk for nearly an hour, then open the group text, making sure that we've covered all the questions asked. Then we send one information dump reply so they know where to find it all.

Me: *December 2nd at four in the evening, just before sunset. We would like to keep the guest list down as much as possible, so no more than a hundred. Uncle Joe, we'd like a lemon cake with blueberries for the main and chocolate-strawberry for the groom cake. Keep the food Southern—meatloaf and fried chicken options served with mash potatoes, green beans, cornbread, and a side salad. Cam and I will take care of the music, then will hand it off as soon as we get that done.*

Cam takes my hand in his and squeezes. We have such a good support system backing us up that I know we won't have any issues getting this done.

The confirmation texts start rolling in. Kayla informs us that she already reached out to Bennett and that he has agreed to help out. She's also trying to contact the designer of her last bridal shoot to see if she can squeeze us in for a fitting.

There's some back-and-forth about the location and such, and then the big question comes up.

Marie: *Okay, it sounds like almost everything is under control then. We'll have a lot to do, but it looks like you will have plenty of help. Who's in your wedding party?*

Cam: *I want Mark as my best man, and Tom and Pat as groomsmen.*

I furrow my brow and look over at Cam. "I thought we'd ask them in person."

He leans over and kisses my shoulder. "Sorry, babe. I've never done this before. I didn't even think about that."

Cam: *Sorry all. I should have asked in person. I didn't even think of how that could affect others.*

Tom: *I think we all know who the wedding party will be. It's fine.*

Kayla: *I accept. Just say it, sis. It's going to drive me crazy if you don't say so now and I have to wait a week to hear it.*

I chuckle. "See what you started?"

Cam shrugs, puts his phone down, and scoots closer, taking me into his arms. He moves the fabric of my shirt so he can kiss the bare skin of my shoulder. "Mmhmm."

I love his kisses, closing my eyes for a moment and just enjoying him. My phone chimes, pulling me back to the present.

"You better answer them." Cam continues kissing my shoulder and neck, making it hard to concentrate.

Me: *Kayla, maid honor. Becca and Kim, maids. Aubrey, flowers.*

Kayla: *You ok, sis?*

I look to my phone and see the text. I quickly stand, getting away from Cam's kisses for just a moment so I can find my head and reply. From the heat in my face, I sure am glad that nobody else can see me right now.

"You have one minute to reply and then you're mine," Cam says. He lifts his phone to send a message himself.

I frantically begin typing.

Me: *I'd like Kayla to be my maid of honor. Becca and Kim, I'd like you to be my bridesmaids, and Aubrey the flower girl.*

Cam's text comes in just after I send mine.

Cam: *We're out. Phones won't be answered the rest of the weekend unless it's an emergency. If so, blow us both up. Talk to you all Monday.*

As soon as I look up from my phone, I see Cam stalking me like I'm a gazelle and he's the lion on a hunt. Oh, this is going to be fun. I love when he's like this.

I toss my phone on the counter and turn to take off upstairs, knowing that I won't make it any further than a few steps before he's on me.

Life is good.

By the following Wednesday, most of the wedding is coming together nicely. We pull off a miracle and get the whole wedding party off work for a few hours at the same time for our apparel appointments. The designer Kayla reached out to also owns the men's side of a wedding shop.

When we pull up out front for our appointment, Cam and I step out of the truck and meet our party.

Cam leans in, giving me a hurried kiss. "I'll see you after." He gives me one more quick kiss before righting himself. "She's all yours."

After watching him walk away, I turn and go into the boutique with the other ladies. I'm taken aback. It hasn't really hit me until now that I'm about to try on the dress that I'll marry Cam in. The girls, clueless to my thought process, are already rummaging through the gowns hanging along the wall to the right.

Marie walks over. "It's a lot, isn't it? Don't worry,

we're all here for you. I have a very good feeling about today. I know you'll find the one."

Though I wish my mom were here with me in this moment, I fight back my tears as best as I can. I'm grateful to have Marie. I don't want her to feel as if I'm not. "Thanks, Mom. It *is* a lot. It's been a rollercoaster of emotions."

The dress shop employee steps forward from the front desk. "Ms. Covington?"

"That's me," I say.

"How about I take you to the fitting room? We'll talk about what you're looking for. I'll come and select a few myself, as well as a few that your friends and family choose, and we'll go from there."

I nod and follow her to the fitting room. I don't really have any idea of what I want or what would look good on me, but Jackie—my personal dress shopper—says she has a few ideas.

In a matter of twenty minutes, she walks back in with a rack of dresses. "How about we start with family and friend picks?"

I do as she suggests, and after four failed attempts, I move on to Jackie's choices. By dress six, I'm ready to give up. Nothing feels right. Nothing makes me feel like a bride, like I can envision myself walking down the aisle toward Cam in it.

Marie knocks on the door before sticking her head inside.

"Come in," I say.

She steps in, bringing a dress with her. "Hun, all these dresses are lovely, but I don't think any hold a candle to your beauty. Nothing screams *Leah*. When we walked in, I saw this one and immediately thought of you. I'd be honored if you'd try it on."

That's sweet of her. I wonder why she didn't have Jackie bring it in with the others.

"Of course, I'd be happy to." At this point, I have nothing to lose.

"Let's get this on you, then," Jackie says.

Marie excuses herself, and I step into my next dress. As I turn to face the mirror, I know right away.

"This is it," I say. I put my hand to my mouth as I fight to hold back tears.

"This is the one?" Jackie asks for confirmation.

I nod. "This is *the* dress."

"Alright, then. Let's show the others."

I leave the dressing room and step up onto the pedestal in the showroom. Jackie straightens out my gown. As she does, I hear gasps all around. My dress is an A-line gown with a plunging sweetheart neck, lace straps, and a deep V-back. The bodice is covered in elegant, floral lace appliqués. Layers of tulle cascade down into a chapel train, edged in what Jackie calls horsehair trim. The best part is that the dress is ivory and rose—I don't care for white dresses. Rhinestones are placed all over the dress, making me shine. This is the most perfect sunset wedding gown I've ever seen. Cam won't know what hit him.

"Oh honey, you're stunning. Cam's gonna fall over when he sees you," Marie says.

"OMG Leah. You're a bride," Kayla says, wiping her tears away.

"Thank you," I say, wiping my own. "I feel like a bride."

"How about we accessorize?" Jackie suggests.

"Please," I respond.

"I have a surprise for the bride," Becca interjects. She looks at the clerk behind the counter and nods. "When we spoke about the wedding, you said no heels since we'll be in a field." She pauses as the clerk brings over a couple bags. Becca accepts one, takes out a box, then opens it. "I hope you don't mind, but I ordered bridal boots. Yours are ivory and rose—I remember you saying you love rose gold—with rhinestones," she says with a big smile. "Ours are blue with little sunflowers. I swear, when I ordered them, I didn't know about the dress."

"You shouldn't have," I say as I accept the tissue I'm given by Jackie. "Thank you, I love them."

Marie steps forward, opening a bag of her own. She produces a veil and hair comb. "This veil was worn by my mom and then me. The hair comb has been in the family for five generations. I'd love it if you'd wear them on your wedding day."

My eyes begin to fill with tears again. I take Marie's hand in mine as a sign of gratitude. "Thank you, Mom. I'd love to," I cry.

"You look amazing, sis," Kayla says. "I can't wait to see this all come together. Now, let's get this show on the road, girls. I have to get back to work."

After I change, Jackie pulls several options for the ladies and Aubrey. I fall in love with a sleek, strapless, mermaid-cut, floor-length gown in navy with a sweetheart neckline. The gown has no embellishments, but the simple elegance is classic.

I hand each bridesmaid a box in gratitude. When they open them, the single pearl necklace set in silver and a pair of pearl drop earrings completes this look. For my maid of honor, I went with a water droplet diamond necklace and earring set. They look amazing.

When it comes time to finding Aubrey a dress, I'm worried that she might not like the ones I want.

"Can I have a pwetty pwincess dwess like you, pweese?" she asks me.

I kneel and give her a hug. "Miss Jackie has a few princess dresses for you to try on. Why don't you go with her, and we'll see what dress makes you look like the prettiest princess possible?"

The second dress is it—it's the perfect fit. The lace that overlays the sweetheart neckline and the layers of tulle do it for me. When they have her turn so we can see the keyhole back and tiny train, I'm sold, and when Jackie adds a navy-blue belt with a sunflower clip to tie it all together, I call it a day.

She runs the color swatch next door for the guys, then we begin to check out and schedule the next fitting. Some minor alterations need to be done to my dress, so we'll pick them up the week before the wedding.

Once we leave the shop, we wait on the guys to finish up. I pull out my phone and reserve a suite at one of the local hotels for the ladies and me for the night before the wedding. We may not be following all old-school traditions, but this is one thing that I want to do.

Chapter Twenty- Five

Two more weeks go by in a blur. Planning for the wedding, finalizing the sale of my apartment, unpacking, furnishing the house, and going trick-or-treating with Aubrey keep us busy. Not to mention my work and training—it's been kicking my butt. Cam is helping wherever he can. He extended his sabbatical to the end of February due to physical therapy and to ensure that there is plenty of time to take care of things around here and get stuff wrapped up with Stalker John and Tillie. There hasn't been much activity from them other than a note saying, "See you soon, Leah," left at my work last Friday and a set of punching gloves left on the patio. Cam and the other guys freaked out and now they watch me closer than ever before. I don't leave the farm, unless Cam or one of the other guys are with me. No more leaving with the ladies. I get it, but still, I hate being cooped up so much.

Today, we have a full day planned. Tonight, we have VIP tickets to the Thunder game. Mark and Becca, Pat and Kim, Mike and Kayla, who have been acting weird since they got back from their trip, and Tom, and Janelle are all coming with us. We have a whole night of festivities planned.

The others trickle in as I grab my shoes and begin to lace them.

"I can hardly believe everyone is able to get together for this," Kim says.

"Agreed," Cam adds.

My phone goes off, alerting me that it's nearly time for us to head to the stadium. Cam and I load up into Mark's truck and head out, the others following closely behind. Mike and Kayla are meeting us there.

As soon as I see the stadium in the distance, my shoulders start bouncing. "I can hardly wait for this. Come on, let's go," I say to Cam. I grab his hand and tug him out as soon as the truck is parked.

We all gather near Tom's truck at the front of the lot, then head toward the stadium box office. After getting our lanyards, we head in the direction we were pointed. At the entrance, I see a few cheerleaders and three golfcarts.

One of them steps forward. "Welcome! I need Mr. and soon-to-be Mrs. Cameron to the front, please."

Cam and I step forward, and she puts a sash over each of our heads. His reads, "Groom," and mine reads, "Bride." Next, she pulls out handcuffs, linking us together. Don't worry, I have the key," she delivers with a wink. She leads us to the golf cart, where another cheerleader sits, and we get in next to her.

"Sorry about her," she says. "Haley gets a little out of hand sometimes. I'm Madison—Maddie for short. Nice to meet you both."

"Nice to meet you too."

"I need the maid of honor and best man next," Haley says, from behind us.

"They're not a couple," I respond. "If you handcuff my sister and his best friend, his wife might have an issue with that."

Maddie and Cam both laugh, but I can only imagine Becca. She likes Kayla well enough, but Mark is not someone she shares, even for antics such as this.

"No cuffs then," she says. "Sit behind the bride and groom, please."

After she has everyone in position, Haley hops in one and takes off. Maddie follows closely behind.

Maddie leans in. "When's the wedding?"

"December second," I say.

"Congratulations. That's awesome," she replies.

"It is," I say, smiling at Cam. "Are you married, Maddie?"

"Oh God, no. I've been with the same guy for six years. I don't really see us going anywhere, but it is what it is. It's so hard to find anyone who'll take me seriously."

"Does your boyfriend not take you seriously?" I ask. "Sorry, I barely know you and here I am, already prying."

"It's fine," she assures me. "No, Ashton doesn't take me seriously at all. He and I have been together since high school. We're basically just friends now. We never do anything unless one of us needs a plus-one for something. He thinks I'm a bit of a ditz, and I can't see past his behavior."

"I don't know you at all and I can tell that you're not a ditz."

"Thanks."

Maddie parks the cart and leads us through the stadium doors into the court. It looks so different when it's empty. There's supposed to be a game in a few hours, but since it's our wedding party, we were able to buy this package that got us a VIP room and the opportunity to meet the squad. This moment is something I know I won't soon forget. Being on the court with the cheer squad and my family and friends is insane.

"She's gorgeous," Tom says, upon approach.

I chuckle. I knew at some point he'd make comments about the ladies. "Who, Maddie?"

"Maddie . . ." he tries on before nodding.

Haley runs over, grabbing Cam and me. She walks us out to center court, where she has a chair waiting. Cam sits, then she directs me to sit on his lap. The squad does some kind of cheer for us in congratulations, then they call some guy from the stands who appears to be a photographer.

Maddie leans in. "I hope you don't mind. The girls love a photo op."

"Not at all, as long as we get copies," I say. I notice Maddie staring at Tom, even though she's talking to me. "You know, he's single, and a good guy."

She shakes her head as if she doesn't understand, then looks at me. "I don't know what you mean. I have a boyfriend."

It's not that I want her to act on it without dealing with her boyfriend first, but she doesn't seem happy. Would it be wrong to be upfront and tell Tom she likes him but is in a complicated relationship right now? Knowing that would give him a chance to walk away or open the lines of communication.

"You yourself said he's no more than a plus-one. I don't mean for you to cheat on him. But I see you checking Tom out," I state as Cam nudges me. "I'm not saying anything other than maybe you should think it over. Everyone deserves to be happy."

She looks back at Tom, then nods as if her mind is made up. "Someone like him would have no interest in me. I'm nothing in real life like I am when I put on this uniform. This job requires me to step out of my norm. Besides, it's not like Ashton will accept me trying to break up again. He never does."

"What do you mean he'd have no interest in you? You're beautiful!"

She really is—dirty-blonde hair with tight curls, beautiful baby-blue eyes, porcelain skin, and tiny waist. Her looks complement Tom rather well. I bet she's at least five foot ten or eleven. She gives Kayla a run for her money in the beauty department.

"And what do you mean he won't accept it?" Cam asks.

"I've said too much already. I shouldn't have even brought it up. Sorry. I'm normally the shy type—quiet, really. I better hush; we have pictures to take." She quickly stands up and joins the huddle to talk to her squad.

"Maddie," I hear from one of her squad members. "That man has eyes for you. If you're not going to make a move, I'm going to slip him my number. He's delicious."

"Leave it be, Kells. You know about Ashton. I can't bring anyone into that drama. Let's just do this. We have a game tonight, you know," Maddie replies.

Cam catches me listening in. "Let them work it out, sweetheart. You already planted the seed. Tom will be happy that you tried."

"All right, Cameron wedding crew, we'll take a couple pictures, then move on to some games. A quick meet and greet with the team, then we'll walk you up to your box," Haley says.

After taking pictures of us with the squad, the whole group gets into the photos.

In the end, Maddie pulls me aside. "I'm going to slip Tom my number. Can you let him know not to use it if he wants to be more than friends? I like him, but I can't start anything right now. There's just something special about him. I can't get him off my mind."

I'm thrilled for Tom, and yet at the same time, she mentioned that her boyfriend is drama. Maybe I shouldn't have stuck my nose out there after all. "I'll let him know." I will, but I need to make sure he knows what he's signing up for too.

Maddie walks over to her squad, so I grab Cam and tell him what's going on. He wraps his arms around my waist, holding me close. Knowing that she has the support of her squad, she appears more confident than before.

Out of the corner of my eye, I see the guys on the team start walking out. The cheer squad moves from their huddle, producing a chair in the center. Maddie sits Tom down in the chair, then leans in to whisper something that causes him to laugh. The squad does some sort of cheer meant just for Tom as the team walks out to the rest of us for a meet and greet.

I get them to sign a foam finger that I brought for the game, a gift for Uncle Joe. They all seem down to earth and easy to talk to. They don't have much time considering that they have a big game soon, so they make their rounds and leave.

Nearly thirty minutes later, Maddie and Haley lead the way to our VIP box.

"If you're free after the game," I say to Maddie, "we're

going to the Smirking Tree Saloon. We'd love it if you can come."

"Give me your number and I'll let you know. If the girls have no plans, I'd be happy to."

After exchanging numbers and showing us to our suite, Maddie and Haley take off to get ready for the game.

Tom beams with pride as he pulls me from Cam, giving me a big ol' bear hug. "Seriously, sis, that was freaking awesome. You can be my wingwoman any day." He looks over at Mark and Cam. "Sorry, guys, you've been replaced."

"I'm glad you're happy, but I want you to be careful. She mentioned that her *boyfriend* is drama. She seems like a good one, but from the sounds of it, she's wrapped up in something heavy."

"She told me. Plus, it's just a friendship right now."

When my phone beeps, I'm pulled from our talk. I take it out to check the text.

Unknown: *Hey Leah, it's Maddie. The girls have no plans tonight. I'm free if the offer still stands. I'll have to run home and grab a change of clothes first though.*

Me: *I can ask my sister if she has a dress that you can borrow.*

Surprisingly, I get a text back right away.

Maddie: *That would be great! Let me know.*

Me: *How about you meet us out front when you're done? We'll go to my sister's after and change.*

Maddie: *Sounds good. Can I give Haley your inform-*
ation? I trust that nothing will happen since I'll be with a
bunch of cops, but better safe than sorry.

Me: *Of course!*

Maddie: *Gotta go. See you in a few . . .*

After meeting Maddie, I nearly forget that we're here for a game, but seeing the smile on Tom's face it's worth it. I just hope that I didn't open a world of hurt for him.

After the game, Mike walks over to Biff's and places a big order to bring back to his place. Since we have Maddie with us now and we still need to get ready, we figure takeout is the best option. The ladies and Cam head back to his place while the guys hang back and wait on Mike.

By the time I walk into Kayla's room, Maddie in tow, most of the girls—Kayla, Becca, Kim, and Janelle—are already stripping down. I produce a dress from my bag and smile—every woman needs a little black dress.

Kayla takes one look at it and shakes her head. "I'm glad I went shopping. I knew you'd do this. We're celebrating a wedding, not going to a funeral. Hold on, I got you." She goes to her closet and pulls out a beautiful, deep-red dress with spaghetti straps, a plummeting V-neck, and no back.

It falls just below my butt cheeks, then has a small ruffle that flows when I move. In the past there was no way in hell I'd wear this out, but tonight, knowing I'll be on Cam's arm, I feel empowered—sexy even. I know that when he sees me in this, he'll barely be able to keep his hands off me. I love knowing that I do that to him. It's a rush.

Kayla attacks each one of us with her glittery body spray as I take my hair down, putting it in hot curlers before doing my makeup.

Once the curlers are out, I leave it down and put on my black heels. I rummage through Kayla's jewelry and grab a white-gold rhinestone lariat necklace that matches my diamond-studded earrings. I move to grab my coat when Kayla stops me.

"Not tonight, sis. That's what Hot Cop's for."

"That nickname is never going away, is it?" I ask, on a giggle.

"Nope! He's hot and he's a cop. It suits him. Just because he's getting married doesn't change that," Kayla adds.

"Don't ever change, sis," I reply, then lean in for a quick hug. "Are we ready?"

"Yes, but one at a time," Kayla says. "These guys won't know what hit them."

That's Kayla—anything can be turned into a fashion show. I wouldn't have it any other way. I love my sister and all her over-the-top behavior.

Janelle goes out first. I hear Tom say, "Where on earth are the rest of your clothes?" I can't help but laugh at that brotherly response.

"What? I'm a single woman; I never dress like this," she retorts. "Let me have fun."

"What he meant," Mark interjects, "is that you look beautiful. Just be careful. There are a lot of jerks out there."

"Thank you, Mark. I have you guys with me. I just want to have fun tonight," Janelle replies.

"As you should!" I yell out.

When Kim steps out, I hear Pat whistle. "Looking good, pumpkin."

I'm over this already and just want to get the night moving, but I can't help but enjoy the responses my friends are getting.

Becca pauses at the door for a moment so I can get a better look at her. Her deep-green and bling-covered dress has a slit up the side to her upper thigh. When she steps out, I hear some whistles and what sounds like Mark choking up a bit. "Damn, baby, you're gonna be the death of me in that dress. How long does Marie have Aubrey again?" he asks.

I can't help but chuckle.

"Not long enough, apparently," Tom jokes.

Kayla steps up to the door, then looks back at Maddie and me as she cracks it open. "You two come out together. You're gonna blow the socks right off those two." She slips through, and I hear Mike grumble, "Damn, Kay, you look freaking hot!"

That is such a Mike reaction. He never has a problem telling her how beautiful she is. I'm a little worried about them, though. There's been a lot of tension between the two of them lately.

"You ready for this?" I ask.

"I guess. I didn't know I'd be doing a catwalk tonight when I agreed to come."

I grab her hand and squeeze lightly. "Sorry about that. It's kind of Kayla's thing."

"I'm just glad she didn't push me out there on my own. Are you sure this is alright? I'm not trying to give anyone the wrong impression."

I take a deep breath, hold it, and let it out. "Tom knows what he's getting into. We had a talk earlier and he knows you're just friends. I don't think you're leading him on. You were up front about it. Just don't hurt him, okay? He's a good man with a big heart, no matter how much he plays around. He's a big softie." I have mixed feelings; I really like Maddie and I would love to see her and Tom together, but I have a feeling that there's a lot more to this Ashton guy than she's letting on and that bugs me.

When she nods, I put my hand on the knob and push the door open. Maddie and I walk out together. Cam has his back to me, but I see Tom's eyes bug out of his head. He hits Cam in the arm, and says something, effectively stopping their conversation.

"Damn, you ladies look good!" Mike says.

"No kidding," Pat adds.

I look over to see Maddie looking a little shy. She must really not like all the attention on her outside of work.

"Boys, how about you pick your jaws up off the ground and get your girls?" Mark states.

Tom snaps out of it. "Looking good, sis. I feel bad for Cam tonight." Then he turns toward Maddie and smiles brightly. "You're the loveliest woman I've ever laid eyes on. Would you allow me to escort you tonight?" he asks, extending his arm to her. "As friends, of course."

"I'd be honored, Tom. Thank you. You look nice also."

As they walk off, Cam comes up to me, taking my hand and lifting it so I can do a spin for him. "You look *amazing*! All the guys are going to be checking you out."

"That may be true, but I'm only going home with you."

Chapter Twenty-Six

I lean over the counter and fix the smudge of mascara under my eye. Today is Thanksgiving, my first as a member of the Cameron family. Well, not officially yet, but considering that my wedding is in *nine* days, I might as well say I'm a Cameron. I've been busting my tail all morning on dinner prep. Now it's eleven o'clock and everyone—both Cam's family and mine—has started showing up. Becca and Mark are here too. Becca's parents don't host the holidays anymore, and Mark's are in Florida this year. Apparently, they travel a lot.

I pull back and flatten out my top, making sure I look good. I have on a pair of high-rise, dark-blue skinny jeans, and a white V-neck tee tucked in and covered by a puffy, fall-orange sweater. I'll be putting on my booties in a minute.

"Hey, sis," Kayla says, walking into my bathroom. "You about ready? Uncle Joe just pulled up and has a car full. The guys went to help unload."

"Yeah. Let me grab my shoes."

We walk downstairs and I have to stop for a moment to take in how much my life has changed in the last year. It's crazy to think that a year ago, it was just Uncle Joe, Kayla,

Mike, and I—Janet was with her kids. This year, our house is full.

Kayla pats me on the shoulder and leans in. "This is amazing, isn't it? I'm glad you found a man that is willing to let your crazy family be a part of his. I don't know what I'd do without you in my life."

I turn around and pull her in for a quick hug. "You'll never have to know. I'm getting married and gaining a new family, but that doesn't mean anything will happen to us. You're always welcome here, Kay."

"She's right," Cam says, sneaking up on me. He leans in and kisses my cheek before looking back at Kayla. "I want you to feel at home here. We're your family too. We'll have many moments to share in the future. I hope you're a part of them." He pulls me to his side and smiles. "One day, we'll be starting a family and they're going to need their Aunt Kay just as much as they will my siblings."

I turn in his arms and give him a tight hug. "I love you, you know that?"

"I do. I feel the same for you."

"Alright, you two. I'm going to go make sure I didn't mess up my makeup," Kayla says, wiping a tear from her eye. "Thank you, Cam. It means a lot to me that you'd want to include me."

Kayla walks back upstairs while Cam and I turn and walk into the dining room that's full of chaos—I love it. Gathering around the table and bar is everyone I love. My heart has never been so full.

The week before our wedding, we have a combined shower and surprise anniversary party for Becca and Mark. It's been fun, but I think my favorite moment is when Becca tells me that they've decided to try for baby number two. After going to counseling with her for the last month or so, Mark agreed that it's time. I'm beyond happy for them.

There have been so many last-minute things to do that the days have begun to blur.

It's the day before the wedding, and Grammy arrived yesterday—she was unable to make it last week due to an illness—so we have a small shower set up at Tom's for the wedding party and close friends and family that want to participate. My bag is packed and next door, ready for my departure this evening. After the party, the girls and I will be loading into a limo and heading to the suite I rented for the night.

"You almost ready, beautiful?" Cam asks as he walks up behind me, placing a kiss on my temple.

"I am. Are you?"

"I'd rather take my bride back to bed and make out like teenagers a little more, but considering how good you look in that dress, I guess I can take you out and show you off."

This dress *is* nice if I say so myself. It reminds me of my wedding dress in a way. It's a simple, thin-line, backless dress, with a rose-colored silk slip and an ivory lace overlay. It floats just above the ground with a small train in the back.

It's not long enough to be stepped on or to be heavy, just enough to be bridal. It makes me feel beautiful. The simple three-drop diamond necklace and diamond-stud earrings I paired with it are perfect.

"Thank you, babe. You look good yourself."

Cam's in a nice pair of black slacks, an ivory button-up dress shirt, and a navy-blue tie. He looks very handsome and very much like a groom.

"If you keep checking me out like that, we might not make it to the party."

I link my arms behind Cam's neck, but before I have a chance to respond, I hear and feel a big boom not far in the distance. Way too close for comfort.

Cam wraps his arm around me, quickly throwing us to the ground. After he makes sure I'm safe, he goes to the side table, grabs his gun, and makes his way to the door. "Stay here and call Dad." Before I have a chance to respond, Cam's out the door.

"Leah!" I hear someone yell from the side door. "Leah, Cam, where are you?"

Turning to look behind me, I see Janelle coming in, looking frantic.

"Over here," I say.

She runs my way. "Are you alright? I was leaving Pat's when I saw the explosion." She pulls me up from the ground, looking me over. "You're not hurt, are you? Where's Cam?"

"Explosion?" I ask. "Oh my God, Janelle, Cam's out there!"

As soon as I fling the door open, I see a huge fire—one that is now engulfing my entire wedding event tent.

"Leah!" I hear from my side. I turn in time to see most of the wedding party running up the walk in their party attire with worried looks on their faces. Before I can say anything, I catch a flash of Mark, Tom, and Butch running out into the wooded area behind the tent.

"Thank God, you're safe," Marie says to me as she pulls me in for a hug.

Stunned, I stare out at the tent immersed in flames. Everything we had for our reception, minus the food and cake, is in that tent. Our wedding is tomorrow. *Oh God.*

Seeing that some of the guys have taken off into the woods, I move to grab my phone out of my purse, pulling up the camera app. I cover my mouth the moment I catch a glimpse.

John.

Seeing his face on my phone again brings back the same fear I had the day he met me in the stairwell. I'm so caught up in the memory that I don't notice Uncle Joe approaching.

"Hey, baby doll," he says as he puts his arm around my shoulders, causing me to jump. I look into his worried eyes, then melt into his arms, letting the tears fall. "Shh. I'm here. All's good now. We'll call in some favors and—"

"It's not that. I don't care if I stand in this living room and say my vows. I'm just tired of always having to look over my shoulder. Is nowhere safe?"

"You're safe here, you hear me? You *are* safe."

Being on an acreage full of cops, I'd like to feel safer than I do, but I don't. He's getting braver by the moment. It's only a matter of time before he's caught or he gets to me.

I see Pat run up the drive with buckets and toss them over to Cam—I didn't even know he left but I'm thankful he did. I slip off my shoes and run out that way, creating a chain as the others follow me. We start passing buckets of water from the pond down to the tent area to prevent the fire from spreading. We aren't making much progress in putting it out, but at least it's not getting worse.

I look out at the drive as I hear tires crushing rock. There's a line of cars following the one volunteer fire truck in Baycliff Valley. My shoulders sag in relief. The fire truck drives around the pond and out into the water-soaked grass near the tent. As the volunteers put out the flames, the neighbors on surrounding acreages pour out of their cars and head our way.

"Is everyone alright?" an older gentleman asks upon approach.

"I think so. I haven't had the time to check on everyone though," Cam replies.

"What can we do to help?"

"I'm not sure. I guess we need to come up with a game plan now," Cam states.

"Come on, ladies," Marie says to Becca, Kim, and a few others who just showed up. "Let's go inside and make some snacks and drinks for our volunteers."

"Mom," I say, "we have a party full of food and drinks. Why don't you send a few to Tom's to collect it, and a few can grab some tables from the garage? There should be plenty to feed everyone."

"Are you sure, Leah? That's for your wedding party."

"I'm sure. The party plans have changed."

Seeing as the fire destroyed the event tent and party supplies and the fact that our wedding is tomorrow, we need to find a new location and décor fast. There's too much to do to party. No matter how much I feel like falling apart, I refuse to do so.

Cam walks over to me and pulls me in for a hug as others mill about around us. "Well," he starts, "we can always postpone."

I pull back and look up at him as tears of frustration burn my eyes. "Do you really want to put off our wedding? That's letting him win. I don't care where we get married, Cam. Sure, I would have loved what we had planned, but that's not a deal-breaker for me." I look around us and see everyone pitching in in some way—some passing out food, others coming back from the woods now, and some trying to fill in the ruts the fire engine left on our lawn. "I don't want to wait," I cry.

"Then what do you want to do? Tell me, sweetheart, and we'll make it happen."

I pull him toward the tables and get everyone's attention. "Do you all think it's possible to come up with the stuff needed to set up for a wedding tomorrow? We have the field Cam proposed in. The altar is still there. If we can divert everyone another way and drive them up there, we have a place."

Cam hugs me again. "Genius. We can drive them through Tom's land, toward the back. We'll all have to use our Gators to get the guest up there, but it's doable."

"I can bring over my tractor and trailer," one of the neighbors says. "I use it for hayrides every year. If someone can help me get it set up, I can get it here in the morning. That'll carry a dozen people at a time."

"I can see about borrowing the event tents from the church," someone else says.

"I have tables and chairs in my garage you can use."

The tears I've been holding back are unleashed as every one of them starts spouting off ways that they can help.

"I'm the manager of the dollar store. I can donate a hundred dollars' worth of décor."

Marie takes over, talking to all of them, pulling things together.

Cam leads me away to help me regain my bearings. This is a mess, and I didn't think we'd be able to pull it off. I'd have been willing to marry him either way, but seeing as this is going to work out, the relief is outstanding.

When three o'clock rolls around, the limo—the one I forgot was coming—pulls up in the drive. I stand, stretching my back. The ache is bad—I've been bent over making signs for our guests to follow for hours.

"Let me walk you," Cam says. He takes his work gloves off and reaches for my hand.

"Cam, I'm not going anywhere. I'm going to go tell him we won't be needing him after all."

He looks me over with a shake of his head. "Sweetheart, look at you standing here in your party dress, covered in filth. You're favoring your back and tomorrow is our wedding day. Go. Have your night with the ladies, get a massage and a manicure, and relax. The guys and I have got this. I promise, it'll get done. Enjoy your last night as my fiancée."

I put my hand on my hip and shake my head in protest. "Babe, there's too much that still needs to be done."

"It *will* get finished, I promise. I want you to go and get pampered. You deserve to go be catered to."

"This shouldn't all be on you."

"It won't be," Tom says. I look over to see him working right next to us, still in his suit and dress shoes. "We won't leave until it's done. You ladies go ahead and go relax."

"Ladies!" Cam hollers, looking around at all the women scattered around us, helping us despite their fancy clothes. "Go change and gather your bags. Your chariot awaits."

I'm done arguing. I really could use this time to reset.

"Thank you." Looking out to all that are gathered here to help us, I can't help but say it loudly to them too. "Thank you all."

"I love you, beautiful. Now let's go get your bags."

"I love you too."

By the time I make it to the limo, all the ladies—Kayla, Becca, Aubrey, Janelle, Kim, Marie, and Grammy—are already in the back. The driver loads my bags in the trunk for me.

Cam pulls me into him for a heated kiss, then pulls back. "I'll see you at the altar."

I can hardly wait. "I'll see you there," I reply.

I get seated in the back with the others but find myself looking out the window at Cam toeing some rocks before turning around and heading back. Not satisfied with how I left it, I roll down my window.

"Cam!"

"Get back in here, Leah. We gotta go. You'll see him tomorrow," Kayla says, tugging at the hem of my dress.

The others chuckle but tell the driver to wait as Cam approaches the limo.

"What is it, sweetheart? Did you forget something?" he asks on approach.

"Yeah." I grab a handful of his shirt and pull him in to me for another kiss. Hearing the cheers from within the limo, I chuckle before pulling back. "I love you," I say, turning him back around. "I'll see you soon, Mr. Cameron." I swat him on the butt before sitting back down and rolling up the window.

He looks over his shoulder and laughs as the other guys cheer him on, then takes a bow. "Show's over. Now get back to work."

I pull out my phone when it buzzes.

Cam: *That was fun. See you soon, fiancée.*

I look up to find that I'm being watched.

Kayla sticks out her hand. "Phone. Now. No talking to the groom until the I-dos."

"But, Kay," I protest.

"Don't argue, Leah. None but Marie will have theirs either. I'll make sure there are pictures taken, but I want you to enjoy this. If you're on your phone all the time, you won't fully be present."

"Fine," I say, handing her my phone.

Kayla takes it from my hand and drops it into Marie's bag. "Now the party starts!"

Chapter Twenty-Seven

Checking into the hotel is quick and easy. They immediately have a bellhop walk us to our suite, carting our bags along the way. Once he unloads the cart, he leaves us to it.

"Holy heck, y'all! I didn't realize how fancy this place was." When I reserved the room, I told the lady it would be for six to eight women for a bridal shower, so she must have set us up in the most glamorous room they have. There are three double queen rooms and one king, all with lush comforters on the bed, a sunken living area, and a wall of windows just below the massive chandelier. This room rivals the one where Julia Roberts stayed in *Pretty Woman*. Thank God my apartment sold; I'd never be able to afford this otherwise.

"No kidding. This place is legit," Kim adds.

"Let's find our rooms. The one to the left of the bar is supposed to be the master. I think it's fair that the bride should get that one," Kayla states.

Everyone starts divvying up rooms while I search for my bags.

"Aubrey, Grammy, and I can share a room," Marie adds.

"Kim and I can share," Becca says.

"That leaves me and Maddie if she's able to make it. I don't mind sharing," Kayla says.

I've had Maddie out to the farm for a few game nights since we met. Since she's been around more often, I invited her to my shower and the wedding. I really like her, and I hope things work out for her and Tom. I don't want to see either get hurt.

After taking our bags into our rooms, I hear a knock on the door. I walk back out and open it to find a hotel staff member wheeling in a garment rack with spa robes and slippers.

"Ma'am, I was informed that Sarah—our spa hostess—will be ready for you ladies downstairs in thirty minutes."

"Thank you," I reply. "We'll be there."

I let him out, then turn back and grab the white, silk bridal robe and slippers. I walk off to my room, letting the others know theirs are waiting on them. Once I'm in my robe, I move to the common area, where I find a vase loaded with flowers sitting on the bar. A card sits next to it, my name written across the front.

Leah,

I know we're supposed to have no contact right now, but I couldn't help myself. I miss you, and I had to know that you were smiling. I know at this very moment, you're holding this card in your hand and have the brightest, most beautiful smile on your face. That's enough to get me through until I hear your voice again. I love you, my soon-to-be wife.

—Always and forever, Cam

He is the sweetest man I know. As much as I hate sounding cliché, I miss him too . . . so much.

The girls all come out and head toward the door, waiting for me to join them.

"I'd like to forgo the waxing and go straight for the massage. Who knew I'd be so sore?" Kayla says. We head out toward the elevator and off to our evening of beauty. The whole while, I can't wipe the smile off my face.

The waxing is not forgotten, but when the spa hostess hears the story of our morning, she makes sure the massages are done to the point of making me feel like Jell-O. My face is smooth and glowing from the facial, and I choose a simple French-tip manicure, with rose-gold glitter for my ring finger. By the time we're back upstairs in our room, I'm ready for a nap. The ladies, on the other hand, have another idea. Mark meets us in our room to pick up Aubrey. He lets me know that the prep work has been finished. He's dropping Aubrey off at a sleepover and then he'll ensure Cam gets to let loose and relax a bit too.

As soon as the door's shut behind Mark, Kim says, "Dinner and nighties time!"

The ladies and I gather in the living room, still in our robes, eating and laughing. Once the gifts appear, I understand where the "nighties" part of that comment came from. I don't know how I manage not to crawl under the bed and hide. The amount of wedding-night lingerie I'm given is insane. Thankfully, since Marie and Grammy are with us, the girls—Maddie included, now that she made it—attempt to keep things PG-13. There are many laughs and some raunchy jokes—mostly thanks to Grammy—but overall, the night is calm.

I'm thankful when Kayla says, "It's time to wrap things up. The bride needs her beauty sleep, after all."

There are some grunts and a bit of argument, but when all is said and done, we head into our rooms to get a good night's sleep. Or at least try to. It's so hard trying to sleep without Cam beside me. I didn't realize how much I've grown to rely on him being next to me when we go to bed every night. Thinking of becoming his wife and knowing that we'll never have to be apart again helps me find the sleep I desperately need.

"Wake up, wake up, wake up!" Kayla says. She comes waltzing into my room, throwing the doors open, knocking them into the wall. "Today's the day you marry the love of your life!"

Squeezing my eyes tight, I squeal loudly as I kick my feet in excitement, then crawl out of bed. "OMG, Kay, I'm getting married today!"

"I know," she giggles. "Shower up. I'll get breakfast."

I shower quickly, humming the bridal march the whole time and throw on the sweat suit that Kim had custom made for me. Once packed up, I move to the common area and eat a quick croissant and fruit breakfast before we head down to check out.

As we pull up to the house, I'm a bundle of nerves. I see Tom standing on his porch and Uncle Joe walking that way. I can't help but wonder where Cam is and what he's doing.

Today is the day that I start the rest of my life. I hate that I said I wanted to spend the day away from him, but I know the time apart will make the reunion that much sweeter. I never thought I'd miss him this much though.

Before they let me walk from the car to the house, the girls surround me while holding up sheets so Cam can't sneak a peek. "You all know this is ridiculous, right?" I say with a laugh. "Cam won't try to look. I asked him not to."

"We're not taking any chances," Becca replies.

Once inside, we turn the dining room into a bridal suite and the office into a changing room. Kayla starts in on my hair and is almost done when Kim starts with my makeup.

"You're stunning," Maddie says. "Let's get you into your dress before we all start crying." She decided to come along and help wherever she's needed.

We all move to the office and get started.

Maddie and Kim work the buttons on my dress, while Becca fusses with my bouquet and Kayla helps me with my shoes.

There's a warning knock at the office door before Uncle Joe and Butch walk in, followed by Mark. I'm glad that they waited until now because the looks on their faces are everything.

"Baby doll, you look so much like your momma on her wedding day. Stunning," Uncle Joe says with tears in his eyes.

"You look beautiful, hun," Butch adds.

Fighting back happy tears is harder than I thought. I can only imagine what I will feel when I see Cam.

"Damn, Leah," Mark says. "You clean up nice."

"Thanks, I think," I reply.

"Mark, that's no way to compliment the bride," Becca says.

"It is when your wife is standing next to her," he retorts. I chuckle, but Uncle Joe pulls something out of his pocket, and the mood grows serious. It's Mom's wedding jewelry. I'd know it anywhere—a floating-diamond necklace and a pair of diamond chandelier earrings—Kayla and I used to gush over Mom and Dad's wedding album. Tears begin to fall. The others excuse themselves to give us privacy.

Uncle Joe holds my hand in the air, allowing me to twirl so that he can take in the whole image, having to wipe his own eyes in the process. "Your mom and dad would be so proud. When you were born, your parents both wrote you a letter in case something was to ever happen to them. It says to give it to you on your wedding day." He hands me an envelope with my name on the front in my mom's handwriting.

I put my hand to my mouth in disbelief and take a seat. How can I do this without Cam? I want him to be a part of this.

I look up at Uncle Joe when he hands me his phone. It's in the middle of a voice call with Cam. "I figured this might be something you'd like to share with your future husband. I'll be in the living room when you're done." He leans in and gives me a quick hug and a kiss on my head before excusing himself.

Holding a letter that my mom and dad once held in their own hands has me in a trance. I look from my mom's jewelry to the letter and back. I can't process what's going on right now.

"Sweetheart, are you there?" I hear Cam ask.

I pick up the phone. "Yeah, I'm here. Sorry, I didn't know Mom wrote me a letter. I don't know how to feel right now."

"There's nothing to be sorry about. Have you opened it yet?"

"No. I don't know if I can do this alone." I know my makeup is ruined by now, but at this point, I don't care if I look like a clown. This is too much.

"You're not alone. I'm here with you. Imagine me there holding you. I'm right here. Can you try and read it to me?"

"I don't know if I can."

"Why don't you ask Mark to read it to us? I know Uncle Joe and Kayla won't make it through if you can't, and Becca's too emotional. I'd do it, but I don't have it with me."

"I wish you were here." I wipe my wet face with a tissue.

"I know, babe, me too."

I hear a phone ring in the other room. Mark says something to the others, then pushes open the office door and squeezes my shoulder before he sits across from me. "If you're alright with me being a part of this, I'd be honored to read the letter."

When I nod, he opens the first of three in the envelope. He grabs some tissue from the box sitting next to him, hands it to me, then takes my hand and begins to read.

Leah,

My beautiful baby girl, you are my pride and joy. When the doctor put you in my arms for the first time, I knew that I got life right. My heart grew so much the moment you looked at me that I thought it would pop out of my chest. Your dad has never beamed so brightly.

You, baby girl, made us parents and have taught us what true love is.

If you're reading this, that means something has happened to me and I can't be there for you on your wedding day. I'm so sorry, precious. That's the last thing I want. I can only imagine how beautiful you are today. Walking down the aisle to your dad was one of the happiest days of my life, next to the day I found out I was pregnant with you and the day you were born. If I'm not there with you today, please forgive me. The jewelry that you should have just been handed is the same that I put on in front of the mirror right before marrying your daddy. I want you to have it, and I want you to wear it. It's my way of being there with you today, even if not physically.

Did I ever tell you that your Uncle Joe walked me down the aisle? He was the only person there for us. As a show of support for your father and me—even though I knew his heart was breaking—he walked me down the aisle and handed me to your dad. It nearly tore me up. I grew up thinking that Joe and I were it. We'd marry and run away one day. But when I met your dad, I knew I was wrong. The support that Joe gave me after was a display of how true love works. Your dad knew all about what Joe and I had, and still accepted him as part of our family, even naming him his best man and godfather of our future children—of you.

You, my precious little girl, are blessed to have two strong men who love you so much. But today, on your wedding day, you are adding another. Hold on to that, baby. Let that love be your strength. Let it guide you. You carry me in your heart every day, but today, I hope you do me the honor of taking a part of me down the aisle with you.

I better hand this to your daddy now. He's practically foaming at the mouth to get his turn with the pen. He's only asked me to let him have his say about ten times since I started. Impatient, that one, but always so loving.

I love you so very much. I am, and forever will be, proud of you, precious.

—Love, Mom

Mark takes a moment to dry his eyes while I breathe in and try to process my mom's words.

Cam is silent at first. I hear a sniffle, followed by, "Are you okay, sweetheart?"

Unable to get the words out without crying, I simply hum.

Mark clears his throat. "We have another when you're ready."

Knowing I need to hear it, even though I'm a wreck, I take the hand he has stretched out toward me for support and nod for him to continue.

Hey, sweet cheeks.

Okay, maybe I need to find a different nickname. I'll work on that one. Just give me some time and I'll find one you'll love, I promise. If you're reading this, then today is your wedding day and I can't walk you down the aisle. I hope that's not the case. Looking at you now, lying in your mom's arms, you're the most beautiful baby girl I have ever laid my eyes on. You look so much like me, but thank God you get your beauty from your mom.

It would be an honor to walk you down the aisle—just please don't get in a rush to get there. Well, if this is your wedding day, you're already past that. So, scratch that. I'm sorry. I'm no good at this, but I'm trying. I'd like for you to do something for me, if you will. If I'm not there with you today and Joe is, give him the honor of walking you down the aisle in my place.

I know most think I should push him away, but when I walked into this relationship with your mother and saw the kind of love he has for her, knowing that he would step back so she could be happy, how could I push him away? Joe's a good man. He can be scary (don't tell him I said that), but he is. I can only hope that your husband-to-be is just as good and that Joe will give him hell for me.

It's my job to ensure my girls are happy and cared for, and if I can't do it, I hope Joe will step up to the plate. I'm sorry I'm not there for you today, but I want you to take a breath, put on your game face, and get out there to marry this man. Your mom and I are so proud of you. I'll be watching and cheering you on. I'm there with you today in spirit. I love you, baby girl, forever and always.
—Dad

To the husband-to-be,
Son, I wish I could be there to meet you. I also wish I could walk Leah down the aisle, to shake your hand and officially welcome you into the family. If my baby girl has agreed to marry you and you have gotten past Joe, you must be a good man. I remember my wedding day to Kelly like it was yesterday. The feelings you'll have in your gut are no joke. As you watch her walk down the aisle toward you looking like an angel, it

will be impossible to breathe. Make sure you have a hankie in your pocket. You might think you won't need it, but I'm here to tell you that is one of the biggest lies you will tell yourself today.

My best piece of advice is to always put your family ahead of everything else. In this life, God gives you the gift of love in the form of our loved ones. You were given the best gift out there when you found Leah. Put her ahead of all else. Continue to date her, build on the friendship at the base of that love, and when anything threatens to rock your relationship, hold on to it like no other.

I approve of today so long as you make her happy. If I'm really aren't there today, she's going to need you to be her rock. Make sure she has you to lean on any time she begins to drift. Take good care of her for me. She's precious to us all. Now, go get started on making us grandparents. Not really, but soon. Babies are a blessing, and if yours are anything like mine, they'll change your life.
—Noah, aka Dad

Mark smiles as he wipes the tears beneath his eyes. "I'll give you two a little bit, then I'll send the girls in to help get you taken care of. Thank you for letting me be a part of this special moment." He pulls me in for a hug. "Your parents sound like amazing people."

"Thank you, Mark. They were the best."

He leaves, but I'm unable to really speak, so Cam and I sit in silence while I process it all. Occasionally, he mutters things like, "I love you," "You're so strong," and "I'm here for you, baby." I love him even more for it, but I can't seem to get control of my tears.

When Uncle Joe walks in and wraps me in his strong embrace, I know this is what I need. After my parents spoke so highly of him in their letters, I needed to feel his love surrounding me.

He takes his phone back. "I'm with her now. I'll get her cleaned up and walk her down that aisle to you soon, son." He hangs up and looks back at me.

I hand him the letters, letting him know that I think that he should read them. When he does as I ask, the tears flow freely.

"I can't believe he felt like that. Loving your mom was never a secret, but I'm glad to know it didn't cause them issues. Thank you for sharing these with me."

"Thank you for loving her so much . . . and for loving us. You *are* a good man, Uncle Joe. Thank you for being a dad to us all these years. I treated you badly so many times. You didn't deserve that."

If there was ever a moment for my tears to dry up, now would be great. I'm sure my eyes are puffy and my makeup is a mess.

"I won't have any of that now. It's time to dry those eyes and put on your game face. I'll let the ladies back in and go check on the guys real quick. I'll be back in thirty minutes." He kisses my forehead, then leans back, smiling. "I love you, baby doll."

"I love you too."

Those thirty minutes fly by. My makeup is redone completely after eye drops and a cool cloth is pressed to my eyes, and Becca does her mom magic to remove a small amount of mascara from my dress. After Kayla puts on my necklace, I'm taken to the mirror standing in the corner of the office. I can't believe it. I look so different and yet still like me. My gown is beautiful, but that isn't what does it for me anymore. It's the whole picture. From the lace, pearls, and bling of my dress to the vintage jewels adorning my neck and ears. The body glitter on my chest and the family-heirloom veil on my head. Kayla did my hair in an updo with a few loose curls, and she gave me a smokey eye and deep-red lips

I hear a throat clear from the doorway. Looking over, I see Tom wiping his eyes. "I'm not crying; you are." He chuckles as he tries to get himself together. "I didn't think I'd ever see this day. *You* are beautiful. Cam is a lucky man to have found you, and I'm lucky to be able to call you my sister." He pulls me in for a hug. "I came to give you a ride. Everyone's up there waiting."

Looking around for the first time in a minute, I realize that everyone cleared out while I was in my head.

"Thank you, Tom. I'm the lucky one to gain not only a husband but a brother who I think of as one of my best friends." I grab my flowers and link my arm with his. "Let's get me married."

Chapter Twenty-Eight

Stepping out of the Gator with some assistance from my girls, I take in the same field Cam asked me to be his wife in. Fairy lights are wrapped around the tree that Tom has parked next to. Just past that is sheer curtains hung to keep me from seeing ahead—or rather, Cam from seeing me.

"No more tears," Kayla says. She pulls me in for a quick hug. "Hot Cop is on the other side of that curtain, waiting for his beautiful bride. Let's not keep him waiting anymore. It's time to make this official." She gets everyone lined up in the order they should be before the curtain is pulled open and then shut after each couple, giving it a moment before reopening.

Uncle Joe walks to my side just before our turn. "Are you ready for this, baby girl?"

I nod.

When the music changes and the curtains open for my entrance, my eyes lock with Cam's, and everything else disappears. It feels like I'm floating down the aisle to my man. I can't keep the tears at bay. He mouths the words, "I love you, beautiful," and I nearly lose it.

When Uncle Joe and I make it to the altar, the pastor asks, "Who gives this woman to be wed?"

Uncle Joe stands up taller, if that's possible. "Her mother, father, and I." He then kisses my cheek and places my hands in Cam's.

The pastor says some words that I barely hear as I get lost in Cam's eyes. "Cam and Leah have decided to write their own vows. Cam, you may share yours."

Cam takes my hand in his and opens a paper with the other. As it begins to shake, I squeeze his hand in a sign of support. He grins. "Leah, my love. When I found you at the bottom of the stairs, I knew that you were it for me. There was no way around it. I would do anything to make you happy. I'm so glad that you took a chance on me. You're the strongest, kindest, and most loving woman I know. You've taken my crazy family and made each member fall in love with you. Hell, you even have Tom falling at your feet. That's no easy task." There are some laughs in the crowd, but he pushes on. "Much like what your mom said, you taught me what love is. I love you, and I love who we are together. The minute you sat down at that table with all of us at that restaurant and Aubrey crawled into your lap, I knew there was no turning back. You floored me when you jokingly spoke of babies and a wedding that day."

I can't help but giggle at that reminder.

"That beautiful giggle is my reason for breathing. I promise to make you laugh until we're old and gray. I vow to challenge you every day. And I promise to always find time to take in this beautiful sunset with you."

I have to wipe my tears. Again.

"I have so many memories with you and look forward to making so many more, to growing a family, and to further growing our love. Sweetheart, I vow to walk through this life by your side, through good and bad, in sickness and in health, until my dying day. These are my vows to you."

I use the hankie Uncle Joe gave me and dab my eyes, careful not to smear my makeup.

"Leah, do you have vows to share?" the pastor says.

I nod, hoping I don't choke up in front of all these people.

"Cam, you know me better than anyone, and somehow, you're still here with me. Even standing here in this moment, it's hard to believe that I'm the one marrying you. You found me at my worst. You stayed by my side before you even knew who I was. There is so much about you that I love, but the thing I love most is that you never give up. We have had so much push against us, but it's only brought us closer. When you fell off that cliff . . ." I have to stop for a moment as a sob threatens to break free.

Cam leans in to wipe my tears.

"Cam, I thought I had lost you that day. Life without you played through my mind. That is not a life that I want to be a part of. I made a promise that if you were okay, I'd happily marry you, tying our lives together forever. You showed me that family isn't about blood. Family is about love. I can't promise you that things will be easy, but I *can* promise you that no matter how hard life gets, we'll figure it out together. I promise to love you with everything I have and continue trying to be worthy of your love every day. I vow to give all of me to all of you. I promise to grow old with you and to never stop loving you. To watch as many sunsets as possible in your arms and, one day, grow a family in our love. My promise to you is that I'll walk through life with you in hard times and in good, through sickness and health. I will love you for all my days."

At the pastor's urging, Cam places the ring on my finger. "Leah, this ring is a visible sign of our vows. It is a token of my love and devotion to you. I pledge to you all that I am and all that I will ever be as your husband. With this ring, I happily marry you, my best friend, and join my life to yours."

When it's my turn, I place the ring on Cam's finger and echo the very vows he just made to me.

"I now pronounce you husband and wife. You may kiss the bride."

"About time," Cam says, causing me to giggle.

After a minute, we hear a bunch of catcalls, causing me to pat Cam's chest in protest. He laughs and pulls away.

The pastor has us turn toward the aisle. "I would like to present to you, Mr. and Mrs. Butch Cameron Jr."

Cam links our fingers together, kisses my hand, and raises our joined hands in the air as we start down the aisle.

"Let's get this party started!" Tom yells out.

The weeks following our wedding pass in a blur. We postpone our honeymoon trip to the Maldives due to Kayla's moving. I hate that she's really gone, but I'm glad that Cam suggested we stay so I could have more time with her. When the day finally comes to hop on our flight and whisk ourselves away, just over a month has gone by since our wedding. Stalker John and Tillie were caught on video at the airport the day after our wedding, leaving the state, and things have been quiet since.

The shuttle is supposed to pick us up at three a.m. sharp for our four-thirty flight, but the driver sends us a message that he's running a little behind. When he still doesn't show up by three-forty, I decide to call the airline. They can't reach the driver either, so Cam and I decide to drive ourselves and park in long-term parking. It's not exactly how we pictured it, but it'll have to do on such short notice.

We find a spot in the parking garage, then Cam gets out of the truck and unloads the bags from the back while I start gathering our carry-ons.

The back door opens behind me.

"I'm almost done, babe. Do you need help?"

When Cam doesn't answer, I turn and look over my shoulder but am met with a prick to the neck instead.

"Cam!" I yell. "Help, Ca—"

Before I can yell another word, a hand covers my mouth, and my body goes limp. My brain is in a fog.

"Your husband won't be helping you any time soon. Don't you worry, Leah. He'll never bother you again."

What did he do to Cam, and what the hell was in that? I can't move. I feel the pressure build in my chest as panic sets in. Now is not the time for this, but as my vision blurs, I know there's nothing I can do to stop it.

When I come to, I have no idea where I am or how I got here. I try to move, but I feel a burning sensation on my wrists, which are tied behind my back. I'm tied to what looks like a wooden pole in some kind of rundown building, maybe an old barn or shop of some sort. The floor is dirt with some remnants of wood as if it's so old that the floor itself has disintegrated.

Straight in front of me are a set of double doors that are practically falling off the hinges. To the left of that are some old boxes, a crumpled McDonald's bag on top. To the right is an empty wall, the bottom rotted out and jagged with one lone busted window. Behind me, I hear something that sounds like an old TV show playing.

Chills run up my arms as a draft hits my skin. I'm *so* cold.

I try to get a look under the wall to make out where I am, but a glint catches my eye. There's a gun sitting right next to the McDonald's bag. If I can get loose of these restraints, maybe I can get to it.

The front door opens a sliver, allowing John to walk in.

He comes over, and turns in a full circle, lifting his arms.

"Like the new place?"

I shake my head, ignoring his question. "Why are you doing this?"

"You should know why, Leah. You put me behind bars, costing me everything. Did you really think that I'd just let it go?"

"You hurt me. You could have stopped it, but you just let me fall and then ran off. What did you expect me to do?" This guy is nuts if he thinks its okay to hurt someone and not have to face charges.

He pulls me up the pole to stand without a care in the world for the torture he's putting my arms through. He lowers himself a bit to get in my face. "That wasn't nice, Leah. You know I didn't mean to hurt you. Yet you still went through with it."

"Let me go, John," I plead. "You don't want to do this. Come on, you're better than that."

He hauls back, pummelling me right across the face. "That's enough! It took me long enough to get you—I'm not letting you go any time soon. Now, shut up before you make me angry."

Good Lord, that hurt. As much as I don't want to concede to him, I swallow the bile in my throat. "I'm sorry." I'll play nice if it means it'll buy me some time. I just hope my family is looking for me.

He circles me like a shark circling its prey.

I stay quiet, knowing the last time I begged, he hit me. I have to conserve my energy until I can find a way out of this. If he hurts me now, I might never make it out.

He hauls back, smacking me. Then again. "You know, the cops went to my mom's house after they found out it was me watching you. *They threatened my mom, Leah.* My dad isn't the nicest man out there, and he put her in the hospital because of it. It wasn't even her *fault*! I have to make that right."

I don't know what he's talking about, but I apologize anyway. "I'm sorry. I didn't know."

I feel sick. He's worse than I thought he was. This guy is deranged. but if he wants to talk and it will buy me time, I'll talk until Im blue in the face.

He smiles maliciously at me.

That's the only warning I get before he punches me three more times in the ribs and face, causing my head to bounce back against the post. I think he might even be taller than Cam, and he sure did beef up while in jail. I don't remember him being this big before.

We hear a noise outside, causing him to stop. I'm relieved, but when he turns back my way, I'm mortified.

He takes my cheeks in his hand, squeezing them. "I'll be back soon, then we can finish up. Stay quiet for me now." He looks me over once. "It sure is a shame to mess up someone so pretty."

When he walks outside, I start struggling with the ties on my wrists while I look around the room for anything that can help me. I didn't bust my butt practicing with the guys just so I can take a beating and wait for someone to come rescue me. If I can get out of this, I will. Each movement of my arms jostles my torso, sending shock waves of pain through me. I can only imagine how much worse this'll get if I don't do something now.

When I hear a slight tap on the window to my right, my head snaps that way.

Oh God, it's Tom.

I can make out his eyes and nose, just enough to tell me it's him. He reaches in through the missing pane and attempts to unlock it. After opening it, he starts to crawl in.

"Where are the others?" I whisper.

"It's only me. I just found you and called it in. They should be here soon. Stay calm, sis. I'm coming."

When we hear the door creak open, Tom closes the widow and lowers himself behind the boxes to take cover. John opens the door and walks over to me again. As he sinks another punch right into my bruised ribs, I see Tom move in the corner of my eye. John must see him, too, because he stops hitting me long enough to turn in that direction.

"No, Tom! Run," I yell.

In slow motion, I see Tillie step into the room, brandishing a gun. Without so much as a warning, she fires it, hitting Tom in the shoulder.

"No!"

"What are you doing? You shouldn't be here. I told you to meet me tomorrow," John says, stepping toward her as she continues to point her gun at Tom.

"I came out here to talk you out of this, but now that I shot a cop, it looks like *we* are doing this together. I didn't want to get involved any more than I already was. You promised me, baby."

I have a hard time believing that she's not as involved as he is.

Tom looks at me from his position on the ground, blood seeping from the wound on his shoulder.

John pulls her in to him for a kiss, which quickly turns into a full-on make-out session. Carefully, Tom starts scooting toward me slowly, making as little noise as he can, but it's impossible to move quietly on this dirty floor.

John sees what he's doing and breaks away, grabbing Tillie's gun, and slamming the butt of it over Tom's head, effectively knocking him out.

"No!" I scream.

Tillie moves my way, grabbing a knife off the table. She stands in front of me and shakes her head. "Do you know what I've been through because of you?"

I shake my head. She's a woman on the edge. I don't want to set her off. She might be more dangerous than he is.

She leans forward to whisper in my ear. "If you were dead, maybe I could finally be happy."

Before I can react, she pulls back and stabs me once on the upper right side, then pulls the knife out and does it again.

I fall forward in shock, blood pouring out of the wounds. She looks me right in the eyes and smiles, then drops the knife on the table. "Have your fun with her, but hurry it up. We need to go."

Blood pools at my feet now, thick and sticky on the dirt floor. Oh God, that hurts. *How am I supposed to get out of this now?* It's getting hard to breathe. When I start seeing spots, I try to get my breathing under control.

John walks past Tom, kicking him in the gut on the way. "Wake up, pig. I want you to watch this. Tillie, tie him up somewhere so he can see."

They move Tom over to another pillar so he's sitting on the ground with his arms behind his back. When John puts his thumb in Tom's gunshot wound, he wakes, yelling, then looks around for me. When he finally sees me, his eyes wander down my body until he locates the blood dripping down my side. He struggles to get free as John walks my way.

"Let her go," Tom growls.

"Just sit there and keep your mouth shut, *cop*," Tillie spits.

"Untie me, John. Give me a chance to defend myself," I beg.

Tillie pushes her gun into the back of my shoulder. "Shut up. You have no reason to talk."

"This isn't a fair fight, and you *know* it," I exclaim, desperate for one of them to listen.

"Shut up, Leah," she snaps in reply. "Hurry up already. We have cops out looking for us."

John hauls back, punching me in the face hard enough that my head snaps back. I grunt and spit out the blood that pools in my mouth from the hit.

"Get the hell off her!" Tom yells.

When John moves in once more, I'm done letting him get his way. I jerk my leg up as hard as possible and knee him in the groin, causing him to double over. While he's tucked in on himself, I knee him in the head, knocking *him* out this time.

Another gunshot goes off, and then a white-hot pain shoots through my leg. Blood begins to soak my jeans as I realize that Tillie just shot me.

"Dammit, Tillie!" I yell, in pain.

She circles around me and gets in my face again.

"Get the hell off her!" Tom yells. He's struggling to break free, with no luck. "Stop this! Take me instead. Shoot me but leave her alone."

Ignoring him, she holds the gun to my head this time.

Oh God . . . she's going to kill me. *I love you, Cam. Please be happy.* A lone tear escapes as I accept that I may not make it out of here alive.

She stares straight into my eyes as she pulls the trigger. When it clicks and nothing happens, I gasp for air as I see *red*.

She had her chance—now it's mine. "You should've made sure it was loaded first." Pulling back as much as I can, I headbutt her. I'm left lightheaded, but when she falls to her knees, I take my legs and wrap them around her neck, clenching my teeth as I try to fight the pain at every tug.

In the corner, Tom is struggling to get free. Watching me fight has him in even more of a frenzy to break his restraints and help.

I can think of only one thing to free myself. I know it'll hurt like hell, but what choice do I have?

"Tom," I say. "I'm going to try something. If it works, grab the knife."

He shakes his head, but no words come out.

With Tillie's neck still between my legs, I gain leverage with my arms behind me, grab the pole as best as I can, and kick her into the table with the gun and knife. Thankfully, it's not that far, so I successfully knock it Tom's way.

Without enough time to get my feet back under me, my body slams down to the ground, hanging me by my arms. The force of the fall sends a jolt up my spine, causing me to see spots. "Ugh!" I growl out in pain. *Everything hurts.*

Tom looks at me with sad eyes, and I know I must be in bad shape. "Hold on, sis." He manages to turn himself just right to grab the knife and free himself before he runs my way.

As he's cutting me loose, I see John stand slowly and move to hit Tom on the head.

"No!" I yell, but my vision gets fuzzy, then fades to black. If we make it out of here alive, I'll do everything in my power to make sure John and Tillie never see the light of day again. I just hope that Tom's okay and that help's on the way.

I'm in and out of it for what seems like forever, but I manage to make out Tom on top of John, his arms behind his back, me lying flat on mine next to them. I turn and look to the other side, finding Tillie tied to the pole I was attached to moments ago.

My eyes are so heavy, I can hardly keep them open. "Stay with me, sis," Tom says.

The door swings wide open. I look over Tom to see a frantic, wide-eyed Cam struggling to get to me as Mark and Butch attempt to hold him back. "Cam," I croak.

"That's my wife!" I hear him yell. "Let me in there. You can't keep me from her."

I never get to find out if he makes it to me or not, because my whole world goes black. Again.

Chapter Twenty-Nine

As my eyes slowly open, I'm so disoriented. I have no clue what's going on, but I feel like I weigh a ton. I don't know how long I've been like this. I vaguely remember coming to a few times, only to black out again. I try to blink my eyes open, but they won't cooperate.

When I finally wake, I don't hear Cam. I don't hear anyone for that matter. But I'm able to open my eyes if only for a moment, grunting in frustration when I can't keep them open.

"Leah? Oh my God, Leah!" I hear Cam fumbling next to me. "Sweetheart, I'm here." He shifts something around, then speaks again. "I think Leah's waking up. She's been making grunting noises and furrowing her brow." He drops something near the head of my bed, and I feel him grab hold of my hand.

My eyes flutter open again, and this time, I see my handsome, unshaven husband's face. He's smiling back at me as my eyes close again.

"Oh, beautiful," he cries. "You'll get there. You keep fighting, I'll be right here. I'm not going *anywhere*. I love you."

I've opened my eyes a few times and squeezed Cam's hand. It's the most I can manage, but I want him to know that I'm trying to get back to him.

I try to stay awake as long as I can, but my body is too weak, and I fall asleep again.

The next time I wake up, it must be morning because my room is bright with light. I grunt, attempting to cover my eyes. By some miracle, I'm able to move my hand this time, bringing it to my face.

"Cam! Cam, hurry up in there. Leah just moved her arm," I hear Becca say excitedly. Someone grabs my hand, then I hear her near my ear. "Hey, girl. Welcome back. Nothing's been the same since you've been here. We all miss you like crazy."

"Sweetheart, I'm here," Cam says, taking my other hand. "Ma, close the blinds, would ya? There you go, beautiful. The room isn't nearly as bright now. You can open those beautiful eyes now."

I open my eyes, looking right into Cam's ocean blues that I love so much.

"Good morning, sweetheart. I'm so glad to see you." Looking over at a now-crying Becca, he adds, "Get the doc."

I hear sniffles coming from further down the bed, and I shift my gaze to see Marie and Uncle Joe, who moves to take Becca's place at my side. Mom looks like she hasn't slept in weeks. Uncle Joe isn't faring much better, his beard beating

Cam's, letting me know he hasn't been working either. If he was, he'd be clean shaven.

I look back at Cam and try to talk. "Ca—" is all I can get out before I flinch in pain from my dry throat.

Marie rushes to my side, pushing in next to Cam with a cup and a straw. "Here, love, take a small sip."

I do as she tells me, watching Cam as I sip a small amount of water into my parched mouth. Tears stream down his face, and I squeeze his hand in reassurance.

The doctor walks in quickly behind Becca. "It's so nice to see you awake, Mrs. Cameron. Do you mind if I look you over?"

I close my eyes and reopen them, trying to communicate that it's fine. As if he knows exactly what I mean, he nods his thanks and gets to work.

"You're very blessed. With the kind of injuries you sustained . . ." He looks at Cam, then changes his tone. "I'm glad they got you here in time. Most of your injuries have had the chance to heal up nicely since you've been here. They aren't completely healed, but in time, we have high hopes."

"What's it going to take to get our girl up and out of this bed?" Marie asks.

"She'll need physical therapy, We'll get started tomorrow if she's well enough. We'll also have someone come in and focus on her mental health. After an incident of that manner, her overall well-being will be our focus."

After his poking and prodding is done, he looks at Cam. "I'll leave you to it and come back in before the end of my shift. We can go over my findings and where we go from here. Let's give her some time to adjust before we jump in."

"Thanks, doc," Cam says as the doctor walks out the door.

"Cam," I say. I pause to take another sip to fight the burn in my throat. "How long?"

"You've been here a little over a month," he replies.

Oh wow.

"Kayla?" I ask. I wish I could ask more, but saying one or two words at a time hurts enough right now.

"She's in New York still," Uncle Joe says, taking my hand. "She calls every day, twice a day. She should be video calling soon."

When things start coming back to me, I'm reminded that Tom tried to save me. Remembering his own injuries, I start to panic. My heart monitor makes a weird noise, and I try to sit up. "Tom!" I cry.

Cam sits with me, trying to soothe me. "Tom is good. Physically, he's doing well. Mentally, he'll be better when he sees that you're awake. He's at his therapy session right now. He'll be here after. Tom hasn't left your side much at all since coming in. Maddie's had to pry him away. She's been good for him."

"I hate to break this up," I hear someone say as they walk in the door. "But I need to check on Mrs. Cameron and give her some meds."

Everyone but Cam moves from my bedside. The nurse walks around my bed to check my vitals and my dressings before giving me meds. Whatever she gives me makes me tired almost instantly.

"Rest. I'll be here when you wake up. I love you," Cam says as my eyes get too heavy to hold open.

I love you too, I try to say, but I'm asleep before the words pass my lips.

I open my eyes to see Cam napping in a chair next to me, holding my hand.

I turn my head and see Tom, who has the biggest smile on his face.

"Tom," I say, smiling as best as I can. "You're okay?"

"I'm good," he says, showing me the sling his arm is in. "A little ol' bullet won't stop me anytime soon." Sobering, he continues. "Thank you, Leah, for everything you did. I came to save you and you ended up saving me instead. I can never thank you enough."

I start to reply but the door opens, interrupting us.

"Afternoon, Mrs. Cameron. How are you feeling?" the doctor asks as he walks in.

"Fine."

"Let's talk about what's going on. Is it alright to talk in front of your family?"

Looking around, I see Tom, Cam, Uncle Joe, and Maddie—she must have come with Tom. Cam did say she's been good for him.

"Sure."

"I'm going to give you a quick rundown and then you can ask me as many questions as you'd like after." When I nod, he continues. "When you were brought in, we had to give you blood and rush you into emergency surgery. We lost you once while you were on the operating table. You had a dislocated shoulder, multiple stab wounds, and a bullet lodged in your leg that we had to get out. It was touch and go for a while. We had to put you in a medically induced coma for the first two weeks, and you were intubated for a while after that.

"Your wounds have begun to heal rather nicely over the last several weeks, and most of the bruising is gone. Mrs. Cameron, you went through a huge ordeal. Most wouldn't come back from that. I'm worried about your mental health after this. Starting tomorrow, I'll have a physical therapist come in twice a day to walk with you. A mental health therapist will come in once a day to start as well. The OB should be coming in for a visit throughout, and you'll see me around also. I'd like to keep you for another week and go from there. Any questions?"

"I don't understand why an OB would come around. He didn't touch me that way."

He looks at Cam with concern. "I'm sorry, I should've led with that, but I assumed you knew. Mrs. Cameron, you're . . . pregnant."

I take in the look of shock on all the faces surrounding me. The only one seeming normal is my husband. Cam must've known already but has kept it to himself for whatever reason.

Tears roll down my face as I start to realize what he's just told me. "Is it okay?"

"I was worried but they seem to be growing just fine. We've been monitoring them very closely."

"*Them*?" I ask.

"Yes, ma'am, twins, about eight or nine weeks. Your OB would be the one to answer questions about them. That's not my area of expertise. Do you have any other questions for me, Mrs. Cameron?"

I shake my head, still in shock. He turns and leaves, letting us know hell check in tomorrow.

"I've been here every day," Tom says. "How did I not know?"

"Same," Uncle Joe says.

"Don't you guys think that their mom deserved to know before everyone else?" Cam says. "I wasn't telling anyone until I had to."

"*Twins?*" I ask again.

Cam looks at me with a huge smile on his face. "Yeah, sweetheart, *twins.*"

"Cam . . . What if John had hurt them?"

His look of wonder turns lethal at the thought.

"They're good, beautiful," he says after clearing his throat and face of any signs of anything but wonder. "I've been here for every single scan. They're growing well. The OB says that they were well protected. They were under stress in the beginning—that's another reason they kept you sedated for so long. That gave you and the babies a fighting chance. It won't be easy with all the healing and therapy you have ahead of you, but sweetheart, these two are fighters, just like their mom."

I lie back and take it in as the others chat around me.

An hour later, an OB and a nurse walk in wheeling an ultrasound machine. "Alright, let's get started, shall we?" She looks over at me and smiles. "It sure is nice seeing you awake, sweet pea. You can call me Winnie, or Doc, if you're not comfortable with that, but there's no need for formalities with us. This here is Sasha. She's the ultrasound tech." She looks around at all the others standing in my room. "Are you alright if they stay, or would you rather they wait in the hall?"

"They can stay."

They all seem to pull in closer at that, nearly surrounding the bed.

The tech covers the bottom half of me before tugging my gown loose from the blankets.

Uncle Joe holds a phone up to the monitor. "It's Kayla and Mike."

"Care to tell me why Mike's in New York with Kayla? Is she okay?"

"He's not. He's at work; I have a split screen going."

I look over at Winnie and smile.

"Any names for the babies yet?" she asks.

"No, I just found out about them. Maybe we will after we see them."

"Then let's get to it," Winnie responds.

"This is going to be cold," Sasha says. She squirts a slime-like clear liquid on my stomach before producing a wand and running it over my skin, pushing hard enough to make me flinch. When I see my little peanuts on the screen and hear the swooshing of their heartbeats, the only thing I can do is cover my mouth as tears begin to fall.

Cam is right there with me, holding me the best he can, then kisses my head. "We did that. Our love in black and white."

"Good babies," the tech says. She clicks around on the machine and then swaps places with Winnie.

"Mr. and Mrs. Cameron, the babies are lookin good. Congratulations."

I look up to see teary cheeks all around, even with the smiles that stretch across so many faces. When the doctor leaves the room, there's so much commotion that the nurse comes in and asks the others to head to the waiting room for a bit to let me get some rest. Once they're all gone and it's just Can and I left in the room, he turns to me.

"Docs right. We should think baby names. Do you have

any in mind?"

"If you wouldn't mind, I'd love to name them after my parents. How about if we have a girl, Kelly Lynn?"

"Kelly Lynn," Cam agrees, smiling through another bout of tears. "What about Noah James if it's a boy?"

"I love it."

"This road's not going to be easy, but I'll be by your side every step of the way. Through therapy—physical and emotional—I'll be there. For all your cravings and midnight runs, I'll be there. I promise, sweetheart, we'll get through it all, and after the newborn stage is over . . . I'll be taking my wife on our honeymoon."

"I'm looking forward to it."

"Oh, I nearly forgot to tell you," Cam says. "Becca's pregnant too."

"That's awesome. I'm so happy for them."

"Me too. I want to hold my family now if you don't mind." He crawls into bed with me on the side that's not all bandaged up. "Have I told you how happy I am that you came back to me?"

"Not in the last five minutes," I reply.

"Well, I'm over the moon," he says, breathing me in. "I love you, Mrs. Cameron."

"I love you, too, Mr. Cameron."

For the first time in a long time, I know I can rest and not have to look over my shoulder. I can *finally* let my guard down.

H K Brown's **Digging Deep** is book one in the Baycliff Valley Series. Keep following along to find out what's going on between Mike and Kayla.

Coming Home—book two of the Baycliff Valley Series —coming soon.

Follow me for up-to-date information.

Facebook- authorhkbrown

Instagram-authorhkbrown

YouTube-HKBrown-author

TikTok-hkbrown_author

Make sure to join my mailing list.

Subscribers get to see cover reveals and receive general

information earlier than those who don't.

https://www.authorhkbrown.com